HER OWN GOOD TIME

By

Barbara Selling

This book is a work of fiction. Places, events, and situations in this story are purely fictional. Any resemblance to actual persons, living or dead, is coincidental.

ISBN: 1-4033-7067-2 (e-book)
ISBN: 1-4033-7068-0 (Paperback)

Library of Congress Control Number: 2002094172

This book is printed on acid free paper.

Printed in the United States of America
Bloomington, IN

1stBooks - rev. 12/02/02

Acknowledgments

I'm grateful, first of all, to our class in Advanced Creative Writing at the Radcliffe Institute where this novel came to life over a period of several years. Our teacher, Professor Alan Feldman, deserves much of the credit for its development and its fruition.

Thanks also to my four children who, along with the emotional support they provided, have served as editors and critics of this book. My physician husband was able to add his medical knowledge to the complicated diagnostic picture I created, and his four children became the computer experts that publishing demands today.

I owe much to my agent, Ed Breslin, whose faith in this novel never wavered. And to all my friends and colleagues who spent hours proofreading and fact-checking, I offer my deepest thanks.

And finally, gratitude to the artist, Miriam Gilman of Newton, Massachusetts, who brought to life and to the cover of this book - in monotype - my fantasy of a decaying Victorian house where this story had to take place. She has exhibited throughout New England and is the winner of a Newton Citywide Contest for Original Artwork and the recipient of a Massachusetts Cultural Council Grant.

Prologue

Margaret MacPherson Bluestone squirmed and wriggled in an effort to find a comfortable position on the cracked plastic seat of her chair. Looking around, she saw that it was too late to move. The auditorium, in the sub-basement of a refurbished old Boston hotel, was filling up quickly. Thank God, this workshop -- *Secrecy vs. Privacy* -- was the last one of the day.

Several times a year, she was required to attend conferences like this one, both to represent the clinic, but also to collect continuing education units -- called CEUs -- to keep up her license as a clinical social worker. While she tried to look at these days as a kind of holiday, a chance to dress up, to have a day off from work, have a nice lunch, and perhaps run into a few colleagues or fellow alumnae from graduate school, today there didn't seem to be anyone she knew. The morning session had been dreary, much too technical for a computer-phobic person like herself, and the lunch heavy, featuring a thick clam chowder followed by classical creamed chicken in a patty shell, both guaranteed to be sleep-inducing.

The leader of the workshop, a shapeless grizzled woman in a wrinkled wool suit, began by passing out sheets of yellow paper. "Now," she said, smiling broadly, "I want all of you to write -- at the top of the paper -- a <u>secret</u>. Do it quickly; don't even think about it; just put down a secret."

Without hesitation, smiling to herself, Margaret wrote: <u>I don't like this</u> <u>session. The leader is smarmy</u>. She put down her pencil, folded her arms and looked around. The other participants were bent over their papers. She wanted to laugh. Wait till she sees what I've written, she thought, realizing that she was acting like a child, a junior high school student seeking to annoy the substitute teacher.

Lately it had seemed to Margaret that she was going through junior high all over again. She wasn't the only one: all her women friends -- like herself, now in their early sixties -- were concentrating on new hair styles, having face lifts, literally kicking up their heels, either in exercise classes or line dancing, flirting awkwardly with each other's spouses, even having one-night stands at out-of-town conferences, or just giggling foolishly over nothing.

For Margaret, herself, it was a time of increased energy, of a new awareness of her own body. She was moving faster, and at the same time, noticing the details of her environment as if she were a traveler from another land. Early that morning, for instance, the view from the road into town along the Storrow Drive had been a sheer delight, bringing tears of joy to her eyes. The surface of the river had been smooth, the color of old pewter in the mid-May sunshine, and across the Charles, she'd seen in the river the reflection of Harvard's variegated college buildings, tall spires interspersed with squat modern structures. Small boats had dotted the Basin, and above the noise of the traffic, from time to time, she could hear the voices of the coxswains as they called out: "<u>Stroke</u> and; <u>stroke</u> and;" in the eight-man sculls.

She was rediscovering the beauty of the world. Maybe this was what one anthropologist had meant when she used the phrase "post menopausal zest." Had anyone, Margaret wondered, ever noted the similarity between the zest of this time of life and the spark of those awkward pre-teen, pre-menarcheal years?

"Okay, now," said the leader, still smiling. "Most of you hesitated too long that time. Try to do your next assignment right off the tops of your heads." Why did the woman keep <u>smiling</u>? "Write down in one sentence a statement that is totally <u>private</u>, something no one knows but you, and something you've never really told yourself."

Margaret suddenly felt warm and very dizzy, as if she were going to faint. She took a deep breath and then wrote quickly, almost as if it were automatic writing: <u>My husband is paranoid, mentally ill, and I don't know what to do about it</u>. She put her pencil back in her purse and folded up the paper, shoving it into her pocket. The room felt hot; she wished there were some open windows. She needed fresh air.

The leader of the workshop spoke quietly, no longer smiling. "You don't have to hand these papers in. Put them away. I just wanted you to understand how powerful secrecy and privacy are to all of us." The workshop continued, but Margaret kept thinking about what her pencil had written on the yellow paper. Her anxiety persisted. Finally, excusing herself, she squeezed past a row of sleepy participants and walked shakily to the deserted Ladies' Room. She stood before the full-length mirror, something she usually avoided doing. Only five feet, one inch tall, she'd always found her reflection a disappointment. Her internal view of herself was quite different from the reality: she pictured herself as tall and willowy, with long, dark straight hair instead of her short, white (formerly blond) curls. She'd always wanted brown eyes and delicate bone structure, but saw instead china-doll blue eyes and a round heart-shaped face.

Right now she looked pallid and sweaty. Her heart was beating fast. What was wrong with her? Could she be having a heart attack? Her blue eyes looked wide open and worried. Her hair, damp with perspiration, was limp. She took the yellow sheet out of her raincoat pocket and ripped it into small pieces, dropping them into the trash basket. Only then did she begin to feel like herself again. It was as if by destroying the paper she had made the written statement no longer true. She decided to go home.

Chapter One

She thought back to the early morning. She'd been sitting at the kitchen table, reading the paper and drinking her coffee. Since she was going to the conference, she'd dressed a little more formally than usual -- her periwinkle blue suit, her mother's pearls.

Henry had stopped to grab some coffee as well. Looking closely at her, he said: "You're all dressed up. Don't think I didn't notice. You and that boss of yours, you're going somewhere special today, together."

Margaret was stunned. Quickly she said: "I'm going to a conference in Boston, one of those day-long things where I pick up CEUs. I won't be seeing Brian at all today." Whatever had put that idea into his head? She was almost old enough to be Brian's mother, for God's sake.

He glared at her, then tossed his coffee cup into the sink. "Lies, lies, that's all I get from everyone these days." And he hurried out the back door, slamming it as he went.

Driving home in a daze, she decided she'd stop only to pick up a pound of scallops. Now, in the late afternoon, the picture had changed. The world she'd fallen in love with that morning had turned fickle. Low-lying black clouds warned of a gathering storm, probably with thunder. Whitecaps corrugated the surface of the water; most of the small craft had already been pulled out, and the last oarsmen were crowding the decks of the crewhouses,

1

hurriedly putting away their long oars, lifting their fragile boats to safety. The wind picked up and she began to drive faster. She was shivering.

As she pulled into her driveway, the rain was just beginning. Hurrying up the back steps, she shuddered, as she did nearly every day, at the condition of the house. She remembered the first time she'd seen it, thirty-five years ago, one of the town's many Victorian "painted ladies," built in the 1880's. She'd fallen in love with it, mostly because the house reminded her of her grandparents' home in Iowa, where she'd spent five years of her childhood during the Second World War. Like Granny's place, it fitted right into the neighborhood, a turret on top, and a barn out back with its own cupola.

Henry had been less than enthusiastic, foreseeing expensive upkeep. Growing up in New York City, he'd known only apartment living, but he went along, mostly because Margaret had inherited enough for the down payment from her father. While they'd had only two children at the time, she felt the need for larger quarters. She was already picturing herself as the mother of a large brood. The house had been let go, but it was structurally sound, so Henry had finally agreed.

This poor painted lady now needed a "make-over" at the very least. With its paint peeling, front porch sagging, and inside, piles of Henry's junk up to the ceiling in several rooms or spilling out into the barn, it almost looked abandoned. The kitchen, still in its original nineteenth century condition, was full of her husband's old tools, computer printouts, and maps. It had no counters, no place to put anything except for some shelves in the dark pantry. Its appliances consisted of an old iron sink, a refrigerator from the mid-thirties -- its round, coiled motor on the top reminding Margaret of the Guggenheim Museum in New York -- and a secondhand stove that Henry had found at the curb one morning. Someone had put it out for the trash collection. Margaret had done what she could, with paint and paper, to bring bright color into this kitchen, and to the other rooms in the house, but orange walls and green stenciled chair rails weren't enough to stop Henry from bringing in more junk almost every day.

Of course, he didn't believe in interior decoration or remodeling. As the kids used to say: "Why bother, Mom? Dad's junk will cover it up, anyhow." They were right; one could hardly see those bright walls now. There was even an old phone booth in the barn (Henry had bid successfully for it at an auction.) Made of solid oak, it had a brass ceiling. In an odd way, the phone booth was quite beautiful. The barn, in fact, was full of other 19th century artifacts and tools -- an old adze, a becket, a brace-and-bit, and a number of devices that Margaret couldn't name.

It wasn't just the money that kept Henry from agreeing to fix up the house. His salary as a low-level but tenured geology professor at a non-Ivy university wasn't princely but it was certainly enough, especially with Margaret's job at the clinic in the last fifteen years, to do the bare cosmetic minimum. But Henry saw the house as just another device -- like the kids, and the costs of their educations -- that would keep him from living out his original dream of a career as a working, non-academic geologist. Lately he'd begun to plan again for this thwarted career. Spreading his maps out on the Mission Oak dining room table, night after night, he would trace the route of a trip West, dreaming of living out of a tent and finally proving his theories about the movement of tectonic plates. Margaret had never understood exactly what these theories were, but she knew Henry believed there was evidence -- somewhere in the mountains of Utah -- that would prove he was right about the origin of certain kinds of earthquakes.

The condition of the house remained an issue with them. Often, when Margaret would complain about something that needed fixing, Henry would say: "We could have managed in a furnished room, for God's sake, with a few sticks of furniture and a manual typewriter." This fantasy of a simple life was his favorite comment, requiring no answer.

One time, not long ago, foolishly, she'd ventured one remark: "But Henry, with four children, we needed some kind of house." As soon as the sentence was out of her mouth, she knew it had been a mistake to say it.

"And whose idea was it to have all these fucking kids?" he'd shouted.

Margaret had caught her breath and her eyes filled with tears. She shouldn't have been surprised at his words. Years ago, when the children were still small, there were nights when several of them were sick at the same time, and she was running from room to room, carrying a basin. When she'd asked Henry for help, he would look at her scornfully, and point out that he had to go to work every day, and that this was the price she had to pay for having such a large family.

She put the scallops in the refrigerator and began to heat water for tea. She'd struggled for years with the question of what to do about her marriage. Her feelings seem to move in cycles. Often, after one of his tirades, she would find herself wishing he'd come down with some dread disease. She'd picture the doctors shaking their heads, saying he had only a few months to live. Or her daydreams would begin with a knock at the door and two uneasy policemen would inform her that he'd wracked up his old car and been killed instantly. But, strangely enough, she never seemed to have a fantasy that she, herself, had left <u>him</u>. It was always some mysterious outside force.

Some of the worst times were the few occasions when Margaret herself was sick. Henry found sickness of any kind disgusting -- hers, the children's, or even his own sniffles. He hated doctors and would never even go for an annual check-up. The kids had learned pretty early to deny their

5

colds (it's just an allergy, Daddy, they would say) but it was more difficult for them when they'd broken an arm or sprained an ankle. At such times, their father would give them the silent treatment until the cast was off.

Most of the time Margaret could hide her own minor illnesses, but it was more complicated when she was really sick. Once when the children were still little, she'd felt feverish and shaky. Dragging herself to the doctor's office, she was not surprised to learn that she had pneumonia.

"Go home and go to bed," the physician had said. "You've got a temperature of 104 degrees. Call your husband and tell him he's got to take over these kids. You need complete rest and ten days of antibiotics. I'll call the drugstore." She nodded, uneasily, collecting Molly from the toy cupboard and stuffing Andrew into his snowsuit.

Picking up the pills on the way home, she mentally mustered her forces: a call to a neighbor who would give the kids supper, chicken broth for herself, a change of diaper and pajamas for Andrew, and a check to make sure his "blankie" was in his crib. By the time Henry came home, the little ones were playing near Margaret, who'd stretched out on the living room floor under an afghan, and the older ones were watching TV.

"What the hell is going on here?" he asked.

Margaret's fever was so high she didn't care what she said. "I have fucking pneumonia," she whispered hoarsely. "The doctor said I had to stay in bed. I'm on penicillin. My temperature is a hundred and four."

"Well, who the hell does he think is going to run this household?"

"I'll give you one guess," she said, feeling somewhat drunk and less cautious. "He suggested you." Looking up at him, she saw that he looked stricken, almost abandoned.

Henry picked up his briefcase and marched into the kitchen. She could hear him opening and slamming the refrigerator door. He came back to where Margaret was lying. "There's nothing in this pesthouse to eat, so I'm going out to a decent restaurant." He closed the door loudly and was soon driving off. He was right: she should have gone shopping before she came home. Years later, her therapist, her voice filled with astonishment, had suggested that most women would have at least asked their husbands to stop off at the supermarket and fill the larder.

"Well, in fact," she said sheepishly, "he did come home with a load of groceries, and later on, it was he who called my mother in Scarsdale, asking her to come and help."

Her mother had called her back the next morning with a different scenario. Margaret could not imagine Caroline Chippen MacPherson taking over the care of four children (Margaret had been an only child), and sure

7

enough, her mother had said: "Darling, you poor thing. I'll send you a check and you can hire a housekeeper. Call one of those agencies in the morning. Whatever it costs, I'll take care of it."

From time to time, she would berate herself for not walking out, trying to figure out why she seemed unable to leave. These days, after all, everybody got divorced. At age sixty-two, with four children grown and out of the house, there was no one to keep her there.

Sometimes, when she was feeling desperate enough to leave, Henry would appear to change for a while and become almost sociable. Perhaps he sensed that he'd gone too far. During these periods, she would be reminded of earlier, happier days, especially of camping trips with the children when Henry was at his best. She would recall the whole family sitting on an old blanket, on a high hill at night in the Berkshires, Margaret holding a sleepy baby on her lap, while he pointed out the constellations.

Sitting now at the kitchen table with her cup of tea untouched before her, she stared unseeing at the rain-drenched back yard. Suddenly, she was startled by a flash of lightning and, after a long minute, the rumble of thunder. Normally that sound, particularly at this time of year, would thrill her: summer was coming. But now she thought about the statement she'd written on the yellow paper. Those words were <u>true</u>.

As a professional social worker in a mental health clinic, she'd been trained to recognize the signs and symptoms of mental illness. It was ironic, a classic case of denial. Accepting this diagnosis would mean that she was in a trap. "In sickness and in health," she'd promised as they stood before the justice of the peace nearly forty years ago. Could she abandon someone who was mentally ill, even if he was a bastard? Or was she just looking for another excuse to stay?

Years ago, when he'd first been appointed to the faculty at the university, he'd come home and complain that his colleagues didn't appreciate him: they didn't believe his theories had any foundation, and often treated him as if he were a wild-eyed visionary. Margaret had done her best then to sympathize with him, urging him to stand up for his beliefs, to encourage his independence and abilities. Her support would cheer him up.

He'd always been a little "different" and maybe even difficult, but it was only in the last year or so that he'd become so suspicious, so certain that people were out to get him. He'd been cruel, nasty and obnoxious for many years, but there'd been a change recently, subtle at first, but slowly growing. His face had begun to show a mysterious smile. It was as if he knew something important that no one else was smart enough to know.

* * * *

She still remembered clearly her first sight of him. In her last year at Wellesley, she'd taken a course in elementary geology to please her father. It was a small class and their professor had arranged for them to have joint field trips with a similar class at M.I.T. The group had traveled together to the White Mountains, and Henry, a graduate student and a teaching fellow, had been one of their instructors.

When she saw him on the bus, she'd been intrigued by his looks. Unusually tall, six foot, six -- he'd chosen a seat on the aisle so that he could stretch out his long legs. He was tan, with tiny freckles all over his face, well-defined muscles, dark hair, and a face like an eagle with a beaked nose and piercing black eyes. She thought she'd never seen such beautiful hands -- long tapering fingers that handled tools with assurance. It was a joy just to watch him tap a stone with his rock hammer. When he saw her watching him, he smiled and introduced himself. A good teacher, he was gentle with the students.

He called her several days later. Soon he was a frequent visitor, but even in the conformist 50's, Henry Bluestone never appeared in flannels, jacket and tie, but stood out in his faded work shirts, jeans and Australian outback hat. This difference was part of his appeal. She was reminded of the father she had known as a small child in mining towns. He, too, had been tall and often had worn work clothes in those days.

But his appearance stirred other feelings as well. From the beginning, she was drawn to him physically. She loved looking up at him, and she had especially wanted to touch those fingers. She began to picture his holding her as he held those tools -- with reverence and care. To someone of her Anglo-Saxon Protestant background, there was a quality of "otherness" about him. He was Jewish and had grown up in the Bronx, the son of a father who'd been active in the Amalgamated Clothing Workers Union, and a mother who ran a left-wing bookstore. His early childhood had been marked with memories of picket lines and protest meetings. He and his much older sister Rosa (named after the famous radical Rosa Luxemburg) had watched their parents march in May Day parades. The two children had learned all the Spanish Civil War songs, and their parents had actually voted for Earl Browder and the rest of the Communist party ticket in 1936. Margaret had only recently learned that children like Henry, with Communist parents, had been called "Red Diaper Babies."

While Henry was basically a scientist, he'd always had an emotional affinity for left-wing politics, and, in fact, had cast <u>his</u> first vote in 1956 for a third party candidate, an unknown socialist. "Margaret," he would say, over coffee in a small working class cafe in Somerville, "you'll always carry with you your middle-class capitalistic prejudices. You can't help it." He would illustrate his point with an appropriate paragraph from Karl Marx. It often seemed to Margaret that she was learning a new game, with a whole set of words to go with it. Henry described his sister Rosa, who was living a middle-class life, as having sold out.

Margaret stood up and dumped her cold tea into the sink. Reviewing the past did not cheer her up, and she was avoiding the question raised by that afternoon's conference session: did eccentricity lead to mental illness? Of course, the answer was no.

Henry's craziness was more recent, alternating with what she had come to call his "good" days, when he was almost his old self, organized, and if not cheerful, at least sardonic. Little by little, he saw himself (or was seen by others) to be out of the main stream, both professionally and socially. As the years had gone by, left-wing politics had become so splintered and its adherents so disillusioned that there was no place for Henry to hang his political hat. While he still called himself a socialist, he'd begun to sound more like an anarchist. He'd had more "bad days" in the years since the breakup of the Soviet Union, and had begun to veer toward the right in a frightening way, attacking the women's movement, labor unions, and minority organizations -- groups he'd once fiercely championed. He'd begun to sound like the proverbial "angry white male."

Margaret, his good pupil, was now the left-wing member of the family. After a few bad experiences, however, she'd learned to keep her political thoughts to herself.

But however it all began, his illness was now becoming full-blown. There were more "bad days" than good ones. He was becoming more suspicious. No matter how careful she was, she could no longer predict what could set him off.

And now it was too late -- either to leave him, throw him out, or even to start fighting back. Why had she waited so long?

Chapter Two

Her thoughts were interrupted by a familiar sound. From half a block away, she could hear the purr of Henry's twenty-five year old apple-green Volvo station wagon. The car had over 300,000 miles on it, but a new engine had been installed not long ago, plus all the latest gadgets, including air conditioning. And the finish looked brand new. Henry had spent hours with Leo -- the chief mechanic at the Volvo dealer -- bringing the car up to snuff. Unfortunately, since it was crammed with boxes, old books, tools, maps, and cast-off clothing, the inside made it look like a dumpster on wheels.

In recent months, when she could hear him coming home, Margaret would try to guess what direction his tirades would take. As he let himself in the back door, she looked up, stiffening for the first explosion. But today he looked different: his face was softer, his eyes more gentle. The lines around his mouth seemed less deep and the furrows in his brow were smoothed out. It had been years since he'd had this soft look: maybe not since he'd come home to announce that the university was sending him, all expenses paid, Margaret included, to a conference in Denmark. So perhaps today, too, would be one of his rare "good" days.

Sometimes, back when they were still having sex, Henry would have that same gentle look as he came to bed, but it had been over a year since that part of their life together had mysteriously ceased. Tentatively, after several weeks of being ignored, she'd asked if anything were wrong. He'd turned his head and refused to answer. Subsequent attempts on her part to be seductive had been brusquely rebuffed.

But today he looked, not only triumphant, but again younger; he was smiling. He was actually still a good-looking man, she thought to her surprise. As a couple, they'd always made a nice contrast: her curly, prematurely white hair and bright blue eyes, with wide cheekbones and a softer, shorter body, and his long, dark, lean look. What could have happened to turn him back, even temporarily, into the Henry she first knew?

Carefully he laid an official-looking manila envelope before her, reminding her of the way their old kitty had presented them with young birds. That cat had been called Richter, named for the seismologist who'd developed a special way of measuring earthquakes. "Here," he said, "you'd better read this."

Picking it up gingerly, almost as if it <u>were</u> a newly-killed fledgling, she saw that the envelope was stamped in red: CONFIDENTIAL.

"Let's have a drink," he waved his hand grandly, "and I'll explain it." Slowly, he lowered himself into a chair. She took down the bottle and poured two glasses of wine. There was an open box of rice crackers on the shelf; she put a few on a small plate. This was the most civil interchange they'd had in private for a long time. Margaret's eyes filled briefly with tears. He still had the power to move her.

He opened the envelope and took out a short memo from the university. "This came the other day. Everyone who was turning sixty-five, in fact, was invited to attend a meeting today." He smiled reflectively. "It was a funny group, people from every level of the university, including the fellow who guards the parking lot, the cook in the faculty dining room, secretaries, one department chair, several full professors, and me. What we had in common was our recent birthdays."

Listening to Henry now, Margaret picked up another change -- a new tone to his voice. He sounded relaxed, comfortable, and almost optimistic. She realized, sadly, that this tone, too, had been missing for several years. She wondered if that meeting today, in which he was treated by the university as an equal member of their staff, rather than as a permanent outcast, or a maverick scientist, had made the difference.

Maybe what she'd written on that yellow paper was <u>not</u> true. She sipped her wine, her mind following two tracks: one, trying to figure out what role, if any, the university had played in the development of Henry's suspicions, and the other, more insistent, observing Henry in this genial role. She'd forgotten what a good story teller he could be.

Henry took out the rest of the papers. "It's probably easier if I just summarize all this." He flipped the pages. "The university has been very up front." Margaret tried to hide her amazement. It had been a couple of years since Henry had called anybody "up front."

"Basically, it comes down to this," he said. "They've figured that if all of us who've turned sixty-five were to stay on, it would cost them a lot of money. Each of us was given a computerized sheet summarizing our situations." He pointed to the top sheet. "Mine was completely accurate. The thing is, Margaret, they're sweetening the pot, the famous golden handshake. They are offering to keep us on the health plan, and are giving us a substantial amount of severance pay, several years of salary. They'll still come out way ahead. In my case, of course, they could replace me with an inexpensive new PhD or whatever."

She swallowed. Oh, God, she thought: life with Henry underfoot every day. What would it be like when she was the full-time target of his anger? Even though she had a job, it wouldn't last forever. Maybe her clinic would start handing out -- well, not golden, but -- silver handshakes. Then they'd both be at home, face-to-face with each other on a daily basis maybe for the rest of their lives!

"I called our accountant," Henry continued, "and he gave me a quick ballpark figure on the tax situation; we'd lose about a third of it right off the

17

top. But the university had warned us about that already." There was a silence, and he looked down at the floor. For the first time, he seemed uncomfortable. He was rubbing his jaw in a funny way that meant he was keeping something back. What was he not telling her?

"There are legal implications as well," said Henry. The rhythms of his speech had slowed down. "So I went to see Paul." (Paul was their family lawyer.) Unfolding himself carefully, he began pacing around the kitchen, his long legs making the circuit several times before he spoke again. "Look, I need to go up and change my clothes. We can talk over dinner." There was an ominous tone in his voice, and Margaret began to feel anxious.

"One thing first," she said. "How much time do you have to make up your mind?"

"I have until June 30, the end of the university's fiscal year. And actually, I could wait a year, or two, or five, whatever. Of course, the money would be less, the longer I stayed." He looked serious, pausing in the doorway on his way upstairs. "But I've made up my mind, Margaret. I'm accepting their offer. Now."

* * * *

Margaret had decided to set the table in the dining room. Something told her this was going to be an important meal in their lives. It required ceremony. She laid out the heavy woven mats, the linen napkins, the

18

Wedgewood plates, the real crystal, the sterling silver, and the brass candlesticks. She opened another bottle of wine, and sprinkled parsley over the *Coquilles Saint Jacques*. Henry didn't appear to notice the formality of the setting, but then he'd always been immune to such changes in decor.

The table, with its shining candles, stood out like an island of civility amid the jungle of Henry's junk: the sideboard was piled high with folders of papers, each stack held firmly in place by a heavy rock, several of them geodes, their interior crystals reflecting the candlelight. There were boxes on the floor almost everywhere, all full of unsorted materials, and several of the chairs were heavily laden. Sitting down at the dining room table made Margaret feel as if she and Henry were a British white hunter and his lady, "dressed" for dinner (actually, both were wearing jeans), pushing back for a few hours the bush that was always encroaching, the dangers of tigers and hyenas temporarily banished.

But the tigers were inside as well. Margaret felt panicky, frightened by what Henry might say and anxious about the future. She'd always assumed that she'd have a little more time to face the problem of Henry's retirement. She was pleased with the way the dinner looked, but her fear seemed to have taken away the taste. She turned to the wine and found in its dry smokiness the courage to ask: "So what's the rest of it? What are the legal implications?"

Henry sighed. "I told Paul what I'd decided about retiring from the university, and how I wanted to live the rest of my life." He shifted in his chair. "I don't have to tell you -- again -- that I've never bought this suburban model of house, wife, and kids, not to mention the goddam lawn (he had never believed in mowing the grass), the fucking holidays, the dinner parties, the whole nine yards." His voice had become louder and he was beginning to sound like his usual self. Margaret was careful not to say anything. They didn't need another tirade right now. "This golden handshake is giving me a second chance, a way to manage my life the way I want. I'm going out west, Margaret. I'm leaving." He paused. "I'm leaving all of this, including you."

"You're kidding!" She felt as if her whole picture of the world had been shaken up, almost like one of those earthquakes that Henry was predicting.

"No, I'm not." His jaw had tightened, but he wasn't looking at her.

"You're planning to leave." Her voice was low, and close to a whisper.

"Yes." Now he looked directly at her, not quite defiantly, but as if to challenge her to doubt him.

He <u>wasn't</u> kidding. Her first reaction was sheer fury: how <u>dare</u> he be the one to make this decision, to have the courage to kick over the traces of marriage, home and family, and just go? This was one fantasy she'd never had, the idea that he would take the decision out of her hands. Had he been

20

thinking about it for a long time, maybe even as long as she had? Of course, he had often <u>threatened</u> to leave -- many times -- but she'd never taken him seriously. Now, in one fell swoop, thanks to the university and their golden handshake, he would turn her from a wife who didn't have the guts to leave, into a deserted wife.

For a few moments, she was speechless. Then the vigilant, watchful part of her, the careful observing self that had always been able to keep its cool when disaster struck, began to fade away into the distance. It became smaller by the second, vanishing into almost nothingness, leaving her with a raw, red anger that seemed to be rising from way down inside her. Then that fury came pouring out of her mouth and emerged as a scream: "You bastard," she shouted forcefully. "All these years I've had to put up with your tirades, your tyranny, and your crap!" Her arms pointed in every direction at the piles of junk that met her eye wherever she looked. "You think you can just walk away from all this, leaving me to sort it out, to try to make a decent life out of this wreckage?"

Henry looked down at his plate. This time, he was the one who was temporarily speechless. Then he looked at her and said quietly. "It sounds as if you might be glad to have me gone." He paused, and then added: "Whatever happens or however you feel, I <u>am</u> going. I'll be out of your life in a few weeks."

21

* * * *

She sat there, staring through the candles, trying to pull herself together, to bring back that observing ego and to begin to deal with the reality that he was presenting. She felt as if she didn't have any choice. He had made the decision.

Once again, by going along with his plan, she would be thrown back to that summer after her graduation from Wellesley. She'd been unable to make up her mind about graduate school, even though she'd been accepted by the Columbia School for Social Work in New York. Part of it was that Henry was urging her to stay in the Boston area and to go to one of the local schools part-time. He was still at M.I.T. and had hoped to finish his dissertation in a year or less.

And she really didn't want to be that far away from him, either. He'd offered to teach Margaret what he called the "art of socialist love." As it turned out, his knowledge in that field came only from books, and they'd learned these arts together, fumbling in the back of his old truck, and later in his furnished room when the landlady was out. Even in those early days of their relationship, lovemaking was what they did best. But neither of them knew enough about birth control, as it turned out.

As a compromise, she'd taken a summer job at a mental hospital right in Boston and moved in with two classmates who had a sublet on Beacon Hill.

Henry was a frequent visitor, but she spent many nights at his place as well. He'd moved to a partly furnished apartment in North Cambridge, with a small bedroom and a kitchenette.

Little by little, she'd begun fixing up his place. Her first purchase was a set of willowware dishes from Woolworth's, and then, her color scheme determined by the china pattern, she bought a blue tweed-like slipcover for the old couch. After a few weeks, emboldened by the fact that Henry either never noticed or didn't mind, she found a pair of brass candlesticks at a second-hand furniture store, and from Filene's, on sale, a blue and white checkered cloth for the card table where they ate. By chance, she discovered some bright red curtains in a thrift shop -- they only needed shortening, hemming, and the sewing on of rings to turn them into cafe curtains. Her final bargain was a blue rug and a red easy chair from Goodwill. All the room needed was for her to hang the landscape she had painted at her art class at Wellesley -- white clouds looming over a lazy blue river with a little red house in the distance. Henry did notice this last addition, and looking around said wryly: "My God, this place looks like the Fourth of July -- all red, white and blue." Margaret laughed. He had a point. In those days, too, the tone of his criticisms was more gentle.

But Margaret loved the feeling of sitting in the red chair in the evenings when Henry was at the library. She could play house to her heart's content, sewing the rings on the curtains and thinking of other things she could do to transform the place into a real home.

By midsummer, she was pregnant. As soon as she was a few days late, she was sure. In those days before instant pregnancy tests, she knew, of course, that she would have to wait another month before checking with a doctor. But nature had its ways of telling young women what was happening to their bodies. In Margaret's case, she found herself inordinately sleepy, constantly hungry for saltines and bread crusts -- she'd even stolen one off her roommate's breakfast plate -- and her nipples were sore. After a few weeks, she began to hear herself talking to the baby: hey, sweetie, you're sitting on my bladder. She knew that Henry would be furious when she finally told him -- he'd often said that marriage was an invention of the bourgeoisie -- but she put it off as long as she could. She became pleasantly passive. It was a lovely feeling to know that something had taken over her life and that nature would just take its own sweet time. There was nothing to do but wait.

Of course, even in those days, there was an alternative. But she knew instantly that she didn't want an abortion, even though she'd known some women at Wellesley who'd gone to Puerto Rico for the operation, and another who "knew someone" in New York. In fact, she very much wanted to <u>have</u> the baby. When she finally told him, Henry was astonished.

"What will you do?" he'd asked. (Not, she noticed, what will <u>we</u> do?)

When she mentioned that she could always go home to her parents in Scarsdale, he was horrified, as she knew he would be. All of a sudden, he became a parent. "You're going to let my child be brought up by those bourgeois, capitalist, conformist suburbanites?" In his lexicon, these were the worst things he could call them.

Margaret shrugged. She felt strangely empowered, and the baby was her ally.

"I suppose we could get married. . ." he'd ventured, hesitantly.

"But you don't believe in marriage," said Margaret, realizing that the game was over and she had won. It had been almost too easy.

"Listen, let's just do it. You'll have to work as long as you can, but by the first of the year, I should have my degree. You can move into my place right away. Get yourself a ring -- I'm sure they have them at Sears (and he was right, they did, fourteen carat gold and only $29.95 in those days; she was still wearing it) and call the City Hall and find out what you do to get a license."

* * * *

And so they were married, in the musty living room of an elderly justice of the peace, whose overstuffed furniture featured hand-crocheted antimacassars. The baby -- who turned out to be Anita, now thirty-nine --

managed to cooperate with the deception by postponing her birth for nearly three weeks. In fact, the months of Margaret's pregnancy and the next two years when all three of them lived in Henry's little apartment were the best times of the marriage. Anita was an easy baby, who looked exactly like Henry, long, lean and bird-like -- twenty-four inches at birth. Henry was enchanted by her. Although he was busy, first with finishing up his dissertation and then with a new job as instructor at the university, he enjoyed domestic life and Margaret's cooking. His mother had never cared much for homemaking and he'd often been left in the care of his sister whose idea of a home-cooked meal was a peanut butter sandwich and an apple.

And Margaret was content. She saw this time as her nesting period, but content was the word to describe the warm, physical euphoria which nursing and marriage had induced. Living closely with Henry, having him available all night long, had repaired a sense of loneliness that being an only child with a cold, distant mother, had created. And the days with Anita in the sandbox at the park left her pleasantly drunk with sunshine.

* * * *

These memories, available until now as reminders of happier days, and of the decision she'd made forty years ago to marry Henry, suddenly seemed painful. Would they now be colored by the events of this day, when Henry was talking about leaving her? What happened to people's happy memories when things turned sour? Would she have to wipe them all out? Or would they just gradually melt down, like these candles?

Picking at the dripping candle wax, she took a deep breath and asked him, trying not to sound sarcastic: "So you never expected me to go with you on your trip west?"

Henry shook his head. "No, you've made that clear over the years. You never wanted to give up this bourgeois existence." His voice was rising. "I have other plans," he said. "I'm going to show all those bastards in the Geological Association that I know what I'm talking about. I'm going to turn their theory of plate tectonics on its head and someday they'll be grateful to me, because I know how to prevent earthquakes." His eyes were shining and he looked as if he could see a glorious future somewhere out there.

While Margaret had never heard him make this last assertion, she wasn't surprised. "So how does Paul come into all this?" She tried to keep her tone neutral, but she was aware that all the anger was still there.

"I went to see Paul because I wanted to do it all properly, to be fair to both of us. Let me tell you what he suggested." Henry sat up formally, almost as if he were in the witness chair in a courtroom. "He recommended that I split this handshake money with you -- right down the middle -- and that I give you the house free and clear, since it was your father's money that gave us the down payment." He looked at her carefully. "And besides, as you know, I never wanted the place anyway." Margaret said nothing, waiting for the final shoe to drop. "I can live on my pension, my social security, and this new money -- my half. I figure you'll have a similar income when you retire, with your own pension and the money from your great-aunts' trust fund, plus the house."

"It sounds as if you are talking about a divorce," she said, her voice now sounding wooden and without feeling. The word "divorce" had a power of its own. It carried all kinds of baggage, from anger to sadness, and included a frightening feeling of loneliness and desertion. The other piece of baggage had to do with her children. All those years when she had thought about leaving him, it was the children whose needs held her back. She'd been convinced that the children of a "broken home" would suffer in all kinds of ways: they'd drop out of school, they'd become drug addicts, and blame her.

"I guess I am." Henry had slumped back in his chair again, perhaps relieved that she had been the first one to use the "D" word. Turning his head, he swallowed nervously, still looking at her out of the corner of his eye.

Now all she could think of was being stuck in this old house, surrounded by the mountains of Henry's junk. And he would be getting off scot-free!

"But what about your stuff?" Her voice rose and she could feel her face getting red. She was really furious. "All those damn phone booths," she shouted, "and your fucking prehistoric tools, and computer print-outs, and" -- waving her hands in all directions -- "all that shit?" Her more rational self was watching this performance as if it were a drama put on by someone she hardly knew, a person who could use four-letter words to good effect.

"Well," he said amicably, and evidently not surprised at her language, "no problem. You can write it into the separation agreement that I have to have all those things out of the house by a certain date. I should probably be leaving by the Fourth of July." Was that a look of relief on his face? Was he telling himself: well, the worst is over? Perhaps he could afford to be generous. Henry was getting what he said he wanted -- a ticket to freedom. Suddenly she wanted to hit him. It wasn't fair, after all these years of her putting up with his tempers, his tirades, and his possessions, that he would be one to get what he wanted. She would be the one who would be left to grieve this marriage, to deal with confused and angry children, and the end of a life that had looked from the outside as if it were at least as good as anyone's. People would be surprised: she had done a good job of creating an impression. It had become almost the real thing.

Chapter Three

Even before Margaret opened her eyes the next morning, she knew Henry had already gone. The bed felt empty, the sheets slippery and cold. Soon, she reminded herself, she would be sleeping alone every night, and waking up by herself as well. She was tempted to turn over and go back to sleep, but there was too much to do. She sat up and looked around the room, feeling disorganized and overwhelmed. Against the far wall, Henry's chest of drawers, covered with the usual mixture of papers and rock samples, was echoed by her own dresser: it was starting to look like a pale imitation of his -- bills to be paid, invitations to workshops, earrings, and yesterday morning's coffee cup. The anger and anxiety of last night had been replaced by a feeling of dislocation, and a kind of numbness.

Climbing out of bed, she moved slowly to the window. Raising the shade and then the sash, she saw that Henry's car was missing. He'd probably gone to the office, as he often did on Saturday mornings. She put her head out. Yesterday's storm had blown out to sea, and it was a fresh May morning. Even her own unkempt lawn was green at this time of year: her feeble attempts to plant bulbs every autumn had sprinkled a few tulips here and there. The lilacs, left over from the previous owners, while becoming more leggy each year, still sported a blossom or two. And on the far edges of the yard, she could see dots of purple and white where her volunteer violets continued to seed themselves.

Regretfully, Margaret turned from the window and began to put on a few clothes. Yesterday's jeans still hung on the back of the bathroom door; a clean T-shirt and a sweater would complete the outfit. Various major tasks presented themselves. To begin with, she needed to come to terms with the fact that she was now going to be in charge of her whole life -- all of it, including this half acre of land, an enormous old thirteen-room house that was falling apart, her finances, her legal affairs, and a divorce. She realized that, with the exception of about six weeks right after her graduation from Wellesley when she'd shared that sublet on Beacon Hill and worked at the mental hospital -- a momentary hiccup in a long life -- she'd either been supported by her father or had been in some way under Henry's wing. Having a husband, even one like Henry, had its advantages. He'd been there, for advice if not comfort, when the car made funny noises, when the furnace broke down, or the water heater leaked all over the basement floor. Now it would all be up to her.

Slowly, lost in thought, she moved into the ancient kitchen and was reminded once again that whatever she did, she'd have to start with the house. Many people would tell her she should sell it immediately, and buy a new, modern condominium and never have to worry again about shoveling

31

snow or mowing the lawn. She tried to picture herself living in such a place. Even the idea felt wrong. From the very beginning, when they bought the house, Margaret had felt the house had a purpose, a role to play in her life. She could not abandon it until this mission had been fulfilled.

All that was down the road, of course. As soon as possible, she and Henry needed to talk to the four kids, either on the phone or by letter. Even though they were no longer children, they should be told that their parents' marriage was breaking up. Perhaps a joint letter, signed by both of them?

But talking to the kids was too much right now. She'd end up reassuring each of them that this separation was a good thing for both of them, and at this moment, Margaret needed some reassurance herself. Also pressing was the necessity to find a lawyer for herself. What it came down to was that she needed to talk to Chloe, her best friend. From her very first months in town, right after they'd bought the house, she'd shared her life with Chloe. Their two oldest children -- Margaret's Anita and Chloe's Athena -- had been inseparable since nursery school. Their mothers often called them "our two A girls" and the girls were still friends today, thirty-six years later, although separated now by 3000 miles: Anita had lived in Seattle for the last ten years and Athena had ended up in New York.

Chloe was the expert when it came to social survival in the western suburbs of Boston; she and Margaret had developed an elaborate on-running game about the kind of family who'd made it in their kind of town. Chloe Pappas Solomon was herself a good example. According to their theory, this mythical family was first of all almost always a mixed marriage. Chloe had been the product of an orthodox Greek family, and her husband Saul's family was also orthodox, but Jewish. Most of Margaret's and Chloe's friends were similarly cross-matched. One little girl, whom Chloe had often quoted, had been overheard insisting authoritatively to a group of fellow kindergardeners that the mothers were never Jewish.

The family in the game lived in a large Victorian house, with a modernized kitchen, shiny hardwood floors, oriental rugs, and antiques that had been passed down from grandparents. They drove a Volvo station wagon, had four children, a dog and a cat. The dog -- a Golden Retriever or a Black Lab -- was usually named something utilitarian and unpretentious -- Fido, Rover, or Rufus -- but the cat (unless it was named just "cat" or "kitty") was the focus of the family's intellectual game-playing and gave them a chance to show off their special fields of knowledge. Cats tended to be called Chomsky, Thisbe, Teller, or Papageno, or, as in Margaret's case, Richter. The families all had summer cottages, of course, in New Hampshire, the Maine coast, at the Cape or on Martha's Vineyard.

The children took many kinds of lessons, beginning with woodworking at age five for the boys, on the theory that they needed regular contact with a

33

male figure since their own fathers were either too busy or knew nothing about tools. Eventually, some of the mothers had got together and hired the same carpenter for a class of their own, since it usually fell to their hands to do the routine inside painting and wallpapering in these old houses. One whole session had been devoted to spackling (and grouting for those who stayed after class). Margaret was a quick learner on that day, since she'd had a lot of experience frosting cakes. Most impressive, however, was one class member who had her own miter box.

After the course was over, Margaret had rented a steamer and had taken off all the wallpaper in her living room and dining room, then repainted both, including the ten-foot ceilings, and later, with her kids' help, had done some of the bedrooms as well. Henry never seemed to notice any of these improvements, even though he'd often had to walk under the ladders.

Following woodworking, the children in this mythical family had piano or cello lessons, and where appropriate, Hebrew, Greek or Chinese, sailing, and ballet for the girls. Eventually, the kids grew up, and after a short detour of experimentation with marijuana, and perhaps a few sessions with a therapist, went on to attend schools and colleges whose names were emblazoned on the rear windows of the Volvo.

Chloe and Margaret often continued the game in which they described the ongoing saga of this archetypical family. Once the children had been launched, the wife "went back to work," as indeed Chloe and Margaret had done, developing a career in human services, academia, or the arts. This wife, and to a lesser degree her husband, would become active in local politics, joining others to support candidates, run campaigns, or at least collect signatures in front of the supermarket for worthy causes -- the dog leash law, fluoridation, and the bottle bill, and many others long since forgotten.

While neither Chloe or Margaret had been divorced, they'd decided several years ago that divorce was, in fact, the fate of their typical couple. Now Margaret needed to tell Chloe how destiny was tapping her on the shoulder.

* * * *

When Margaret called Chloe she explained that she needed a good lawyer. Quickly, Chloe came up with the name of Eleanor Baxter, describing her as very bright and tough when she had to be. Margaret jotted down the name in the back of her address book. Chloe, of course, had a Rolodex. And she probably put her whole Christmas list on the computer.

"What kind of legal problem do you have?" Chloe asked.

Margaret realized she needed to see Chloe's face when she told her the news. She'd often felt that an event wasn't real until she'd threshed it out with Chloe and they had classified it, put it in context with its wider implications. "Can I tell you in person?"

"Of course. Come for lunch."

Several hours later, showered and dressed appropriately, driving over to Chloe's house, she found herself remembering what had happened when her mother died six years ago. The nursing home had called early in the morning to say that her mother had died in her sleep, "a blessing," as they put it. Margaret was able to make the necessary phone calls -- first to Chloe who said she'd be over in an hour, -- and then to the funeral home, calls to the local papers, her children, and the few distant relatives. She had no difficulty with any of it, even the purchase of the other half of the cemetery plot. She told herself that her ability to do all this so effectively was because she and her mother had never been close.

And then Chloe had come over. She had made Margaret get off the phone, and sit down. She'd made coffee, and insisted Margaret eat breakfast. And when Margaret started to say how easy and simple it all had been, hearing the news, making the calls, Chloe shook her head.

"Nonsense," she said. "You think, just because you weren't close, that this will be easier for you? Don't you understand? You've spent your whole life hoping against hope that your mother would change and turn into a real mother. You've been a good girl all your life, and for nothing. As it turns out, <u>you</u> were the parent. And now it's too late. It's got to be harder for you, not easier."

There was a long silence. Finally, after a long minute, Margaret had begun to cry.

* * * *

And once again today, Margaret was sitting on Chloe's patio, seeking solace. Saul was a great gardener and at this time of year, his perennials were in full flower. Puddles of late-blooming red tulips dotted the emerald green of his recently fertilized lawn, and his early yellow irises were clumping under the evergreens. Once again, Margaret thought of her own poor back yard. Maybe the time had come for her to think of hiring one of those companies that sent an army of men to mow, clean out the leaves in the fall, and perhaps even shovel snow.

"I made us a fruit salad. Good for my diet," said Chloe with a smile, for she was always dieting. Margaret loved the way Chloe looked, fat or thin, her hair still dark (except for one long white streak), twisted into a knot at the back of her head, and that long line that ran from her forehead to the end of her nose -- a classic Mediterranean profile -- her black sparkling eyes and olive skin. Compared to Chloe, Margaret found her own looks both uninspiring and ordinary. Her bright blue eyes were her only outstanding feature, and they had been likened, variously and not very originally, to bachelor's buttons, or periwinkles (the flowers, not the snails). A potter once told her that one of his prize glazes was exactly that shade of blue. Margaret, herself, thought that the color and texture of her hair was her best feature. It was now pure white, fluffy and soft, as it had been since she was thirty-five. Of course, the people at the beauty parlor were always suggesting that she color it, but Margaret liked it the way it was. Because she was short, she had become accustomed to people patting her head, particularly at cocktail parties. Sometimes it helped, if the offender wasn't too drunk, for her to draw herself up to her full five feet, one inch in height, and to say, in the accent of her Boston aunts, the Misses Chippen -- "I <u>beg</u> your pardon. . ." Most of the time, the person would begin to apologize profusely, but occasionally she would have to add: "Please, don't embarrass yourself."

But no one would have dared to do anything like that to Chloe, who always looked regal and unapproachable. None of Chloe's children had her Greek beauty (she had four daughters), but they were a handsome family, with some of the kids inheriting Saul's gray eyes and sandy curls combined with some of Chloe's features. The two friends had often agreed that ethnic mixing made for beautiful children, but they were admittedly biased.

"So tell me," said Chloe.

Margaret sighed. How to begin? Although she'd often talked to Chloe about Henry and her marriage, she had never really told her how desperate

38

she was or how crazy he'd become of late. Some sort of residual loyalty had always made her minimize the worst of it. She'd also worried about creating gossip that might destroy Henry's already shaky reputation at the university, since Saul Solomon had a friend in Henry's department. She took a deep breath. What the hell, she told herself. It's time.

She took her fork and tried to pick up a seedless grape, and then frowned because she kept missing it. Putting the grape in her mouth with her fingers, she looked up at Chloe. "Henry and I are getting a divorce."

"Oh," said Chloe, obviously not sure whether this was good or bad news. She was looking closely at Margaret's face. "You don't look devastated or down-hearted. You do look -- well, sort of surprised." Chloe spoke carefully, as if she were tip-toeing into an invalid's room.

"Maybe that's it. I'm feeling as if someone just unlocked the gate. I'm free, or I am until someone remembers and comes back to close it." She sighed. "That's part of it. The other piece is that I'm really angry. I don't know if I'm angry at Henry or at myself. Maybe that's it. I'm furious that I sat there and waited for him to make the decision."

"Are you going to be all right? Financially, I mean," said Chloe, always the practical one. "I know Henry has always been such a miser. I can't picture his being generous with alimony when he wouldn't even fix the front porch."

Margaret explained about the golden handshake and Henry's decision to split the money and give her the house. "He went to see our lawyer about it. Which is why I need a lawyer of my own. I want to make sure the arrangement is fair to me." She didn't add that, of course, she was scared.

Chloe sat quietly, moving the strawberries around on her plate. "So you're both glad and mad. How about sad?"

"Oh, Chloe, trust you to get to the heart of it. Of course, I'm sad, not just about the end of a forty-year marriage, but I feel I've failed somehow, failed maybe to be the kind of wife Henry should have had." Margaret wondered if she really meant that last statement. It came out sounding almost sugary-sweet. She paused, and then found herself going on to tell Chloe something she had never before shared. "Although, of course, Henry never wanted any kind of wife. He didn't believe in marriage -- still doesn't, I suspect -- and I'm sure he would never have married me if I hadn't been pregnant."

Chloe smiled. She didn't seem surprised. "I suspect there are a lot of men like Henry out there who say they don't believe in marriage, but secretly, they're like kids with their noses pressed to the candy store window. They're hoping the proprietor will find an excuse to invite them in. Pregnancy can be their good excuse."

"You may be right," said Margaret. "But I was not above using it myself as my ticket into that candy store. For some reason, I just wanted to have that baby. It was true of all of us, I think, our whole generation of women: something was driving us to have all those children. Henry used to say that we were all lemmings rushing to the sea of over-population. I certainly wasn't thinking of what was good for him when I encouraged him to get married. Someone like my mother would probably have told me that a good wife would have been thrilled when he told me yesterday that he was finally getting the chance to do the research he believed in. I should have been willing to go out West with him and live in a tent while he tested out his theories. Come to think of it, my mother, for all her uptight, Brahmin inflexibility, actually did live with my father for a number of years in mining towns. But when Henry told me last night about his opportunity to retire early, I don't think it occurred to either of us that I might want to go with him. What occurred to us was to get a divorce. And of course," she added softly, "we haven't been living as man and wife for over a year."

Margaret's eyes filled with tears. "It's funny, "Margaret said, "we sleep in the same king-sized bed -- even last night, after talking about divorce. But nothing happens. He just doesn't want to anymore, I guess."

The long silence that followed Margaret's statement was broken, finally, when Chloe asked quietly: "You're not thinking that there is someone else in Henry's life?"

Margaret shook her head. "Of course, I wondered about that for a while, but except for when he's at work, he's actually home every evening, working at the dining room table, planning the trip that I guess he's finally going to take. But I wish I knew what made this change take place; it seemed to be all of a sudden."

That last phrase made it sound as if the coldness and distancing had come just from Henry. Margaret had to admit that most of the time, these days, she was too angry at him even to think of going to bed with him. What it came down to was the fact that, although she really didn't want to have sex with the Henry of today, she wanted to have sex with someone -- someone like the person Henry used to be, when they both wanted each other and all the bad things hadn't happened yet, or maybe with a whole new man out there somewhere.

She cleared her throat. "So now he'll be leaving home. For good."

Chloe frowned. "I was always curious why you never got angry at him, no matter how much he humiliated you. You were the old-fashioned good wife. Remember in colonial days, they called married women Goody? You've been Goody Bluestone."

"Shit," said Margaret, suddenly anxious to change the subject. "Well, the good news is that now I can throw out all his junk."

Chloe smiled. "I can see the signs tacked up on the telephone poles: Giant Yard Sale! Antique Phone Booth. Stone-age Tools. I can hardly wait."

"Don't laugh. I was thinking the same thing. I think I <u>will</u> have a yard sale. In fact, I told Henry we couldn't get divorced unless he promised me to get rid of all his junk. And he said -- can you believe it? -- quote: 'no problem.'"

"What will you do with the house? Sell it? Or fix it up?" Chloe's eyes lit up.

"I've decided to take my share of the money and put a good portion of it in the stock market, and then the rest of it in the house. In the long run, I think it will give me a better return on my money." Margaret stopped, blushing. She'd never been able to admit to Chloe how painful it had been for her to live in such a neglected, dilapidated house. She was sure everyone was sorry for her. Most of the time, she made a joke of it, calling it the Bluestone Folly.

Chloe frowned. "I know a wonderful contractor. Gretchen Donabedian, your friend the economist, thought the world of him. He did over her whole house. He's a big Danish fellow. Gretch always called him The Great Dane."

"How's Gretchen doing? I haven't talked to her in a long time." As Margaret spoke, she thought about Gretchen and her strange life: unhappily married, she lived for her romantic interludes with a colleague at their annual conventions.

"She's getting divorced, actually," said Chloe, "and moving away somewhere to live with some guy."

"Well, good for her," Margaret heard herself say. "What's happening to her kids? As I recall, they are still quite young."

"Her husband's keeping them." Chloe shook her head. "No matter what happens, the kids are the losers, that's for sure."

Margaret took out her address book and under the name of her new lawyer, she wrote: Contractor. . . "So what's the name of her contractor?" She wasn't quite ready to talk about the effect of divorce on children.

"Jensen. Erik with a "k" Jensen. He's in the book. He's taking care of his handicapped son, so he likes to work close to home."

Surely, Margaret thought, a man who took care of a handicapped child would be -- what? -- she wasn't sure what she felt, but there was something reassuring about the phrase.

Chapter Four

After lunch, the skies clouded over and a cold wind began to ruffle Saul's tulips. Shivering, Margaret pulled her sweater around her shoulders. But it wasn't just the sudden drop in temperature. She felt apprehensive, as if they were heading toward areas she really didn't want to deal with. Chloe, who had been silent for a few minutes, looked up. "Oh, Margaret, you're cold. Come, let's move indoors and have some coffee. That should warm you up." She paused. "There are gingersnaps as well."

The cups were set up on the coffee table in the big living room, and there was a fire already going in the fireplace. Margaret had always thought Chloe's living room was perfect, maybe almost too perfect. It was funny, she thought, as they settled down inside, that she and Chloe, for all their cleverness in social satire, had never made this kind of interior decor a part of their joint game. Many of the couples they talked about had living rooms that proclaimed to all the world that theirs was a family whose members, even down to the youngest child, had his or her one special talent. One musical family, whom both of them knew well, featured, on a music stand, the score of an opera one of the children had composed, and across the room, leaning on a bookcase, the cello seemed to be awaiting its ten-year old owner who would surely be back in a minute to play the Brahms concerto. The seven-year old daughter in that family, Margaret recalled,

45

played the harp quite well, and that instrument, too, was in place next to the child's little chair. A bust of Mozart sat on the piano, next to the metronome.

Chloe's living room gave the impression of being a workshop or display gallery for the whole family's art work. There were changes -- you could call them new exhibits -- every time Margaret came to visit. Chloe's hobbies were evident both in the loom in the corner, with its half-finished baby blanket, and her photographs of small children that filled one whole wall. Saul's metal sculpture dominated the area over the fire-place -- a copper bas-relief of a group of excited and protesting faces, crowded together: you could almost hear the shouts. The children's paintings were carefully hung nearby.

Every table had piles of books, some dog-eared old favorites, bound in leather, others the latest novels or treatises on biology (Saul's field). Every time Margaret saw those piles of books she wanted to go home and rearrange her own living room (which was nothing special, except for the paintings by her son Charles). She also couldn't help but wonder if someone were actually reading Religio Medici or dipping into the Sonnets from the Portuguese, or whether these artifacts represented an attempt to create an atmosphere of study. Somehow she had never wanted to put Chloe on the spot by asking her which was her favorite Elizabeth Barrett Browning poem.

Across from where Margaret was seated at the coffee table was a new item, a pencil drawing obviously by one of Chloe's grandchildren. She got up to take a look.

Chloe had written at the bottom of the drawing -- by Theo, Age 3. It was an astonishing picture for such a young child. Stick figures of children were running toward the viewer, but in the background, much smaller figures were fading into the landscape. Even the houses in the distance were smaller than those in the foreground.

"My God," said Margaret. "That's some drawing. He seems to understand perspective."

"Yes," said Chloe, "he told me quite firmly that everyone knew things got little when they got far away. I had to admit he was right." She shook her head. "Poor kid. He did that two years ago. Now he's in kindergarten and the teacher doesn't like the way he draws. She thinks he's too 'constricted.' So now she's got him doing abstract things, dripping finger paintings like all the other kids. He looks very upset when he visits me and sees that drawing up there. I think he's ashamed of it now." While her voice sounded upset, her face glowed with pride.

Margaret laughed. "Now you know how traditional painters felt in the 1940's when Pollock and de Kooning took over."

There was a long silence. Chloe's hand hovered over the gingersnaps and then withdrew, regretfully, it seemed. She must be about to ask something difficult, Margaret decided. Then Chloe said: "Have you told your kids about the divorce?" Her face had become softer. For Chloe this would be the real bottom line. She had always been close to all of Margaret's children, particularly with Anita.

Margaret shook her head. "Not yet. I'm giving it some thought, but you know I've always been careful not to put Henry down. It's probably written somewhere in Doctor Spock: *'Don't say bad things about your spouse.'* But then if you decide to leave him, the kids think you're abandoning a perfect husband and father." She laughed nervously. "I'm sure they know things haven't been wonderful, but I think they'll be surprised, and probably dismayed. Even though they're all grown up and on their own, they probably like to think that the home fires are still burning."

"What do you think their reactions will be?" Chloe frowned and leaned over the table.

"The one I'm really worried about is Anita. She was never good about changes. When Charles was a toddler and we still lived in Cambridge -- she was only three or so -- she told me I'd ruined her life by having that baby. She would hardly speak to me. And that's when she attached herself to her father. Even now, at 39, she's still Daddy's girl, and, of course, she looks just like him. Of all the kids, she's certainly the one he's closest to. Sometimes, watching her face at home when she was growing up, I had the feeling she thought I was the wrong wife for him."

"Oh, Margaret," said Chloe, leaning back, "that's just classic Freud. All four of my girls used to think I didn't understand Saul, either. They were always telling me I didn't handle him properly."

"But I suspect Saul didn't go along with it, whereas Henry really ate it up. Anita is a lot like him, too, being a scientist. They often talk on the phone. She calls him for advice about work. I think she's going to blame me for all of this." Margaret frowned. "Maybe you always worry about your first child. I know I do. That whole generation of kids had a hard time, a lot of pressure left over from the sixties." Margaret paused. "I worry that she's thirty-nine and still not married."

Chloe looked down. "But at least she has that fellow, doesn't she? Everett?"

"Oh, yes. But I don't have any sense of where it's going. None of us have met him. I guess she's not planning to have children. She seems happy in her job, so I should just shut up and let her run her own life. Which is actually what I do. But I feel disconnected from her."

Even as she was speaking, she was wondering about Chloe's oldest daughter, Athena. For a long time Margaret had worried about this child.

She'd always been incredibly thin, beginning in High School, and continuing, as far as Margaret knew, to this day. She'd been briefly married, had never settled down to any special career. A brilliant, all-A student in High School, star of all the plays, she was early decision at Dartmouth. But even then, Margaret worried about her. She felt that Chloe and Saul were always pushing this child. Currently, so Anita had told her, she was working off and on as a "temp." She wondered if Chloe and Saul helped to support her.

Yet in spite of their closeness, Margaret and Chloe had never really talked about Athena. In the old days, in their grandparents' time, it used to be money that friends didn't discuss. For Margaret's mother's generation, it had been sex. Now, it seemed, one did not reveal worries about grown children. She wasn't even sure if Athena had ever had any professional help. She suspected that she had, but Chloe had never said.

"Do you worry about Athena, too?" she asked tentatively.

Chloe nodded. "All the time," she said slowly. "All the time." Now she picked up one of the cookies and began to eat it. She looked at Margaret. "I wonder if <u>you</u> could talk to her. I'm so afraid of saying the wrong thing. All she ever says to either Saul or me is 'Get off my back.' She always seemed more at ease with you, Margaret. I thought she spent more of her time at your house than mine."

Margaret smiled and said: "That's what I used to tell Anita, that she seemed to prefer you to her own mother!"

The two women sat quietly for a moment. Strange, Margaret thought, that in all these years, they had never shared this strange irritation, envy -- or was it jealousy? -- about their relationships with each others' oldest children.

Margaret sighed. "I wish Anita were closer to Molly and her two brothers. The three of them are like a little club, and I think Anita feels left out. Of course, she does live far away, and that was her choice."

"So you think the other three will take it pretty well?"

"Molly may be upset because her wedding is in February and she'll want her father to walk her down the aisle. Maybe he'd be willing to fly East to do that. But she's got too much on her mind to worry about us. And Andrew's wife, you know, is having their first baby in October, so they'll be preoccupied as well. But I may be in for some surprises."

"And what about Charles?"

"I hate to dump all this on him right now." Margaret was thoughtful. "He has his own troubles." She was glad Chloe did not ask for details. Now Margaret was the one holding back. "Of all the kids, he'll be the one who will worry most about me, and who will be -- quote -- on my side."

Margaret stood up to go. Chloe gave her a big hug. "I'm on your side, kiddo. And if you don't like Eleanor Baxter, I can probably come up with another name."

* * * *

On Tuesday morning Margaret took several hours off from work and drove to Wellesley to see her new lawyer. The sun had finally come out and the leaves had that fat, juicy look of late May, still not full-grown, but bursting with hormones like teen-agers. In a few weeks they would be mature, darker green and capable of providing shade from the June sunshine or to act as little umbrellas all summer long.

Moving quickly up the steps of Eleanor Baxter's office building, she felt both grown up -- here she was consulting her lawyer, taking care of her legal needs -- and on the other hand, she was as frightened as a child. What if this woman asked her: why did you wait so long to leave this man?

Margaret had often felt that, by not leaving Henry, she was somehow letting the side down -- the side defined by feminism. She assumed that Eleanor Baxter would be relatively young, a career woman who thought all men were chauvinists. And Margaret would be judged as a passive, old-fashioned breed of woman who had never stood up to her husband about anything, following him two steps behind all the way.

There was no point in telling a woman like that how often she had struggled with the problem in her own mind. It was so much more complicated than anyone thought. As a socialist (or Communist, anarchist, whatever he was or had been) Henry actually was a strong believer in women's rights. It was only recently, when he evidently felt threatened from all sides, that he'd begun to speak of the women's movement in derogatory tones. He'd always been pleased that she had a career. In fact, it was the years she spent having and taking care of the kids when they were little that he resented. As soon as Andrew started first grade, Henry began to push her to go back to graduate school, <u>any</u> graduate school, get her degree, and then to get a job.

The flip side of Henry's attitude, alas, was that he also expected her to arrange for and solve the child care problem. Not only was he never willing to stay home when the kids were sick, but he wouldn't take time out to attend school plays or teacher conferences. "You were the one who wanted all these kids," he'd say.

Henry was actually no different from most of the other fathers whom Margaret knew. Even loving husbands like Saul Solomon left the child care entirely up to their wives. Margaret and many of her friends worked a four-day week as long as they had small children at home and used that extra day to be the neighborhood "Mom," especially in the summer and during school vacations. They supervised lemonade stands, sat on the bench during swimming lessons, car pooled to Cub Scouts and Brownies. It all worked somehow, and the children grew up almost as part of a large extended family.

* * * *

Eleanor Baxter (who asked to be called Eleanor) was, in fact, very young-looking, petite and almost fragile. But from the beginning she treated Margaret with respect, and took careful notes as the story unfolded. Finally, Margaret finished her dreary tale.

Eleanor looked up from her notebook. "Your husband's lawyer seems to have come up with a pretty fair plan for both of you," she said. "Tell me about your husband. What's he like as a person?" She leaned back, putting her pencil down.

Margaret sat quietly, trying to decide how much to share about Henry's instability, his temper, his suspicions, his paranoia. Well, she told herself, this woman is my lawyer and she wouldn't be asking if she didn't need to know. "He's always been a difficult man, angry at everyone and everything. I don't mean that he hits me or anything like that. He's just furious all the time. Perhaps you'd call it verbal abuse, although he never actually calls me obscene names. He doesn't like the way we live. He wants to live simply, just travel and sleep in a tent. But at the same time, he collects things, all kinds of stuff that he's picked up, thinking it might be worth something someday." Margaret sighed, hearing herself beginning to wind up. "He should never have got married, or had children, or bought a house."

Eleanor picked up her pencil again. "He's an eccentric, that's what you're telling me? With a nasty disposition?"

"I suspect that's what many people have always thought, including his lawyer. I wish it were just that. In the last year or so, he's become -- well -- paranoid. He collects old nineteenth century tools. They're all over our house, some in strange places, too. Not long ago I found an old-fashioned drill in his underwear drawer, but when I asked him about it, he claimed that someone had put it there on purpose, just to confuse him." Margaret sighed. "Even worse was the time he accused one of the kids, who happened to be visiting at the time, of stealing a set of screw drivers; he insisted on hunting through my son's luggage to make sure he wasn't taking it with him. He thinks people are plotting against him. And he has some strange ideas. He's a geologist, you know, with a specialty in plate tectonics. You know what that is?"

"Something to do with underground faults and earthquakes? Continental drift?"

"Right. Well, he has his own theory about how all that works, a different theory from anyone else in the field. He thinks he has the key to preventing earthquakes, but no one will listen. And someday, they'll all be sorry, but then it will be too late. Los Angeles will have fallen into the Pacific Ocean."

"But maybe he's right, "said Eleanor, smiling. "Well, I'll just keep things calm and simple," she said. "I'll push for a settlement right away, so you'll get your money and the full title to the house before your husband leaves town. We'll get both of you to sign it. If you get it in the mail ready for signing, you should feel reasonably secure about the divorce, itself. We probably won't get a court date until early next spring -- January at the earliest -- but you should be all set."

Margaret walked down the steps to her car, carefully choosing where she put each foot. Somehow, she had the feeling she could trip.

Chapter Five

As it turned out, in spite of their agreement to write a joint letter to all four kids, the news began to leak out, like plastic peanuts from a packing box. Margaret's comforting fantasy that this was going to be an amicable separation, followed by a friendly divorce, became just that: a fantasy. She realized there was no way they could have cooperated in a joint effort at this point, and soon both of them had reverted to their usual patterns of family communication.

Anita had called Henry with a professional question and during the conversation Henry had mentioned he might be in Utah in a month or so and could maybe drive up to Seattle to visit her. (Anita worked for what used to be called the Weather Bureau in Puget Sound.) From the look on his face, Margaret suspected he'd let slip something about their up-coming separation and divorce. She decided she'd better talk quickly with Anita.

As always when she got in touch with her oldest child, it turned out to be more complicated than just a simple phone call. She had to remind herself that there was a three-hour time difference between Boston and Seattle, and the best time to call usually turned out to be midnight, Boston time. By that time, at least, Henry would be in bed, so she wouldn't have to cope with the stress of a three-way call, Henry on the upstairs phone, his voice echoing strangely, and she on one of the downstairs phones, or, even more distracting, when both of them were in the same room, Henry's waving at her and mouthing something he wanted her to add. But no matter the time or place, it was always hard to talk to this prickly child.

On this particular evening, she decided to phone from the den. Sitting at the desk, staring at the phone, she found herself picking up one of Henry's old diagrams. She turned it over and began to make a few squibbles on the back where a wet glass had made a spidery stain. Doodling seemed to make difficult calls a little easier.

Since the night was warm, she'd opened the window. Soon the June bugs were flinging themselves against the screens. She smiled, recalling that when Anita studied entomology and Latin in college, she'd nicknamed these bugs *Bangus Screenus.*

Anita answered on the first ring, as if she had been expecting the call. "Mom?" And then she added: "What's happening out your way?"

"Well, your favorite June bugs are trying to get in. Warm and muggy here." There was a silence. The ball was in her court; she'd made the call. "Anita," she said, "I'm sorry. We didn't want this news to come as a shock, but it must have slipped out."

"Mom, I'm not even sure what the news <u>is</u>," said Anita. "Dad said he was coming west, but that's all I know."

Margaret began to add a head to her arachnoid creature and several bulging eyes. She wasn't sure whether that <u>was</u> all Anita knew, but she went on bravely. "I don't know if your father told you he was retiring early and that he's got a chance to do some of the research he's always wanted to do, which would mean traveling to Utah, to begin with. It's a great opportunity for him."

"Mom, somehow by the tone of your voice and his nervousness on the phone, I get the impression you guys are getting divorced. Correct me if I'm wrong." Trust Anita to hit you with it straight on.

"Actually, we are," said Margaret, quickly, relieved that the worst was over. "But you must understand that this was a mutual decision, with no hard feelings." That sounded pretty good, Margaret thought. She began to put hair on her spider's legs.

"No hard feelings?" Anita was shouting. (Margaret held the phone away from her ear.) "Are you kidding? You two have been having nothing <u>but</u> hard feelings, as far as I could tell, for years. I don't know why you ever got married."

This was not the time to tell her <u>that</u> piece of information, thought Margaret. Now she noticed that there was another little stain on her doodle paper, looking like a baby spider, a few inches away; she drew several tiny legs on it. "Anita, there <u>were</u> a number of good years. All our family trips. You of all people should remember them."

"But Mom, you didn't like those trips. You were the <u>home</u> person, the one who did the holiday dinners and the token ethnic and religious rituals."

Strange how each person remembered it all so differently, Margaret thought. "Anita, whenever and whoever did what, it's over, and Dad will be leaving on the Fourth of July weekend. I was hoping all you kids could come for a few days before that and see him off. We'll have one more family dinner and maybe a yard sale to get rid of what he doesn't want." Now Margaret was beginning to have a vision of the whole family waving goodbye as Henry drove into the sunset. Suddenly she remembered Chloe's description of her as Goody Bluestone. She made a web for her little spider family, stretching the lines to the edge of the paper. In the corner, she drew an innocent fly, a blue-bottle -- or was it a Goody Bluebottle? -- obviously the next meal for her spiders.

"A yard sale! Is that the way to end a marriage of forty years? Good God!" Anita paused. "I'll come, of course. Let me talk to my boss and the airlines and I'll get back to you." She laughed nervously. "We should probably all buy him some kind of present." She was more like her mother than she knew, Margaret thought: presents were a good idea. Anita went on. "I'll ask my colleagues to recommend the latest gadget for geologists."

The next day, before she left the house, Charles called to say he would be in town and wondered if he could meet her for lunch at the museum cafeteria near her office. He was waiting for her when she arrived at noon. Although he'd been named for Margaret's uncle Charlie, he looked nothing like that side of her family. He had the face of a Chippen -- her mother's relatives -- a straight patrician nose and a firm chin. No matter how he dressed, he always looked like a Boston Brahmin. Even in paint-spattered dungarees, his usual uniform, he appeared to be an aristocrat temporarily slumming. Today he had on pressed chinos, an oxford button-down shirt, and relatively new running shoes.

"You're so dressed up. You must have just gone to the gallery," she ventured, after giving him a big hug.

"Yup," he said, "they sold one of my paintings last week."

"Oh, Charles, that's wonderful!"

"So I brought them another, a study of the backyard of that cafe."

"Where you took us to dinner last summer?"

Charles nodded.

"There was such a wonderful light that night," said Margaret. "The sky was that strange almost green color you sometimes get at sunset."

"Exactly. It made a great contrast, with the dark tables and their umbrellas, and the roof aerials."

Having a son who was a painter was gratifying, but his success sometimes made Margaret envious. For a while, she, too, had hoped for a career as an artist, but by the time she'd reached her senior year in college, she knew that she just wasn't good enough. She had a good eye and an excellent critical sense, but not that extra creative ability that could translate what her mind envisioned and her hand could do. She'd often wondered if her easy acceptance of her pregnancy with Anita was her way of producing a work of art.

"Come, let's have lunch," she said, picking up her plastic tray. It was always a pleasure to see Charles. Of all her children, he was the one who could pick up on her mood and make a quick assessment of how she was feeling. In fact, he was sensitive to the emotional temperature of everyone in the family. The flip side of this ability was that he often fell into the role of peacemaker or mediator. Occasionally Margaret wondered: who looked after Charles and his moods?

Today, he looked a little down -- not the usual - - Hi, mom, just thought I'd drop in and have lunch at your expense - - but more serious. It occurred to her that he might have already heard from Anita. She looked closely at him. "You've talked to Anita," she said. "Anita told you."

He nodded, and then reached out and put his hand on her arm. "Mom, are you going to be okay? Financially, and emotionally?" He slid his tray along the counter. Luckily, the cafeteria was empty today, and they could talk.

"I'll be fine." She tried to speak briskly, but she knew her tears were just behind her eyelashes. A little sympathy could often do this to her. She swallowed. "This can be a new beginning for both of us, Charles. I'll have a chance to do some special things as well." Even to herself, her voice had an artificial ring.

"Mom," Charles interrupted while he chose a corner table. "You don't have to sugar-coat this thing for me. You've been married -- what? -- forty years or something, and now suddenly it's over."

"Charles," she said, gently. "For many of those years, I was certainly not happy. I'm sure you knew that. Your father has not been easy to live with, to put it mildly, but I guess I felt the good outweighed the bad. And the last few years have been kind of scary; your father has been more difficult lately. Honestly, I'm a little mad that he came up with the idea before I did, but mainly I'm relieved."

Charles sat quietly, looking down at his pasta salad.

"Does all this surprise you? Anita seemed to think it was inevitable. It was as if she were amazed that we lasted as long as we did."

There was a long silence. "Mom," he said, speaking slowly, "I don't know how anyone stays married these days. I'm the last one to pass judgment. As you may have guessed, Elena and I are probably not going to make it." He paused. "I'm just the baby-sitter at this point." His voice trailed off and he pushed his lettuce around the plate.

Margaret sighed. She'd often worried about his marriage. Charles had always picked women who were needy, so needy, finally, that even Charles couldn't supply whatever it was they were looking for, and sooner or later, they would turn to someone else. She wondered if it was somehow all her fault: perhaps she'd given him a role model that encouraged his choices. "Maybe it's catching. But I'm sorry. Your father and I -- we've had our turn. I was hoping better for you two, even though you were very young when you got married." She didn't add that Elena had been pregnant then. Margaret shook her head. "Well, I'm glad you came today because I wanted you to know that your Dad will be leaving sometime during the Fourth of July weekend and I was hoping all you kids could be there. Anita's coming and I'll be talking to Molly and Andrew. Anita's going to buy him a present."

Charles looked startled at first but then he seemed to fall into the spirit of a party. "Maybe I'll make up a care package of foods for him to go camping with," said Charles. "Is he taking a lot of stuff? And what about all his junk?"

"I'm thinking of a yard sale," said Margaret.

Charles looked up, surprised. "Mom, you're kidding."

"Well, I've got to do something about all that stuff. He obviously can't take it with him. I was hoping you could bring your kids. Matt especially would be helpful in carrying heavy things out of the house and barn, and Katy could be the cashier since she's so good with numbers." Matt was fourteen and Katy was ten. "School should be over by then, so you'll be free as well."

"Katy will be at sleep-over camp by that time, but I'll bring Matt. He says he's too old for camp this year, and even though he's nearly six feet tall, the world seems to think fourteen is too young to work. He'll be at loose ends."

* * * *

Although he'd been eating out a lot lately, that evening Henry was home for dinner. Fortunately, there were several chicken breasts in the freezer, and Margaret was able to find a few mushrooms, some left-over rice, and a little wine. Henry seemed, if not peaceful, at least non-combative, so as he sat reading the paper and waiting for her to sit down, she told him that she had seen Charles. She began by saying that he'd sold a painting, and then she said: "I think he'll be getting divorced, too."

"What do they say? Fifty percent of all marriages end that way?" He shook his head sadly. "It's the death of a bourgeois tradition, I guess." He paused. "Did you talk to Anita? I'm afraid I messed up that call."

Nodding, she put the food on the table and cleared her throat. Bravely, she continued. "She and Charles are both coming to say goodbye to you."

He snorted. "And if I know you, there'll be the equivalent of the fatted calf. Or the reverse of it -- the children sending off the prodigal father or something." Margaret recalled that he'd refused his Department Head's offer of a retirement party for him.

"Well," said Margaret, getting defensive, "we'll all have to eat while they're here. I'm hoping Molly and Andrew can come as well. For the whole Fourth of July weekend." She went on, bravely. "Would you object to a yard sale during that time? It would help to clean out the house and might make a little money. Charles said he'd bring Matt to help carry out the heavy stuff."

Henry looked at Margaret as if he thought she'd gone mad. After a minute he said: "I don't know why I'm surprised. It's the kind of thing you always think of when events are getting out of hand and everyone's upset: you <u>organize</u> a sort of spectacle; you <u>civilize</u> the whole environment." He sighed. From the set of his mouth, Margaret suspected he was about to go into one of his tirades. "Bye-bye Bargain Basement at the Bluestones. Is that it? Are you tacking up signs on the telephone poles yet? Might as well bring the whole town into it." He got up from the table and began to pace. "Can't you get it through your head? We're getting divorced. I'm leaving you. It's not some kind of picnic." He slammed his chair against the table and stalked out.

* * * *

The next morning before they were out of bed, Molly called. Clearly, she'd already heard from Charles and was up to date on the news. Easy to talk to, with a great sense of humor, she was Margaret's most organized child. Now thirty, she was a financial planner, engaged to a broker, and in the middle of arranging her wedding.

In fact, the wedding was uppermost in her mind. "Will Daddy be able to walk me down the aisle? We're getting married Valentine's Day weekend, on Saturday night."

"Let me get your father and you can ask him yourself. He's right here." Margaret was glad Henry could have his turn at talking to the kids, dealing with their reactions. As she pulled on her bathrobe and headed for the kitchen, she could hear enough to figure out that Henry had agreed to fly East to be part of the wedding. Nevertheless, she decided, over coffee and a piece of toast, that it might be a good idea -- since she wasn't expecting her first client until nine -- to go to the office a little early and talk to Molly a little longer, just to make sure she was not at least a little upset at this news.

Margaret's office was more than a haven for her: it was her sanctuary. Unlike the house, with its piles of junk and decay, this special space represented the person she thought of as her real self: a professional adult, someone with good taste, excellent judgment, and a measure of control over her life. While the Chadwick Clinic had been established nearly a hundred years ago, it had struggled along in cramped quarters for most of that time, surviving on the generosity and whims of its founding family, and the uncertain support of Federal and State grants, sliding-scale client fees, and health insurance. Then fifteen years ago old Josiah Chadwick had finally died -- at the age of ninety-eight -- and left the clinic his twenty-three room mansion just over the Boston line.

The legacy also included the untouched principal of the family fortune, with the codicil specifying that the treatment of clinic clients should never be terminated because of inability to pay the fees. However, as public funding declined, and Managed Care cut back on insurance benefits, the clinic still found itself falling into deficit. Her job, in addition to seeing clients, was to write grant requests to private foundations.

As the part-time grant writer, Margaret had been given the old library for an office, and she'd made the most of it. Its best feature was a working fireplace; she'd found a set of andirons and fireplace tools in polished brass to set if off, and two Victorian love seats where she could have conferences on cold winter afternoons. A low table was set for tea. Over the mantelpiece she'd hung the portrait of Hannah Chadwick, wife of the original benefactor, and on the other walls, scenes of Boston Harbor, crowded with sailing ships, a reminder that the Chadwick fortune had come from the slave trade. In the corner, above her desk, was a Mary Cassatt print -- the classic mother-and-child painting -- and below it, the recently purchased computer. The clinic had dragged its collective feet for a number of years before its accountant had put his foot down and forced them to succumb. But, for the most part, Margaret had managed to ignore the intrusion of this pale gray monster.

After she'd made herself a pot of coffee, she dialed Molly at her office. It was easy to picture this daughter, since she looked so much like Margaret at that age. "Mom," Molly said, "divorce is no big deal. David's parents have been divorced for over ten years, and everyone gets along just fine. His mother and step-father will host the rehearsal dinner and his father and step-mother will come to everything." Somehow, the underlying message was: whatever you do, just don't mess up my wedding. She did agree to come for the Fourth of July weekend and would bring a present.

"And by the way, Mom," said Molly in a tone of voice that long experience had alerted Margaret to big news, "I should tell you that David and I have decided to have a Jewish wedding." Margaret was astonished. While she knew that David had been brought up as a Reform Jew, it had been her impression that neither parent -- both now remarried, his father to a Roman Catholic -- would have insisted on this kind of ceremony. This must have been the kids' idea.

"Does your father know about this?"

"Well, I didn't actually tell him," said Molly sheepishly. "I figured you could kind of let him know gradually. You've always been good at that."

"Molly, I'm not going to do your dirty work anymore. Your father and I are getting divorced: you kids will have to deal with him directly." She paused, to let this sink in, but mainly because she liked the sound of it. Margaret wondered if she would have had the courage to make that statement if she were calling from the house instead of the office. "And besides," she said, "he still hasn't recovered from Andrew's Bar Mitzvah."

It had been fifteen years since that Bar Mitzvah, and it was still a sore subject for all of them. Margaret had always known that moving to the suburbs had been a shock for Henry in many ways. Not only had he ended up as a homeowner, a father of four children, a commuter, and the caretaker of a large lawn, but he'd found himself in a community that was at least one-third Jewish. For a man whose left-wing parents had scorned all religious faiths, the fact of his own Jewishness was something Henry had never dealt with. While a number of the Jewish families were mixed -- like theirs and Chloe's -- most of them were affiliated with temples and took their religion seriously. The public schools were closed on Jewish holidays and many local employers and stores also shut down. Over the years Margaret began to learn about a whole new culture, and as the children grew older, they began to ask why they couldn't have Chanukah presents; they were invited to their friends' Bar and Bat Mitzvot.

At the same time, mostly because she couldn't bear to give it up, Margaret continued to observe Christmas. The first time she brought home and set up a tree, Henry was outraged.

"What the hell is that . . . that thing? How many times have I told you that religion is the opium of the people? You will be feeding a narcotic to my children."

"Henry, I'm not doing it as a religious ritual. It's part of my culture, the way I was brought up. It involves giving and receiving." She continued, cautiously, reminding him that they'd always celebrated Columbus Day, and that he'd used the occasion to tell the children what it must have meant to the Native Americans to have a European culture foisted on them.

Henry had laughed. He'd had more of a sense of humor in those days. "And you make spaghetti because it's an Italian holiday!"

Eventually, Henry got used to Christmas and even enjoyed getting presents. Margaret did all the shopping, of course. Gradually, with a small twinge of guilt, she added Chanukah to the family rituals, beginning with simple gifts -- usually books, on the theory that the Jews were a literate people -- on the first night of the holiday. When Henry's sister Rosa heard about her growing interest, she sent them a Menorah as a gift, and from then on, Margaret and the children lit the candles for each of the eight nights. Henry did his best not to notice.

Margaret had never had the courage to introduce Easter to the family calendar although the children spoke longingly of chocolate bunnies and colored eggs, but once Chanukah had become routine, she began to think about putting on a Seder. As it happened, Henry's elderly parents were visiting at Passover time, and she wanted to give them a festive meal. She knew, of course, that theirs had not been a religious home, but she suspected that both of them must have had childhood memories of this holiday, so she decided to make a stab at it.

She wasn't exactly sure what to prepare, but she asked various friends and ended up with a few basics -- matzos, a bottle of Kosher wine, some bitter herbs, a plump chicken, and some green vegetables. When Henry walked into the house that evening, he was -- for once -- beyond speech. He looked at his parents for support and saw his father wearing a yarmulke

72

(also a gift from Rosa) and beaming at the formal table. The children, then ranging in age from sixteen down to five, were dressed in their best clothes, and seemed to be looking forward to the occasion -- with the exception of Anita who was showing her usual adolescent disdain by rolling her eyes and shrugging.

After they were all seated -- even Henry, whose sighs were almost as exaggerated as Anita's -- Margaret swallowed and began the speech she'd mentally rehearsed.

"Tonight is the first night of Passover, a holiday that celebrates the freeing of slaves, not just the Jews from Egypt over three thousand years ago, but freeing slaves everywhere, even today." She paused, hoping someone would come to her assistance. And somehow, with the help of Henry's father, the meal gradually turned into a real Seder. Charles, even at fourteen aware of the need for participation, began to talk about the exciting escape across the Red Sea, and eventually, Andrew had a chance to do his part as the youngest member of the family and ask the Four Questions. Finally, Henry and his father had a friendly argument about the politics of ancient Egypt, and Anita began to explain to Molly how the original Matzos were made without having a chance to rise.

The family continued, as the years went by, to have informal, somewhat abbreviated Seders as long as the children were at home. Henry was able to

73

turn them into opportunities for political education and the children made no objection. Of all of them, only Andrew seemed to have any real interest in the religious aspects. When his best friend, Jeremy Greenberg, began to take Hebrew lessons, Andrew begged to go along, and soon he was learning his letters as well. Henry's father, who in his old age was beginning to take an interest in Judaic history, was happy to pay for the lessons. No one should have been surprised when Andrew began to talk about his Bar Mitzvah.

As the time grew near to Andrew's thirteenth birthday, Margaret finally had to speak to Henry about the child's insistence on going through this rite of passage.

"So who's stopping him?" said Henry.

"It's not as simple as that," said Margaret. "Even in a Reform ceremony, the parents, especially the father, are expected to participate, up on the altar, or whatever it's called. The whole affair also costs money, although I guess your father would be willing to take care of that part of it."

"You might as well know, Margaret, that I am going to put my foot down in this matter. I am not going to 'participate,' as you call it, in an archaic, atavistic, ancestor-worshiping ceremony that goes against all my principles. You can do whatever you want with Andrew, and my father can be my substitute if he wants to, but I'm not going to be involved."

Margaret was pretty sure he meant it. But she had two more irons in her fire. "Will you explain all this to Andrew, then?" she asked.

"Oh, no," said Henry. "You're the one that got us into this mess. You let him take those goddam Hebrew lessons, so you'll have to tell him that I'm not playing."

The other recourse was the rabbi. Margaret went to see him in his office at the Temple. She'd met him several times when she dropped Andrew off and he'd seemed like a reasonable young man. He listened to her story without interrupting, and then sat quietly, looking at her intently.

"I'm sure you're aware that this Bar Mitzvah is only the tip of a dangerous iceberg. But you're not asking me to save the Titanic -- just to rescue one little boy."

"Thank you for understanding that," said Margaret. "Have you dealt with anything like this before?"

"I have. But they're all different. I take it you'd like me to call your husband or see him?"

Margaret nodded. "But I have to warn you. He can be very difficult."

She never knew what transpired between the rabbi and Henry, but it ended up that Henry was at least a minimal participant at Andrew's Bar Mitzvah. Henry's father was able to brush up on his Hebrew and actually read a portion of the Torah on that occasion, but Margaret and Henry never discussed the subject again.

* * * *

After her call to Molly, Margaret decided she might as well complete the task and talk to Andrew. Somehow, she'd thought this would be the easiest call. But Andrew surprised her. He and Julia had planned their entire lives together neatly, beginning when they met as freshmen in college. They went through medical school together, and both got residencies in Atlanta. The baby, they admitted, was unplanned, but they'd taken the news in stride and had quickly evolved some new planning, including a nanny who would arrive just in time to coincide with the baby's birth in October. Julia was going to take a few weeks off, evidently, and then return to Plan A. Margaret had wondered if a little thing like Andrew's parents' divorce would get in their way.

But Andrew sounded very upset, almost tearful. "Mom, I can't believe any of this. Molly thought the decision had been made. Are you really going to be divorced? Is Dad actually leaving -- Molly said the Fourth of July?"

"Yes, Andrew, it's true. You sound so surprised."

"Lots of my friends' parents got divorced when I was a kid, but I always thought we were the 'chosen people' who had it all. We celebrated every kind of holiday, and we had wonderful discussions at the dinner table -- all about labor unions and peace marches. We learned lots of things that other kids knew nothing about. I remember the time we went, somewhere in upstate New York, and Dad showed us where the Bluestone rock, the stuff they use for flagstones, came from. I always thought we were very special, being Bluestones. You and Dad -- sure, you were nothing alike -- but you.." He stopped, evidently unable to conjure up any examples of their devotion.

Margaret couldn't help but compare the difference between Anita's and Andrew's views of the same events. "Andrew, it <u>was</u> good for many years." Suddenly, it seemed important to Margaret to give Andrew this gift. "It's just the last four or five years when they've been less good. Since you went to medical school, you haven't been here to see, but we've been going our separate ways, and your Dad, he <u>needs</u> to have a chance to develop his theories, and I have things to do here, projects at the clinic. It's going to be okay, really." For a minute Margaret felt as if he were still her little boy and she found herself reassuring him. "You know it's nothing any of you kids did."

Margaret wondered why, of all the children, this news had hit him the hardest. Anita had been bothered, too, but she wasn't able to admit it. Maybe the fact that he was about to become a father had made him more family-oriented. But she remembered to ask him if he could come to what she now thought of as the "good-bye party." He seemed to think that the timing was good, that the new interns would arrive the day after the holiday and that he, at least, could come.

"Don't forget to get your Dad a small present," she said.

Then she wondered if she should give Henry a present as well. Taking off her shoes, she began to pace around her office. The Chadwick oriental felt good on her stockinged feet. Automatically, she asked herself: why not?

But instead of asking why not, she tried to answer the other question: why? Something was compelling her to do all this -- the yard sale, the dinner, and the gifts. It had something to do with her finally getting what she wanted: getting rid of Henry without throwing him out. She wanted to be forgiven for wishing he'd go; she needed to put on a show, almost a three-ring circus in which every elephant did his part perfectly, and no tight rope walkers slipped even a little. She was the ring-master.

She sat down on one of the love seats, looking into the empty fireplace. What should she give him? Whatever it was it should somehow give a message -- it should say: this has been a good time in your life, Henry Bluestone. You've been a good teacher and you've launched four children into the world. Now is the time for the next chapter, whatever it may be.

And then she knew. She would put together a photograph album, memorializing these last forty years, a small collection with just the highlights.

Chapter Six

By the middle of June, Henry had begun to sort and pack his possessions. Margaret found it almost impossible to watch. He seemed to have no system whatsoever. And from time to time, she found herself wondering if he knew what he was doing and where he was going, but she was afraid to ask. All she saw were piles of papers being shifted from one place to another, never quite making it, either to the trash bags she had so carefully laid out, or into the Volvo. He'd certainly have to buy a roof rack, she thought; the old wagon could only take so much. But she said nothing. Coming home from work, she'd often find him whistling tunelessly as he crated various kinds of scientific equipment. Or he'd spend the day in the basement and in the back yard, carrying out his old tents and sleeping bags to hang in the sunshine.

Watching him prepare for his journey, she was reminded of the time, shortly after Pearl Harbor, when she was almost six and living with her parents in a small mining town in the Colorado mountains. As soon as the war was declared, her father's National Guard Unit was called up and made part of the Regular Army; Duncan MacPherson decided that Margaret and her mother would have to stay -- for the duration, as the phrase put it -- with his parents in the Southeast corner of Iowa.

Margaret still remembered watching her father pack. He, too, had whistled, but he'd been a much more careful and deliberate packer than Henry was now. He, too, seemed happy about the upcoming change. It was as if the war had given him and many other men a chance to shake up their old lives and start over. A cheerful second-generation Scotsman with an optimistic outlook, he was tall and broad-shouldered, blond with a large, square head. He had thick, blond eyebrows over piercing blue eyes and big, capable hands. He was for Margaret the strong, caring parent, in contrast to her mother who was, first of all, always a lady, but timid, dependent, and frightened at being left behind.

Brought up by two maiden aunts after the death of both parents in the 1918 flu epidemic, Carolyn Chippen MacPherson was used to quiet and order. Her clothes were modest and inconspicuous. Her light brown hair was pulled neatly into a tight bun in back. Thin and pale, her posture was always erect. If she hugged Margaret -- a rare occasion -- Margaret could feel her mother's bones.

The aunts had lived frugally in the Back Bay at the bottom of Beacon street, and after the 1929 stock market crash, their capital had shrunk drastically. Somehow they'd managed to hang on to the family brownstone, crowded with rickety antiques, hundreds of old but flourishing plants, all dimly seen through the rare authentic purple glass window panes. To make ends meet, the younger sister -- Aunt Emily -- had finally been forced to take a job as assistant librarian at the Athenaeum, while Aunt Jane had stayed home to care for Carolyn.

Carolyn had met her husband's parents only once before, at her own wedding in Boston in 1934. Her aunts had done their duty by their niece and had put on a small but elegant tea to celebrate her marriage. From their point of view, she was marrying an uncouth cowboy from a family no one had ever heard of. Actually, Duncan MacPherson was a graduate of Harvard and his father a respected lawyer in the Midwest, but to the Misses Chippen, these were not real credentials: the MacPhersons were not Bostonians.

"Can't we go where your unit is, Duncan?" Margaret's mother had asked, as the packing and dismantling continued. "You'll probably be stationed there for a while."

"I want you and Margaret to be safe," he said. "An Army base is no place for a woman like you. You're no camp follower. My parents will love having you and it will be a normal life for our Maggie."

And so, in two weeks, he'd packed them all up, his things to go to the Base, most of the furniture to be sold, and her mother's and her clothes to her grandparents' home. Gradually, the rented house became empty, echoing as Margaret ran from room to room. At night, however, she could hear her mother crying, and once she'd sobbed: "But you're so glad to be going!"

And so it was for Margaret now. Even though she told herself she would be free, it bothered her, too, that Henry seemed to be so glad to be going.

* * * *

In those days before the interstates, the drive from Colorado to Iowa had taken three days. Her father had taught her to read maps, and she was able to trace their route to her grandparents' home. They'd taken US 34 -- then mostly a two-lane road -- all the way from the steep mountains of Colorado to the flat plains of Nebraska. Put to bed for the winter, the farms looked quiet and almost deserted, but along the roadside were the perfect entertainments for a little girl who had recently learned to read: Burma Shave signs. And on the sides of the barns, big ads for chewing tobacco, Doctor Pepper, Clabber Girl, Barbasol, and farm machinery.

On the road, her father had told her stories about his family. His parents had six children. Uncle Hugh at thirty-six was the oldest and he was retarded. Dad explained to Margaret that no one knew why Hugh hadn't grown up to learn to read and write.

"We're all very proud of your Uncle Hugh, Maggie," her father went on. "He's very helpful around the house, mows that big lawn and shovels all the snow. Your granny taught us that it wasn't nice to tease him or make fun of him. I used to take him fishing and rabbit hunting, and he was always in charge of our dogs." Her father seemed to be remembering those days with both sadness and happiness in his voice.

Margaret's father was the next child, followed by Elizabeth who was then thirty and living with her husband in California. Helen, at twenty-five, was a second-grade teacher and Ian, now in the Navy, was twenty-three. He and his young wife Gladys had been married at Thanksgiving while he was on his last leave before joining his ship, and Gladys was going to have a baby in the spring. "And the baby of the family is my little brother, Charlie. He's sixteen now, born when I was in college." Her Dad laughed. "He inherited my room eventually."

* * * *

Margaret and her parents arrived at her grandparents' home two days before Christmas. As they drove up the long driveway, Margaret saw a big house at the top of a hill. In the late winter afternoon the whole building glowed with a deep rose color, the white pillars that held up the wrap-around porch picking up orange glints from the dying sun.

The house was a classic Victorian, built in the 1880s, during an expansive period in American history, when lumber was plentiful and carpenters had the time and inclination to carve little designs under the eaves, and put gingerbread cut-outs on the overhangs, with scalloped shingles on the upper stories. Grandfather had bought the house in 1910 and had it all done over, expanding the porch, adding flush toilets and other indoor plumbing as well as central heating. The turret at the top had windows all around; it was to become Margaret's "lookout" for six years.

When her father stopped the car, he pressed down on the horn three times. Suddenly they were overwhelmed with hugs and shouts. Someone lifted Margaret out of the back seat (it was grandfather) and carried her into the house.

"Here's your one and only grandchild, Granny," he announced, and she was passed into the arms of an almost tiny, white-haired lady with bright blue eyes who was swaddled in a wrinkled apron and seemed to be covered with flour. Margaret looked around. The living room was dominated by a huge Christmas tree with piles of presents underneath.

"Come, child, let's you and me check on that turkey," Granny had said, leading her by the hand into a huge kitchen, full of wonderful smells and shining pots. After a quick peek at the giant bird, Granny took her upstairs. "As long as your Dad is here, you'll sleep on this daybed here in the sewing alcove. See, I've given you this quilt. My granny made it." Margaret reached out and stroked the quilt. It was soft, and had a faint circular design. She traced it with her finger. Granny smiled. "That's called the wedding ring pattern. She made it before she got married -- to put in her hope chest.

After your Dad has left, you and your mother will share Elizabeth's old room, since she probably won't be back until the war is over; both she and her husband have jobs in a defense plant out west." Margaret went in to take a look at the room. She saw twin beds, with a long bookcase by the window. There was a whole row of books about the Bobbsey Twins, a half shelf of Oz books, and a number of Nancy Drew mysteries.

Dinner that first night set the pattern for the next five years. Granny believed in setting out a spread. Nine of them sat at the table, including her grandparents, Margaret and her parents, Uncle Hugh, Aunt Helen and Charlie, plus Ian's young wife Gladys, a pale, round, sad-looking girl with frizzy red hair.

Looking back on the meals she'd had in the "big house," as the family often called it (to distinguish it from the smaller place they had lived in years ago), Margaret remembered them as beige, creamy, bland and runny. There were mashed potatoes or rice, chicken in cream gravy, creamed onions, white bread, roast pork, freshly made rolls, bread pudding, veal cutlets, whitefish, and custard. It was a far cry from her Boston-born mother's bright green salads, lamb chops, roast beef, with string beans, carrots and squash.

The best part of living at her grandparents' was the people. Grandfather was a lot like Margaret's Dad, tall, cheerful, and warm. Uncle Hugh was quiet but he always made her feel special. He taught her to ride the two-wheeler Grandfather gave her for her seventh birthday. And he was the one who showed her how easy it was to walk on stilts: he'd made the stilts for her himself. It was Hugh who took her for walks in the country, to track rabbits in the snow by their funny foot-prints. When it snowed and school was cancelled, Aunt Helen -- tall and thin, with sparkly eyes -- was always there to help her figure out the words in the Bobbsey Twin books, or she would let Margaret try on her "ball gowns" for dress-up games.

Charlie was her special favorite. Small and fair like his mother, he was clearly everyone's pet. The family was very proud of his report cards; he was active in sports, the star pitcher on the High School team at a time when baseball was an obsession in Iowa: Bob Feller had grown up on a farm not too many miles away. Feller had won 25 games for the Cleveland Indians in the 1941 season, but was expected to be drafted into the Navy any day. Margaret loved to peek into Charlie's room when he was at school. There was a big poster of Bob Feller on one wall, with the young right-hander's left leg stretched high in the air as he wound up to pitch, a Harvard banner on another wall, borrowed from Margaret's Dad, and over the bed, a big map of the world on which Charlie kept track of the progress of the war over the years. Charlie and his two best friends, Donnie Peterson and Bert

Walker, talked about the war all the time. They were afraid it would all be over before they turned eighteen and could enlist.

* * * *

Margaret's mother was miserable for all the five years they lived with her in-laws. After her Dad left, Margaret found herself forced to listen to her mother each night in their shared room, as she whispered complaints about life in the "big house." Margaret would often pretend to be asleep, trying to breathe slowly and evenly, but then she would remember that her Dad had told her to take care of Mom, and she would murmur something about maybe the war would be over soon and Dad would come home. Often it seemed that her mother was talking to herself as well.

Strange to look back now at those years and to realize that the "big house" had meant prison to Carolyn MacPherson. Her poor mother, Margaret realized now, was living in a place where none of her own values counted for anything. When she looked at her mother, across the big table at Granny's, she could see that she was drawn and thin -- she'd never learned to like the food -- and it made her feel guilty, as if she were not doing her job, but she really didn't know what to do.

Margaret, on the other hand, although she missed her Dad, loved everything about living with her grandparents. As the only child of parents who had moved nearly every year from one mining town to another, she liked staying in one place, living in a real house, and having, finally, a best friend. Rebecca Peterson, almost exactly the same age, lived two doors away. Like her brother, she had pale, blond hair and big front teeth. Soon the two of them began a collection of paper dolls, and as their drawing became more expert, the outfits of their fragile subjects looked more and more glamorous. Rebecca liked to make bridal gowns, and several times, they set up a whole wedding party, complete with flower girls and a ring bearer. Eventually, they developed story lines for the lives of these paper creatures, as well as elaborate names -- Margaret's favorite was the Princess of Monte Crisco. The dolls' escorts in these wartime years were always soldiers or sailors.

Best of all, as she was soon to discover, was getting to know Granny. Margaret saw, even as a young child, that Granny had a real talent for running a house. There were no servants (with jobs in war plants so easy to get, "hired girls," as they used to be called, were no longer available), but everything got done, cleaning, laundry, and cooking for eight people, because Granny had it all organized. Margaret, too, had her special jobs, counting out the towels and pillow cases on bed-making days, or helping Gladys put away the silver. As she grew older, her responsibilities increased.

Margaret's mother, who had not been a particularly talented housewife, resented being given assignments like dusting or vacuuming. She especially disliked being paired with Gladys; Granny had evidently thought they would be a natural team -- both daughters-in-law with husbands in the service, but the two women avoided each other. Margaret sometimes wondered if Granny thought she was being judged by the speed at which she worked. Granny moved faster than anyone she'd ever seen; she could crimp the edges of a pie in seconds, and iron a man's shirt in ten minutes. Margaret loved to listen to Granny who tended to think out loud: "Now the beans are cooking; there's just enough time to run up to the bedrooms and close the windows since it looks like rain coming."

"How can you tell, Granny?"

"Look, child, you can see the backs of the leaves, a sure sign of rain, especially when you look at them poplars." Granny also took time to explain to Margaret, as they hung out the wash together, about the clouds and what they were called. The wide flat countryside of that part of Iowa encouraged the development of some lovely thunderheads, or on clear days, white puffy clouds that sailed by like the sheets on the line.

Hanging out the clothes also gave Margaret a chance to check on the Purple Martin bird-house. Almost an exact miniature of her grandparents' house, painted in the same rosy mauve with a little turret on the top, it had round holes instead of windows. In Rebecca's yard there was a tiny replica of the Peterson house as well. Granny said it had been years since any martins had nested there, but Margaret kept hoping to see a family of baby birds. That first year in Iowa when she started school, she learned a new song: America the Beautiful. For many years, until she saw the printed words, she sang out bravely -- For Purple Martin Majesties. And why not?

* * * *

For Margaret, it was a time of stability, of living in a place where people acted as you expected them to act. This was how life was supposed to be, even including gas rationing, meat stamps, and war bond drives. Every week had its special rituals. Saturday night, the farmers came in from the countryside, parking their rattly old trucks on the diagonal around the square, their children dressed in "funny" hand-me-downs. On Sunday mornings, the whole MacPherson clan (good Scotch Presbyterians) went to Church (except for Carolyn who claimed status as an Episcopalian and slept in). Even better were the Thursday night Church suppers where Granny's special dishes had a chance to shine, and where Aunt Helen cast longing glances at the assistant minister.

The effect of the seasons was more pervasive. In the early spring, it was time for plowing. Then, depending on rainfall and sunshine, the corn, the main crop in that area along with the hogs, would be knee-high, as the farmers said, by the Fourth of July. In a good summer, the economy grew along with the corn (and the fatness of the hogs), but in the drought years, everything dried up and faces got longer. The farmers stopped coming to town on Saturday nights. Autumn, in a good year, was harvest time, and everybody had a garden. In the fall Granny started her canning, a process that took over the whole kitchen for more than a week, but it ended with rows and rows of bright-colored jars, full of wonderful reminders of summer. All winter long, as the snow fell and covered the landscape, the family ate the fruits of Granny's labor.

* * * *

Two events did not follow the expected pattern in the years of Margaret's sojourn in Iowa. In May of that first year, six weeks before her baby was to be born, Gladys and Margaret were in the back yard, hanging out the towels on the line. Granny had said: "Gladys, I don't want to see you hanging up them towels any more. Maggie can do that job by herself. They always say it's not good for your baby if you put your arms up over your head. You don't want the cord wrapping around its little neck."

But Granny had gone inside to check on the pies and Gladys, without thinking, had begun to help Maggie again, pinning up the towels on the higher line that Maggie couldn't reach. Suddenly she drew in her breath and cried out. That night, in the little County Hospital, Gladys had been delivered of a stillbirth, a tiny red-head, Aunt Helen told Margaret. She'd seen the baby before they whisked him away. Aunt Helen also said that it was just an old wives' tale that reaching your arms over your head would hurt the baby. But Granny told them later that the cord <u>had</u> been wrapped three times around the baby's neck. He'd have been named Malcolm if he'd lived.

It was against hospital rules, but Granny took Margaret to see Gladys. She looked small and pale, almost the color of the sheets. But her hair was still red and so were her eyes. Her mother and father had come down from Des Moines to take her home when she was well enough to travel. Aunt Helen told Margaret several years later that Gladys had written Ian a "dear John letter." After the war, there was a divorce.

Margaret's mother said privately that perhaps it was for the best, but Margaret had been looking forward to having a baby in the house. Granny was quieter after the loss of the baby, her mouth often a straight line and she seemed to work harder and faster. The only person who cried was Uncle Hugh. Margaret never saw Gladys again.

* * * *

After Charlie graduated from High School-- he'd been valedictorian -- he joined the Marines, along with Donnie Peterson and Bert Walker. Margaret hadn't seen Granny cry at the loss of Gladys's baby, but there

92

were tears in her eyes when the family went down to the station to see the boys off. The Petersons and Walkers were there, as well, along with a few other families Margaret knew.

One morning late in February of 1945, when Margaret was almost ten and home from school with the flu, the doorbell rang. Since Granny was in the basement, Margaret, still in pajamas and bathrobe, answered the door. An early winter thaw had turned the snow into puddles and rutted the roads. Ben Dobbin, the Western Union man, had come out to the house on his bicycle. He looked uneasy.

"Is anyone else at home?" he asked. "I have a telegram for your grandfather."

"Just Granny," Margaret said, sneezing from the sudden change in temperature, "She's down cellar; I can take it to her."

"Better go tell her I need to see her," he said, shifting his muddy feet back and forth on the welcome mat.

Margaret walked down the basement stairs. "Granny, Ben Dobbin is here. He has a telegram for Grandfather. He wouldn't give it to me."

Granny was putting bluing -- an early version of bleach -- into the wash tubs. She turned around and looked at Margaret. "Dear God," she said, drying her hands on her handkerchief. She took a deep breath and moved slowly and heavily up the staircase.

93

"I'm sorry, Miz MacPherson," said Ben. He held out the yellow envelope. "Don't know no way to make this easy for you." He sighed. "And I got two more of these to deliver this morning."

Granny took the envelope and put it in her apron pocket, unopened. For the first time, Margaret thought she looked like an old lady.

In a wooden voice, she said: "I hope your next stop isn't to the Peterson's."

"Yes, Ma'am, it is. And I've got one for the Walkers as well." He stepped out on the porch and walked down the stairs to his bicycle, riding quickly away.

After a minute, Granny looked down at Margaret. "Charlie's been killed in that awful war. And Donnie and Bert, too." Now she began to cry. Taking off her glasses, she rubbed her eyes with her handkerchief, covering her face with bluing. "Here," she said, "you read it. I can't see." She opened the telegram and handed it to Margaret.

REGRET TO INFORM YOU CORPORAL CHARLES EDWIN MACPHERSON KILLED IN ACTION FEBRUARY 19, 1945. MY SYMPATHY IS EXTENDED.

It was signed by the name of the Company Commander.

"You better call the operator and ask her to tell your grandfather to come home."

They later learned that the place was called Iwo Jima.

* * * *

Katherine Campbell MacPherson -- Granny -- actually lived into her hundredth year. Margaret had flown out to Iowa for her grandmother's funeral just ten years ago. After the service, she and her Aunt Helen had sat together over tea. "Margaret," her aunt had said, "I need to tell <u>someone</u> something I've just learned about your grandmother, and it should probably be you." She paused, frowning. "I was going over her papers, for the undertaker, you know, and I discovered, when I saw her marriage license, that she was actually pregnant with Hugh when she and Dad got married."

Margaret felt both shock and sympathy. "Poor Granny. It must have been hard back then. Not like now, when everyone -- at least in my children's generation -- seems to live together and then get married when they become pregnant." She paused. "Maybe that's why she was always so nice to Gladys."

Helen nodded. "Looking at the dates, I figure my Dad must have been still in Law School then. They lived up in Des Moines for several years when they first got married, and by the time they moved back here and bought the big house, I don't think anyone gave it a thought." Helen shook her head. "But you know what else I figured out? Granny took her religion very seriously. I suspect she decided, when Hugh was born and there was obviously something wrong with him, that it was God's punishment for her sin." Then she added: "And I had another thought. I suspect my mother made a sort of bargain with God -- something along the lines of: 'If I'm good, and take care of everybody, and do my work all day long, maybe God, someday, you'll give me another little boy, an extra one, a perfect one, to make up for Hugh.'"

Margaret sat there, remembering how Granny worked at top speed all the time, and how she organized the whole house. Then she looked at Helen, her eyes wide. "Was that extra boy Charlie?"

"Yes. He was born long after the rest of us."

"Now I know," said Margaret, "why Granny was so certain that the telegram was about Charlie. I didn't question it then, but as I've grown older, I've wondered why she didn't even wonder if it were bad news about my father or Ian: they were both overseas then, too. She must always have expected that this would happen to him, that her bargain with God would only last just so long. Maybe she always knew she wouldn't be able to keep him."

Helen sniffled and her eyes filled with tears. "It's funny," she said, "I can cry for Charlie -- and that was more than forty years ago -- but not for my mother." She stood up to add more hot water to her teacup. She was no longer the tall, thin reed that she'd been for so many years. She moved awkwardly, her sweater straining across her breasts. "I guess the worst part of it is that my mother and I never really hit it off. She was little and pretty and good at everything around the house, and I was six feet two, skinny and homely. She just didn't know what to do with me." Helen wiped her eyes. "And I never found out, until now, that my mother wasn't perfect after all."

Margaret sat musing. It was strange: she'd always thought of Granny as perfect, too, but she certainly hadn't been the perfect mother for Helen. Maybe there was no mother who was perfect for all her kids.

Chapter Seven

Margaret's children began arriving several days before the long Fourth of July weekend. Charles and his son Matt had driven down on Wednesday from Portland, and as Margaret hurried out to meet them, she saw that Matt had shot up several inches since Christmas -- his bare ankles were visible below his jeans -- and he'd turned up the sleeves of his T-shirt to show off his biceps. He even had the beginnings of a faint moustache. She felt a little tweak of anxiety: time was moving too fast. Soon even this younger generation would be adults. Where would she be when that happened?

"Hi, Gran," said Matt, grinning and casually turning his head to the back. "Good God, what have you done to your hair?" There was a faint design on the back of his head, sculptured on his scalp. "I thought only African-Americans did that!" Charles smiled. "Mom, every generation has its own way of rebelling." He sounded as if he'd recently read this statement in a magazine article, and was trying to convince himself that these various manifestations were normal. "What did you do at fourteen or fifteen to shock your parents?"

"Actually, if you must know," said Margaret, aware that she might be opening a Pandora's box, "I ran away from home."

"I never knew that," said Charles. "How far did you go?" He seemed stunned.

"About three hundred miles," said Margaret, smiling at his discomfort.

In the long silence that followed, Charles stood there, chewing on his lip. "So how's Dad's packing going?" he asked, probably, Margaret thought, to change the subject. He looked at the Volvo wagon. "Not much more room in there. I brought a small box of camping goodies as a present. Where should I put it?"

"We'll probably give him all his presents in the dining room when we have the big dinner on Friday night, and the yard sale will be all day Saturday. Your father plans to leave early Sunday morning, to get a head start on the holiday traffic which should be worse on Monday." As she heard herself speaking she wondered why she sounded as if this were just an ordinary business trip Henry was about to take. He's <u>leaving</u> me, she told herself. He's not coming back. Forty years of marriage were about to end and she was talking about traffic jams, for God's sake. It was no wonder the kids were finding it so hard to believe.

Charles went into the house to drop off the box. When he came out, he looked worried. "Mom, this place is a mess! Didn't you tell me that in the separation agreement, Dad promised to get rid of all his stuff?"

"I never really believed that," said Margaret. "The agreement does give me the right to dispose of what's left. One reason I'm having this yard sale is to get rid of as much as I can. But, of course, a lot of it is just trash. I really don't know what I'm going to do with it all by myself, when all of you are gone." She sighed. "I'll need one of those huge dumpsters, not to mention someone to help me carry it all out."

"Why don't you hire me, Gran?" Matt said. "I need a summer job. I could stay here and work for you, clean up all this trash, do whatever you need done."

Margaret looked at Matt, and then at Charles. She tried to imagine dealing with a live-in teenager again. As the first grandchild, Matt had always had a special relationship with her, but he was no baby at this point. How would she handle the situation if it didn't work out? She'd be at work all day and he'd be on his own.

"What do you think?" she asked Charles. "My first thought is that it would be a godsend to me, at least for a month to six weeks. Sometime in August, I hope to take some vacation -- the Solomons have invited me down to the Vineyard."

Charles beamed. "It would be a great help to me -- I could get some real work done, since Katy will be at camp until August. I'm sure Elena would be pleased as well. She'll be occupied this summer with other things," he said, vaguely. "But mostly, I'd be happy for Matt. Let's talk about it later, and maybe we can work something out."

Matt walked up to Margaret and put out his hand. "Deal?" he said.

She smiled at him, but said: "Let's both sleep on it, Matt. We'll talk about it after your grandfather has gone." Why was she even thinking of this scheme? Hadn't she been looking forward to having the place to herself? She certainly needed help if she was ever going to get the place cleaned out, but, of course, she could get someone else to do the job, someone with a truck, perhaps. She hoped to God she wasn't just trying to prolong the period of motherhood, grabbing at the last straw for one more chance to play Goody Bluestone.

She could hear Chloe now. "There you go again. You're setting yourself up for a big disappointment. Can't you remember kids at that age? They're impossible." Perhaps she and Matt could work out a business-like relationship. She certainly had no intention of baby-sitting this six-foot Adonis. Nor would she cook elaborate meals for him.

"Well, come on, you two," she said. "Take your backpacks up to the third floor while I throw together something for dinner."

* * * *

One by one, the rest of them trickled in. Molly drove up from Philadelphia on Thursday, and that night Charles went to the airport to meet Andrew. Anita flew in on Friday afternoon and promptly lay down for a nap, in an attempt to straighten out her jet lag. Throughout all the comings and goings, Henry was strangely distant, almost as if he had already gone from their lives, polite, but still preoccupied with his packing.

Margaret had been busy all day, preparing a family favorite, a paella that included bits of lobster, mussels and clams, as well as shrimp and rice. Andrew had brought several bottles of Pouilly-Fuisse and Charles had made a layered salad. Molly had put together the dessert -- a raspberry torte -- and when Anita woke up, she took from her suitcase a sourdough loaf from Seattle. Everything in the dining room looked lovely, partly because she'd insisted that Henry take his things out of this room first, but also because she'd gone to a lot of trouble to make the occasion memorable. She'd polished her mother's candelabra, and had even ironed the linen tablecloth.

This was the first time she'd had all four children together since -- God knew when -- she figured it out as she deveined the shrimp: it was at Andrew and Julia's wedding, three years ago, right after they graduated from medical school. Thinking about it made her eyes teary, probably because that meeting had been part of a happier time. Henry had not yet begun to be so miserably suspicious; he wasn't having those good and bad days. Today, she had no way of knowing how he'd behave, or even if he'd show up.

Following the family custom, a pile of wrapped gifts sat on the sideboard. She'd prepared Henry for the fact that the kids would want to give him small tokens for his trip, and she'd told everyone that dinner would be at six, since they all had to get up early to put things out for the yard sale, which was to start at noon on Saturday.

So when Molly poked her head in the kitchen just before six, Margaret quickly told her to tell everyone that dinner was ready. Silently, they all trooped in. Henry had put on clean slacks and a fresh shirt, and Margaret, herself, had chosen a bright blue sun dress with a white wool shawl, but no one else had dressed for dinner. Matt looked quite decent, in a clean jersey. But the four grown children, following the tradition of their generation, all looked as if they had been camping -- torn, grungy jeans seemed to be the order of the day -- and they were not happy campers. Anita, since babyhood always cranky after a nap, was scowling; Charles, forever the peacemaker, was looking from one to the other as if expecting violence to break out, and the younger two kept whispering to each other. Matt seemed to be the only one who was his usual self, with his hungry adolescent attention focused on the big paella platter. Henry sat impassively, somehow giving the impression that he was not responsible for this occasion.

Once seated, everyone began to talk at once, almost as if each of them had decided on an opening statement or question to cover what he or she assumed would be an awkward or silent beginning. "So, Dad, are you going all the way on the Interstates?" This comment from Charles chimed in with

Anita's weather report -- an unstable front would intersect with a high pressure area. And Molly's enthusiastic comments on the wine were countered with Andrew's delight in the sourdough bread. Although some of these remarks were directed to him, Henry said nothing. After several uncomfortably long silences, Margaret decided that opening the presents -- normally in their family a project that accompanied dessert -- had better begin right now. Somewhat hesitantly, she stood up and moved to the sideboard. "Well, Dad, I see everyone has brought gifts for you." Even to her ears, this phrase -- especially her calling him "Dad" -- sounded artificial, but where in the etiquette books were the rules for this kind of occasion? Perhaps it would help if someone poured the wine. She glanced over at Andrew and pointed to one of the bottles. He filled the glasses, and in his nervousness, poured one for Matt as well.

Margaret picked up the first package. It was from Andrew. "Here," she said to him, "perhaps you'll read the card." She returned to her seat and began sipping the wine.

Andrew's smile seemed artificial as well. "We thought you might need a medical emergency kit for this trip, Dad, so Julia and I put one together. The card explains some of it." He read: "The razor blade is not because we're trying to make you shave every day, but it's there in case of snake bite. We've also included some antivenom, and five days of penicillin, some painkiller, ace bandages and Band-Aids, and water purification tablets." He handed the package to Henry, and then added: "Good luck," raising his wine glass and draining it completely. Margaret noticed that Matt followed suit.

Henry opened the carefully packed medical kit and managed a weak smile. (He must have decided to be a good sport and go along with all of this, Margaret thought, gratefully.) "Thank you, Andrew," he said formally. There was something about Henry's voice as he thanked his son that reminded Margaret of the quaver of an old man. She looked closely at him. Of course, he was probably exhausted from the weeks of packing, but there had been a strange look to him all day, almost as if he had been -- what was the word? -- sanctified. He certainly looked and sounded, all of a sudden, much older than sixty-five.

The combination of Andrew's present and another glass of wine for each of them somehow helped to ease the dinner party, and they were able to enjoy the food and the rest of the gifts. Molly's offering was a set of gift certificates to a motel chain. The card explained that they were to be used only when he'd reached the point where he just _had_ to have a shower and a night in a real bed. Everyone laughed, albeit somewhat over-enthusiastically, since Molly was always the one, when they were on camping trips, for asking plaintively: "When can I have a shower?"

Charles's present was a box full of instant camping foods -- trail mix (gorp) and even something called "instant water." Anita had come up with a complicated new-fangled kind of compass -- "so you'll never get lost." There was a long silence, during which the only sound was of Matt emptying the wine bottle.

"I think we could all use another drink," Margaret said, and Charles went into the kitchen to look for the corkscrew. Quickly, she stood up and went over to the sideboard, and brought back her own present to Henry. "And this is from me." She hadn't wrapped it or written a card, so she just handed it to him.

After he had glanced inside at the first page of the album -- a picture of the four children taken at Andrew's engagement party -- he said very quietly: "I'll save this until later. Thank you, Margaret." She found herself thinking of a better word than sanctified to describe the way Henry was behaving: dignified. And he had never been dignified in his life. She looked at the children. They all seemed almost blank, unsure of how to respond to this interaction between two people about to separate.

The rest of the meal went a little more smoothly. Margaret said very little but she was thinking about what a nice bunch of kids they were: they'd indulged her by participating in this dinner, and had honored their father. And perhaps he understood why they were there, for he was uncharacteristically mild and gentle. She reached for another glass of wine, and glanced over at Matt. His eyes were closing.

Somewhat later that same evening, when Margaret was straightening up in the kitchen -- the kids had done the dishes, but had forgotten where everything was kept -- Andrew came back into the room and sat down at the table. "Mom," he said in a serious tone of voice, "have you noticed anything lately about Dad? Is he becoming more forgetful?"

Margaret was startled. "Not that I've noticed. His memory seems still good, but tonight, yes, he seemed almost withdrawn, sort of pale and quiet for him. And he's tired, of course. He's been working like a packhorse. Is that what you mean?"

"I'm not sure what I mean. Of course, I haven't seen him for a while. He looks a lot older all of a sudden. He's not paying attention to us the way he used to. He didn't even yell at anyone, or argue, or pontificate his latest theories." Andrew looked pensive. "If I didn't know him, and if he were a patient, let's say, I'd describe him as a passive, quiet elderly man in his late seventies."

"Well, Andrew, you know he would never go to the doctor. He hasn't even <u>got</u> a doctor. A few weeks ago, I did suggest maybe he should have a check-up before he drove across the country. But he just snorted. And started talking about 'the quacks.' You know how he gets."

"Maybe you should bring it up again, suggest anti-tetanus shots and a few other immunizations to encourage him to go to see someone."

"Let me remind you of one thing," said Margaret, using as mild a tone as she could manage, "we're getting divorced. I'm not responsible for him any more. After tomorrow, he's on his own out there. <u>You're</u> the doctor in the family. <u>You</u> talk to him." Margaret paused, wishing Andrew had been there earlier in the week when Henry had been his old nasty self. "One thing I should tell you," she said, "he has his good days and his bad days. This happened to be one of his very good days." She turned on the dishwasher. She yawned. "I'm going to bed. Put out the light when you're through in here."

"I thought I'd call Julia and then I'll be heading for sack as well." He paused. "Mom, I hope I didn't upset you. At this point, I'm not sure whether I'm speaking as a doctor or as a son. I do think he's changed. But I wasn't trying to tell you what to do." He leaned over and kissed her. "Goodnight, Mom. That was a nice dinner." He smiled. "Someone will have to teach Matt how to hold his liquor."

* * * *

The yard sale was something else. Fortunately, it was a bright, sunny day. From the moment they were out of bed, Molly had taken charge. She reminded them that she was the only member of the family who understood profit and loss. "The rest of you, I hasten to say," she said, "are all involved in not-for-profit activities."

It was true. Henry had spent his working life at the university, Margaret at the clinic. Anita worked for the Weather Bureau; Charles was a teacher as well as a painter, and Andrew a hospital resident. Molly had bought a bunch of tags, and right after breakfast, she went around putting prices on everything. "Now listen," she said, "if any of the customers want to bargain, you just send them to me. The rest of you would give away the store."

Other members of the family also took on special tasks. Charles and Andrew, with the assistance of a slightly hung-over Matt, carried the heavy things out of the barn, agreeing that the ancient phone booth was to be the centerpiece of the sale. They placed it so that anyone coming up the driveway would spot it first. Their father also had a collection of other early appliances -- a mechanical copier, an old manual typewriter, and several gadgets none of them could identify. All these things were displayed on the old picnic table.

Anita had found a rope which she stretched across the foot of the driveway, and she put up a sign that read: <u>Yard Sale -- 12 Noon.</u> Margaret continued to brings things out of the house, concentrating on all the old kitchen equipment she'd been wanting to get rid of -- old metal eggbeaters, rusted muffin tins, a flour sifter and a number of things she'd inherited from her mother. Then she remembered the old mangle down in the basement and asked her sons to bring it out into the area in front of the barn. From the attic, she had Matt carry down a box of broken Christmas ornaments, and a number of childhood games -- Candyland, Chutes and Ladders, Clue, Stratego, and Risk. As she went in and out of the house, Margaret occasionally had a glimpse of Henry, still packing and seemingly able to ignore the activity around him. Thank God, she thought, he's not objecting to the whole idea.

No one had prepared them for the hordes of people who'd appeared as early as ten o'clock (they'd seen the signs Matt had put up all over the neighborhood), and they were begging to be let in early. At eleven o'clock, a well-dressed middle-aged gentleman came up the front walk, ignoring the crowd and the restraining rope. He approached Margaret and introduced himself as an antique dealer. He'd spotted the phone booth and wanted to make a special bid for it.

Trying to keep a poker face, and wishing Molly were with her, Margaret asked him how much he thought it was worth. She was tempted to give it to him for nothing.

"I'm prepared to offer you three hundred dollars," he said. "Even at this distance, I can see that it's the old kind, solid oak and brass."

Margaret was astonished, but tried to appear uninterested. "Actually," she said, "it's a special favorite of my husband's. He was planning to refinish it."

"That makes sense," said the dealer. "If I refinish it myself, I could probably get a couple of thousand for it."

"Let me get him," said Margaret. "Selling it has to be with his approval."

Henry was in their bedroom, putting toilet articles in a small canvas bag. "Henry, there's an antique dealer outside who seems very interested in your phone booth. I thought it made sense for you to talk to him."

Henry looked completely astonished. "You're going to sell my phone booth?"

Margaret felt a chill run through her. Oh, God. Where could all this be leading? "But Henry, you promised, in the separation agreement, that you'd remove all personal property or let me dispose of it. And you said, when we first talked about it -- I remember -- you said: 'No problem.'"

"But surely you weren't thinking of the phone booth!" His voice rose and he began shouting. "Clearly, if some dealer out there wants it, it must be valuable and shouldn't be sold."

"Well, he did say he'd give us three hundred dollars for it." She decided not to tell him about the two thousand. At this point she didn't care about the money. She wanted to get rid of the damn thing. "You'll just have to take it with you," said Margaret. Her voice became louder as well.

"You want me to tie it to the roof of the Volvo?" He asked. "Well, maybe I'll do just that." Margaret pictured that giant phone booth, perched on the roof of the Volvo, but gradually teetering and falling off on some super-highway, causing a multiple car accident. She could see the headline in the Boston Globe: <u>Phone Booth Kills Three. Traffic Tied Up For Six Hours. Professor Held</u>.

Charles suddenly appeared, peacemaker to the end. He'd evidently heard their shouting. "Wait a minute, Dad. Let's work something out here. If you want to keep it, we could ship it to Aunt Rosa's in Cleveland. She could put it in that big garage of hers."

"I don't see why it can't stay right here in the fucking barn," said Henry. "It's mine."

Margaret could not bear the thought. Somehow, having the phone booth right there on the property was like having Henry, himself -- forever. It certainly meant he would always have a foothold. And the phone booth represented the worst of Henry. But before she could put these thoughts into words, Anita came into the room. "For God's sake, you two, the whole neighborhood is listening. All those people clamoring at the gate can hear your every word." And then, as Margaret was sure she would, Anita turned on her. "Haven't you done enough over the years, Mom? You've always put him down, and now you're trying to get rid of the one thing that has any value to him."

Anita had never said these words before. Margaret wondered if there was any truth in her point of view. It had always seemed that the putting down was more Henry's role. She sighed. Surely this was not the time to make an issue of it.

Charles was quick to speak up. "Anita, I'm sure there's a compromise possible."

"You always think there's a compromise somewhere, Charles. Sometimes, dammit, there isn't. You want everybody to like each other and to like you. But it doesn't work that way." Now Anita was shouting. Henry seemed to be enjoying the spectacle.

Margaret realized that, once again, in order to keep the peace, she would have to give in. "Charles, ask Andrew and Matt to help you move that beast back into the barn. I'll explain to the dealer that it's not for sale." She wanted to go somewhere and just cry. But there wasn't time. There never was.

* * * *

By dinner time (they'd sent out for pizza; Margaret said she would do no cooking that day), they were all dirty and exhausted. With the exception of Henry (who was arranging things in the Volvo) they were all sitting on the back steps, watching the fireflies. Molly was counting the proceeds. "It's hard to believe," she said, "that we made over twelve hundred dollars. Who would have thought that people would pay real money for all those old games and toys?"

Margaret could hardly move. She had switched over to the old aluminum chaise (which had almost been sold by mistake) and was stretched out listening to all of them as they recalled some of the more outrageous customers. ("Did you see that guy in the yellow shirt -- he was trying to steal our old galoshes!"), and ("How about that strange lady who paid five bucks for that rusty eggbeater!")

Somehow it felt like the end, not only of the era of her marriage, but of motherhood (especially since Anita's angry words), and the micro-managing of this whole family. From here on out, she thought, they're on their own. They can deal with their father on their terms. Goody Bluestone was hanging up her cleats.

When Margaret woke up the next morning, Henry had gone. He had left without saying goodbye.

Chapter Eight

By Tuesday morning, all of Margaret's children had gone. Waking up to an empty house was strange. Everything echoed. Automatically, she drifted downstairs to the kitchen and set out two mugs. It was not until she started to measure out the coffee beans that it hit her: Henry was really gone. She now lived in this enormous place all by herself. She had six days to be on her own; then on Sunday night, her fourteen-year old grandson, Matt, would be back to start work on clearing out all the trash. Now was perhaps the time to make a sober, unromantic decision. Did it make any sense at all for a single woman to continue to live in this mausoleum?

Wandering into the living room, Margaret set her mug down on the glass-topped table. She sank into her mother's old wing chair and looked through the wide double doors toward the front hall and beyond to the dining room. Squinting to block out the boxes of Henry's junk and the overflowing trash barrel, she tried to recall the foyer almost as she had first seen it thirty-five years ago. Then it was a dark, but dignified entrance hall, quite similar to her grandmother's in Iowa, with a fading, elaborately patterned wall paper. In fact, behind the mirror were still vestiges of that old paper which even the steamer hadn't been able to remove. She tried to imagine what it <u>could</u> look like. She could paint the foyer a pale greenish yellow and put a green pottery lamp on her old cherry table. An umbrella stand might be good there, too. She smiled. Clearly, she was not ready to dispose of this house. She wanted to make it look the way she'd always imagined it. Somebody out there -- probably Chloe or whoever it was that passed judgment on one's interior decorating skills -- would have to give her a more than passing grade, maybe even an A plus. Only then could she decide about getting rid of the house.

Driving down to the clinic, she thought about her schedule for the day. She had a session with her client Deborah Breen at 9:30, then an appointment at the Foundation Library near the wharf at eleven, and finally an interview nearby at the Boston Fund at one-thirty.

Something about this first client made her anxious. Margaret's legs felt rubbery, her heart a little louder in her ears, and it was difficult to swallow. The obvious answer was that her client's issues were similar to her own, and the temptation was to lump the two of them together in her mind. She needed to remind herself that they were two different people. Deborah's husband, for instance, had a history of losing jobs, and often these periods of unemployment would make him verbally abusive and paranoid. Margaret had also begun to wonder if he had problems with alcohol. Lately, a new and exciting job had changed his whole outlook, and when she'd seen Deborah last week, the woman had looked radiant, her usually pale face pink and glowing, her light brown freckles picking up the auburn color of her curly hair.

When the secretary announced the client's arrival, Margaret went out to the front desk to meet her. She hardly recognized her. Deborah's hair was stringy and unkempt. She was wearing a wrinkled cotton plaid skirt, a flowered blouse, unevenly buttoned, and a dark green running jacket. Her face was bruised and she moved slowly and dejectedly. It was clear to Margaret that she'd been beaten. She looked old, although she was only thirty.

"Sit down, Deborah," she said quietly. Her gut feeling told her that at this moment she needed a kind of symbolic caretaking: in Deborah's culture -- Irish-American -- a "cuppa" was the first thing you offered at a time of crisis. And while Margaret had never offered this service to a client before, it felt right. "Shall I have the secretary bring us some tea?"

The client nodded, and then looked down at her lap, her body language proclaiming her status as a whipped puppy who knew it had deserved this punishment. Margaret sighed. Where to begin?

"How often does it come to blows?" Margaret said, forgetting about her own anxiety and concentrating on this poor woman.

Deborah was silent. Then she said slowly: "I didn't want to tell you. I couldn't." Margaret thought: here it comes. She's going to tell me that it's partly her fault, that she should have known by now that he hated being questioned, or something like that. "But these . . ." Deborah paused, "bad times usually end up that way." She took a deep breath. "He was drinking, too." She sighed, perhaps relieved to have confessed to this part of the story as well. "He was fired again, of course. I shouldn't have even asked what happened. Why can't I learn to keep my mouth shut?" Yup, said Margaret to herself, she's blaming herself. Of course, these men, when you do have a chance to talk to them, say exactly the same thing: the wife should never bring up whatever the touchy issue is.

Sounding more like her usual self, Deborah went on. "Part of the problem is that he loses his temper at work, too. He can't handle anyone telling him what to do. I think all bosses remind him of his father, who treated him like shit, pardon the expression."

Oh, dear, thought Margaret, these battered wives learn so quickly, thanks to all the self-help books on the market, to be amateur psychologists. How much easier it is now to assign blame to a previous generation. But it wasn't going to help at this point, for Margaret to try to topple the whole structure for Deborah.

There was a long silence, while they both waited as the secretary set the teacups on the table. After she had taken a few sips, Deborah began to cry. "What can I do? The kids are too little still for me to work full-time. I can't leave them with him, either. I don't trust him not to take everything out on them. Now you see why I haven't left." Margaret thought: well, there are a thousand reasons women can't leave. We'll have to get to know Deborah a lot better before she and I will know the "why" of her situation.

"Have the children seen him hitting you?"

Deborah nodded. "I know what you're thinking, that it's not good for them. I don't want Emmy to think this is the normal way for a man and wife to relate."

"I was actually thinking of the boys," said Margaret. The clinic had discovered that, as they got older, boys like this would begin to hit their mothers when they were being disciplined, but Deborah wasn't up to hearing all this right now. What to do? Whatever decision Deborah made, it had to be her own. They'd talked about restraining orders at her last visit, but she hadn't want to go that route. Things would probably have to get much worse before she'd be willing to consider that option. "Deborah, does it ever occur to you that your life might be in danger?"

"I wish I could say: 'Of course not. He loves me.' And, in fact, he does love me. But you're right. He gets so angry; he doesn't know what he's doing. I'm scared."

Normally, Margaret never gave advice, but this was a life-and-death risk. It was a tricky situation. She didn't want to frighten the woman, but she needed to be aware of the risk. "Let me tell you," she said finally, "what the experts recommend, just as a safety measure. You have your own car, right?" Deborah nodded. "Sometime when he's not around, pack a minimal suitcase for yourself and the kids and put it in the trunk. Start saving up bits of money, whatever you can, and make sure the gas tank is full. Then think about someplace to go, somewhere safe where he can't find you, perhaps to a friend he doesn't even know about, maybe even a shelter. Then the next time -- it will probably be a while since these things go in cycles -- you'll be ready."

"You're right. They do go in cycles. When I get home tonight, he'll have ordered flowers, and he'll promise never to hit me again." She'd stopped crying, but then hiccuped. "But now I know better." She smiled wryly. "Can I call you if I need to?"

"Of course. I'll give you my home number. And here's your next appointment."

As they stood up, she added: "Be careful, Deborah."

* * * *

Margaret left the offices of the Library and turned toward the harbor. On this bright day, perhaps she could spend her lunch hour just walking about the waterfront. How long had it been since she'd strolled the streets of downtown Boston? When, if ever, had she done so by herself? It was time, long overdue. A stiff wind was blowing, making little whistling noises as it found its way between the wharf buildings. The flags were slapping briskly. Boston had really done a lot to its waterfront in the last several years, Margaret thought, approvingly, with new hotels, a dock for whale-watching cruises, and some shops that specialized in shipping equipment. Standing in front of the display window of one of these places, she admired the polished brass, the shiny instruments, and an exhibit of nautical knots. Dimly, she remembered learning some of them as a Girl Scout back in Iowa.

Suddenly, she was aware of a new sensation: I'm happy, she thought, standing here in the sunshine. I don't have to worry any more about Henry and what his moods might be. I'm just myself.

She strolled along toward the new hotel. Maybe she should go inside and have lunch on their terrace overlooking the water. She could have a sandwich and a beer. Her money was as good as anyone's, she told herself, and she entered the restaurant.

"One for lunch?" asked the hostess. Margaret nodded, and then wished she'd brought a book. What did one do, as one waited for the order to arrive? She answered her own question: one sips one's beer and looks out at the view, and maybe sneaks a few glances at the other patrons. Sitting at the bar were several other singles; next time perhaps she'd sit there, too. She could always talk to the bartender. One man was obviously looking in her direction. Was this how the single life began? If she returned his glances, would that mean she was encouraging him? She had a lot to learn.

That evening, back in the chaos of her house, thoughts of Henry kept intruding. It was hard <u>not</u> to think of him since she was surrounded by reminders: he had left his spoor everywhere. Walking from room to room with a little notebook, trying to list which kinds of things should be saved, and which discarded, she found, on the lower shelf of the bookcase in the den, a tattered flyer advertising a Soviet film festival, scheduled for the fall of 1968. They had actually gone to some of these movies. Margaret had a dim memory of Russian soldiers riding on tanks, with girls holding flowers and cheering them on. Suddenly, her eyes filled with tears as she recalled those times in her marriage when they had gone out together in the evenings; they even had dinner in a Central Square cafe. She picked up the flyer and smoothed it out; should she keep it? Shaking her head, she told herself that this was not, after all, an archeological dig. Most of the stuff would have to go. The best thing, she decided, was to make a wide swath, to keep <u>nothing</u>, except for a few pieces of furniture. She would buy a gross of large trash bags, and a bunch of tags in varying colors, so that Matt would know what to save. And a big dumpster might be a good idea at that.

In spite of her relief at the prospect of getting rid of it all, she found herself worrying about Henry. Since he'd left Sunday morning -- very early

-- and supposedly headed west, she'd assumed he'd be stopping for a day or two at his sister's in Cleveland, a journey of two, or at most, three days. He should be there now. Even while telling herself he was no longer her responsibility, she found herself starting to dial Rosa's number. The two women hadn't talked since Henry's decision to leave home, and she wasn't sure what Rosa's attitude toward her might be. She didn't even know what Henry had told her. Perhaps nothing. But she completed the call.

"Rosa? It's Margaret. I'm calling to see if you've heard from Henry. For some reason, I'm worried about him. He left without saying goodbye to any of us."

"Oh, Margaret. I'm glad you called. We're worried as well. I did hear from him late on Sunday." She sounded as if she were trying to reassure herself. "He sounded rather strange, actually, and he said he was lost in Albany."

Albany? Margaret was puzzled. That would be less than two hundred miles from home. He should have been way up in the Finger Lakes by now. "You haven't heard from him since then?"

"No," said Rosa. "I thought he might have had trouble with his car. Is he still driving that old Volvo?"

"Yes." Margaret began to worry. "Did he actually say he would stop off at your place?"

123

"Oh, I'm expecting him." There was a long silence. Then Rosa added, speaking carefully, "Margaret, I was sorry to hear that the two of you were separating. At least that's what Henry implied a few weeks ago when he told me he was heading west. But I want you to know that George and I have always been fond of you. I'm sure he was a difficult man to live with. And I hope we can keep in touch and that your children will continue to be part of our family." Suddenly, she could picture Rosa, pursing her lips.

"Thank you, Rosa. I was sure you'd say that. Actually, the separation was originally Henry's idea, inspired, I guess, by the chance to retire early with some extra money." She paused. "I don't know why I'm still worrying about him. It must be habit. But I'd appreciate it if you'd let me know when he's arrived safely."

* * * *

But on Sunday evening, when she went to the bus station to meet Matt, she still hadn't heard from Rosa. Surely it wouldn't take six days for Henry to get to Cleveland!

Matt was the last passenger off the bus. At least, she assumed it was Matt. He was completely transformed into a look-alike of any number of adolescent boys she'd noticed on the streets. Beneath his baseball cap, two sheaves of blond hair fell on each side of his head; the back, which had displayed a sculpture last week, had begun to grow out. She was startled to note that he was wearing a silver earring on his left earlobe. An oversize T-shirt hung down over his knee-length baggy shorts, and his untied sneakers flopped along on his sock-less feet. Under one arm, he was carrying a skateboard, and under the other, a plastic bag, presumably holding his clothes. His expression, possibly assumed for the benefit of two teen-age girls who were standing nearby, combined a sullen stance with an uncertain frown.

Margaret quickly decided that this was no time for a hug. Casually she said: "Hi Matt. The car's down the block."

Driving home along the Storrow Drive, she glanced at him, and then remembered visiting his father when he was at the Rhode Island School of Design in the early eighties. Many of the students, Charles included, had affected what could only be called a bizarre presentation -- green or purple hair, nose rings, garish T-shirts and ragged dungarees that often revealed their owners' underwear. One of Charles's friends had even had a safety pin through his lip. Matt's mother, Elena, had always looked in those days as if she were in another world -- and thinking about it now, Margaret suspected the girl was probably stoned a good deal of the time. It'd been a shock to her when Charles told her they were getting married. The fact that Elena was pregnant was the least of Margaret's worries. She'd even wondered, especially since Elena seemed to have more than one boyfriend at any time, if, in fact, the baby was Charles's. But Matt's birth had settled that question, since he was a dead ringer for Charles, with a straight patrician nose, a firm chin and the general look of Margaret's mother's family, the Chippens. They'd named the baby Matthew Chippen Bluestone. If one looked at the whole process from a bird's eye view, Matt was just being conformist, right down to the last untied shoelace.

Passing through Brighton, she stopped to pick up some Chinese food. She said that she hadn't planned to do much cooking this summer and she hoped he wouldn't mind if they just had pizza, take-outs, or an occasional fast-food restaurant meal.

"Well, Gran," he said, sounding relieved perhaps that she wasn't going to wait on him, and a little more grown up than she'd dared to hope for, "I can cook some stuff, hamburgers, hot dogs, and I can even roast a whole chicken if you like. We could use paper plates, too, so we won't have to do all those dishes." He grinned. "We're both going to be working all day, after all," he said, sounding like a serious day-laborer.

What a nice kid, she thought. There'd always been an easiness to him, reminding Margaret not so much of Charles, his father -- who was more uptight -- but of her youngest child, Andrew. She'd actually seen a lot of Matt over the years, since only a hundred miles separated Charles and his family in Maine from Margaret and Henry in Massachusetts. Matt had stayed with her for six weeks when Elena had been ordered to bed in the latter part of her pregnancy with Katy, Matt's younger sister. At that time, Matt had been just four, and he'd explored Margaret's attic, discovering various treasures that had belonged to Margaret's children. He was particularly entranced by a full set of match-box cars that had belonged to Andrew, and by a big box of plastic dinosaurs that Anita had collected over the years. Margaret remembered how he used to line up all the dinosaurs, naming each of them correctly, and separating the carnivores from the plant-eaters.

"You know, I was thinking, Matt, that you wouldn't need to work <u>all</u> day. Why don't we say you'll work each day from 8 until 2, with an hour off for lunch -- that's five hours a day. I was planning to pay you five dollars an hour, if that seems fair."

Matt nodded. "That's okay." She couldn't tell if he thought that was a lot or a little.

"It's going to be hot, heavy work, with lots of dust, too. You could take the latter part of the afternoon off, maybe go to the Lake. You might meet some kids there, someone your age."

Matt brightened. "You know I've got a certificate as a life guard. I wonder if they'd hire me for a few late afternoon hours."

"Well, that's something you can check out for yourself," said Margaret. "When we get home, we'll take a quick look at what's ahead of us, go from room to room, and figure out where you should start tomorrow morning."

When they'd finished supper and completed the tour, Matt went back into the sun porch, having spotted their old hi-fi set. Margaret had just settled down to work on her checkbook when she heard him call: "Gran, who had these old albums? I found some Pink Floyd, a couple of Doors records, and some Led Zeppelin!"

Margaret laughed. "Those were your father's. I'm sure he wouldn't mind if you played them."

"Man," said Matt, "I never knew he was so cool."

* * * *

Gradually Margaret and Matt settled into a routine. Each morning they would agree on that day's tasks, and little by little, the line of big green trash bags at the curb grew longer. Sometimes Matt would question whether an item really should be thrown out, and once he asked if it was okay for him to keep some things for himself -- parts of an early Victrola, the kind you had to wind by hand.

Occasionally Matt would turn up items of Henry's clothing. Eventually, they had quite a pile. "Would you like any of these things?" She asked him. She sounded wistful, almost as if Henry were still in her system.

Matt grinned. "Could I have some of these hats?" He put on an old hard hat that Henry had worn for rock climbing. "Is Grandpa a famous scientist?" he asked, with a little note of hope in his voice. How could she answer without disillusioning him?

"He has his own theory about what causes earthquakes, but he still has to prove it. That's what he's working on right now. If it turns out he's right, he <u>could</u> be famous." Quickly, changing the subject, she pointed to a weather-beaten Australian outback hat and a long-billed cap. Matt took both of them.

In the middle of Matt's first week, Rosa finally called to say that Henry had arrived. She asked if Margaret wanted to talk to him, and more to please her sister-in-law than anything else, she agreed. Henry's voice sounded faint and very tired, and Margaret could hear Rosa in the background, almost as if she were telling a small child to say hello to Grandma: "It's Margaret, Henry, wanting to know about your trip."

"Hello," he said, obediently.

Margaret wasn't sure what to say, but asked if the car was performing well. "I was afraid it might overheat with the heavy load you were carrying." Since he made no comment, she went on: "So how long are you staying with Rosa and George?"

"I'm not sure," he said, "a few days."

"Where will you stop next?" she asked.

"I'll camp out somewhere," he said, and she felt he was being evasive. Well, of course, they were getting divorced, and it was none of her business, but she was curious why it had taken so long for him to get to Cleveland. "Well, have a good trip and drive carefully," she said. "Matt's staying with me, and he says hello, too."

Again there was a silence. "Matt's there?" he said finally.

"Yes, he's helping me clean out the house." More silence. "So send us a postcard," she said. He did not reply. Quietly, she hung up the phone.

Matt did find his way to the Lake that week, and was evidently able to help out with some minor life guarding duties. During one hot spell, Margaret asked him if he'd mind if she went to the Lake occasionally after work. While he didn't seem enthusiastic -- she felt somehow that it was his turf now, and perhaps he was afraid she'd embarrass him -- he didn't say no. She concentrated on swimming laps and kept out of his way except for a brief nod, but she did notice that he seemed to have made friends: there were several young girls who were "helping" him carry equipment.

In the evenings, Matt usually settled into the sun porch, playing his father's old albums, and discovering other treasures -- Charles's high school yearbook sent him into stitches. He quickly programmed Margaret's VCR -- it had been flashing 12-12-12 ever since she'd brought it home from the store

130

last Christmas, and he'd begun renting a few videos with his princely salary. He also tinkered with the old Victrola, trying to get it back into working order. Margaret spent those hours in the den, composing fund-raising letters for the clinic, hunting and pecking on their old typewriter. One night, Matt seemed restless and came wandering in to see what she was doing.

"Gran," he said, sounding puzzled, "why don't you use your computer? It's sitting right there and would make your life so much easier."

"Matt," she sighed, "I hate to admit I don't know the first thing about it. I have one at work, too, but I've managed to avoid it."

He looked completely astounded. "You could use it just like a typewriter if you wanted." His fingers began twitching in anticipation. "Here, I'll show you. Okay?"

"Be my guest." Margaret had never even touched the keyboard. It had belonged to Henry, and she was always afraid she'd ruin something. "The bill for the on-line service turned up on my Master Card bill the other day, and your grandfather even gave me the password. It's in this drawer." She handed him a slip with a four-digit number. Matt soon had it in operation. "What are you working on?" He spoke with a note of authority in his voice, but he was kind. Little by little, working a few hours each evening, he was able to teach her to write letters, and look up information about foundations. Gradually, she lost her fear of the computer, and even began to think about using it to organize her household accounts. She'd been spending hours trying to straighten out the mess in Henry's old checkbook. He'd always taken care of their finances and done a good job. But this last year of checks and bank statements made no sense to her; nothing balanced, and often she couldn't read his figures. His writing seemed to have gotten a lot smaller. She couldn't help but think that something must have happened to Henry if even his handwriting had changed.

Her uneasiness led her decide to call Rosa again. She wondered if Henry had gone.

"Yes," said Rosa almost tentatively, "he left last Saturday." She paused, as if wondering whether to continue. "Margaret, I hated to see him start out, and to think of his planning to go all the way West. He just wasn't himself."

Margaret felt a chill of apprehension. "How do you mean?"

"He was so forgetful, especially at first. After a few days, and maybe after he'd caught up on his sleep, he was better. He explained his earthquake theory to George and me one night at dinner. He was quite lively and we were fascinated. But when it was time for him to leave, even George said: do you think he knows where he's going? We got out the map and tried to have him show us how he would travel, but he became impatient and just drove off. I begged him to call us but we haven't heard from him since. I thought about calling you right after he left, but I decided to wait a few days.

Perhaps we'll hear from him soon. But if you hear anything, be sure to let us know."

After she'd hung up, Margaret sat with her hand on the phone. There was nothing she could do, she told herself. Henry was no longer her responsibility, but maybe in a few weeks, she'd call Anita in Seattle to see if she'd heard from her father. If he thought to call anyone, it would probably be Anita.

* * * *

Matt was about two-thirds finished with his summer's task when one day Margaret decided to come home for lunch. She'd been at a meeting nearby and it seemed foolish to go to a restaurant. Parking the car on the street, she walked up and let herself in the front door. Glancing quickly at the mail, she moved slowly toward the kitchen and stopped in shock: sitting around the big old table were Matt and a group of teenagers -- two boys and two very young women. They were all drinking beer. A half-finished six-pack sat on the table and another on the floor. The boys looked familiar. They were lifeguards at the Lake, a little older than Matt.

For a very long minute, no one said anything. The room smelled of a mixture of pungent adolescent sweat and the yeasty odor of newly opened beer. A noisy fly buzzed over the table and then settled into a little pool of liquid. It was evidently up to Margaret to begin. "Matt?" she said, feeling a mixture of disappointment and something akin to fear. Perhaps that was only her old self-blame. Had she, indeed, set this up by being too trusting?

"Gran, this was the first time. Honest," said Matt. His glance met hers and then he looked down at the wet table. He looked sullen and yet scared.

"And it's the last time as well," she replied, trying to think what to do next. The plump, dark boy rolled his eyes and began drumming on the table.

"Hey, cool it," said Matt to him. The kid put his hands in his lap.

The other boy -- he was blond with hundreds of freckles -- quickly said: "Matt said he was sure you wouldn't mind."

Matt's head snapped up and he looked at the boy. It was clear to Margaret that he'd said nothing of the kind. "That's a lot of crap," he said finally, moving his chair a few inches farther away from the boy. "But I did say probably no one was home."

After a long silence, Margaret turned to the girls. "How old are you two?"

The thin, dark girl looked at her friend, a small red-head. "Thirteen," the first one said. "My mother will <u>kill</u> me."

"I'll need your phone number," said Margaret.

Reluctantly, the girl gave her the number. "My friend is from Vermont. She's staying with me. Her mom's away."

"Where did this beer come from?" said Margaret. She was sure that no store would have sold it to such a young group.

Matt spoke up. "We got it at Dave's house." He pointed to the blond boy. "It was in his fridge." The boy turned his head. "It was a dumb thing to do," said Matt. "You guys had better go home." They all stood up.

"I'll have to talk to your parents," said Margaret. "You're all under age." No one spoke. She passed around a piece of paper. "Just put your names and phone numbers," she said. No one picked up the pencil. "Well," she said firmly, "the Life Guard office at the Lake will know who you are." That was mean, she thought, but effective.

Quickly, the boys scribbled the information. "See you," said the dark, plump one to Matt. The girls slid out and ran down the back steps. Margaret could hear them begin to giggle as they rounded the corner of the house. Matt did not even look at them. Margaret sat down at the table across from him. She felt defeated, and as if the good relationship the two of them had developed had never existed, as if it'd been a facade.

Matt got up and took a sponge from the sink. He began to wipe up the spilled beer and to straighten things up. But he left the bottles of beer alone. Then he sat down again, still not looking at Margaret. Suddenly she remembered the time, Lord, it was twenty-five years ago, when she and Chloe had discovered Anita and Athena smoking pot. That time, too, the adults had sat there, not knowing what to say or do. Other times, other problems. Somehow they'd all lived through it, although for a few months, Margaret had found herself secretly blaming Chloe's child, and she was sure, now that the dust had settled, that Chloe had probably blamed Anita.

At the moment, Margaret had an almost primordial urge to pour the contents of each bottle down the sink, like the enraged wife of an alcoholic. It also crossed her mind that it might feel good to smash them all. Instead, she just sat there, trying to sort it all out. She would have to tell Matt's parents as well, she thought. He <u>was</u> only fourteen. Thank God, none of them had seemed drunk.

"Gran," said Matt, his eyes now filling, "I'm sorry. You're not going to believe it, but I've had a great summer with you."

"I thought it was great, too," said Margaret. "You've been a big help. But I'm not going to be comfortable leaving you on your own in the house after this. Maybe we were both expecting too much of you. I suspect it's hard not to yield to the pressure of new friends." She shook her head.

Later that evening, after she had talked to the parents, including Charles and Elena, they all, with one exception, agreed to go along with the idea of the blond boy's father. He said he would bring his truck over and that he would supervise the group of kids while they finished cleaning out the house. The thin, dark girl's mother, on the other hand, blamed her for leaving Matt alone in the house and made vague threats to report Margaret

to the Department of Social Services for child neglect.

The place was free of trash by Friday night. The job was done, and Matt

went home for good. As she saw him off on the bus, Margaret's eyes filled

with tears. It was also starting to rain. She took off her glasses and tried to

wipe them with the hem of her shirt, but they were smeared both inside and

out.

Driving home from the bus station, she began to ask herself: how she'd

got herself into this mess? Had she -- by leaving Matt on his own all day --

set the whole thing up to fail? What had made her accept his original offer?

It probably did have something to do with her own runaway, although it was

different in so many ways. She'd run away to her loving Granny, away from

a mother she saw as not listening and not caring.

Oh God, she thought. Here I am, getting ready to fix up this old house

so it will be as nice as Granny's house, and how I'm trying to be Granny,

the loving grandmother, able to be a better parent than the real mother.

She pulled into her driveway and sat listening to the rain as it fell

steadily on her car roof. She felt vaguely ashamed, as if she had done

something not very nice. It all must have started when Charles had implied

that Elena was "occupied" this summer, and was neglecting Matt. Without thinking, she must have fallen into the "Granny trap," - - I'll be the good fairy grandmother and make it all better.

And it'd all resulted in a situation that was no good for anyone. She smiled bitterly. The person who might end up being cited as a neglectful parent was herself, if that girl's mother really meant it when she threatened to report Margaret to the Department of Social Services.

For the first time in forty-eight years, she began to understand a little of what her parents must have felt when she ran away from home.

Funny, when she ran away she had been Matt's age exactly - - fourteen.

Chapter Nine

Margaret's father came home from the war in the spring of 1946, arriving just in time for her eleventh birthday. A few weeks after his return, he took Margaret's mother with him to Chicago, for a second honeymoon, and to talk to his former employer -- the copper company -- about prospects for employment. The upshot of these discussions was that he was offered the position of Chief Engineer for the Central Division of the company, and the family would be moving to the North Shore of Chicago, probably in the late summer, but at least in time for Margaret to start school. Her father had bought a house for them, an "English cottage" in a suburb on Lake Michigan. Margaret would be going to a large junior high school that included the sixth, seventh and eighth grades. Margaret's mother began spending time in the Chicago area, decorating and furnishing their new house.

All summer long, before they moved, Margaret and Rebecca played together as they'd always done, except that now they were part of a "gang" that included several boys -- Dan Harkness, the minister's son, and his best friend Dick. The boys built tree houses which became forts, and when they moved to other battlegrounds, the girls turned the houses into models of tree-top domesticity. Margaret pretended that she'd never leave.

The day finally came when she had to drive off with her parents, the car loaded with suitcases. Margaret looked mournfully back out the car window, watching Granny grow smaller and smaller. Her childhood was over, she told herself. She would no longer be Granny's girl.

Driving the three hundred miles between Granny's town and the North Shore of Chicago, Margaret made a decision: she would not like the new house, the new town, or anything about it. She was determined to be miserable. She began answering her parents only in monosyllables; she learned to shrug her shoulders when asked questions; and even when they stopped for lunch in a restaurant, she said that she didn't care what she ate. It was not all pretense.

Arriving at the new house, she could see that her parents had hoped she would be pleased, or at least impressed, by its luxury, by the recently purchased furniture, and most important, by her own room. Her mother had obviously gone to great lengths to coordinate colors -- in this case, pink -- and current styles. There was a fluffy pink rug by the bed, a dressing table with a pink ruffled skirt, and a desk with a view of the manicured lawn, set up to encourage good study habits. On the bedside table, was a small pink radio, her mother's concession to Margaret's burgeoning interest in singers like Frank Sinatra, and on the closet door, a full-length mirror. Margaret had her own bathroom, with big, fluffy pink towels.

"I hope you like it?" Her mother had begun to suspect that pleasing Margaret at this point was not necessarily predictable.

Margaret knew that shouting out loud -- I <u>hate</u> it -- would be less devastating than a conventionally polite response. "It's okay," she said in a neutral tone. How quickly she was learning the fine points of getting back at her parents!

Her father's mouth had become a tight, thin line. "I hope you realize, Maggie, that your mother went to a lot of effort to find just the right things for you." Margaret remained silent, and he went on: "I should think you'd appreciate finally having your own room, after years of having to share space with your mother."

He was right about that, of course, and suddenly, she realized she would need a place to be by herself, a place where she could go and slam the door, causing them to worry that their child was unhappy. Some whole new part of her found pleasure in knowing that she had the power to make them feel guilty about forcing her to change her whole life, just so they could enjoy their new world.

Margaret was aware, of course, of the changes that were supposed to be taking place in her body. While her mother had never discussed these subjects, Rebecca's aunt outlined to both the girls a timetable of what would be happening, showing them the equipment they'd be needing. On

Margaret's twelfth birthday, in April of that first year in Junior High, her mother had left on her daughter's bedside table a little booklet, put out by one of the manufacturers of sanitary products, *Marjorie May's Twelfth Birthday*. Despite her fury at this round-about way of communicating, Margaret read the booklet, leaving it looking pristine and untouched, in the exact same spot where her mother had placed it. But none of the events foretold in slightly oblique language took place: she did not discern a slight swelling in her upper chest. Nor had she any need for the little razor set her mother had bought for her on that same occasion.

While she hated the fact that she still looked like a young child, when they went to gym and she had a chance to see how the other girls looked, particularly some of the eighth graders, she was horrified. She wondered if she really wanted to have hair <u>down there</u>, or full breasts, or even hair under her arms. Maybe she would always look like this: maybe by wishing hard enough, she could remain a little girl, Granny's girl. She knew she ought to ask her mother about these ideas, but somehow her mother would get a funny, frozen look whenever anything about people's bodies was discussed.

* * * *

It was her father who first told her that her mother was expecting a baby, and he seemed to expect Margaret to be pleased, but all she could think of was how embarrassing it was going to be: <u>no</u> one her age had a pregnant mother. She was sure of that. She tried to push from her mind altogether what Rebecca had told her about how pregnancy took place. She could not imagine <u>her</u> mother doing anything like that!

One afternoon, shortly after Margaret had come home from school, she heard her mother moving around in the kitchen, and then she heard her gasp. "Oh, no; oh, dear." And then, softly, "Margaret, I need your help. Please bring some towels, a lot of them."

Margaret hurried down the stairs with an armful of pink towels from her bathroom. She was frightened: she'd never heard her mother sound so helpless. "What happened, Mom?" Her mother stood in the middle of the floor, blood streaming down her legs."

"Don't look, Margaret. Just hand me the towels."

"Did you cut yourself?"

"It's called a miscarriage, Margaret. It means I'm not pregnant any more. I won't be having the baby." She began to cry. Margaret had never seen tears on her mother's face. "Call your father. His number is by the phone."

Her father came home an hour later. While they waited, Margaret took her mother to a chair and wrapped her up in a blanket. She was shivering. She made her some tea, and as the tears continued to run down her cheeks,

Margaret wiped them awkwardly with a soft napkin. She didn't know what else to do.

At one point, her mother said: "I'm sorry. I wanted this baby partly for you. I wanted you to have a little sister." She kept on crying. "Your granny probably will think I can't do anything right." Margaret patted her head. Then Dad drove her to the hospital. For those few minutes, Margaret had felt close to her mother, but they never talked about the event again, and gradually, they became their distant selves once again.

She had a similar miscarriage two years later, at the age of thirty-eight, and after that, there were evidently no more pregnancies. Margaret remained an only child.

* * * *

The new school seemed enormous. Most of Margaret's fellow classmates had known each other in elementary school and that first day was punctuated with squeals of delight as old friends found each other. From the very beginning, Margaret felt that she just couldn't catch on to the <u>rules</u> of this new place, not so much the school's regulations, but the unwritten rules that had been set up by the students.

You were classified by several kinds of categories: by the neighborhood you lived in, by the kind of lunch you brought each day, or by the shoes you wore. Certain kinds of kids, for instance, <u>never</u> brought their lunches. They bought lunch at the cafeteria, and they were the athletes, the tough kids. Margaret's mother had given her a bright new lunch box, but she found out after a week or two that a brown paper bag was more acceptable. Margaret felt that she was always catching on just a little too late.

She found a few kindred souls -- thin, short boys with thick glasses, a very overweight girl and a girl whose main interest was field hockey -- outcasts like herself who would never make it socially. There was a girl in her home room who was a different kind of outcast -- Vera Mudge was one of a small group of students who were bussed in from the farm country, and she was truly a farm girl. Margaret felt an immediate kinship with Vera, not just because she liked to read a lot of the same books -- Jane Eyre, the Count of Monte Christo, Rebecca of Sunnybrook Farm, and Uncle Tom's Cabin -- but because she reminded her of the kids in Iowa, particularly the ones from the outlying farms. She loved to listen to the way Vera talked and found herself letting her own Iowa accent (which she'd tried to bury at first) come to the fore. Part of her began to hope that the other kids would think that she was also a "farmie."

Margaret had a part in one of the school plays. Not exactly a real part, she told herself. She was chosen to read the narrator's comments in "Our Town," even though the script called for a male. Her parents, of course, came to the play. Her mother's eyes were shining, the only time Margaret could recall her being proud of her in the three years of junior high. She hugged Margaret enthusiastically. Margaret decided that her mother could love her only when she was playing a part, when she was not being herself at all. The real Margaret was probably someone her mother would not care for, just as her mother -- in later life -- was more comfortable playing the parts of other people, than she was being herself.

* * * *

By the time she was fourteen and almost ready for High School, she was filled with dread. By the fall, so she fantasized, everyone would be dating except for her. It was a Regional School, even bigger than the Junior High. She would be lost in a sea of strangers. There were other changes, of course. Like many of her classmates, she had braces on her teeth, and finally, the week after her birthday in April, she was able to use the kit that had come with the booklet her mother had given her two years before.

She'd come home from school, feeling achy and sleepy. Her stomach was cramping and she was cold. No one was home -- it was Wednesday, her mother's bridge day -- so she decided to crawl into bed, after a quick trip to the bathroom.

It was one thing to read about this event in a pamphlet, but she was not prepared for the brightness of the blood, for the feeling of being wounded, of having a cut that would not heal. She felt betrayed: in spite of all her

146

wishing, she was going to grow up. Struggling to use the introductory kit, she thought: this isn't fair. Boys don't have to do all this, she told herself, grumbling.

* * * *

Emboldened perhaps by her new status as a real adolescent, she began to beg her parents to let her spend the summer at Granny's. After pointing out that she was now too old for camp and not old enough to get a job, she said: "I could go on the train by myself; you wouldn't have to take me. There's <u>nothing</u> to do here, and I'm going to <u>hate</u> that High School."

Her mother sighed. "Margaret, there's no point in carrying on. You might even like the new school. It's time you adjusted to life <u>here</u> on the North Shore."

Margaret's eyes filled, but this time she let herself become openly angry. "You <u>never</u> let <u>me</u> do anything <u>I</u> want, only what you want <u>for</u> me. If you really cared about me, you'd see that I really <u>need</u> to go back to Iowa." She paused. "I'm <u>homesick,</u> don't you understand?"

"But Maggie," said her father, looking puzzled. "This <u>is</u> your home."

She could tell by his face that he was tempted to let her go, but her mother was adamant. "I don't want my daughter to grow up with those small-town values, with Granny's homemaking, and Helen's old maid school teacher mentality. It was bad enough that she had to spend her formative years in that God-awful place, but enough is enough."

Margaret looked to her Dad and saw that, once again, her father had chosen what she secretly called the United Front, at least in front of her. That night, as she lay in bed, she could hear them arguing. She imagined that he hadn't liked what her mother had said about his family.

One day, early in July, when Margaret was in downtown Chicago having her braces tightened, she saw in the railroad station the timetables for the Chicago, Burlington and Quincy line, the trains that went to Granny's town. She took one and put it in her purse, and on the way back to the North Shore, she studied it. There was a train leaving every day at ten in the morning. It would arrive at Granny's at four in the afternoon. Tickets were $14.50 round trip; she had more than that left over from her recent birthday plus some baby-sitting money. Leaning back in her seat, she found herself thinking: I could run away. Granny would let me stay.

She began to plan. She'd pack a suitcase, get it out of the house without anyone seeing her, walk the mile to the commuter rail station, and then ride into Chicago, transferring to the "big" train station to catch the ten o'clock train to Iowa. She'd have to pick a day when her mother was out, Wednesday, to be on the safe side.

* * * *

The trip went exactly as planned, so neatly that she didn't really feel anything until the train crossed the Mississippi. She was back in the land of black soil, tall corn, and fat hogs. She began to get nervous. What would her parents do to punish her? She tried to imagine something worse than having to go to that big high school but nothing crossed her mind.

The train began to slow down. In a few minutes she would be there. Looking out the window she saw the water tower, the old Buick place, and the paint factory. She was almost there! Picking up her suitcase, she moved toward the end of the car. "Anyone meeting you, young lady?" asked the conductor.

"I'm just going a few blocks," she replied enigmatically, and stepped off the train.

It was true. It was only about six blocks to Granny's. Her heart beating fast, she hurried along. And then there was the house, still looking exactly the same.

She ran up the porch steps and opened the screen door. "Granny?" she called, "Are you home?"

"I'm coming, I'm coming," said the familiar voice, "Who's there?"

"It's me," Margaret replied, as Granny came into the living room.

"Oh, child." Granny heaved a deep sigh and wiped her face with the dish towel she was carrying. "Oh, Maggie, we've missed you so. You're a sight for sore eyes. And you're all grown up, taller than your Granny." She laughed, with pride in her voice.

"I'm just five foot, one inch," said Margaret, reaching out to hug her. Granny felt just the same, soft and squishy around the middle and a little bony in the shoulders. It was going to be okay. She even looked the same, with the same old apron.

"Are your parents outside? Why didn't you all tell us you were coming?" Granny moved to the screen door to look out at the driveway.

"No, Granny, it's just me. I came on the train. They don't know where I am. I ran away. I wanted to see all of you, especially <u>you</u>, Granny." Now Margaret began to cry, as if she'd held those tears back for a long time. "I want to live <u>here</u>, Granny. I don't belong on the North Shore. I never have. I hate those big schools."

Now, suddenly, Granny looked sad. "Child, we'd love to keep you, but you belong to your Mom and Dad. I'll have to call them right now: they must be frantic, wondering where you are."

* * * *

. Although she didn't hear all the telephone calls that first night, she had the impression that there was a lot of back and forth talking between her parents and her grandparents. And Margaret did talk to her Dad for a few minutes. He kept asking her: "Are you all right, Maggie? You're not in

150

trouble?" A year or two later Margaret finally figured out he was asking her if she were pregnant, but at the time, she just kept saying: "I'm fine, Daddy, I just wanted to see Granny."

As soon as she'd unpacked -- they'd put her in the same room she'd shared with her mother for so many years -- they encouraged her to call Rebecca and invite her for dinner. Dinner that night was like one of Granny's celebrations, reminding Margaret of the festive spreads they'd had when -- first Ian, and then her Dad -- had come home from the war. It was now, of course, a smaller group, just her grandparents, Uncle Hugh, Aunt Helen and Ian. But this time, Margaret was the traveler come home.

Rebecca Peterson was now a tall, willowy blond, her large front teeth now tamed by the magic of orthodontia, "Oh, Rebecca," said Margaret, "you're so gorgeous! And here I am, still a shrimp, and just starting braces." Even as she spoke she asked herself why she couldn't talk like this to the girls on the North Shore.

The days fell into a rhythm, with mornings spent helping Rebecca baby-sit, and afternoons at the local pool where the boys with whom she and Rebecca had climbed trees were now life-guards. Dan Harkness was almost l6. When he and Dick went off duty, they walked the girls home to Rebecca's house where her aunt gave them cokes.

On Saturday night the four of them went to the movies, Margaret's first real date, and Dan even put his arm around her in the darkness. When he walked her home, they stood in front of Granny's screen door. He couldn't seem to think of anything to say, but his feet seemed permanently stuck to the porch floor. Margaret moved a little bit closer and looked up at him. Then he planted an unsteady kiss on her wondering lips. It felt sort of like a mosquito bite, but it was a start. She'd got the message.

On Monday, when Rebecca had to help out in her uncle's store, Margaret's Uncle Ian -- now a law student up at Iowa City -- asked her if she wanted to go with him on an errand. He was spending the summer at Grandfather's law firm as a para-legal and had to go out into the country a few hours away to get a signature from a farmer who lived near Keokuk.

It was a day of bright blue skies and high white puffy clouds. The corn was tall, almost ready for picking. Somehow, things looked <u>right</u>. For the rest of her life, when she thought of Iowa, she remembered that ride through the countryside. Ian even drove her to see the house -- on the outskirts of a little town called Keosauqua -- where Granny had been born and brought up. She felt comfortable talking to him and when he began to ask her why she'd run away, she tried to explain about the differences in what she'd called the rules. And then he told her about a similar escapade in his younger life.

He'd also been fourteen. Margaret was surprised. Why would anyone want to run away from Grandfather and Granny?

Ian laughed. "My Dad wasn't -- and still isn't -- an easy task-master. We were at swords' point every time he asked me to put up the storm windows or mow the lawn. So I ran away to your Granny's brother, my Uncle Grant -- named after President Ulysses S. Grant, of course. He was an old farmer, maybe ten years older than my mother; he raised hogs and chickens down in this area. I thought I wanted to lead the 'simple life.' It's sort of like what you've been saying about why you came here. But I soon found out that the simple life involved slopping the hogs and feeding and killing chickens. He could see that I wasn't going to be much help, so he sent me home."

He slowed down as they came to the center of Granny's home town. "My folks used to point out where the river had flooded when Granny was a girl. I think maybe you can still see it." He slowed down and then she saw the dark line way up above the first stories of the office buildings. "Running away is sort of like that. You'll always have a little dark line to remember about this time in your life. It will be part of you."

Margaret smiled. She knew that Ian was only thirty-one, and somehow this grown-up conversation made them contemporaries. Suddenly she found herself wondering what Charlie would have been like now if he'd lived.

On the next day, Tuesday, her father arrived by car to take her home. He didn't seem to be angry at her, and Margaret suspected that he'd offered to come instead of her mother because he knew that her mother would be furious, and perhaps blame Granny. All the way home, he probed gently, trying to understand why she'd run away, but it was not as easy as it had been with Ian. Finally, in desperation, and with tears running down her face, she tried to explain it.

"I've been so confused, Daddy, these last three years." She sniffled but went on. "I just can't find the right way to fit in. I don't understand how to behave." Now she was crying steadily. She'd held back these tears for a long time. Her Dad handed her his handkerchief. She caught her breath. "When I'm at Granny's -- in Iowa -- I sort of know who I am and what the rules are." She glanced over at his face. He was keeping an eye on the road but clearly listening. He looked puzzled. "Daddy, haven't you ever been in a place where you couldn't quite figure it out? Someplace where no matter what you did, it felt wrong?"

Her father laughed bitterly. "As a matter of fact, Maggie, I was in a place like that. The Army. For five years. And it was hard." He paused. "The first day in the National Guard, on our schedule it said 'Recreation,' so I sat down under a tree for that half hour and started reading a book of poems I had in my pocket. Boy, I never heard the last of that one. The

Sergeant started calling me 'our local poet' and worse. It turned out that when the Army talks about Recreation, they mean volley ball or something like that." Maggie smiled, still sniffling. "And another time some of the guys threatened to beat me up when I told them -- by this time I was even an officer -- that I would have to report them if they looted in some of the bombed-out German cities. It was probably a hopeless proposition -- everyone was stealing things right and left, champagne from factories we captured, cameras, and even tennis rackets. I finally gave up. But I know what you're talking about." He smiled. "Has it been that bad?"

It didn't seem quite right to compare her life on Chicago's North Shore with the war. "Maybe some of it was my fault. Maybe I didn't try hard enough. But I love the way things are at Granny's and in Iowa. When I'm there, I don't have to try. I guess I've been hoping you'd give up and we could all come back to live there."

"I'm sorry, Maggie, but it's just not possible, for several reasons, not just my job."

Margaret knew he was talking about her mother, because he sighed. "But maybe your Mom and I can figure out another solution." He frowned. "I guess it's not too easy being an only child," he said sadly. "We tried to do something about that, but I guess it wasn't meant to be."

"I know, Daddy, and I'm sorry." There didn't seem to be anything more to say.

* * * *

Several weeks after they'd returned home, her parents sat down with her one evening and told her that they were going to send her to her mother's old boarding school in Connecticut. She would never have to go to that big High School. And as it turned out, during her first year at the new school, her father was transferred to the New York office of the company, and the family moved to Scarsdale.

Chapter Ten

On the morning after Matt had gone home to Portland, Margaret decided it was time to start calling contractors, and begin planning what she was going to do to the house. She sat at the kitchen table, the Yellow Pages open to *Building Contractors*, her hand on the phone. Now what? The easiest thing to would be to call the contractor that Chloe had recommended, the man with the handicapped son, the one Gretchen had called the Great Dane. Running her finger down the columns in the phone book, she found his ad: Victorian Restorations, Erik Jensen, Member of American Institute of Architects. So he was an architect. Taking a deep breath, she dialed the number, and they made an appointment for the following Saturday afternoon.

"I'll be there around two. I drive an old red pickup," he said, sounding businesslike but friendly. Her mention of Gretchen seemed to bring a little warmth to his voice.

Sitting in the kitchen, a week later, listening to the Saturday afternoon opera on the radio, she heard the sound of the truck pulling into her driveway. From her kitchen window, she could see that he'd parked in front of the barn.

A tall, slightly plump, red-bearded man climbed out of the pickup and moved quickly to the barn door. He was wearing chinos, a faded plaid shirt, and had on work boots. When he turned around, she saw a shock of curly, sandy-colored hair that seemed to blend into his beard, a round face with thick wire-rimmed glasses, and behind his ear, almost hidden in that mass of curls, a pencil. While his very bulk was reassuring, his glasses made him appear vulnerable.

What would it be like to have a man in the house <u>again</u>? -- <u>this</u> man, who was attractive in his own way, over a period of months, with his own ideas, his very <u>presence</u>? And it would be someone she would be paying -- God knows how much at this point. And how would she know if it was the right amount, that she wasn't being cheated, or taken advantage of as a woman living alone?

She watched him as he looked at up at the old barn and then peered into its windows. Walking slowly around the structure, he nodded his head and smiled, as if in delight and astonishment at something he was seeing. Yes, he seemed to be saying, I was right! Well, the barn, at least, had passed his inspection.

Facing the main house, he made notes on a clip-board. As he moved out of view, she decided it would be a good idea to put on something a little less grungy, perhaps the blue cashmere sweater and a clean pair of jeans. She hurried upstairs and washed her hands and ran a comb through her hair. After she'd changed her clothes, she looked in the mirror and was pleased to see that her cheeks were flushed. She looked <u>good</u>, she thought, as she added a little lipstick, wondering at the same time if women ever stopped trying to improve their appearance when a man was coming to call!

Shortly after two, he rang the back doorbell. Turning down the radio, she opened the door. "Hello," he said. "Erik Jensen." His voice was deep and loud. "You have a wonderful house, and an even more wonderful barn." He chuckled, a rumbling laugh that seemed to reverberate. She tried to locate his accent: it certainly wasn't Boston, since the 'r' in the word 'barn' was fully extended; she heard echoes of the Midwest, but without the twang that always seemed to creep into Iowan speech.

She stepped back to let him in. He <u>was</u> big, and the thick reddish hair that sprouted out above his shirt and below the shirt sleeves looked fuzzy: she wanted to reach out and stroke it. What in the world was she thinking? At her age! At the same time, she felt as if she had been invaded by an enormous bear. There were soft brown eyes behind the thick round glasses; he reminded her of someone or something. What? "Margaret Bluestone," she said, feeling her own hand almost swallowed up in his large paw. "Do you really like it?" It had been a long time since anyone had complimented the house, and she wondered if this was a ploy to persuade her to give him the job. She was tempted to say: I bet you say that to all the houses.

"Absolutely. But then," he said laughing, "I've never met a Victorian house I didn't like. And the best thing about yours is that it hasn't been tampered with." He was looking around the kitchen as he spoke. "I smell coffee," he said cheerfully, but before she could fill a cup for him, he put up his hand. "I'd like to go down into the basement and look at the underpinnings, and the plumbing and wiring. Then we can talk, and I'll have some of that coffee." He certainly appeared to be a take-charge person. Did she need another one of those, after forty years of Henry? But, of course, even if he were the one she was going to choose, he'd only be around for a few months!

She pointed him in the direction of the cellar stairs and began rummaging around for some cookies. She thought about her friends' kitchens: they were either antiseptically white, laboratories with buttons to push, places to move food from freezer to microwave, or cheerily countrified with chintz curtains and heart-shaped mottoes on the walls. Neither of these images appealed to her. She'd done well with this kitchen as it was, Margaret thought, and she'd made some great meals on that old stove. Six of them had sat around the big table and it had never mattered that the chairs didn't match. Of course, the kitchen had never had cabinets or counters, but she'd managed, thanks to the old pantry in the back where she kept her dishes, and to her creative use of various surfaces -- the table, itself, the top of the portable dishwasher, and the old wheeled service cart. She kept most of her canned foods and cereal boxes in a tool cabinet a friend had given them, and she'd hung up a spice rack near the stove. Curtains tacked below the old sink hid her cleaning supplies. A little later, coming up the stairs, he said: "Now for coffee." That was pretty bossy, she thought; she wanted to remind him: say 'please.' He seated himself at the table. Although it was a big kitchen, he overwhelmed the room. He was quiet, sipping his coffee. She began to wonder how old he was. From the window, she'd thought he was in his forties, but now she could see more lines in his face and realized he might be somewhat older.

"So what do you think, Mr. Jensen?" she said, pointing to the clipboard. She wasn't sure just what she should call him. "Is the house worth fixing up?"

He smiled broadly. "Please, call me Erik." He paused. "Well, Margaret" -- he smiled as he said <u>her</u> name -- "the structure is good; it was well built, probably around 1880, and built to last, like most of its generation." Pausing, he added: "You seem to have almost new wiring."

Margaret smiled. "We had no choice. The insurance man told us it would be a fire hazard the way it was."

As he continued to talk, stressing the soundness of the plumbing, the excellent condition of the roof, and the fact that there was no sign of termites, she watched his face. Here was a man who obviously loved his work. When he set down his coffee cup, his hands moved, almost on their own, to shape a large box, or to outline the curve of the gingerbread decorations. It was as if he could hardly wait to get started.

He looked closely at her, perhaps sensing that she was not really listening. "Except for the kitchen" -- he waved at the room -- "we're talking about a face-lift, putting on makeup, and color."

She began to laugh. And then she thought: he seemed to have made up his mind, without even asking her what she wanted. "A little mascara and some blush and we're done?" She knew that she sounded sarcastic. "What about the front porch? Maybe we should consider plastic surgery instead of a simple face-lift."

"I'd recommend getting rid of it altogether," he said, evidently ignoring her tone. "I think the days are gone when families sat on their front porches in the evening and waved to the neighbors as they passed." He paused, looking at her face. "Or am I assuming too much?" He was certainly making assumptions. Perhaps she should have spent more time in advance, thinking about exactly what she wanted.

Margaret sat quietly for a minute, thinking about the porch. She began to realize it was Granny's porch that she was feeling sentimental about, those long summer evenings when it had been too hot to stay in the house, when the family gathered out there, greeting their friends who lived nearby. Granny'd even had a porch swing. But this porch, what had they used it for? Thinking back, she remembered snow shovels stacked near the door, skis and sleds parked there during the snow season, and rakes in the fall. But no one ever seemed to sit out there. There weren't even any porch chairs. Once in a while, Charles would sit on the steps and play the guitar, but that was it.

"We could give you a <u>little</u> porch," said Erik, "just big enough for people to stand on while they waited for you to answer the bell." He smiled. "And we'd make you a new set of double doors with a Victorian oval glass."

Margaret liked the picture he described, but she felt as if she were being rushed into something. Trying to slow things down, she asked: "without the porch, would it still be" - - she paused -- "authentic? I know you're into restoration." She kept thinking of Granny's house, with its wraparound porch. Of course, she reminded herself, this was <u>her</u> house. It was not Granny's, and it was not Erik Jensen's. She could do what she wanted with it.

"Don't worry about it. The Victorians did all kinds of things to their houses. I suspect that porch was added later on; it's a different quality of wood, less good. You'll find, I'm sure, that if we take it off, it will lighten up your living and dining rooms, and the front hall. Cheaper, too, not to replace it." He was thinking. "If you want somewhere to sit, we could make you a deck here off the kitchen, connected to the back porch." He stood up and opened the back door, and pointed. "Right here."

"A deck out back might be nice." She tried to picture herself sitting out there, watching the birds. God, what was all this going to cost? "But wouldn't that be an expensive project?"

"Not too bad. Am I getting the message that you don't want to spend a lot of money?" Margaret was glad he'd brought the subject up. She saw little frown lines between his eyebrows, and now that she was looking at him more closely, she saw that his hair was not sandy, but a kind of grayish red, fading toward white.

"I'm newly separated from my husband," she said slowly, realizing that this was the first time she'd said those words aloud. "I'm not sure what I want to do with the house eventually, but I think what I want right now is for it to look nice, just for me. I suppose I might sell it one of these days." She paused. "But I don't have a lot of money." Maybe she should have told him that right away, she thought, frowning.

"I wasn't thinking of a lot of changes. Why don't you tell me what would be the minimum you need done."

"The porch, painting the outside, redoing the kitchen completely, and maybe another bathroom or two. And I think I'd like the floors sanded and some interior painting as well." She smiled. "That seems more than minimal."

"It shouldn't be too bad, even with the deck. Why don't we walk through the whole house so I can get a feel for it, and then we'll come back to the kitchen."

* * * *

Erik was quiet during the tour of the house until they reached the living room. Then he stopped and looked up at the paintings that decorated the walls. Most of the work had been done by her son Charles. Charles had a gift for using light -- especially from night skies -- that illuminated his pictures in a special way. Her favorite was a painting done shortly after sunset in downtown Boston, the tall buildings defined as they stood in silhouette before a fading, dark orange sky.

"Those are my son's paintings," she said. "He's a professional painter."

"They're damn good," he said. They moved slowly on to the sun porch. On the back of the chimney wall she had hung the painting she had done when she was a student at Wellesley -- the red, white and blue farm picture that had decorated their apartment when she was first married. Here, too, the best feature was the sky.

"Was that an early painting by your son?" he asked.

165

Margaret laughed. "That was an early painting by his mother, who realized even back then that maybe her talents ran in a different direction."

He looked at her curiously. "And what did that turn out to be?"

"I work for a clinic -- the Chadwick -- as a social worker."

As they started up the stairs to the second floor, he said: "You sound like me. Many of us who became architects still think of our profession as a second choice. We were the kinds of kids who showed talent in drawing, whom they pushed to think about attending art school, and then gradually we discovered we weren't cut out to be painters." She wondered if there was any regret in his voice, but she couldn't tell.

As they toured the various rooms, she stopped at the little sewing alcove. Like Granny, Margaret had put her sewing machine there, but then she discovered that she really hated everything about sewing or mending. The space now had an abandoned look.

"I think I'd like to have a door put here, to give me an extra guest room. And maybe you could squeeze another bathroom up here somewhere." He made a note on his clipboard.

Back in the kitchen, with more coffee for each of them, he began to look around the actual structure. "Where does that door lead?" He asked, pointing to a closed door on one wall.

"That's what we always called the 'maid's room.' We've never used it for anything but storing junk." She stood up and opened the door. "As you can see, it's really two rooms. There's a small, non-functioning bathroom back there, too."

He stood up and moved into the area. "Did you want to do anything with this part of the house?"

"I'd thought, when you did over the kitchen, that you might want to include some of this space."

He looked back at the kitchen. "I don't think so. You've got a lot of room here, as it is, especially if we absorb the pantry. I would recommend making it into what they call a mother-in-law apartment, but without its own kitchen since there's one right here. It gives you an added feature to advertise if you ever sell the house." He was at it again, she thought, imagining all kinds of improvements without asking her opinion.

Margaret frowned, trying to picture what he was talking about. "I'd like to put aside that idea for a while, but in the meantime, can we discuss the kitchen?"

"I've been thinking about it," he said, "and I'm wondering if we really want to change it that much." Erik looked at her, obviously to see her reaction.

167

Margaret was surprised. She'd been sure that anyone she brought in would want to remodel the whole place from top to bottom. "That's funny. While you were down in the basement, I was looking at this room, and thinking that I rather like the way it's laid out. This big table has been useful, and I like the big stove."

"Well," he said slowly, evidently really listening to her now, "we could re-create that big table by having a marble-topped island here, with a Tiffany-style lamp hanging over it, pretty much as the original owners probably did. There'd still be room for a big family to gather around. And we could get you a double-sized oven, some other big appliances, and of course, some cabinets and counters. I'll attach some sketches to the estimate, and drop it off in a few days." He stood up, as if to leave. "I don't think you actual need any structural remodeling here." Well, that was good news, she thought.

"Thank you for coming over so promptly," said Margaret. She swallowed and hurried into the statement she'd planned to make. "You realize, of course, that I'll probably get a few more estimates. But I like your approach to the kitchen." She was pleased with the way it sounded, business-like, but friendly. He didn't seem surprised.

"Whoever finally does the job, there's one thing you could do yourself, as a kind of homework assignment. You should go over to the library and take out a book or two on the way the Victorians painted their houses. In San Francisco, these houses, as you probably know, are called 'painted ladies.' If you want to be 'authentic,' you might want to do the job in at least four colors." He grinned. "You'll have a good time picking out which ones you want. It might be a good idea for you to drive around town, maybe even to Cambridge, to get some ideas on how other people have done their houses."

"Thank you. That sounds like fun." As she stood up to show him out, she thought of another question she wanted to ask. "When would you have time to do this job? I was hoping to have it all finished by Thanksgiving when all my kids will be here."

"I could start by the first of August, and be done by November. I'll put all that in the estimate." He stood awkwardly, as if he, too, had a prepared statement. "Could I ask you a favor? Could you unlock the barn and let me look at it? I've a feeling it's a real gem, an example of an early kind of barn, built like a church."

"The key's right here," said Margaret, reaching behind him, "I'll come with you and see what you're talking about." She'd never gone into the barn, unless she could help it. It'd always been Henry's domain, a messy place where he kept more junk.

169

"Good," he said, "and then maybe you could explain to me how you happened to have that wonderful old phone booth in there. I saw it when I peeked in the windows."

"It was my husband's," she said briefly, as they walked together out to the barn. "He collected a lot of old stuff." Opening the big door with the old rusty key, she gestured up toward the ceiling of the barn. "It's all yours." Then she looked up and could see what he meant. The barn had a sort of nave, with an aisle on each side. The rafters even reminded her of the arches that held up the roof of a church.

"Wonderful!" He said. "I was almost afraid to hope. It was made in the basilica style, like a cathedral! I suspect this barn was here long before most of these houses. It probably belonged to the original farm that covered this part of town." His face was lit up.

"I can see why you're into restoration," she said. "You really love this stuff." Margaret was enjoying the look on his face; he was opening a window to his inner self. Suddenly she knew what he looked like -- a barn owl. He even had the same plumage!

Margaret glanced up and saw, coming in from the southwest, beams of sunlight, almost smoky from years of dust in the atmosphere. She was reminded of the barns in the Iowa farms that her grandfather had owned. She smiled, lost in those memories.

"When I was growing up in Iowa, my grandfather used to take me with my best friend to visit one of his farms, and we'd go out to the barn and jump from the loft down into the hay. The sunlight coming in looked just the way it does here."

He'd found the ladder, and, after testing the rungs, he started up. When he reached the loft, he called down to her. "Margaret, I have to say it: I covet this barn. I've been looking for one like this for a long time." After a pause, he said: "Come on up, it's wonderful up here."

Nimbly, Margaret mounted the ladder. She was ten years old again. They sat on the ledge of the loft, legs dangling. "It's too bad there's no hay for us to jump into," she said, looking up at him, suddenly aware that this whole relationship was feeling magical, a revisiting of an idealized childhood. What was there about this man that made it so easy to slip into this easy assumption of shared memories? She'd certainly never experienced that kind of mutuality with Henry. His appeal had been his otherness, the differences between them. With this man, she felt that they had once inhabited the same mythical kingdom. It was scary, but a little too close.

Hoping to change the atmosphere, she asked: "What would you do if you had a barn like this? Would you haul it away and take it somewhere?"

"That's the trouble. I have nowhere to put it. When my wife left four years ago, Will and I moved into a condominium. This is just a dream. But it

171

would make a wonderful office for someone in my business, especially if I could keep that antique phone booth."

Margaret laughed. But she was thinking that the barn might make a good office for herself. After she retired from the clinic -- or even before -- she could turn this space into a place for a private practice. She could see clients here, she thought, although it would require a few little details like electricity, plumbing, and heating!

In the silence that followed, she thought about his remark that his wife had left him. And she found herself wondering how it had happened that he was the one who became the custodial parent. Perhaps it had been something like Gretchen's story. It was, of course, none of her business. But she was curious. "You mentioned that you and your son live together now," she said tentatively.

"Yes," he said, matter-of-factly. "He's disabled."

"How old is he?"

"He's seventeen, born when I was forty years old," he said. Margaret quickly figured that he must be fifty-seven in that case, five years younger than she. "He has severe cerebral palsy, and goes to a special school just a few miles from here. A bus picks him up every weekday." He seemed comfortable talking about him.

"How do you manage on weekends?" She asked, wondering. "Like today?"

"He usually stays with my sister in Wellesley on Saturdays, and she's offered to take him for a whole weekend. One of these days, I'll take her up on it. She has kids near his age and they're great with him. It gives us both a break from each other."

* * * *

During the next week, Margaret managed to interview two more contractors, an unpleasant man whose estimate would have wiped out her whole investment account, and an intriguing feminist organization whose two partners ran Margaret ragged as they moved rapidly through the house. Theirs was the lowest bid, but she realized that, from the beginning, she really wanted Erik. She found time to go to the library and take out a book about painting Victorian houses, and even discovered a book about old barns which she decided to take with her on vacation. Then, after several trips up and down Brattle Street in Cambridge, she made up her mind about the colors she would use in painting her own house. The Victorians seemed to have concentrated on muted off-shades, so Margaret chose a soft mauve as the primary color, with a cream trim, and the accent colors would be a deep purple and a light blue.

* * * *

One evening, shortly before she left for the Vineyard, she was sitting at the phone, trying to get up the courage to call Anita. No one else had heard from Henry and while she knew Anita would still be angry at her, blaming her for 'driving her father away,' she might be the one person whom Henry would call. She punched in Anita's number. Hesitantly, saying she was worried, she asked if Anita had heard from him.

"Mom," her daughter answered, her words sounding as if they were being bitten off and spit out, "even though Dad drove off under his own power, you know that you abandoned him. Not just on the Fourth of July weekend, but several years ago. You've been systematically abandoning him to the point where you never gave him any support about his earthquake theories. And you did nothing to stop him from going, even though it was clear to me, at least, that he was in no shape to drive three thousand miles across the country." She seemed to be getting more and more wound up.

Finally there was a silence. "Anita, just do me this one favor. If you hear from him, will you let one of us know? Andrew, or Molly, at least? You know, Anita, if I thought there was anything seriously wrong with him, I would not have let him go. And if I thought he couldn't drive, I'd certainly have notified the police. But he was rational. I didn't see <u>you</u> trying to stop him." At that point, Anita hung up.

She and Anita had always had their battles, especially during her teenage years, but she'd never hung up on her mother, and she'd never taken a stand so completely on her father's side. And in all those years, Margaret had kept to herself the mental and verbal abuse Henry had directed to her; she hadn't shared with her children their father's intermittent distaste for family life. Anita, in particular, had never understood that Margaret's attempts to "normalize" the family with ritual celebrations were her efforts to make up for Henry's derelictions. And it was too late to start telling her now.

More frightening for Margaret was a recurrent nightmare she'd had for the last several weeks, that Henry had been swallowed up by one of the earthquakes he'd been studying, and that no one would believe her when she insisted he must be underneath all those rocks. It was not such a crazy idea, she would tell herself when she woke from the dreams. She remembered all too clearly the eruption of Mount St. Helens some years ago. Some of those people were never found.

Chapter Eleven

Margaret tried to remember when she'd last taken the road to Woods Hole. Chloe and Saul Solomon had built their new house on the Vineyard ten years ago. Although she and Henry were often invited, they'd never seen it. Henry had always said that a second home was a prime example of "conspicuous consumption" and had refused to go, leaving Margaret to make excuses.

She and Henry had gone to the Vineyard on their own more than thirty-five years earlier. Anita had been a toddler, and they'd rented a tiny cottage in the backwash of the village of Menemsha. They'd put the portable crib out on the screened porch, overlooking a backyard filled with marsh grass and reeds. The house came with a small rowboat, and on occasion, the three of them had donned life jackets and rowed out into the harbor. Margaret remembered spending most of her days sitting up to her waist in the warm water, running her fingers through the strands of seaweed, with a blissfully happy Anita splashing beside her. The tides had left a variety of shells for the baby to play with, and Margaret began a simple collection.

She sighed. Her world had changed. For the first time in her life, she was truly alone.

Taking a trip, going on a "vacation" made it a reality. Henry was gone, and Anita was still not speaking to her. The rest of her children were busy with their own lives. Except for Chloe, most of her friends were not aware that she and Henry had separated. But she could imagine Chloe saying to Saul: we should do something for Margaret, invite her to the beach for a couple of weeks.

Margaret had agreed to meet the Solomon's daughter, Athena, at the ticket office for the ferry. When they first met, she and Chloe used to call their two daughters -- Athena and Anita -- the two A's. Lately, Margaret had been too busy to think about what it would mean to see Athena again. It was probably four or five years since they'd last met, but now she realized she was becoming anxious at the prospect. At thirty-nine Athena was seriously troubled. She'd been anorexic since her late teens, and following a brief, unhappy marriage, deeply depressed. Margaret found herself wondering why Chloe had invited both of them to the Vineyard at the same time. Was she being asked to take on the role of caretaker, confidante, or perhaps buffer? One of the problems with being a social worker was that people often thought that a few words from you would magically solve complex family problems.

In the crowded ferry office, she looked around, hoping to spot Athena before she herself had been seen. She wasn't there. Finally, she saw a bulky young woman with a yellow complexion and lifeless, lanky hair, moving slowly toward the building. Surely, she thought, this could not be Athena, and then realized that the bulkiness was simply an enormous gray sweat shirt, hanging down over a thick pair of pants. Of course, it was Athena, bundled up in spite of what looked like the beginning of a very hot day. She was reminded of some of the pregnant teenagers she'd counseled, girls who were trying to hide their condition by heavy clothing. But in Athena's case, the picture was reversed: she was covering up her extreme emaciation. Athena was traveling light, Margaret saw, with only a small day-pack on her back, a toothbrush extending out of its top flap.

Margaret decided to act as if this were the same Athena she'd always known. She gave the girl a big hug and began chatting about family news, plans for Molly's wedding, the fact that Andrew and his wife were having a baby. She just couldn't bring herself to ask even the simplest questions such as: how <u>are</u> you? what are you doing these days? are you working? Or, the most obvious question of all -- aren't you dying of the heat in that heavy sweat shirt?

She and Athena chose chairs on the bow of the boat, looking toward the Vineyard. The seats were bright blue plastic, damp from ocean spray or early morning fog.

"How is Anita?" The young woman asked. The two of them had been friends since nursery school. "She writes and keeps asking me to visit in Seattle, but I've been so busy." Margaret realized this was Athena's first spontaneous comment. It would be heavy going, trying to carry on a conversation with her.

Margaret turned and looked directly at her. The close-up view was even more frightening: Athena's face was a skull, with eyes that seemed both dry and glittery, and her breath was foul, in spite of the toothbrush. "I think you'd find her pretty much the same," Margaret replied. "Still working for the Weather Bureau -- I guess they call it NOAA now -- and still living with Everett after ten years. They've moved to a new apartment that looks out on Puget Sound." She had trouble thinking of what to say next, since she and Anita were not speaking at the moment. Anita was still blaming her mother for "driving Daddy away."

Suddenly, Margaret realized she was exhausted. She leaned back in her chair and closed her eyes. Through the thin skin of her eyelids, she could sense the warm red sun; the wind in her face smelled of salt, and the squawks of the gulls competed with the murmurs of the passengers. Now her body began to remember that summer when she'd first seen the Vineyard. One night, a few days before they were to go home, it had been too hot to sleep.

"Let's go skinny-dipping," Henry had suggested. "We can hear the baby if she cries. Look, the moon is making a path for us right on our own little beach." They'd dropped their clothes on the lawn and moved into the delicious water. It was the same water they'd been swimming in all day, but in the darkness, it felt like velvet on her bare skin. The moonlight fooled her into thinking she could see Henry's freckles under water. He looked like a speckled trout as he dove toward the bottom. Margaret had not even thought about putting in her diaphragm before disrobing -- could a woman get pregnant under water? they'd asked each other later, giggling. Yet after nine months, Charles was born.

Margaret opened her eyes. How was she ever going to get over Henry if she kept revisiting memories of scenes like this?

* * * *

The Solomons' house was in the Chilmark section of the Vineyard, on a round pond, one of the brackish inlets separating the main part of the island from the long barrier beach that ran along its southern side. The cottage was set back from the water, but if you walked half-way around that clear pond you would suddenly come upon the open ocean, with a heavy surf washing up on a clean white beach. The house itself was simple and sparsely decorated, and except for the deck that faced south, only lightly furnished. Out on the deck were lounge chairs, tables, and on the railings a scattering of bright colored towels and wet bathing suits. A small sailboat was tied up to a simple dock.

They settled into a routine: Margaret and Chloe would get up fairly early, eat a light breakfast and move out to the deck to read the newspapers, the latest novels, or play Scrabble. By eleven, they'd put on bathing suits and head for the big beach. Saul slept a little later than they did since he usually sat up late into the night, working on revising the textbook he was writing. He was a biologist, specializing in Genetics. Margaret could see the light on in the living room when she got up to go to the bathroom, even as late as 2 AM. Depending on the tides, he often spent the morning in his sail boat, exploring some of the other inlets. Athena usually didn't appear until nearly noon, and they would spot her walking along the ocean in her long, gray sweatshirt. She would go far beyond the official Chilmark beach. Although they never saw her in the water, they assumed she'd been swimming since, at the day's end, when she returned to the cottage, she would hang her wet bikini on the railing next to the rest of their bathing suits. Sometimes, if it was a little warmer, she would wear her long red towel robe, bringing back in its deep pockets a collection of wave-scoured rocks and seashells which she lined up on her window sill.

Once Athena brought home an unusual shell, a mirror image of one she'd already made part of her collection. She showed it to Margaret, placing it side-by-side with its twin. "Athena," she said, enchanted by this treasure from the sea, "It's in perfect condition, with that row of bumps there on the shoulder -- like little epaulets." She picked it up and ran her fingers down the whorls. "I remember seeing something about one just like this in one of your mother's books. Let's look it up." And sure enough, in the section on whelks, there was a picture of their shell -- *Busycon Perversum*. The book said that these left-handed whelks were only rarely found in New England.

Margaret and Chloe often packed a lunch for the beach, but when they suggested that Athena join them, she'd quickly answer that she'd just had a big brunch. Once in a while she would go sailing with her father, lying on the foredeck, peering into the clear water, trying to see what was on the deep bottom.

Dinner was a special problem. While lavish in her praise of the menu, Athena would push the food around on her plate, only occasionally putting something in her mouth. Margaret could not bear to watch. Without discussing it, the three adults (it was difficult not to think of Athena as "the child" even though she was thirty-nine years old) had evidently made a compact not to comment on what she did or did not eat. Margaret wondered if she were forcing herself to vomit after meals, even the little that she ate, or if she were taking laxatives. In fact, once when Athena was at the beach, Margaret had sneaked into her room and looked around, but she was afraid to open anything.

No one talked about the fact that Athena was starving herself to death. Even with all the padding she wore, she seemed thinner every day. Once or twice Chloe would urge Athena to try some special seafood dish, but most of the time they discussed public affairs in a desultory fashion. Margaret found she was counting the days until she could leave. This vacation, like so many other pleasures she'd counted on, had ended up being devoted to someone else's problems. Once again, she felt pushed to bury her own needs.

There never seemed to be time for her.

On the morning of Margaret's fourth day, when the two women were playing Scrabble and Athena was sailing with her father, Chloe looked up from the board and said quietly: "You know, I don't think I can stand it much longer." Her eyes were filled with tears.

Margaret felt as if a lump in her stomach had moved up into her throat. She swallowed and said: "You're talking about Athena."

Chloe nodded. "It's as if she's angry at us, torturing us on purpose, punishing us for God knows what misdeeds."

Margaret thought about Chloe's life-long battle to lose weight. She had her own issues with food.

Chloe shrugged. "And the worst part," she said, sniffling, "is that sometimes I think we're getting back at her by not saying anything, and even pretending not to notice. It's our secret way of fighting back. It's a war, and no one is winning." Chloe began to cry in earnest.

"I think I've been playing that same game," said Margaret, reaching over to take her hand.

"I think we're losing her, Margaret. We're losing her and nothing can stop it. She's going to die." And now Chloe struggling with long, deep sobs.

Looking at her, as she sat there in defeat, Margaret realized that Chloe had already begun to mourn this child. Somewhere inside herself she'd accepted the fact that Athena would be lost to them, and that waiting for it to happen was almost the worst part.

Chloe looked up at the sky, and spoke more slowly, as if she were remembering someone who'd already gone. "Athena was our star child, the one who got the 800 on her SATs, who got the lead in all the plays. And now it looks as if that star is about to burn out, like one of those supernovas."

There was a long silence. Margaret continued to hold on to Chloe's hand. "You're feeling helpless," she said. "We all do."

Chloe nodded. "But it helps to have you here," she said. Then, after a long pause, she added: "I never told you, but when her marriage was breaking up, she made a suicide attempt, taking a lot of pills. Luckily, her husband was still around, and he found her in time."

"What does Saul say?"

"Well, of course, being a specialist in genetics, he thinks it's all in the genes, that there's probably nothing anyone can do. Now he wants to yell at her, put his foot down, and hospitalize her. We did that a few years ago, you know," she said, wiping her eyes with the back of her hand. "We sent her to a place in Connecticut that specializes in eating disorders. But it didn't work." Chloe laughed harshly. "All those patients, mostly young women who looked a lot like Athena --- my God, you'd think they were all part of the same weird species, all skin and bones, and exercising all the time -- they got together and sort of went on strike. Of course, they'd all had to promise to cooperate in order to get admitted, but eventually, this whole group refused to eat and wouldn't let the nurses put them on intravenous feedings. Finally, they were all expelled. And those poor crazy kids called it a civil rights issue."

In the long silence that followed, Margaret thought about the fact that anorexia was a slow form of suicide, and that some victims did end up killing themselves by other means, tired of waiting for their bodies to do the job. One thing puzzled her. "Chloe, why do you suppose she came here to the Vineyard this summer?"

"I don't know. That's what made me think she was punishing us. She could have stayed in New York and starved. But that would be too easy."

She paused, and then said bitterly, almost as if she were spitting out the words, "she wants to <u>stick</u> it to us. You must think I'm crazy, or at least paranoid?"

Margaret shook her head. "You're probably right." She thought about it. "Unless . ."

"Unless what?" said Chloe.

"Could she be giving us all one more chance to do it right?"

"But what the hell <u>is</u> right? She must know we love her." Chloe began to cry again. "God, she was my first child, such a loving baby and so good to all her sisters. Maybe I shouldn't have had them; maybe she should have been an only child. I don't know. I don't know anything. I just want her to be happy, no matter what that means to her."

As Chloe spoke, it suddenly came to Margaret that <u>she</u> was the one who would be seen as the last resort. It was going to up to her to save this child. Jesus, she thought. What a position to be in! And what did these people think she could do?

After another long silence, during which she, too, wiped her eyes, Margaret said tentatively. "I have a feeling you want me to talk to her. Is that why I'm here now?" The subject might as well be on the table. She looked directly at Chloe.

Chloe glanced up at her. She seemed uncomfortable. Biting her lip, she spoke tentatively. "Would you, Margaret? It couldn't hurt. Please?"

Margaret was quiet. It felt almost as if she were being set up. Damn Chloe, anyway. Right now, she'd like to get up, call a cab and go to the ferry. But how could she refuse? It was presented as a life- and-death matter. And perhaps it was. Oh, shit.

She sighed. "Okay, but I'll have to pick the time. You'll have to trust me to do that."

She paused, knowing that she must add one more thing. "Chloe," she spoke slowly, feeling her way. "Don't count on me to make magic. No one seems to know how to handle this disease."

* * * *

One morning Chloe joined Saul for a morning sail, and Margaret set out for the beach. She waited on the sand, watching the surf come in, but keeping an eye out for Athena. Finally she spotted her walking along the edge of the pond and heading for the ocean. She was wearing her long red robe. After a half hour or so, Margaret began to walk in the same direction, slowly, as if she were looking for shells. When she reached the section of beach where Athena had spread out her towel, she waved cheerfully. "Hi, can I join you for a moment?"

There was no way Athena could refuse. They sat side by side in silence for a while, watching the waves and listening to the terns squeaking as they dove for unseen fish. In spite of the warm sun, Margaret felt shivery. She wrapped her arms around her knees. Then Athena sighed. "I imagine my parents told you to talk to me." She looked directly at Margaret.

Tired of lying and glad she didn't have to play any more games, Margaret said: "They can tell you're unhappy. I can see it, too."

"I'm just so tired," said Athena. She spoke slowly, as if every word were an effort. "They want me to be happy. But they mean married, with kids underfoot. They think there's still a few ticks left in my biological clock. For Christ's sake -- at thirty-nine!" She paused for breath, after what for her was a long speech.

Margaret found herself wondering if she'd ever given a similar message to Anita. That same clock was ticking for her, too. Was Anita feeling some hidden pressure from her, that made her fight back by not speaking? It was something to think about, but not now.

Then Athena looked directly at Margaret and said: "My mom thinks she's being subtle when she asks me: 'anything new in your social life?' She keeps telling me about all my high school friends, sending me clippings about their new babies." Her words were spoken flatly, as if nothing mattered any more.

Oh, this poor child, Margaret thought. What could she say that would make a difference?

"Athena, you just have to be yourself, not what you think anyone else wants for you."

"I'm so jealous of my sisters," Athena said in a more forceful voice, "And not because they're all married and have kids, but because they never had to be anything but themselves to be loved by Mom and Dad." Now she began to sound angry. She was speaking at normal speed. "They didn't have to get good grades or high SAT scores, or be gorgeous or get leads in all the plays. They could just be funny, like Helena, or klutzy like Diana. And let's face it, Sophia is just plain <u>fat</u>, and everybody loves her."

Margaret didn't dare say that by now, everybody would love to see a fat Athena. Instead she put her arms around that bony body. "I've loved you for thirty-six years, ever since you and Anita met in nursery school. I love you, whatever you are, and I know Anita feels the same."

"Please, Margaret," Athena said after a few minutes, "don't tell Mom and Dad about this conversation."

* * * *

Later that day, Athena seemed more cheerful. She was quite chatty over dinner, and the conversation went a little more easily. Margaret told them all about her long- ago vacation on the Vineyard, and Saul regaled them with stories about other vacation spots the Solomons had visited, including a trip to what had turned out to be a nudist beach in the South of France. They all laughed as he described the reactions of their four children to the whole scene. Athena listened intently and even ate an almost decent meal -- a real serving of fish, one potato and a small salad.

Then she spoke up. "I liked it best of all when we stayed home for the summer."

"Really?" said Saul, clearly astonished. "I wonder why."

"Because we could play," said Athena. "We hung around the neighborhood, sold lemonade from the front lawn, put on dramatic productions in the garage, and on long rainy days, we played Monopoly; sometimes one game would last all afternoon." She smiled, dreamily.

"But didn't you kids play when we were at the Vineyard?"

Athena shook her head. "No," she said firmly. "We had lessons -- tennis lessons, sailing lessons, riding lessons, even square dance lessons."

No one said anything for a few minutes. Margaret decided to keep her mouth shut.

"But," began Saul.

"No wait," said Chloe. "Tell us more about those stay-at-home summers, Athena."

"The best part was sneaking into your bedroom, Mom, crowding into that unmade king-sized bed, all four of us, and sometimes Anita, too." She smiled at Margaret. "I bet you didn't know about that." Margaret shook her head, not wanting to break the spell. "We watched television, re-runs of all those old shows -- *I Love Lucy, Hawaii Five-O,* and *Route Sixty-Six.* Sophia kept losing her pacifier, and one of us would have to crawl under the bed, with all the dust bunnies, to find it, so she wouldn't cry and ruin the programs."

"Oh, Athena, you're telling all my secrets," said Chloe, "even telling Margaret that I didn't always make the bed." But she was grinning. "What else?"

"We used to sneak out, after you thought we were in bed, and play all those wonderful games with the other kids in the neighborhood -- Red Light, Hide and Seek, and best of all, that one where you have to say 'May I?' to take two giant steps or three baby steps." Then suddenly, Athena began to cry, softly but not bitterly. Chloe reached over and took her hand. They all sat quietly, evidently absorbed in their own thoughts. And Margaret found herself thinking about Anita, wishing she could talk to her at that moment, and ask her about those long-ago days when children played innocent games.

After dinner, hearing from the weather report that the next day would be cold and gray, they all decided to drive into Edgartown in the morning to shop and visit the museums.

Just as Margaret was about to turn out her reading light and go to sleep, there was a little knock on her door. It was Athena. "I've decided to give you this." She held out the left-handed whelk. "You're the only person I can think of who'd appreciate it."

"Oh, Athena, it's so beautiful! Are you sure you don't want to keep it yourself?"

"No, it's for you. Honestly. Take it."

"Well, then I will, and thank you. Good night, honey, I'll see you in the morning. We'll have a nice day in Edgartown." After Athena had closed her door, Margaret lay in bed. Feeling the whorls and ridges on the shell, noticing with satisfaction that they all came together at the base.

* * * *

The next morning, Margaret, Chloe and Saul were up early and having breakfast together when Chloe said: "Someone should check on Athena. I'm pretty sure she wanted to go with us."

"I'll go," said Margaret. She went down the hall and knocked gently at Athena's door. There was no answer, so she pushed it open cautiously. The bed was made, and it looked as if it hadn't been slept in. She wasn't in the bathroom, either. Margaret looked around. On the bureau was an envelope addressed: *Mom and Dad.*

Oh, God, she thought. Quickly, Margaret returned to the breakfast table. She put the envelope down between them, and stood, frozen in fear, suddenly remembering that Athena had given her a valuable gift the night before. For a minute, no one moved. Then Saul reached out and took the envelope, ripping it open.

He read: "I'm sorry. It's just too hard. I love you. Athena."

"She must have decided to go back to New York," said Chloe, after a pause. "Let's go check her clothes." She and Margaret ran back to Athena's room, to see if she'd left anything, but as far as they could tell, all her clothes were still hanging up or in the drawers of the bureau, even the gray sweatshirt. When they told Saul what they'd found, he got on the phone to the police to report her missing. Margaret walked out onto the deck; Athena's bathing suit was still draped over the railing. The pond looked gray and forbidding, and a fog was beginning to form, but Margaret went quickly down to the little dock. There, on the small beach, were Athena's flip-flops, side by side. She hurried back to the house to report this new fact to Saul. He was still on the phone, and when he heard her news, he said: "Better bring divers."

Margaret glanced over at Chloe. She was sitting on the couch, her face white and without expression. It was as if what was happening had been predicted, and that there was no hope.

"Come on," Saul said to Margaret, "there isn't time to put up the sails. Let's take the dinghy and look for ourselves."

Margaret wasn't sure this was the best of ideas, but she didn't argue. Kicking off her shoes, she followed him down to the dock, and they stepped into the little boat. Saul pulled the cord to start the engine, and when it didn't catch immediately, he grabbed up the oars and started rowing out to the middle of the pond. Margaret was trying to see through the gray mist. Then he threw out the anchor and stripped down to his underwear. "What are you going to do?" Margaret asked.

"I'm going down to see what the bottom is like, and to look for my child," he said, almost defiantly, as he slipped over the edge of the dinghy.

"But Saul, it's so deep, someone said at least twenty feet."

"It's better than doing nothing," he said. And then he was gone.

Oh, God. If he never comes up, what will I tell Chloe? Finally, with a big gasp of breath, he broke the surface. Suddenly he looked old, with his gray hair plastered to his forehead, the corners of his mouth turned down. Margaret found herself thinking that Saul would never look young and full of energy again.

"The bottom is full of weeds," he said. "And it's murky. I couldn't see at all, and all I could feel were these long reeds." The faint look of hope was gone. Then they heard the sirens.

"Come on, Saul. We should let the experts take over. You need to be with Chloe now."

"I had to try, Margaret, or I couldn't have lived with myself."

* * * *

All morning, police cars kept coming and parking on their road. The officers questioned Saul and Chloe, both together and separately. After the policeman had talked to Chloe, her face took on the lineaments of a Greek tragic heroine, stricken and guilt-ridden. Clearly, no matter what happened, Chloe was going to blame herself. She'd assumed the persona of Medea, Margaret thought, shuddering.

They didn't find Athena until nearly noon, her poor skeletal body wrapped in the long red robe, its deep pockets filled with as many of her colorful rocks as she could push in. None of them had noticed, when they'd looked in her room, that the shells she'd collected were still there, but the stones were gone. Sobbing, Chloe leaned over and kissed her as they put her gently on the stretcher. "Goodbye, sweetie," she whispered, her face softening briefly.

Saul put his arms around his wife. "We have to let her go," he said, stroking her hair.

It was time to call the other kids, and the funeral homes, both on the Vineyard and the one at home. Margaret had made coffee for the divers, and she heated it up again for the three of them after the ambulance had pulled away. Saul began to close up the house, bringing up the battens from under the deck. He pulled the boat up and took down the mast, stowing it under the deck along with the dinghy and the oars.

"Don't you have a caretaker to do all those things?" Margaret asked. It seemed so strange to see him so organized.

"I have to do something," said Saul.

Margaret thought, as she began putting things away, that some people react to this kind of tragedy by <u>doing</u> things. Others might become immobilized. This couple was somehow grieving by closing up the house.

Chloe, too, was stripping the beds, doing a laundry, and packing their bags. Margaret, watching them, began to think that they would probably never come back to this place again. "Do you want me to stay?" she asked.

"Oh, please," said Chloe. "I couldn't bear it if you go."

Saul arranged for the local funeral home to pick up the body and prepare it for shipping. Following the orthodox Jewish tradition, even though Chloe was Greek, they'd decided to have the funeral the next day, at eleven in the morning.

As they continued to work around the house -- like automatons -- to close things up, Margaret tried to comfort them. "Athena died of a terrible disease; no one knows the cause. You gave her a wonderful childhood: I know, because I was there." She paused, trying to decide what to say.

Warily, Saul stopped trying to fit the battens into place and looked at her. Chloe, too, stood motionless.

"I did talk to her yesterday," she said carefully, watching their faces. "Obviously, it didn't help, although she was so cheerful last night at dinner, I couldn't help but hope that I'd done some good."

I'll probably always blame myself for failing that mission, she thought. She'd had only one suicide in her practice, a long time ago, and she remembered the feeling that it was her fault. Her supervisor had said: "Margaret, you're not God, and we can't save them all. You did your best. You have to let it go." But this experience today was different. This was not a client. This was the death of a young woman she'd known for more than thirty-five years, someone who'd sat on her lap when she read to both girls, someone she'd comforted when she skinned her knees.

Margaret could see that they wanted to know more. "We talked on the beach," she said, "while you two were out sailing. What I remember most about our conversation was the way she said: 'Margaret, I'm so tired.' And she spoke so slowly, as if every word was a special effort. I told her that both of you knew she was unhappy, that we all loved her, and wanted her to live her life the way <u>she</u> wanted, whatever that was." She paused, realizing that this had been a highly edited version, but it was as much as she could say without resorting to fiction. "I think she had given up on herself, just as we all had."

"She didn't tell you what she was so unhappy about?" Chloe asked, almost angrily.

Margaret shook her head.

Then Saul spoke up. "Did you ask her what we were doing wrong?"

Oh, dear, Margaret thought. They'll always think I didn't go that extra mile. "I don't think Athena was blaming you guys for anything. When people commit suicide, they're blaming <u>themselves.</u>"

But a few minutes later she thought of something else. She could tell them about the whelk. "You know, last night, just after I'd gone to bed, she came into my room. She gave me that left-handed whelk that I'd admired. I should have remembered that it's a danger signal when depressed people start giving away their prized possessions." Margaret began to cry. "I should have guessed."

Now it was Chloe's turn to try to comfort her. She reached over and took her hand. "I guess we're all going to be thinking of things, for the rest of our lives, that we wished we'd handled differently. Maybe we have to start by forgiving ourselves."

All of a sudden, Margaret wanted to call Anita, first to tell her this terrible news, but also to touch base with her first child, and try to make things right between them. "May I call Anita?" she said. "I know she would want to be told." But it was more than that. The loss of Athena reminded her how valuable and how tenuous relationships with ones own children could be.

"Of course," said Chloe. "Go in our room, so you can have some privacy." She sat down on the couch and put her head on Saul's shoulder. They needed a little privacy, themselves, Margaret thought.

But when she called, she got Everett. Anita was out but expected back shortly. Telling him the story, she asked that Anita call them at the Vineyard as soon as possible since the funeral would take place the next day. In a few minutes, Anita called back, in tears. "Mom, it makes me feel I didn't do enough for her."

"That's what suicide does to people, Anita. We're all feeling that way here, too."

"I want to come to the funeral. I'll call the airlines and get back to you as soon as I know when the flight is. Can you meet me at the airport?" The underlying message, thank God, was that she didn't want to be angry with her mother any more.

"Of course, I'll be there."

Chapter Twelve

Chloe and Saul drove Margaret from the ferry landing in Woods Hole to the parking lot in Falmouth where she'd left her car. No one said anything. It was as if the life had gone out of all of them, and they were just going through the motions. Standing there, helping her with her luggage, Saul looked smaller, his shadow, under the arc light, tiny and foreshortened. In the background, they could hear the deep voice of an old bull frog, calling out from a nearby pond. "Will you be all right, driving alone?" asked Saul. "We could take you home and send someone back for your car."

"I'm picking up Anita early in the morning, so I'll need my car. I'll be fine," said Margaret. "And you two, drive carefully. I'll see you tomorrow at the service."

Watching them as they drove off together into the night, she was grateful to be alone, to sort out this terrible experience, and to pull herself together. She'd felt fragmented, not just that day, but for the past week and a half.

Driving slowly along the dark roads, she let the post-ferry traffic move past her. One of the cars turned out to be the long black hearse that must have been the one taking Athena home. She shuddered, and then, opening the window, let the soft night air bathe her face. The sounds of the katy-dids were also a comfort, a part of normal summer life. There was a hollow, empty feeling inside her, as if an important piece of her life had vanished. Then, all of a sudden, it occurred to her that, on top of everything else, she might be hungry. None of them had felt like eating any dinner (nor lunch, either, she realized) although they'd cleaned out the refrigerator and made feeble efforts to set up a buffet for themselves.

She'd reached the traffic circle and was about to cross the bridge over the canal.

There, on her right, was a fast-food place. It looked as if she'd be the only customer.

"That egg thing sounds good," she told the counterman. "I'll have two of them. And some French Fries." She was becoming hungrier by the minute. "And a chocolate shake."

As she waited for her order, she figured out that living in the same house with an anorexic had probably put a brake on all their appetites. Enjoying food had become obscene. Tonight was the first time she'd felt like eating for over a week. When she brought the loaded tray to her table, she decided she'd never seen anything that looked so good. There was no reason to feel guilty about being alive, she told herself.

Driving home, her odd euphoria began gradually to wear off. The rain that had been threatening began to fall. Her wipers seemed sluggish and the streets looked slippery. She was tired, and the thought of another hour on the road seemed intolerable. She had to keep going. The radio was no help, just a lot of static from the storm. She remembered that Henry used to employ a number of memory tricks to keep himself awake on long drives. His favorite was the exercise of mentally alphabetizing the fifty states. It was worth a try. Alabama, Alaska, Arkansas -- no, she'd forgotten Arizona. This was going to be harder than she'd thought. Fortunately, she was still working on the Ms -- there were so many of them! -- when she drove into her own driveway. But she'd made it safely. Thank you, Henry, wherever you are.

The house was dark. She set the alarm for 5 A.M. She wanted to reach Logan Airport in time for Anita's plane. She grabbed a nightgown from the hook on the closet door, too tired even to brush her teeth. But once in bed, she couldn't sleep. All the pieces of the day replayed in her head. She saw Athena's letter on the bureau, Saul's face when he came up from the bottom of the pond, Chloe's agony as she kissed her child for the last time, and the blinking of the lights from the police cars, going round and round.

She'd taken a vacation to get away from the sadness of her own life -- the end of her marriage and her estrangement from Anita -- and had fallen into an even worse situation in which she was feeling somehow responsible, not only as a social worker, but as a friend who'd failed her mission.

* * * *

Margaret arrived at the airport at six. She waited at the baggage carousel before it had disgorged its first suitcase. A whole parade of bags was humping around, with a few now-familiar repeaters reappearing before she saw the first group of sleepy-eyed passengers from the Seattle plane. As always, Anita was easy to spot. Six feet tall, she had many of her father's best features -- the hawklike nose, his freckles, his tannish skin, and his very white teeth. Normally, when Anita carried herself well she looked like a Native American princess. Today, she seemed almost stooped, her carry-on luggage appearing to be weighing her down. Her dark hair, usually pinned up into an elaborate French knot, had begun to droop down over her neck. Her face was pale, her eyes reddened, her expression searching. When she saw Margaret, she hesitated.

Margaret reached toward her to give her a big hug, yearning to say to this daughter, her first-born child: don't worry; everything is going to be all right; there is nothing to be afraid of. But, of course, she couldn't say that. Anita's world had changed. Athena was perhaps her first close friend who'd died. Her own death and that of everyone she knew was more of a distinct possibility. She could no longer tell herself that only old people died.

After they'd picked up Anita's luggage, they walked to the car. They were both quiet but it felt as if they were together in their sadness. "I brought a black dress," said Anita, as Margaret paid the parking toll. "I hope that's okay."

Margaret was touched, first of all that Anita had asked for her opinion, but also because she hadn't known that Anita owned any kind of dress, let alone black. Her child had grown up.

"I haven't thought about what to wear," Margaret said. "When we get back to the house, maybe you can help me pick out something. I've been living in shorts and bathing suits." At that moment, her spirits picked up. Anita was home and they were talking. That part of Margaret's world was still intact.

* * * *

The funeral was held in the small chapel of the Greek Orthodox Church. The priest, a heavily bearded man in his sixties, shared the pulpit with a tall, thin rabbi. Saul and one of his sons-in-law were wearing yarmulkes. The printed program listed three speakers: Athena's sister Diana, the man who had taught drama at the high school, and her supervisor at a home for teenage runaways where she'd worked for the last five years.

The last person listed on the program was a baritone soloist who would sing a song by Ralph and Ursula Vaughan Williams called "Procris." The words were printed at the bottom of the page. Margaret's eyes ran down the lines; they seemed to burn her brain.

Where in the world had someone found this poem? Reading it made yesterday perhaps a little more bearable. That must be the function of poetry, she told herself. Margaret wondered why someone had chosen this poem. In the Greek myth, Procris (an unhappy woman) actually dies by accident. Was someone trying to suggest that Athena's death was <u>not</u> suicide!

* * * *

Margaret sat with Anita about half-way down the chapel. Chloe and Saul with all their surviving children and grandchildren were sitting in the first two rows. In many ways, she felt as if she'd cried all the tears she could, but she noticed that Anita's tears streamed throughout the service. She, herself, had trouble focussing on what was going on, especially when the Greek Orthodox priests sang in ancient Greek. She smiled a little when Diana, described by Athena as the klutzy one, tripped over the microphone wire as she approached the podium. Diana's words were simple, stressing how Athena had always been the leader, the mischief-maker when they were children. At that point, Margaret reached over and took Anita's hand. She missed most of what the teacher said, but found it fascinating to learn about a whole new side of Athena as a counselor to troubled adolescents who'd run away from home. She was able to reach these kids when no one else could.

When the rabbi's turn came, he told a story. He said that the ending of Athena's life reminded him of a close friend. They'd gone together to a school concert to hear the rabbi's nephew play the violin solo. After half an hour, his friend tiptoed out, and when the concert was over, the rabbi found him sitting on a bench in the lobby.

"I'm sorry," his friend said, "I have perfect pitch, and I can't tolerate dissonance. Your nephew was very good, but some of the players were not in tune. I had to leave."

"Athena," said the rabbi, "was like my friend. She could hear the dissonance in our world that most of us can't hear. She had a kind of perfect pitch. She had to leave."

Then he began to say Kaddish for Athena: "Yit-gadal ve-yit-kadash shmei raba." Margaret began to cry -- for the little girl she once knew, and for the waste of it all.

Driving home from the funeral, Anita said suddenly: "You know what I'd like? I'd like to stay through the weekend, and for us both to go to Philadelphia to visit Molly. I've never seen her apartment, and after today, I'm beginning to feel I should see more of my only sister."

"What a great idea! I'm on vacation until next week," said Margaret. "Let's call her."

Molly was pleased with the prospect, as well. David would be away on business.

* * * *

Waking by force of habit at 7:30 the next morning, Margaret first tip-toed down to Anita's room, just to make sure she was all right. The sight of her, sprawled out -- all six feet of her -- in her old bed, was enormously reassuring. Her long black hair was fanned out on the pillow. There was a little frown on her forehead, possibly because the sun was coming in right on her face. She was breathing peacefully. Margaret lowered the shade and gently shut the door.

When she returned from the supermarket, she found Anita in the kitchen, eating a cracker and looking a lot better than she had the previous evening. As they unpacked the groceries, Margaret felt, for the first time on this visit of Anita's, some return of the tension that had existed between them, an awkwardness, and a formality.

Finally, Margaret spoke up. "Anita," she said firmly, "I think we need to finish up some old business. I watched Chloe and Saul <u>not</u> talking about important stuff. Let's not go that route."

"You mean Dad." Anita seemed relieved. "Everett told me I was wrong to get so involved. He said no one can see inside another person's relationships, and that I shouldn't judge you."

Margaret was touched to hear that Everett had stood up for her. "I realized," she said, "after all of you left last month, that you probably felt someone -- yourself, if no one else stepped forward -- needed to look after your father's interests. You felt I was abandoning him." Anita looked a little sheepish at that point. "Maybe I was. I was glad to see him go."

Anita seemed to be listening carefully, but made no comment. She seemed wary, as if speaking up would commit her to whatever Margaret was about to say.

Less confidently, Margaret continued. "By the time he left, I guess we were all concerned that he was driving off into the wilderness, possibly not in the best shape for a journey like that. Andrew had some questions. But I don't think any of us could have stopped him. And he left without saying goodbye."

"Didn't you think that part was weird, in itself?" Now Anita was sounding angry. Margaret wondered if maybe part of the problem was that Anita's feelings were hurt that her father hadn't at least said goodbye to his oldest child. "He might have been mad at you, Mom, but wouldn't you think he would have wanted to say goodbye to his kids?"

"You're right. I felt bad for all of you. You'd come a long way and brought him such nice gifts. I blamed myself for the way he left: I thought he'd had enough ceremony and ritual, and that he just wanted to get on with it." She paused. "At least that's what I thought then. But now I'm wondering, since none of you has heard from him -- not even his sister -- whether something is wrong."

"It's a terrible feeling," said Anita, now sounding more sad than angry, "to think of him out there, not knowing where, or if he's alive or dead." Now she glared at her mother.

"I agree, Anita. Even though we're getting a divorce, I feel as if I can't, as they say, 'get on with my life,' until I know he's all right." There was another long silence. "You don't stop loving someone just because he's dead, or because you've both decided you can't live together anymore." Anita looked startled at this idea. Then Margaret said: "Maybe the best place to start would be with his lawyer; perhaps you could do that."

"Of course. Give me his name and number. I'll do that right now." Now she sounded brisk and efficient, the expert taking over.

But Paul Kosinski didn't know Henry's whereabouts, either. He told Anita that her father had given him power-of-attorney, that he could check the bank, and see if there were any transactions in his account in the last month. "But your father told me," Paul said, "that he was going to take travelers' checks with him and probably wouldn't be needing to use that account for a while. He has credit cards, too."

Anita relayed all this to her mother, adding: "From what the lawyer said, it does sound as if Dad had made some sensible plans. Maybe we're wrong to worry about him."

* * * *

On the long train-ride to Philadelphia, while Anita slept, Margaret looked out the window. This particular route was one of her favorites, the train hurtling through the little towns in Rhode Island, and then along the shore of the Long Island Sound in Connecticut. She'd made this trip often as a boarding school student going home to Scarsdale for weekends, and later, when she was at Wellesley, at the end of each semester. She'd always felt particularly <u>safe</u> on trains. No one could find her, but she was being taken care of. She was free to let her thoughts wander.

If one looked carefully, there were places along the shore where one could see whole families of swans: the cygnets of long ago had now grown up and were raising broods of their own. Further on, one could see a whole stretch of beach where the locals had put up platforms for osprey nests. It had been a long time since she'd made this journey.

Now she'd reached a new stage in her life, single again, and was looking toward the future with both apprehension and excitement. For a minute or two, she felt, in fact, that she was exactly that same young person who had traveled that train forty years ago. But then who was this tall

211

stranger sitting beside her, now waking up and suggesting they go to the club car for lunch?

* * * *

Molly met them at the station. No one would think that her two girls were even slightly related. Molly was short, and looked a lot like Margaret at that same age, with her curly blond hair. But she was a bundle of energy and organization, more like Margaret's Granny. Even as a toddler, this child had been in charge of herself. Not yet two, she'd marched into the kitchen one morning, announcing: Me use da potty now. And that was it.

She had, of course, organized their whole weekend, but it turned out to be fun for all of them. After they'd dumped their luggage in the apartment, and Anita had admired its layout and furnishings, she took them on a walking tour of the historic district. Soon it became obvious that fine food was the main preoccupation of Philadelphians. They visited a famous ice cream emporium, and then a special place for Philadelphia sticky buns, and later on, they'd had dinner at a French restaurant where Molly had made reservations. They'd had frogs' legs.

Back in the apartment, Margaret stretched out on the couch. In the background she could hear snatches and phrases as the two women discussed and compared Molly's fiancé, David, and Anita's long term companion, Everett. She wanted to hear the whole conversation, but her week of exhaustion had finally taken its toll. There was also something enormously soothing about knowing that her two daughters were safely ensconced in this lovely apartment, enjoying each other's company, well-fed and alive.

Chapter Thirteen

Margaret spent the long Labor Day weekend up in Maine with Charles and his kids; for two of those three days, the weather was perfect for sailing -- a southwest wind -- Charles explained. From the time he'd moved to Portland ten years ago, Charles had been fascinated by boats and sailing. He'd taken courses in both seamanship and navigation from the Coast Guard, and every summer he'd crewed on other people's boats. Finally, this last spring, he'd become the proud owner of a used, but seaworthy thirty-seven foot fiberglass sloop. In keeping with their last name -- Bluestone -- he'd named the boat *Sapphire*. Hesitantly, Margaret agreed to join them in an overnight trip.

The scariest part turned out to be the moment at the dock when she'd had to step down into the heavily laden dinghy. "Come on, Mom. Just do it!" said Charles.

"I will, I will," she said, as they all waited impatiently. But she wanted to do it in her own good time, when <u>she</u> was ready. But even though Charles held her hand, with Matt steadying the little rubber craft, it took a suspension of disbelief and a supreme act of faith for her to make that step. Once she'd transferred into the bigger sailboat, and was settled on her special seat in the little well that held the wheel, she felt somewhat more comfortable, but still a little apprehensive. What would they ask her to do next?

An unspoken undercurrent was the absence of Elena, Charles's wife and the children's mother. When Margaret arrived, she'd asked Charles, in what she hoped was a neutral voice, where Elena was. He'd shrugged and said, implying by his tone of voice that it was no big deal: "Oh, yeah, I forgot to tell you: she's away for the weekend." Okay, Margaret had said to herself, the message was clear: now keep out of it. But she'd felt a familiar twinge in her gut, a mixture of sadness and fear.

Once they were at sea, however, all these thoughts and feelings became muted. Life aboard seemed to have its own rhythms: intense, almost frantic activity, followed by long periods during which one could stare into the choppy waves, lulled by the mixture of colors and motion, and by the iodine smell of the sea. Her only task was to keep an eye out for red "nuns," and green "cans," -- channel markers -- or to warn Charles so that he could avoid the bright multicolored lobster pots.

On the second day, he offered to teach her how to steer. To her surprise, just holding the wheel steady was very difficult: it involved constant attention and the ability to make small adjustments, a whole new skill. She learned to keep her eye on a certain spot on the horizon -- a distant lighthouse, or a whale-shaped island. Fortunately, the weather held and the southwest wind made it possible for them to rely on the sails most of the time, with only occasional use of the motor. Charles was pleased that they were able to cruise at almost six knots. After a bit, Katy offered to help, and Margaret found it very comforting to have that small, wiry body pressed against hers as they struggled to keep on course. It occurred to her, too, that perhaps Katy was missing the opportunity to nestle into the loving arms of a woman.

She was amazed by the way Katy had mastered the navigational system, and astonished to find out that the new electronic aids made it possible for a child of ten -- or anyway, this particular child of ten -- to calculate their course so accurately. Charles evidently trusted her figures, although he checked them unobtrusively from time to time. Margaret loved hearing Katy's serious voice on the radio-telephone, talking to other boats or someone out there. On the first afternoon of their trip, Matt had spotted a small pod of whales -- two adults and a juvenile -- so Katy got on the horn: "This is Sapphire, this is Sapphire," and then, after giving their exact position, she reported: "Whales three hundred yards to starboard." And sure enough, several boats changed course and headed in their direction to see the whales.

Margaret had never seen these animals up close before, so she was gratified when Charles steered the boat toward the area where they were last seen. The whales were evidently not afraid of these human beings in their small craft, and either by chance or to entertain them, put on a little show, diving and then coming up where one least expected them, one even under the boat, then up on the other side, spouting up a steamy fountain, breathing heavily and stertorously. Margaret was a little frightened at first, while Katy squealed with delight.

Then, as suddenly as they'd appeared, they were gone. The show was over, and the ocean was again a lonely place, where human beings were left to struggle on their own in an element that was not always so friendly to them. And it was so quiet.

She was impressed by the way Charles carried out his role of skipper; he was both firm and reasonable, but the children understood that when he gave an order on board the boat, it had to be obeyed instantly. Margaret, too, felt that she had to move quickly when he spoke. She found she wanted to please him, an interesting role-reversal for a mother and son. She ended up as bottle-washer, and later as cook, and found she enjoyed the little galley, trying to figure out how everything worked, and pleased to see that everything had its place. Using the supplies Charles had purchased, she was able to put together a big pasta salad for the first night, and a stew for the next day.

She slept well in her narrow berth, rocking at anchor near a small island. Best of all was going out on deck at midnight, all by herself, looking up, with no city lights to interfere, to see a multitude of stars. The Milky Way was more like clotted cream. And the stars were so big, so close! She reminded herself that what she was seeing was a picture of the past: those bright stars she was looking at might not even be there any more. She shook her head, wondering. The skies must have been like this thousands of years ago, Margaret thought, when ancient shepherds charted out the movement of the constellations. What would they have made of those same skies today, where numerous spacecraft and airplanes could be seen bravely plowing their routes?

Margaret was reminded of nights in the Berkshires with Henry and the children, when the glow from nearby cities dimmed the brightness of the stars. Henry would have liked this display, she thought, wondering if he would ever have the opportunity to sail in this boat with his son and grandchildren. And once again, the curtain of sadness descended, wiping out, with its tears, the glories of distant millennia.

* * * *

Driving home in all the post-holiday traffic, Margaret tried to come to terms with the fact that soon she would be temporarily homeless. Just before she left for Maine, Erik had sat down with her and explained that soon it was going to be difficult for her to go in and out of the house without disrupting someone or something, especially when the kitchen was being torn apart, the floors sanded, new bathrooms installed, and the interior repainted. "You can stay if you want," he said, "but it would be complicated for you, and the air will be full of plaster dust."

"How long will it be before I can use the house, even just to camp out?" she'd asked.

"At least until Halloween, maybe later," he said. "Do you have somewhere to go? It should probably be somewhere nearby, so you can drop by and check on things. I'll be wanting your advice from time to time, and you'll want to see how things are going."

The obvious place for her to go was Chloe's, but Margaret was hesitant to ask her. Ever since Athena's death, there'd been a delicate fraying of the tie between them; Margaret suspected that Chloe and Saul blamed her for not "saving" their daughter. And even if that were not the case, Margaret was aware that she was angry at them for having put her in that position. Every time these thoughts went through her mind, she would end up feeling guilty: she should have found the right thing to say to Athena, the magic phrase that would have made all the difference. Whenever she'd told Charles this sequence of thinking, he'd, of course, reply: "There you go again. You think you're God, with the power of life and death."

Maybe she needed to go over to Chloe's and say all this to her face. But it seemed too soon, after everything they'd all been through. She'd call her and tell her that she and Saul would be her first dinner guests when she moved back into her house.

So where should she go? Her elderly next-door neighbors, Ron and Ethel Larson, had offered her their "guest room" on the second floor of their little house. They would be away all fall, visiting their daughter on the West Coast. Margaret had thanked them at the time, and said she'd get back to them if she needed the space. So, the day after she returned from Maine, she called to tell them she'd like to accept their offer. While the house had a worn-out feel to it, it <u>was</u> next-door.

* * * *

On a happier note, at her own house, the outside work was almost finished, including the painting, and even on days when she didn't drop by to pick up something, she felt good just pulling into her neighbors' driveway, and looking over at her own house. The colors she'd chosen -- mauve, with a cream trim, and deep purple and light blue for accents -- were just right, and the new little front porch, with its Victorian double doors and oval glass, was perfect. As September ripened, she found excuses to go into her own yard. Full of the kind of energy that autumn often inspires, she would tie her jacket around her waist, and begin to rake the leaves.

Wistfully, as she stuffed the leaves into the special recycling bags, she recalled the days of her own childhood when the grownups would make big bonfires at the curbs. The world had smelled better then.

She found excuses to peek inside, as well, especially when the red pickup truck was parked out in back. One late afternoon she came home to find Erik standing next to his truck, checking his clipboard. There was someone in the passenger seat. She moved slowly in their direction.

"Good evening, Margaret," said Erik, stepping from behind the truck. "I don't believe you've met my son, Will." He gestured toward the young man who was looking out the window. "This is Margaret, Will. She lives here."

Margaret put out her hand to the boy. He had red hair and brown eyes like his father and his thick glasses gave him the same owl-like look that his father had. When he began to speak, she could hear that he had some difficulty. He also had a little trouble grasping her hand.

"My father is fixing your house," he said slowly and carefully. "Making you a new kitchen." Understanding him wasn't easy but she could figure it out. He had a warm smile.

"Would you like to see what I've been doing, Will?" his father asked.

The boy nodded eagerly. Erik went to the back of the truck and took out the wheel- chair that had been folded there. He opened it up and brought it to the door of the passenger side. Obviously an expert after long years of

221

practice, he transferred his son into the chair and pushed him up to the kitchen door. The boy was almost fully grown and no doubt quite heavy, Margaret thought. Nevertheless, his father could still lift him and the chair up the back steps and into the house.

Pushing the plastic barrier aside, the three of them moved into the kitchen and Erik hooked up the temporary light. The old wood had been removed and the place now looked as if it were almost ready for its new life. "We've been putting in a new floor," said Erik, "and tomorrow, we'll install the windows. See, Will, where the windows will go, in those openings." He turned the chair so that Will could see. Margaret found herself watching Erik, observing the patience and careful attention he gave his son. It appeared that Will had little or no control over his legs, but one arm seemed well-coordinated and the other could point at the places where the windows would go.

"Did you make the windows, Dad?" he asked, again slowly.

"No, they came from a special factory. I told them how big they should be, and they sent them in a big truck. They delivered the windows today." Margaret looked at Eric, trying to imagine what it would be like for this father -- an architect and a builder -- to know that his son would never be able to use his hands creatively.

Will sat quietly, looking around. Then he said to Margaret: "My Dad is a good fixer, isn't he?" His eyes were shining.

"He's wonderful," she said. And then she added: "He's a good Dad, too."

"Time to go," said Erik, looking a little embarrassed by her compliment, "and thank you, Margaret, for letting Will see your kitchen." He began lifting the chair out the back way again. Will was pulling on his father's jacket.

"But Dad," Margaret could hear Will saying as they moved toward the truck, "why isn't it blue?"

"Why isn't <u>what</u> blue?" Erik asked, his annoyed tone indicating perhaps he'd had enough questions for one day.

"The house," said Will. "You told me you were working," he said slowly and deliberately, "on the <u>blue</u> <u>stone</u> <u>house</u>." There was a long silence.

"Oh, my God," said Erik, after a minute. "You thought I meant a <u>stone</u> house -- a house made of stone -- and that it was <u>blue</u>? Oh, dear. Margaret's name is Bluestone. Bluestone is her last name."

There was another long silence. "Oh," said Will finally, "she's <u>Mrs.</u> Bluestone?"

"Right," said Erik, and bundling the boy back into the pickup, he folded the chair and put it into the rear, and then drove off. Margaret watched them go, wondering what it must be like to have to go through these motions many times every day, not to mention probably dressing him, toileting him, and -- as this little visit showed -- constantly clearing up his confusions, educating him about the world, and how it worked. You did all these things automatically as you brought up small children, but you always knew there would come a time when you could let go, and let them take care of themselves. With a son like Will, that time might never come. Yet the boy seemed bright.

* * * *

Nevertheless, occasionally even one's healthy grown children needed care. Toward the end of September, Charles called to tell her what she had been expecting to hear for some time, that he and Elena were definitely getting a divorce. Margaret thought: Oh, my poor Charles. The surprising part of the news was that he would have full custody of the two children. Elena was going off to Florida with her new love. Margaret found herself thinking, Oh, that bitch, always looking out for herself! Some mother!

Margaret had always known that Charles was a wonderful parent. Evidently, Elena had recognized this fact as well. Still, what must the children feel when they know that their mother had chosen to give them up? Even as these thoughts ran through her mind, she asked herself if she were being sexist: if the mother gets custody of the children, no one would think twice about it. Clearly, Charles was the more nurturing, more involved, more loving parent, and it made a lot of sense for Elena to have done it this way.

"It's hard to tell with the kids," said Charles, when Margaret asked about them. "I've tried to tell them that it's okay for them to be angry about the whole situation, but they -- especially Matt -- keep saying it's no big deal. Katy seems very quiet since we told them." He sighed. "Of course, this agreement just puts a legal sanction on what has been going on for the past year. Elena hasn't been around much, and I've been in charge of the kids, as I'm sure you've noticed."

"Are you going to be able to manage without help?" she asked. Maybe she shouldn't have made him sound so helpless. It was certainly hard to be the parent of an adult child!

"Luckily, my teaching schedule pretty much matches their hours, and one of my neighbors has offered to baby-sit when I have to stay late. She has a daughter just Katy's age." He was making it sound so easy, but she knew Charles: his first defense was organization. He went on: "Matt says he's going to get an after-school job. The real problem will be finding time to paint." Charles sounded on top of it all, but underneath, Margaret was getting a different message: please don't give me any sympathy.

"Perhaps I can come up sometimes, or have the kids down here, so you can get some real time in." Margaret tried to picture what their lives would be like now, and then she remembered that she had no home to offer them right now. "Of course, my house is completely torn up at the moment and won't be habitable until after Halloween. But why don't I plan to come up for Columbus Day weekend? I'll keep them out of your hair and you can paint." She felt she'd hit the right tone now: availability without pressure.

Or was she kidding herself?

After they'd said goodbye, Margaret's first reaction was a guilty, queasy feeling: she must have done something wrong: her child was getting divorced. She and Henry had not exactly given their kids the picture of a happy marriage. She wondered if it would have been better for Charles if she'd left Henry years ago. She smiled ruefully. If she could have followed that course of action, she'd have had to have been a different person, someone who could have put her foot down, or even someone who knew how to fight back.

* * * *

One warm Sunday morning early in October, she walked over to her own yard and climbed up on the deck. She'd taken a couple of beach chairs out of the barn and placed them there in case she wanted to sit and enjoy the sun or read the paper. And she'd made herself a big pot of coffee, carried it over as well, and had just settled down with the *Sunday Times* when she heard the noise of the red pickup, a now familiar sound. At that moment she realized she'd actually planned for this event: why else had she set up two chairs in the first place? Brought extra cups? Made such a big pot of coffee? And she'd even washed her hair. The answer, of course, was that Erik had told her on Friday that Will would be spending the weekend at his aunt's house.

What was the phrase her mother had for a woman who'd taken up with a much younger man? She'd have said that Margaret was robbing the cradle. She wondered, not for the first time in recent weeks, whether five years was too big a gap. The other question she kept asking herself was an old one: what would people think?

"Good morning," said Erik. "I was hoping to get in a little extra time on the cabinets." Ooh, thought Margaret, perhaps this would be a good time to bring up her question about that tight little corner in the place where the pantry had been. But she was aware that this would not be easy. She had a feeling he wouldn't like what would feel like criticism; but she told herself that, after all, she was paying for all this.

Temporizing, she asked him first: "Would you like a cup of coffee?"

"Of course." He sat down in the vacant chair and smiled. "I brought some doughnuts," he said, passing her the large-sized box. "You know," he said, clearing his throat, "this deck was a great idea, if I say so myself."

Nodding, it occurred to her that now it would be a little harder to bring up her problem. She cleared her throat. "You know," she said, "that reminds me. I've been meaning to ask you about that little corner -- you know, where the pantry used to be -- I'm afraid it may be a little tight, especially if someone wants to open that window back there. I seem to recall you're planning to put cabinets along that whole wall."

He frowned. "I think you could squeeze in there, Margaret. It would look a little strange if we left that last cabinet out." There was a long silence as they sat sipping their coffee. Since she didn't reply, he went on. "Well, I'll look at it today, but I suspect we're committed to the way I put it on the blueprint. I'd have to change a lot of things, I'm afraid, if we alter that corner."

"Let me know," she said, unwilling to let it go. She had a feeling that she'd destroyed a golden moment, but she wasn't sorry. She had to keep reminding herself that it was <u>her house.</u> She took a deep breath, and unlaced her sneakers and dropped them off the edge of the deck, wiggling her toes. If he didn't like what she was saying, he could lump it; she wasn't going to let this conversation ruin a gorgeous day. She looked up. The sky had that wonderful deep blue of October.

Erik picked up the travel section of the paper and began looking at the ads. "Will you be going somewhere this next weekend -- Columbus Day?" he asked, also evidently wanting to get back to more neutral subjects.

Margaret sighed. "I'll be going up to Maine to stay with my grandchildren while their father tries to get in some painting time." Her face fell, as she was reminded of the new status of that family.

"You're not happy about it," he said. He was looking over at her with concern in his face, somehow picking up her tension, lifting up his eyebrows and widening those owl-like eyes.

"Charles called me the other day to tell me that he and his wife will be getting a divorce. She's given him custody of the children." She looked up at him, shading her eyes against the sun. "I keep worrying about the kids, how they must feel that their mother has deserted them. And she has, in fact, deserted them." Once again, she felt the stabbing fear of the unknown. "There's another man in her life now; they've gone to Florida. I wonder if the kids will ever see her again." The idea was terrifying. "Charles is a wonderful parent, but . . ." She didn't know what else to say. And she was afraid she would start to cry.

Erik leaned back in the beach chair, putting the newspaper down on the deck. "You're talking to an expert in that situation," he said. "Four years ago, my wife walked out on me and our only son, leaving me to explain. What could I say? Mommy needs to have a new life? A new husband? And what do I say to a disabled child, who probably thinks that he's the reason she left?"

"Well, of course, that wasn't the reason," said Margaret, an anxious feeling beginning to gather in her stomach.

"That was <u>exactly</u> why she left," he said explosively. "I could see where she was coming from. Will was fourteen, growing up and getting bigger. He was too heavy for her to lift, and he was beginning to develop, reaching puberty. It was no longer appropriate for her to be bathing him, changing his clothes, or toileting him. But I suspect what she couldn't handle were his questions about sexual matters, and his masturbation." Oh, God, thought Margaret, and I thought I had problems. But she was impressed that he was able to talk openly about all this. Perhaps it was because he knew she was a social worker; one of the major disadvantages to her choice of profession was the fact that people felt they could discuss <u>anything</u> with her.

"So how did you handle her leaving?"

"I told him that, of course, Mommy wasn't mad at <u>him</u>, that she was angry at me, and didn't love me any more." Margaret looked at him as he said this. His jaw was set and he kept clenching his fingers. "But I'm not sure Will bought it," he went on, shaking his head. "The other day, in fact, one of my sister's stupid in-laws asked him if his mother wrote him or called from time to time, and Will said something like: 'I think she's mad at Dad and me.' There's a lot of truth in that, too. She was angry at me for wanting to have a child in the first place; she'd just had a promotion at work. And we were both over forty when he was born."

Margaret found herself wondering what it would be like to be forty years old, doing well in a career, and then to have a husband who was insisting that she have a baby. She looked over at Erik, seeing him in a new way, as someone who maybe thought he knew what was best for others, who perhaps rode, not exactly roughshod over their wishes, but slipshod. And then, of course, when the child turned out to be less than perfect, it would be not surprising if she'd blame the man who got her pregnant.

Margaret was immediately aware of a need, on her part, to reach out and try to comfort this man, somehow to make it "all better," or at least to offer to help. At the same time, she realized that he was not asking for this kind of assistance, that he was managing very well on his own. There were some problems -- and this was undoubtedly one of them -- for which there were no solutions. Not everybody needed a Goody Bluestone to make things right. Her eyes filled with tears, but she tried to look the other way.

Erik was not fooled, and he reached across to touch her arm. "Don't feel so bad, Margaret. I wasn't looking for your sympathy, you know. It's probably better for Will that the person taking care of him really loves him." Then he looked at her, and grinned. "You know, it may even be better in the long run for your grandchildren that the parent who is taking care of them is able to do such a wonderful job."

She turned to him. He was comforting her.

"Well, back to my cabinets," he said, pulling himself out of the beach chair.

* * * *

When Margaret went back up to Maine for the Columbus Day weekend, she found it hard to be upbeat for the kids. It was awkward, since she didn't have Charles's permission to talk to the kids about their mother and her absence. The down feeling that she'd been coping with ever since the summer's end found its echo in Charles's family as well. Katy, for instance, was much more clinging. Margaret tried to distract her and at the same time help her feel good about herself by asking her help in learning how to use the spreadsheet on the computer. Matt, on the other hand, was hardly there. Charles told Margaret that he'd been staying out late, hanging around kids that Charles didn't know.

But there was good news, in among the bad tidings. When the phone rang on Saturday morning, it was her son, Andrew, calling from Atlanta, to tell them that his wife, Julia, had just given birth to a healthy baby boy, eight and a half pounds, and he would be called Duncan. There would be a ritual circumcision on the following Sunday. Could Margaret come?

"Of course. I wouldn't miss it for the world." Goodness, thought Margaret. But she shouldn't have been surprised. Andrew was her only "Jewish" child; meeting Julia had solidified his connection with that part of his heritage. He'd even been married under a Chupa.

"You can stay with us, if you don't mind sharing quarters with a newborn." Andrew paused, clearing his throat, and then asked, in a more formal voice: "Listen, have you heard anything from Dad? We want to invite him, too."

Margaret explained that she hadn't heard a word from him, and that, as far as she knew, none of his siblings had, either. She began to wonder how many big family events would take place that Henry would never know about. Was it possible he could be among the permanently missing?

"Are you still there?" asked Andrew.

"I'm sorry. I was thinking about your father and how sad it was that he might never know about Duncan. Well, kiss that baby for me. And I'll call Anita to tell her."

When Charles came into the main part of the house from his studio (it was in the barn) he looked downcast. He was carrying a paint brush. Thinking to cheer him up, Margaret told him that he'd just become an uncle: Andrew's wife Julie has given birth to a little boy. Charles made no comment.

"What's wrong?" said his mother. "Anything special?"

Charles looked up, and then angrily threw his brush in the sink. "Nothing's wrong. I just can't paint anymore!" Margaret didn't know what to say. She couldn't ever remember a time when Charles was unable to put brush to canvas. Even when the kids were babies and they were short of money, he always seemed to find the strength, energy, and inspiration to keep working. Sometimes he discarded things that he'd been working on, but he usually went right back to painting.

Katy was looking at her father with consternation. It occurred to Margaret that she'd found out just recently that her mother was no longer reliable. She didn't need to see that her dad had his troubles as well. Putting her arm around the child, Margaret said: "Painters and musicians and writers all get this way sometimes, Katy. When it happens to writers, it's called 'writers' block.' I don't know what they call it when it happens to a painter. But sometimes it helps if the painter sits down and has some lunch. Let's make your dad a sandwich and a cup of tea."

Katy went to the refrigerator and took out some cheese and tomatoes. Then she opened up a loaf of bread and spread it with mayonnaise. Thank goodness, thought Margaret, Charles was smiling at his daughter and starting to eat. "So you have a new baby cousin," he said, obviously making an effort to ease his child. "What's the baby's name?"

"He's called Duncan," said Katy. "Gran said he was named after her father. Would that be my great-grandfather?"

"That's right, smarty," said Charles, now smiling a little.

After the kids were in bed -- thank heaven Matt came in on time -- Margaret sat down in the living room with Charles. "You're going through a bad time, son, and you shouldn't be too surprised that it's difficult to paint." She wondered if that sounded corny. "A divorce is probably the hardest thing to go through, maybe worse than losing a spouse by death, because it's so easy to blame yourself." It was so much easier to say things like this to a client than to a member of your own family!

"Well," said Charles, "when you come right down to it, if she'd been really happy with me, she wouldn't have fallen in love with someone else, isn't that right?" His handsome face looked lean and drawn; he kept rubbing his forehead.

"I didn't know Elena as well as you did, Charles, but she always struck me as someone who was continually looking over the fence at the next back yard. This man, the one she's gone to Florida with, I wonder if he'll satisfy that yearning, either."

Charles looked thoughtfully at his mother. "You never liked her, did you, Mom?"

For a long moment -- too long, Margaret thought -- she didn't answer. She was trying to think of something to say that would be both true and comforting, and finally she settled for truth. "When you first started going with her "she said slowly, "I was fearful for you. She seemed so -- well, needy, or maybe greedy -- and I wondered if you, or any man, would be enough for her." Looking around the room, she tried to think dispassionately about Elena. The room, itself, told a lot about Charles's wife. It was both wild and beautiful. There were some lovely antiques that she'd refinished. Margaret remembered being impressed by her patience, as Elena had sat on the floor, rubbing an old table that she'd found in some farmer's attic. But it was strange; she'd never had that kind of patience with her children.

The wildness was unpredictable. She'd collected a number of strange objects and displayed them on the walls or on top of the furniture: the varnished head of a werewolf, its teeth bared; a stained glass portrait of 'modern life' that featured hypodermic needles, aborted fetuses, and nooses; a photograph of one of the more obscene frescos from Pompeii. Margaret had always wondered how Charles felt about these objects, and how long it

236

would take him to realize he could get rid of them. At the moment, he sat

there, in one of the chairs Elena had refinished, drumming on the arm, and

impatiently tapping his foot.

* * * *

When she got back to Boston on Monday evening, she called Anita to

tell her about the baby. Anita told her that she'd had a postcard from her

father.

"I'm afraid it's not going to help us much, however," she said. "When

we came home from camping yesterday, we found it in our mailbox. He'd

sent it to our old address. The street number was wrong, but I guess the

postman figured out it was for us, and eventually it was forwarded here.

And, of course, there's no return address on it."

"What did it say?" said Margaret, feeling as if Henry were just slipping

away.

"It was hard to tell," said Anita. "It was in very tiny writing, and we

could pick out only some of it. Let me get it," she said, putting down the

phone. A few minutes later, she picked up the receiver again. "It starts out --

Dear Anita. I could read that part, and then there's some words, followed by

'good camping weather,' and then something about rain, and got sick, a

cough. Cold in the mountains, he says, and then there's a line I can't read at

all. And finally, Love, Dad."

"What's the postmark and the date?" said Margaret.

Anita explained that both were illegible, but she offered to send Margaret the postcard so that she could try to decipher it. "But, Mom, at least we know he's alive -- or was in August or September." Margaret shivered, trying to convince herself that this was good news. But her stomach told her otherwise: there was an ominous ring to her daughter's words. It was strange that his handwriting could have changed that much.

* * * *

On Saturday morning Erik came by to oversee the kitchen wiring, and to tell her that he'd been unable to change the design of the "tight corner." Margaret had been sitting on the back steps, just enjoying the Indian summer sun. She didn't know what to say. "I hate to give you bad news when you were looking so comfortable," he said. Finally she just shrugged. She blamed herself for not bringing the whole subject up earlier, when something could have been done. "Why don't you say something?" he said. "Chew me out or tell me to go to hell. What are you thinking?" He sounded exasperated, and his face was as red as his beard.

"Actually, I was thinking that, if this glorious weather keeps up, I'd like to go on a picnic tomorrow, up in apple tree country." She turned to him suddenly. "Would you and Will like to go? One of our staff members has a cousin with an apple farm, about an hour from here, up toward Athol. I've been there before. It's fun, with hay rides and you can pick your own apples." She looked up at him, wondering if she was over-stepping some imaginary boundary line. But it had felt right, as if it were a spontaneous idea.

A flush of pleasure came over his face. "Margaret," he said, "are you sure you want to take us on for an afternoon? It's complicated, with Will. You have no idea. He can get pretty cranky when he doesn't get his way."

"Well, you'll have to do all the heavy lifting, but I'll make the picnic. The family who own that farm are lovely people. They'll take good care of us."

"Thank you," he said quietly, "we'll be over shortly before eleven tomorrow."

It turned out to be a long day, complicated, as Erik had predicted, but it had been fun for the three of them. Will had two rides on the wagon, had been able to stroke the horse's nose, and feed him sugar. The farmer had set him up on a hay rick so that he could pick apples right from the tree -- a nice, old low one -- and they were able to observe, and even help, the making of cider. At one point, bathrooms had been a problem, to the point where Erik became irritated, especially when he saw the long lines at the outhouse.

"I <u>told</u> you," he said to Margaret, "that it would be complicated." Margaret wanted to say something to the effect that outhouses were a part of life in the country, but she just stepped back and let the two of them figure it out.

Later, when Will was just watching the hay wagon fill up with other tourists, Erik lay back on the grass and fell asleep. Seeing him relaxed and comfortable made Margaret a little guilty that she hadn't done more at the outhouse scene. Still, she told herself, if it didn't ruin his day, so why should she let it ruin hers?

Then Will spoke up: "You like my Dad, don't you, Margaret?"

"Yes, I do," she said, simply, and wondering, as he spoke, if he was <u>actually</u> retarded, or whether his cerebral palsy -- plus some anxiety -- made him speak so slowly and carefully. One of these days, she'd have to ask Erik.

They were all a little sleepy on the way home, full of cider and sandwiches. Margaret dozed off as they entered the suburban area, and then suddenly woke up as Erik pulled into her neighbor's yard. "Home again, Maggie," he said. And then he laughed. "I don't know why I called you Maggie, but I've always felt Margaret was too formal a name for someone so bouncy and lively as you."

"My father's family always called me Maggie," she said. "I've always liked it." She climbed down out of his van while he unloaded the remains of the picnic. "Thank you for coming, Will," she said. "It was fun."

"Here, let me get that door for you," Erik said, as he handed her the basket. There was a silence as they looked at each other. He leaned down then and kissed her very gently on the cheek. "I'll see you soon," he said. "Thank you for a really lovely day."

She stood in the doorway, watching them drive off, her hand on her face where the kiss had landed. A feeling of warmth stole over her: she had rejoined the living.

* * * *

After the picnic adventure, there was a subtle change in her relationship with Erik. After work each day, she'd walk over to her own house, and by some magic, he'd also be there. Occasionally, they'd share a beer, and then one day, he asked her if she'd like to come to his place for dinner. "I'll make something simple like hamburgers. Will has been begging me to have you."

"Okay," she said. "I'll just leave a message on my neighbors' machine with your number. I'm a little worried about one of my clients." It was that simple. She climbed into the red pickup and they drove the few blocks to his condominium.

His townhouse was spacious, neat, and sparsely furnished, perhaps in order to have room for Will's wheelchair. The walls were decorated with Red Sox posters -- Erik had told her Will was a real baseball fan -- and with Erik's architectural drawings. As he settled Will and started dinner, she strolled about the living room, trying to figure out what buildings were portrayed. One whole wall was devoted to various renderings of the same dwelling, a large house or office building entitled: <u>Able House</u>. It reminded her of a clubhouse, a small college dormitory, or a community center.

As the three of them were sitting over Erik's "simple" dinner -- a wonderful *chile con carne* decorated with cut limes, and a big salad -- she asked him about the drawings. Erik grinned. "Those are pictures of a dream house, the place where Will might live someday, if we can put it all together." He said no more at that point, but Will looked pleased, so Margaret assumed she'd hear more about it later. In the meantime, she watched as Erik unobtrusively helped Will with his dinner, encouraging him to use his good arm, reminding him to wipe his mouth and keeping the conversation at his level. After dinner, Erik excused himself so that he could get Will ready for bed, promising coffee and liqueurs for the grownups later. Watching him, as he pushed the wheelchair toward the back of the apartment, Margaret thought about how long and exhausting Erik's day must be. Then she heard Will, angrily complaining: "But it's early, Dad," he said in his slow, precise way. "I haven't even watched my show."

Erik didn't answer for a minute. Then Margaret heard him say, with what sounded like forced cheerfulness, "Now let's get those teeth brushed." But he was angry, too.

"No!" said Will. "I want to talk to Margaret. You said she was <u>our</u> guest." Clever boy, thought Margaret. Let's see how Erik handles that one.

"I'll make a deal with you," said his father. "I'll tuck you into bed and tonight you can watch your show in your own room. I'll bring in the little portable."

"But," Will said slowly, recognizing he had lost this round, "it's only black and white." Margaret was reminded of many battles with her own kids, both lost and won on both sides. Guiltily, she found herself happy that she no longer had to deal with problems of this nature.

Margaret felt an easy sense of relaxation. She should probably get up and do the dishes. Wait, someone else was in charge, she told herself, someone who knew what he was doing. She leaned her head against the back of the couch and closed her eyes.

She wasn't sure how long she slept, but she was awakened by a gentle tap on the shoulder. "I'm almost sorry to wake you," he said. "You looked so peaceful. But the coffee is ready." She sat up and saw on the low table before her a tray with cups and saucers, cream and sugar, two small brandy snifters, a dark bottle of something mysterious, and a plate of after-dinner chocolates. How lovely to be waited on!

After he'd poured her coffee and brandy, he sat down next to her on the couch. "You've never said much about your marriage," he said. "You're separated?"

She hesitated, feeling a little uncomfortable to be talking about Henry. But after a moment, she decided it was time. "We're supposed to be going to court in January, for the divorce, but not even his lawyer knows how to reach him. He's a geologist, doing research in the field, somewhere out west is the best anyone knows."

"How long were you married?" he asked. She sensed that he was feeling his way.

"Forty years," she said quietly. "We'd been growing apart for a long time."

"So what happened to end it, after all those years?"

"The university offered him a way to retire early with some income. So he decided to leave, and go out on his own to do the research he'd always wanted to do -- about earthquakes." She shrugged. "So that was that. In a few weeks he was gone."

Erik stood up and began pacing around the room. "So where does that leave you in your feelings? Do you feel deserted or abandoned?"

"Oh, no," she said quickly. "I was actually glad to see him go." She looked up at him. "I'm just beginning to know what it's like to be happy." She looked down at her brandy snifter, embarrassed to be so open. "It's only been five months."

He stood, looking at her, as if trying to decide what to do next. "Maggie," he said, pausing, and beginning to bend over. It was the first time since the picnic that he'd called her that. She looked up, waiting. She was breathing a little faster, focussing on his corona of red hair and beard, realizing that she wanted him to move toward her so that she could reach out and run her hands through all that fur. And then the phone rang. He walked into the kitchen to answer it, and when he returned, he said, with a question in his voice, "It's for you."

"Mrs. Bluestone -- I mean, Margaret. It's Deborah Breen." She was almost whispering. "I'm sorry to bother you, but you said I could call. I did what you said. I packed the bags and got ready, just in case. Then today, all of a sudden, he got angry. I think it was because I was talking to my friend on the telephone, and I laughed at something she said. Joe grabbed the phone out of my hand, pulling it out of the wall, and began hitting me." Deborah went on to tell Margaret how she'd got away and that she'd gone to her girlfriend's place in Jamaica Plain. "But, Margaret," and now Margaret could hear the fear in her voice, "I see his car, right in front of my friend's house. He's just sitting in it, but I can see him."

"Deborah, I want you to hang up and call the police. He's stalking you and that's against the law. Tell your friend to lock the house. Then in a few minutes, call me at the other number -- I'll be leaving here right away -- and tell me which police station you called and what the number is. Tell them I'll talk to them. Okay?" Her heart was beating fast as she hung up. She took a deep breath, and looked at Erik. "I think I'd better go home. The husband of one of my clients seems to be stalking her. Shall I call a cab? You won't want to leave Will."

"No, he'll be okay for a short period. I'll drive you." As he gathered up his keys and their jackets, she looked at him. She saw the face of a sad, round-eyed owl.

"I'm sorry. This was a lovely evening." She didn't know what else to say. As they drove back to her neighbor's house, she kept wondering: what would have happened if the phone hadn't rung just then?

Chapter Fourteen

It <u>was</u> a long night, and more complicated than Margaret had imagined to locate the right policeman at that precinct. Sergeant Walker finally called her long after midnight to say that he'd driven over to where Deborah Breen was staying and had suggested to her husband that he go home.

"But he was stalking her!" said Margaret in a voice more shrill than she'd intended. "Isn't that against the law?"

"Well, that's one way of looking at it," said the Sergeant. "But he said he was concerned about the welfare of his wife and kids, and that he just wanted to make sure they were all safe. It's not the greatest neighborhood, you know." He paused, and then went on with some irritation in his voice. "Ma'am, you know she hadn't taken out a restraining order. I told him to go on home before he got into trouble. He didn't argue, just drove off."

Margaret was non-plussed. "What's to keep him from going over there again?"

"Nothing at this point. She needs to take out that restraining order, and maybe find another place to stay, one he doesn't know about, like a shelter."

Margaret sat on the edge of her bed after she had hung up the phone. There didn't seem to be much she could do until morning, so she made herself lie down, hoping to get a few hours of sleep. But as soon as she closed her eyes she began to think of Erik and their aborted evening. For the

247

first time she began to wonder if he, too, was beginning to think of their relationship in a different light -- that they might be more than just friends. There had been a look in his eyes as he turned to her and called her Maggie, just before Deborah had called. And for the first time in several years, her own body was telling her that something new and exciting was happening to her as well. Who would have thought that her sixty-two- year old body was still giving out signals? And pretty strong signals at that!

The next morning, from the office, she called the number Deborah had given her. Deborah's friend answered the phone. "Deb's gone back home," she said. "He called her this morning, right after breakfast. She was going to drive the kids to school and then go back to her house. I hope you can convince her that she's foolish. I don't trust that guy at all."

Margaret started to dial Deborah's number, then remembered Joe had pulled the phone out of the wall. Perhaps this was a good time to call Eric, to thank him for the dinner and to apologize for having had to leave early. He picked up the phone on the first ring, but then he sounded distant, preoccupied. "Oh," he said, "I thought you'd be busy with your client." Good Lord, Margaret thought. He was miffed that she'd left so suddenly.

Quickly she said: "I'm calling really to apologize for prematurely ending such a lovely evening. You made us a wonderful dinner, and the coffee and brandy afterwards were a real treat." As she talked, she found

248

herself a little miffed as well. "I was really worried about my client," she said, and when he didn't reply, she asked herself why she should have had to defend her professional judgment. Not for the first time, she asked herself: if she'd been a physician and had been called out at a social event to attend to a patient, no one would have thought twice about it. But people evidently thought that what a social worker did was lower on the scale, not like life and death, although God knows, this thing with Deborah Breen could have been a life and death matter. "Well, thanks again," she said as she hung up the phone.

She sat there, looking at the phone, both angry and sad about the way her hopes for a new kind of relationship with a man were evaporating into mist while the demands of her professional life continued. And it didn't sound as if things were any better for Deborah Breen, either. All morning, Margaret felt uneasy about her as well. But at noon, Deb called.

"I'm at the store," she said, "getting bread and milk." The young woman's voice sounded breathless, as if she didn't have long to talk. "I knew you'd be worried about me." She paused. "Joe called me at Bev's this morning, and told me he was really sorry. He was crying. I began to realize that he's sick, and that I can't leave him, not now. And I know, even if he gets a good job, it won't last. But he needs me, Margaret, he really does."

"What about <u>your</u> needs, Deborah? And the kids?"

"That's part of it, too. After I saw how my friend was living, in that crummy neighborhood -- she left her husband last year and now she's on her own -- I realized it was important to me for my kids to live in a decent place, and to keep going to this good school and being with their friends. I certainly don't want to bring them up in a shelter."

"I hear what you're saying, Deborah. But I hope you can keep your appointment with me next week. If you're going to stay with him for the long haul, we need to talk about some strategies." Back to the old drawing board, she told herself.

"Oh, I will," said Deborah. "And I'm not sorry I took your advice last night. I think my actually leaving was good for him. That's what he said this morning, that it made him realize how much he loved me and that he had to learn how to control his temper." Oh, dear, thought Margaret. We have a long way to go here. There was a silence, and then Deborah said: "Listen, I have to go, or he'll be wondering what the hell I'm up to. I'll see you next week."

* * * *

While Erik had originally promised to have her back home by Halloween, he'd had to tell her, rather formally, Margaret thought, that problems with plumbing suppliers had postponed the big day. Ever since their truncated dinner party at his house, they'd not been able to return to their easy, friendly way with each other. The new "M-Day," when the movers would return to put the furniture back where it belonged, was put forward to November 7.

Finally, the big day arrived and she was able to come home. Matt and Katy came down on the bus to spend the long Veterans Day weekend helping Margaret unpack her book boxes, the china, and the glassware. Charles had accepted her offer to stay in Portland and get in a weekend of painting.

Matt took a look at the twenty-nine boxes of books and immediately decided that they should be shelved alphabetically. "But, Matt," said Margaret in dismay, "that will take you forever!"

"Nah," he said, "leave it to me. We'll put the whole thing on computer while we're at it, so you'll know what you've got and where it is." She'd forgotten what a good worker he was. But after a couple of hours her beautiful, well-organized living room was filled with piles of books, several stacks of A's over by the front windows, and the three Z's down at the other end behind the rocking chair. It was easier, though, not to look, Margaret decided, as she moved into the kitchen to help Katy with her job of washing all the glassware. Katy, too, was into organization and counting, and had soon figured out a way to set up the china closet so that all the wine glasses were lined up by size and shape. And it really did look nice, Margaret had to admit, not like her own house at all, but more like those places she used to go for fancy lunches.

As they worked together, Katy began to talk about her pleasure in having things 'just right.' "My mom, you know, didn't really care about things like that. We didn't really have <u>meals</u> at our house very often. Most of the time, for breakfast or lunch, we'd end up standing in front of the refrigerator and trying to find something to eat."

Margaret wasn't sure whether she wanted to encourage this kind of conversation -- in which Elena would turn out to be the bad guy -- so she said something casual to the effect that lots of young people seemed to live that way these days, and it didn't seem to have harmed their children. But, even as she was speaking, she changed her mind about sending out for pizza for dinner.

"What would you like me to make for dinner tonight? Maybe you could help me."

"I loved that stew we had on the boat. Could we make that?" Katy's incredibly curly hair and green eyes suddenly reminded Margaret of Elena, and the almost begging look in her eyes helped her see what it was that had attracted Charles to this child's mother. It was easy to feel the sadness that Katy was struggling with, along with the anger, but Margaret realized that Charles must also be suffering. Perhaps he'd had a head start on these feelings, a foreboding that it was all going to end sooner or later. But he needed some comforting, too. She was glad all her children were coming for Thanksgiving. It would do him good to be around the whole crew.

"Of course," she told Katy. "The stew is a great idea. And how about gingerbread for dessert?" Suddenly Margaret felt as if she had turned into her own granny.

* * * *

During the three-day weekend, Erik turned up from time to time, more like his cheerful self again, as if something or some project was making him more optimistic, and certainly more friendly. He came first to adjust the kitchen faucets, and then to work on the outside lights. Just having his physical presence on her property, bustling about as he did whatever it was he was doing outside, was both exciting and reassuring. Looking out the window, Margaret could see that he was also going in and out of the barn -- still obviously his favorite part of her property -- and she was curious to know what he was doing. He seemed at ease with her two grandchildren, and after watching Matt work in the living room on Sunday, he told Margaret that he'd be back on Tuesday to make one last check.

By Monday night, everything was finished. The kids had done a magnificent job. Margaret was particularly pleased with how grown up Matt had been. He'd even cleaned up after himself when the books were all in place, taking the boxes down to the trash bins, and sweeping the living room floor. Margaret was too tired, after taking the kids to the bus station, to do anything but fall into bed. She'd arranged to take Tuesday off, since the carpet cleaners were coming to deliver and lay the oriental rugs that afternoon. She woke at eleven that morning, aching all over. Partially restored by a long hot shower, she inched her way down the stairs, deciding that she would not go into the rest of the house for its first real inspection until she'd had at least <u>one</u> cup of coffee, maybe two.

Walking into the kitchen, she found a fresh pot all made, with Erik's trademark, a box of doughnuts beside it. There was also a note: *Good news! The job is completed. When you finish breakfast, come out to the barn for the final touch. Erik.*

She glanced out the window and saw the red pickup truck. He must be somewhere around, maybe in the barn. But first, she decided to sit down and drink a cup of coffee and even wolf down two doughnuts. Then, walking slowly and carrying her second cup, she drifted from dining room, to living room, to sun porch and library, all of them now complete, with shiny floors, alphabetized books in the book-shelves, china and glassware neatly lined up, everything looking even better than she had imagined. Finally, it was time to call Chloe and Saul, since she'd promised them they'd be her first dinner guests.

But first she had to find out what Erik had meant in his note. Putting on her old woolen jacket, she went out to the barn and knocked gently at the door. Erik opened it grandly.

"Welcome," he said, with a big grin on his face. She looked past him into the big interior. The whole place had been cleaned, even the windows. From the upper story, the sun now came pouring in, no longer filtered by decades of dust. Erik had hung all of Henry's antique tools on the walls -- almost like an art exhibit -- and cleared away a wide space on the floor. In the corner was the antique phone booth, the brass all polished. As Margaret gazed about her, he said: "All you have to do now is call the phone company and we'd be in business. It's ready to be hooked up." She wondered if he were serious.

"But what would I do with a phone in the barn?" Suddenly she felt as if she were a stranger in her own place. He seemed so pleased with himself. But why hadn't he asked her permission? It was her barn, maybe even the site of her future private practice. Or perhaps she was feeling that it was still Henry's barn.

Something in her face must have alerted him, for he said quickly: "I was kidding, of course." But when she looked at his face, he seemed wistful, with those round owl eyes blinking, and it occurred to her that he wanted that barn for himself. She started to say something comforting. "It's so beautiful out here . . ." And then she stopped. She realized she was angry at him. She remembered then that he'd pushed his wife to become pregnant when she was over forty and doing well in her career. Was he now being intrusive with her? Bossy? Was he fixing the barn because he thought it was best for her? Not even asking her what she'd like done with it?

She'd lived so long with Henry -- forty years -- and put up with all kinds of things against her will, mostly because she was afraid he'd blow up if she objected, even to things in her own area of expertise. Now at last she was in a position to be in charge of her own life. What would happen if she stood up to Erik? Right now?

She looked up at him, suddenly aware that she was only five foot, one inch tall, and he was over six feet. But now was the time to speak up, to discard her Goody self.

"Erik," she said quietly but firmly, "I'm feeling angry about all this. I know you must have thought I'd be pleased by what you've done out here. But it's my barn and I hadn't really thought about what I wanted to do with it yet -- if anything. You didn't even ask me." As she spoke, she realized she was close to tears, and she remembered that one reason she hated to lose her temper was that she would always cry.

He looked stunned. "I thought . . . No, you're right. I didn't think. I just assumed. I acted as if I knew you better than you know yourself." He sighed. "Shit," he said. "Even Will tells me that I'm always deciding what's better for him, that I treat him like a baby, and I don't ask him. And he's right."

Margaret didn't know what to say next. Maybe nothing. If she started talking, she'd probably rescind half of what she'd said. No, she'd said it all, and by God, he'd heard her.

He looked around the barn. "To be honest, I'll have to confess that I didn't do it for you -- I did it for me. This barn was one of the things I fell in love with the first day I came." He sighed again. "Who was it that said each man kills the thing he loves? You'd think I'd learn eventually." He looked down at her sadly. "Forgive me, Margaret, if you ever can."

He walked to his red pickup truck and drove slowly out of her driveway.

So this is what happens if you speak up, said Margaret to herself. People leave you.

The rest of the day, even though it was bright and sunny, felt dreary. Even when the rug men put the clean orientals on her shiny floors, Margaret felt no particular thrill. Her house was, after all, just a house. Half the fun of fixing it up had been the planning with Erik, getting to know someone who enjoyed the place, and wanted to make it beautiful.

257

And now it seemed he was gone from her life, leaving a bigger gap than she'd realized. She'd thought of the two of them as partners, and lately, as even more. She was even missing Will. She smiled wryly as she remembered that, just yesterday, she'd sent Eric the final payment for his work. She'd written, on the lower left corner of the check: *How can I thank you?*

* * * *

Giving herself a week to catch her breath, Margaret invited Chloe and Saul for dinner the following Tuesday. Of course, Chloe's life had changed. Perhaps she would never again be that deliciously sharp-tongued person she'd been as they played their game about life in their suburb. Margaret was quite certain that they'd never play it again, either. But Margaret had changed, too. She hadn't needed the daily interchanges with Chloe in the same way any more. Much of the time the two women had spent together, all those years, was a sort of echo chamber, with the two of them having similar reactions to the various developmental stages of their lives -- motherhood, car-pooling to nursery school, followed by their pregnancies with subsequent children, graduate school, career plans, teenage drug problems, and then the gradual emptying of their nests.

Fortunately, Chloe arrived by herself, coming in the back door, out of old habit. Saul, she explained, would be a little late. Margaret took her coat and hung it in the new mud room.

"Well, then, I'll wait to give you the tour until he gets here. Why don't we have a glass of sherry here in the kitchen?"

Chloe took a chair and leaned back, looking around. "Oh, Margaret. This kitchen! You know, it looks gorgeous and much lighter, more opened up, but it's still the same old wonderful room. With this marble island, you've kept the concept of the round table. And it still looks just like you." Even as she said these words, Chloe's eyes filled with tears, and suddenly, she sounded like the old Chloe, Margaret thought. She wants us to be close again. She's not blaming me for Athena's death.

She didn't know how to say all this out loud, but she reached across and took Chloe's hand. "I've missed you. I keep thinking of you, wondering how you can get through each day."

Chloe squeezed her hand. "It's not easy. The other kids have helped." She sighed. "It's Saul I'm really worried about. He's changed."

"How do you mean?"

"You'll see when he gets here. He's shrunk into himself. He's thinner, almost as if he's taken on Athena's illness." She laughed wryly. "I've gone the other way, eating all the time, trying to fill up that emptiness." She looked more closely at Margaret. "You, on the other hand, look terrific. I think you've <u>lost</u> weight, but it's not just that: you're more alive; you look younger. Getting rid of Henry has been good for you!"

The back doorbell rang. "That must be Saul," Margaret said, opening the door.

Chloe was right. He looked like a different person, older, drawn, and smaller. But he was trying to put a good face on everything, and he spoke with forced cheeriness, almost as if he had rehearsed his opening statement. He was also carrying a big package.

He stepped into the kitchen as he shed his coat. "Smells good, like chicken with forty cloves of garlic -- right?"

Margaret hugged him. He felt like skin and bones. She wanted to feed him and fatten him up. "Welcome, Saul. I should have known your nose would guess the menu. Come, now that you're here, take a glass of sherry, and I'll give you both the grand tour."

"But first we have to give you your house present," said Saul, handing Margaret the big package. "Better put it on the table to unwrap it. It's fragile."

She took his advice and laid it carefully down, gradually pulling off the paper. It actually felt like two paintings. Finally, she had it unwrapped. There <u>were</u> two of them, whatever they were, and she turned them over.

They'd given her two antique prints, one of a beautiful, big artichoke, in the same lovely green that was her kitchen color, and the other of a stalk of Brussels sprouts, also in green. There were two spaces on her kitchen wall that had been waiting for just these two prints. "How could you have known I was looking for that kind of thing? I didn't even know, myself."

"We called Erik, just yesterday, and this is what he suggested."

Ah, thought Margaret. A wave of relief washed over her. He was still thinking about her, still tuned in to her tastes and unconscious wishes. Now she had the perfect excuse to call him, to thank him for suggesting these gifts to Chloe and Saul. It would give her a chance to let him know, just by her tone, that she didn't want him out of her life at all. If only he could understand that it was still <u>her</u> life. She had another thought, as well: she would invite him and Will to Thanksgiving dinner.

* * * *

After Chloe and Saul had gone, she picked up the phone, and dialed his number.

"Erik Jensen," he said crisply.

"It's Margaret," she said, and before he could interrupt or hang up, she went on as quickly as she could: "I'm calling to thank you for that wonderful suggestion you made to Chloe and Saul. Those two prints are just perfect; how could you have known they would be exactly what I wanted?" She was running out of breath . . . and courage.

"Margaret, Maggie, can you ever forgive me? Please, don't ever let me make any assumptions about you. In fact, I was almost afraid to suggest those two prints because I thought you might think I was doing it <u>again</u>, figuring out what would be best for you without checking."

Margaret took a deep breath. "Erik, I'm sure we can figure all this out. Just don't drive away when we're having an argument. Maybe we need to learn how to argue. I've never been very good at it, but I need to find out how to do it without making people disappear." There, she'd said it, and it was something she could live with.

He was quiet, evidently thinking all this over. "Thank you for being willing to give me another chance," he said. "When can I see you again?"

"Well, actually, I was also calling you to invite you and Will to Thanksgiving Dinner. Can you come?"

"I wouldn't miss it for the world."

Chapter Fifteen

Thanksgiving was certainly Margaret's favorite holiday, probably because it had been Granny's: an opportunity to cook bountiful meals and see all the people she loved. This year, all the kids and their children were coming, and Anita was even bringing Everett for the first time. And, of course, Erik and Will were coming, giving her twelve at the table, the perfect number.

On the day before the holiday she woke up early, partly to get a headstart on making up the beds, and then to prepare the Wednesday night supper -- by tradition, an informal affair that began with fish chowder and ended with Indian Pudding. But she also woke because she couldn't wait for it all to begin. Of all the changes in the house, the two she liked best were the former "sewing alcove" on the second floor which was now a small guest room where Katy would sleep this weekend, and, off the kitchen, the old servants' quarters that had been made into a guest suite. She'd already decided to put Andrew and Julia there, and had borrowed a crib and rocking chair to make it a temporary nursery, convenient to the kitchen and laundry.

Throwing on an old pair of jeans and a sweatshirt, she took one more look at the little upstairs guest room. From the cellar she'd brought up the sturdy spool bed that her mother had slept in as a child growing up on Beacon Hill. Several days ago she'd even gone to the fancy linen store and brought two pairs of sheets decorated with little eyelets and stitched with flowers, just for this room. At the foot of the bed she'd put the old pastel quilt that Granny's granny had made. Since Katy would be sleeping there for the long holiday weekend, she'd found herself yesterday, while in the florist buying flowers for the table, picking up some white roses with baby's breath to finish off that room.

She decided to make a quick tour of the whole house, and was delighted to find out that when she closed her eyes, there were wonderful smells everywhere she went. In the living room, a combination of lemon and oil -- furniture polish, of course -- and of freshly cut wood in the fireplace. She sniffed again, and was able to recognize the almost chemical odor of pine, the oily scent of walnut, and the acrid smell of cedar -- where had that come from, she wondered? Oh, yes, Erik had found he needed to put new shingles where the old porch had been.

Opening her eyes, the combination of colors was another kind of feast. One favorite was the burnt orange of the dining room: it brought out the warmth of all the woods. She was also particularly pleased with the pale yellow-green hallway, and the stark white of the living room, which helped to emphasize Charles's paintings. Best of all, of course, was her choice of color for her kitchen. The combination of bright green with brass fixtures made her feel as if she were outdoors on a sunny spring morning.

While she sipped a cup of coffee and finished up the remains of last night's quiche (one of the advantages of living alone was that you could eat anything you wanted for breakfast), she began making a list of tasks to be done. She'd need to leave for Logan Airport by one o'clock to pick up, first of all, Anita and Everett who were due shortly before two, and then, if all this complex planning worked out, the three of them would hurry over to the other side of the airport to meet Andrew, Julia and baby Duncan. Perhaps she should listen to the weather report. The skies looked heavy and she began to worry about those plane schedules. She turned on the radio.

"Snow," said the weatherman, with repressed excitement in his voice, "beginning in the afternoon, becoming heavy by evening. Accumulation today, four to eight inches, by noon tomorrow -- Thanksgiving Day -- twelve to eighteen. Then clearing by mid-afternoon."

Now she began to worry about Molly and David who were driving up from Philadelphia, and Charles and his kids who were coming down from Maine. Well, she'd try to leave by noon, and work faster now, to get it all done in case she was stuck at Logan waiting for those planes. Like Granny, she began to talk to herself out loud: "Good thing I soaked those beans last night. Now where's the salt pork I bought? Might as well take out the cabbage and let the food processor do the chopping for the cole slaw. Maybe I should make the base for the fish chowder now."

By 10:30 the Indian Pudding was in the oven, along with the baked beans, and she was just starting to make the pie crust when the back doorbell rang. It was Erik, carrying a huge pumpkin. The sight of this large man, with his big, round eyes and glasses, struggling to carry this monstrous round vegetable would normally have made her laugh out loud, but there was also something endearing about the whole scene. And it was so wonderful to see him again. It had been more than two weeks since the incident of the barn.

"Good morning," she said, grinning with pure pleasure.

He grinned, too. "Let me set it down here while I get the important part." He went back out to his truck and brought in an enormous stock pot. "It's starting to snow," he said. "I'm certainly glad I have a plow on my truck. This is a funny, sideways sort of snow -- tiny, with stinging, sharp little needles." He stamped his feet as he came into the kitchen to shake off the snow.

"It's beginning to look like that famous blizzard of Seventy-Eight." said Margaret. "That was the way it fell at first -- sideways, as you said. The weatherman predicted it would keep up all night and maybe end up with over a foot." She felt better, nevertheless, now that he was here: his very presence was reassuring. Some of her tension and anxiety disappeared; she felt more light-hearted. "This is an exciting day," she said, looking up at him, "the real test of a new kitchen. I'm already finding that it's a lot easier this year to do things, thanks to you. Two ovens, what a luxury! And the whole house looks lovely. I checked it out this morning." She laughed. "I even walked around with my eyes closed, just smelling everything, even the new cedar shingles."

"That's a new one," he said. "We should write an article for the Architectural Journal -- Quote: <u>Victorian Restoration and the Sense of Smell.</u> Unquote. You and me, joint authors." Suddenly, she wanted to give him a big hug. She loved the sound of that phrase: you and me. But she didn't dare; it was still not clear where this relationship was going.

"So what did you bring, along with your pumpkin?"

"My contribution to tomorrow's dinner. Pumpkin soup. It's in the pot here. But we're going to serve it in the pumpkin. I hope you hadn't planned any other soup. I asked you about the menu the other day and you didn't mention any first course." Then his face fell. "Margaret, am I doing it again? Assuming you'd like something, but never remembering to ask you?" He looked woebegone. "Bite my head off, please, but don't kick me out of your life: it hurts too much."

"It hurts me, too," she said softly, and quickly, before he could respond to that unintended admission, she added: "But no, I hadn't planned anything. And it's a great idea! You actually serve the soup in the pumpkin?" She peeked into the stock pot and saw a lovely, creamy pale orange liquid.

"Yes, but I have to prepare the shell. It will be better if I come a little early tomorrow morning, after I finish plowing your driveway." He stopped. "Oh, God. You won't mind if I plow for you?" She shook her head, smiling. He was learning fast. "The pumpkin shell takes about forty minutes to roast. Fortunately, as you said, we gave you two ovens when we planned the kitchen." Suddenly, it felt like last summer: they were friends again, but now there was a new tension, a delicious feeling of anticipation.

He eased himself into a chair. "You're busy; I shouldn't stay." But he nodded when she passed him a cup of coffee. "Are you on schedule?"

"After I heard the weather report, I began to hurry. So now I'm ahead of myself and I can afford to relax." She joined him at the table.

He looked at the list she'd made. "So many things crossed out already. You're an efficient woman. But what's this? -- Birds? I thought we were going to have turkey."

"Oh, I wanted to put out more bird food, especially if it's going to snow a lot. Could you go down to the basement and bring up that fifty-pound bag of sunflower seed? -- it's too heavy for me." He was already rising to his feet. "You remember, we set up the feeder so it could be filled from this window here without anyone having to go outside." The window was in the corner where the old pantry had been, the area they'd argued about last summer. It was still an issue, as far as Margaret was concerned.

Erik came back, carrying the bag. "Here I'll open it." He took out his Swiss Army knife and slit the top stiching. There was a special scoop just inside the bag.

"The window seems to be stuck," she said, trying to open it. "Must be the new paint."

He moved into the tight space. "Don't breathe," he said, reaching past her and pushing up the window. "You were right," he said. "This corner was my mistake. I'm sorry; sometimes I get stubborn and I don't listen." Reaching out, he filled the bird feeder. Then, closing the window tightly, he turned to her and without another word took her carefully into his arms. Margaret sighed a long sigh. It was sheer relief. She felt as if she'd been waiting much too long. She put her arms around his neck.

"You can get stubborn," she said, pressing herself against him, "and bossy, too. I'll remind you." And then her body took over and she forgot everything.

"Oh, Maggie, Maggie, Maggie," he said, and he began stroking her hair. "I was so afraid I'd lost you."

Her eyes filled with tears, and as his hands touched her face, he leaned back and smiled. "You're crying, too," he said, his eyes also wet. And then he began kissing her, slowly at first, and then with more urgency. They moved out of their tight corner and into the middle of the kitchen. "Maggie," he said, "isn't there somewhere? Where we can at least lie down?" He had

that helpless look that men seemed to wear at this stage of lovemaking.

"When do you have to leave for the airport? I have to pick up Will at one:

it's a half day at his school."

Margaret looked over his shoulder at the kitchen clock. It was just past

eleven. "There's time," she said blushing. She went to the back door and put

the chain on it, and as they walked into the front hall on their way upstairs,

he chained the front door. Margaret felt both bold and pleased with herself.

"Now I know why I put flowers in the new guestroom."

* * * *

Afterwards, she remembered a mixture of feelings -- first, the

enchanting discovery that this man was a furry red bear all over; then some

anxiety about what he'd think at the sight of her body, with its scars, and its

menopausal flabbiness; then a <u>fear</u> that she would have forgotten <u>how</u> after

all this time, (but it turned out to be like roller-skating: your body never

forgets); and finally, some embarrassment at her eagerness (but he seemed

to like that). Lying together, sweaty and somewhat sleepy, they exchanged a

few questions: when did you decide that we'd be more than just friends?

was her query. And his answer: the very first day I saw you, even before I

fell in love with the barn. And you? When you had me for dinner.

Erik's eyes were closing. "Look," she said, "why don't you take short nap? I'll jump in the shower and get dressed for the airport. I'll wake you in about ten minutes, I promise." Getting out of bed and draping herself in Granny's quilt, she headed for the master bedroom and her bathroom. On the way, she laughed to see a big puddle of his clothing where he'd stepped out of them, and then a smaller puddle of her own things.

Before she could turn on the shower, the phone began to ring. It could be one of the kids to say the plane would be late. She picked it up. Then she heard Henry's voice, sounding very far away and very old, almost raspy. "Margaret?"

"Where are you?" she said, picturing a phone booth on a deserted highway in Utah. "I can hardly hear you." Perhaps he had a cellular phone. Was he calling to wish them all a happy Thanksgiving? "Are you still out west?"

"No, no." He sounded a little closer, but irritated. "I'm here."

"What do you mean, 'here?' Are you at Rosa's?" (She'd hoped he would go to his sister's in Cleveland for the holiday.)

"No, I'm here in town," he said. "In fact, I came by the house about a half an hour ago. Of course, my keys didn't work since you put in all those new doors, front and back. But I rang the bell. Your car was here and some truck."

Oh, God. Margaret tried to organize her thinking. What if he had somehow got in? Thank God they'd put chains on both doors. "I must have been up in the attic," she said, marveling at her ability to fabricate. "The contractor was checking the insulation because of the coming storm. How come you're here?"

"I came for Thanksgiving, to see the kids. I assume they'll be coming." There was a long silence, while Margaret tried to think of what to say.

"Henry," she said finally, "I really don't think this is appropriate. We're separated, and we have a court date to get a divorce in January." Improvising, she said: "I think what most people in our situation do is that the father takes all the kids out to a restaurant the day <u>after</u> Thanksgiving. All the kids will still be here. Why don't you call them on Friday morning and they can meet you wherever you choose, some nice place?" Even as she spoke, she recalled stories of other families where the various husbands -- the first, the second, and so on -- were all having Thanksgiving dinner together. Well, good for them, she thought. I'm not going that route!

"But where am I supposed to stay?" he said, sounding now like a whining child.

"You have lots of friends in town," she said, wondering if, in fact, he did. "I'm sure many of them would be glad to put you up and give you Thanksgiving dinner as well." Since Henry didn't answer, she went on, "or you could stay at a motel." Then quickly, before he could dispute her, she said: "Listen, I have to change and get to the airport. Call us on Friday." She hung up.

While she was in the shower, she could hear the phone ringing and ringing. She decided to ignore it. I probably should have told him about Andrew's baby, she thought, and was aware that was the only thing she felt guilty about.

When she went back to the former sewing alcove, warmly dressed in her MacPherson clan kilt and yellow sweater, Erik was sitting up on the edge of the bed, putting on his socks. "You look lovely, Maggie. Here, sit by me while I put on my shoes." Then he looked at her face. "What's wrong? You look as if you've seen a ghost."

"I've just talked to one," she said. And then she told him.

"Are you upset? Is he going to cause problems for you tomorrow?"

"I don't think so. I told him to call on Friday." Then she trembled.

"What's wrong?"

"He told me he was here a little while ago, that he tried both doors and couldn't get in, but he saw your truck. I told him we were in the attic, checking the insulation."

"Why, Maggie, I didn't know you could be so devious!" He put his arms around her.

"It was sheer self-preservation," she said, shakily. "Here, you'll have to stand up. I've got to remake this bed -- my grand-daughter will be sleeping in it -- and get to the airport."

"I'll help you," he said, and together they put on the clean sheets and tucked in the blankets, as if they had done it that way for years.

* * * *

Driving to the airport was difficult. It was hard to see with the snow moving across her windshield, a strange sensation. There was also a lot of traffic: everyone seemed to be going to Logan. Several drivers had put on their brakes too quickly and had spun out on both sides of the road. She had to concentrate, but she kept thinking about Erik, rescrolling the scene at the birdfeeder. I'm sixty-two years old, she kept telling herself. She'd had no idea people her age could still be caught up in that wonderful young frenzy.

Reliving it was like carrying a warm secret inside herself, something precious and delicious that made her indifferent to the storm that was whirling past her car. Whom could she tell? No one, it seemed. Not Chloe. She couldn't imagine it becoming just another chapter in their little game. And she certainly couldn't tell the kids.

Miraculously, Anita's plane was on time. They'd run into snow only as they'd crossed over the Berkshires. Anita was smiling as she introduced Everett. He was shorter than she by a few inches, and he seemed somewhat older.

"It's very comforting to travel with your daughter, Mrs. Bluestone," said Everett, shaking Margaret's hand. "She knows what's about to happen before it takes place! As a weather person, she was privy to the fact that there would be a snowstorm hitting Boston just as we were about to arrive. So here we are, along with the snow." Margaret was immediately taken by him. He seemed comfortable in what could have been an awkward occasion: he was meeting, for the first time, after ten years, his live-in girlfriend's mother. When Margaret and Henry had visited Anita in Seattle four years ago, Everett had been away on business.

Margaret grinned at both of them as she shook snow out of her wooly hat. "Are you familiar with our New England winters?" she asked Everett.

He shook his head. "No, I grew up in L.A. Anita made me buy this scarf and these mittens, just yesterday." When he took off his matching hat, Margaret saw that he was quite bald. "I can't wait to get out in the snow."

"Well, first we have to hurry over to the other side of the airport to meet Andrew's plane. It, too, is supposed to be on time. Then we'll take you outside and you can make your first snowball." She looked down at their feet. "I see you both have boots; you'll need them, I suspect."

"Mom, do you think it makes sense," said Anita, "for you to drop us -- on the way home -- at Chloe's? We could stay awhile and then walk home those few blocks and give Everett a taste of the weather. I could call Chloe from here if it's okay with you?"

Margaret nodded. "Yes, what a fine thought to see her now. It takes a lot of courage for you to have thought of it."

"Bringing Everett will make it a little easier. I'm not sure I could do it by myself."

"While you're there, be sure to tell her to drop over sometime in the next few days to see Andrew and Julia's baby. She'd like that," said Margaret.

While Anita called, Everett picked up their luggage from the carousel and Margaret stood outside the phone booth. Anita nodded as she came out. "Chloe seemed pleased. I'm glad I thought of it." She looked at her mother. "Mom, you look terrific. You look as if you've just had a face-lift." She laughed. "You're the first person I've ever seen who had her house done over and somehow she got her self done as well."

Clever girl, thought Margaret. She'd hit the bull's eye. But if I tell her, it will just bring back all that stuff about my abandoning Henry.

And Henry, she kept forgetting, was <u>here</u> in the Boston area. She'd have to tell the kids at supper, when they were all together.

* * * *

Back in the house, following a quick tour of the downstairs, Andrew took a much-needed nap (he'd been on duty at the hospital until 4 A.M.), while Julia sat in the rocking chair in the kitchen, nursing the baby and keeping Margaret company as she finished up the fish chowder. They were going to have supper at this big round marble island in the kitchen, all ten of them. There'd been a message from Molly on the machine saying they'd be there by six. And Charles was due any minute. Feeling a little more settled, Margaret lit a fire in the kitchen fireplace, a real luxury.

There was time, finally, for her to concentrate on getting to know, not just the new baby, Duncan, but also Julia as a mother. Julia's face seemed fuller and her cheeks were pink, maybe from the heat of the fire, but Margaret was reminded of some of the Botticelli madonnas, with her reddish hair and blue eyes. "Who does he look like?" Margaret asked.

"No one seems to know. He doesn't look like either Andrew or myself," said Julia. "Andrew is so dark -- like his father -- and Duncan is so fair. Here, let me turn him so you can see his face." The baby had thick, yellow hair.

"I think you named him appropriately," said Margaret, laughing. "My father, whom you kids never knew, had this look, and his father before him. It's the MacPherson face. They were both tall, and blond, with imposing heads, like this boy's." She paused. "You seem pretty pleased with him."

Julia's whole face lit up. "He's really the biggest surprise of my life. I had no idea I could feel this way. I don't know if Andrew has told you, but we've canceled the live-in nanny. I'm going to stay home for a while, at least till he's weaned. The hospital has given me a six months leave without pay."

"Oh, that's lovely," said Margaret. "I hated to think of your missing this time with him." The baby had gone back to sleep. "Why don't you let me take him and maybe you can get a little nap as well. I think I hear Charles's van. Katy will be delighted to help me baby-sit."

Julia disappeared into the guest room and Margaret opened the door to the whirling storm. "Come in quickly, before we freeze this baby." She pulled the blanket over him.

"Hi, Mom." The three of them pushed in. "That was no fun," said Charles, "let me tell you, driving for three hours in that stuff. It sure stings like hell on your face, too. Reminds me of the famous blizzard." He flipped back the blanket. "My, he's a big one!"

Margaret closed the door behind them. "Oh, it's so good you all got here. I was worried. Come, stand by the fire. Katy, take off your coat and then you can hold the baby -- your new cousin, Duncan. I've got to finish this chowder." Katy looked as if she had been inducted into Paradise.

* * * *

By the time Molly and David arrived, covered with snow, but on time and hungry, the baby's eyes were beginning to close. Whispering her greetings to David, and kissing Molly on the cheek, Margaret took Duncan and eased him into his car seat. For Margaret, the sight of Molly, who was in so many ways physically a newer version of herself -- small, with curly blond hair and amethyst eyes -- usually made her feel guilty. Molly had always been so competent, so organized, and so in charge of her own life, even as a child, that Margaret would often catch herself thinking, particularly in a crisis: "Well, I don't have to worry about Molly right now. She can manage. I did at her age." And it always turned out to be true. Molly did manage, and very well, too. Margaret was free, then to devote her energy to Anita's prickly disposition, or to Charles's habit of bringing home lame ducks, or to Andrew's position as baby of the family, which seemed to require special handling as well.

So Molly, it seemed, never received much of her worried attention. At the same time, just the thought of this child -- and now again the sight of her

-- gave Margaret such a lift, such a feeling of pride and identification that her eyes would often fill with tears. The guilt came because she'd never seemed to have the time to <u>tell</u> Molly all this; she just hoped Molly wasn't being competent just because she'd never been given any other choice. Once in a while, Margaret would make some observation -- about how a row of shuttered houses looked along a winter beach -- and Molly would catch her eye and say: exactly, Mom; and then Margaret would know that it was okay, that Molly knew she had a special role after all.

But of course, Margaret didn't know David at all, Molly's choice of a man to spend her life with. She would arrange to sit next to him at dinner and try to figure out why this special child -- her Molly -- had selected him. Here Margaret hoped Molly would have done a better job than she'd done forty years ago, that she might have picked a man who could be . . . what? more loving, more giving, than Henry had been? What did Molly need in a man?

She looked at David now, as he hung up his coat in the new mud room. He was tall, dark, and perhaps heading toward plumpness, a little bald with a bushy mustache. As she glanced at him, she saw him look over at Molly, and quietly beckon to her to sit down on a nearby chair. Then, carefully and with no comment, he gently pulled off her boots, one by one, and set them neatly on the newspaper Margaret had put down for that purpose. And

Molly beamed. She'd found a man who would look after her needs. She put her hand on his arm, and then turned to the baby who was sleeping in his car seat on the kitchen floor. "Hi, baby Duncan," said Molly in a lilting voice, and just then, Anita and Everett arrived, with red cheeks and their new knitted hats frosted.

"Come and sit down, all of you," said Margaret. "We'll look at the house after supper. Right now we could all use some hot soup." She sounded just like Granny.

"Soup's on!" shouted Matt, the constantly hungry adolescent. Everyone moved to find a chair and Margaret managed to put the two "unknowns" on either side of her -- David and Everett. For the first few minutes, as everyone helped himself to chowder and home-made bread, Margaret just looked at the group around her. She sighed happily. It was a moment worth working and waiting for, finally arrived.

Directly across from her was Matt, still wearing the disguise of a teenager -- floppy clothes, floppy hair, and floppy shoelaces -- but underneath one could spot (and hear in his newly acquired bass voice) the emergence of a grown man. And when he caught her staring at him, he did a grown-up thing: he winked. Dear Matt.

He was seated between Julia and Anita and seemed delighted to be talking to both of them. Margaret could almost imagine Julia saying to herself: don't tell me that in fifteen years Duncan will be like this! Margaret also noted that Julia's right foot was rocking the little car seat from time to time, obviously hoping that the baby would sleep through dinner. Although it was hard to hear across the big table, she picked up enough phrases to figure that Matt and Anita were talking about computers and their use in weather prediction. "So you guys," said Matt, clearly impressed with his aunt's knowledge, "knew last week that we would get this storm today?"

While her attention had been diverted, her own two dinner partners had fallen easily into shop talk, and were conversing, literally and figuratively, over her head. Both were in what Margaret called "money" -- Everett an accountant and David a broker -- and seemed to be happily into the subject of taxation, mutually sympathizing over the obtuseness of their clients. As Margaret appeared to be listening and paying attention, they gradually changed their focus to family matters. Everett, who, it turned out, was an only child, seemed enchanted by this large family. His eyes kept glancing in every direction and his questions to Margaret had to do with time management, sibling rivalries, and the assignment of household tasks. But what had impressed her at the airport, his flexibility and the ease with which he absorbed them all, continued to be her picture of him. He was a social animal and was loving every minute of this dinner. Before turning to David, she introduced Everett to Katy, who was sitting next to him, telling him that

Katy was instructing her in the use of a spread sheet. Soon they were speaking a language that Margaret hardly knew.

David, on whose left was his own fiancé, Molly, was clearly less easy to get to know. He was a serious young man -- only 30, (Everett, she'd just found out, was 50!) and would probably have preferred a smaller gathering. He'd only had one sister, he said when asked, and Margaret remembered that his own parents had been divorced, and that both had been remarried. It was perhaps no wonder that he didn't regard families in the same way that Everett did. And then Margaret wondered if her own upcoming divorce would modify her children's view of family life. It probably would, she thought. After a few minutes of effort, she redirected the conversation with David to his clients, commenting that she also had clients, and soon they were enjoying the difference and similarities between people with financial problems and those with emotional problems.

Molly, on the other hand, was talking quietly and seriously with Charles. It appeared that Margaret had got her wish: Charles was getting some support from his siblings. Molly was nodding her head, and interjected sympathetic grunts as Charles talked. "But Charles," Margaret heard Molly say at one point, "no one could say that you didn't help with the kids! It always looked to me as if you raised them all by yourself!"

Margaret also overheard some of the conversation between Anita and Andrew. Andrew had asked her how it had gone that afternoon at Chloe's. Anita sighed. "It was sad. But I was glad we went." Anita's face suddenly reminded Margaret of a look Henry sometimes had, when he was confused, and not sure what was happening. "Chloe showed Everett some recent photos of Athena -- not the nice ones we saw at the funeral, but some that must have been taken this year. Oh, Andrew, she was so thin in these pictures. I wish I'd seen more of her in recent years." There was a long pause, as Andrew put his hand over Anita's. Gradually, everyone at the table stopped their private conversations and began to listen. Anita went on. "I guess suicide does make everyone feel guilty." She caught her breath. "I wonder if that guilt feeling ever goes away." And then Anita began to cry.

Margaret thought that Everett's presence had perhaps given her permission to do this. She'd never have let her guard down like that in front of so many people. Everett reached across the table and touched her shoulder. "Honey," he said, "you talked to her a lot on the phone. You were good to her. You went to visit her last year in New York, and we kept asking her to come and see us. But she never came."

Everyone was quiet for a while, and then Matt whispered: "Is there more chowder?" Trust Matt, thought Margaret, to break up a solemn moment.

"Gran," Katy asked, after Margaret had ladled out more soup for almost everyone, and before the noise level rose again, "how many people are coming for dinner tomorrow? I just counted the places at the dining room table. There are twelve. Who else is coming?"

Margaret smiled, delighted to have a chance to say his name. "I've invited the man who renovated the house -- the architect, Erik Jensen. You and Matt met him a few weeks ago, remember? And he's bringing his son, Will, who's in a wheel chair."

"What's wrong with him?" said Katy.

"He has cerebral palsy. He was born that way. Maybe your uncle Andrew can explain it better than I."

Andrew looked up, smiling wryly. Margaret wondered how often people put him in this position -- the expert, who was supposed to know everything.

He shrugged his shoulders. "We still don't know why some babies are born that way." He paused, and then said: "Actually, Katy, your aunt Julia's the expert in this field -- she's a pediatric neurologist -- so I'll pass the question to her." Oh, good for you Andrew, thought Margaret.

Julia smiled. "Andrew is right. We really don't know." She turned to Margaret. "Does he have some mental retardation as well?"

"I'm not sure; it's hard to tell, because his speech has been affected. He's seventeen and goes to a special school here in town. A bus with a wheelchair elevator picks him up every day. He lives with his father. Usually, they have their holidays with Erik's sister, but she was going to be away this Thanksgiving, so I invited them here."

As the conversation moved in other directions, Margaret was trying to think how to bring up the subject of Henry. Finally, when there was a lull, she said, as casually as she could, "Your father called today."

"You're kidding. Where is he?" said Anita. "Is he all right?" Suddenly, her features became sharp; she looked wary, like an animal defending its wounded cub.

"Well, you won't believe it," said Margaret, trying to sound both concerned and light-hearted at the same time -- not an easy combination -- "but it turns out he's here in town. I'm not sure where he's staying. He sounded as if he were recovering from a bad cold, rather hoarse. But he wants to see you kids, so I told him to call on Friday morning and you could all go out to dinner someplace nice. I'll baby-sit Duncan." There was a long silence. Of all of them, Andrew looked the most concerned, but he said nothing. Margaret waited to see if anyone was going to ask why she hadn't invited him to dinner tomorrow, but no one mentioned it. She thought it was strange that all of them, including Anita, seemed less interested in Henry now that he was here in the flesh, than when he was a mysterious, long-lost wanderer in the desert. No one could blame her for abandoning him or driving him away. Kids, she thought, realizing she was pretty angry!

After supper, and the obligatory house tour, Anita's jet lag caught up with her and she and Everett retired to bed. Julia followed, not too long afterward. The two kids went into what was now called "the computer room," and David evidently decided to join them there. That left Margaret and the "gruesome threesome," as they still occasionally called themselves, in the kitchen. On the night before Thanksgiving, they fell into their traditional roles -- Molly taking on the painful and fingernail-destroying task of roasting and opening the chestnuts (destined to become part of the stuffing Margaret would make in the morning). Charles, as always, was peeling and chopping the apples for two pies, and Andrew was filling two other pie shells with pecans, molasses and corn syrup. As soon as Margaret finished the supper dishes, she decided to take herself off to bed.

"Oh, Charles," she said, "could you and Andrew move the cars so that Erik can plow in the morning? Good night, kids." She looked at the three of them. It was a wonderful feeling having them in her kitchen again. "And thanks so much, all of you, for coming." She dragged herself up the stairs.

She was aware of a slight feeling of disappointment that the kids appeared to have taken all the renovation and decoration for granted. Of course, she reminded herself, they probably liked it the way it had been. It was home to them. And she didn't fix it up to please them: She did it for herself. In her mind's eye, she'd never seen it the way it actually was, but always as she hoped it would one day be.

A few minutes later, just as she had climbed into bed, she heard a knock at the door.

"Mom, are you in bed?" It was Charles.

"Just about," she said. "What's wrong?"

"Dad's outside." He opened the door to her bedroom.

"What? Where?"

"He's in his car," said Charles. "He was planning to <u>sleep</u> in his car. And it's damn cold out, a howling blizzard. We think he probably meant to sleep in the barn, but the door was locked."

Now Andrew came into the room as well. "He doesn't look well, Mom." Andrew was frowning. "We can't let him sleep outside. He'd die of exposure." He paused, as if trying to put something simply. "He looks lost and confused, Mom."

Margaret thought quickly. "Okay, bring him upstairs and put him in your old room, Andrew. The bed is all made up. There are extra blankets in the cedar chest. I don't want to see him tonight. I'm just not up to it." She thought for a minute. "You know that armoire in the hall? Matt and I put all of your father's clothes in there. You may find some warm pajamas, or even

288

long johns in there." She sighed. "I'll deal with all this in the morning. Maybe he could use a hot bath or something, or some soup. There's some left in the refrigerator. Goodnight, and thank you, both of you, for doing this."

* * * *

She thought she would fall into a deep sleep, but once she was in bed, she found she was wide awake. The years of problems with Henry seemed to have come back with a vengeance. She should be used to them, she told herself, but she was not the old Goody Bluestone anymore. She'd tasted freedom, independence, and perhaps love. Why should she have to go back to that old life? What if Henry settled into the house for good? What would happen to the divorce, with the court date in January?

She should be calling her lawyer right now, but Eleanor had taken this long weekend off to visit her parents in North Carolina. She could hear her saying: Margaret, whatever you do, don't let that man back into your house. In fact, it had been Eleanor who'd insisted she should change the locks. And she'd done so. But tonight, she felt as if she had no choice. She'd been trapped.

Henry would undoubtedly be here for Thanksgiving dinner, either by default or because the kids would not want him turned out into the storm.

There would be thirteen at the table. Margaret was not superstitious but the thought had an ominous ring.

She tried to picture Erik and Will at the same table with Henry. It felt all wrong. She should probably call Erik right now and tell him the latest development. But it was her problem. She'd have to deal with it in the morning.

Chapter Sixteen

The alarm went off at six, but Margaret had been awake for several minutes, trying to deal with an uneasiness in the pit of her stomach, the feeling that something bad was about to happen, or perhaps had already taken place. Then she heard the wind. Snuggling deeper into the blankets, she tried to shut out the noise, an insistent, intrusive, invasive kind of wind, not so much howling as whistling sharply and ominously. It was trying to get in. Crawling out of bed, she moved to the window. All she could see was swirling snow. The cars, the barn, and the whole back yard were all invisible. It must have been snowing all night. She turned on her little bedside radio. Every report spoke of the storm, and described it as a true blizzard that would continue throughout the day, tapering off by midnight. "Eighteen inches of snow," the announcer said, almost gleefully, "with more expected by afternoon."

Today was a day for layered clothing, she thought, beginning with thin silk long johns. As she dressed, she asked herself why she was feeling so threatened? She'd lived through snow storms like this before. The house was in good repair: Erik would not have left any way for that wind to get in. All her children and grandchildren were tucked into bed, the refrigerator was full of food, and somewhere -- she would ask Katy exactly where -- there were candlesticks and boxes of candles. Even if the power went out, she had a gas stove, a basement full of newly delivered firewood, and fireplaces everywhere.

The wind was not the real intruder. <u>Henry</u> was in the house -- the man who came for Thanksgiving dinner. Thanks to the wind and the snow, she might have to deal with him for longer than just today. And if Andrew was right and Henry was ill, goodness knows what would be involved. Well, Andrew and the rest of them would have to deal with him. She had other things on her mind today. Tiptoeing out of her bedroom, she glanced quickly down the hall. The door to what used to be Andrew's room was closed, and she heard no sounds of anyone stirring.

Downstairs in the kitchen, all was quiet. The baby was giving his parents a little extra time to sleep; she would try not to make any noise. Her list was tacked up above the sink, with everything in its proper order. First: make the coffee, then turn on the oven for the muffins she'd made last night. It was going to be a long and busy morning, but as various family members awakened, she would have plenty of help. Right now, while she had the privacy, she wanted to call Erik.

He answered the phone immediately. "Maggie?" he said. He seemed to have been expecting her call. "Are you okay over there? I've been worried about you. It's snowing pretty hard." His words were soothing, almost as if he were stroking her hair.

"I'm fine," Margaret said, "now that I hear your voice." It was true. She realized she'd been afraid that what happened between them yesterday had been -- well, not exactly a dream -- but a one-time magic moment, or maybe just a one-night stand. But, of course, that was not the case: she could hear it in his voice.

"I'll be coming over soon to plow, if I can get out of my own driveway," he said. "Do you still have heat and power?"

"So far," she said. "But listen, I need to tell you something." She paused. "Henry is here. He came last night." She went on with the story, and with each pause, she heard Erik make a sad, but sympathetic little groan. "I suppose he'll be here for dinner. Will you be comfortable with that?"

"Whatever you want me to do, I'll do," he said. "I'd like to come. I can certainly manage Thanksgiving dinner, as long as you're there. Don't worry about me."

Now she felt a little better, safer, and more able to move ahead with her busy day.

* * * *

As she'd expected, the first person up was Katy. The two of them worked quietly together as Margaret told the child what had been happening. "Your grandfather turned up last night -- he's sleeping in your Uncle Andrew's old room -- so we may have to add another place to the

293

table, maybe in the middle on the far side." She looked quickly at Katy, whose green eyes and keen mind were already sorting the possibilities. "Maybe later, you can do the place cards. But right now, remind me where we put all the candlesticks when we unpacked all those boxes. With all this wind, I suspect we may have a power outage and we need to prepare for it."

As she spoke, Margaret was aware that this was the first Thanksgiving in which the children's mother would not be there. Elena had always slept late when they held these family affairs, somehow avoiding the chores of preparation "Oh, you've done all the work already? Can I help?" she would say, coming downstairs at noon. But she'd been a fun person to have around, witty, and so lovely to look at.

The early morning went easily. After a sleepy-eyed Matt had devoured three muffins and a tall glass of orange juice, Margaret put him to work bringing up armloads of firewood, with orders to lay fires in some of the rooms -- the kitchen, dining room and living room, and her own bedroom, to begin with. Shortly before eight, she heard the reassuring sound of the plow. Thank God, Erik was here. And at nine, just after she'd put the turkey into the oven, Andrew emerged from the guest suite, with tousled hair and rumpled pajamas, carrying a hungry Duncan who was rooting around looking for his breakfast.

"You've got the wrong parent," he said to the baby, with a gentle smile.

Suddenly, Margaret wanted to store this memory away in some special place. Whatever else happened today, there would be these little scenes to treasure.

"Good morning." Andrew looked at his mother with a clinical eye. She felt as if he were taking her emotional temperature. "I've just changed this young man, but I wanted to see how you're all doing before I gave him to Julia." He looked out the window. "Some storm! Mom, you haven't heard anything from Dad, have you?"

Margaret shook her head. At this point, she was concentrating on the possible loss of power, and she'd tried to avoid thinking about Henry and where he'd fit in.

"Well, as soon as I get some clothes on, I'll go up to check on him." By now, the baby was howling, and Andrew took him back into his room to be fed.

* * * *

Ten minutes later, Andrew came out, carrying his black doctor's bag. Even though he was wearing jeans and a heavy sweat shirt, the look on his face -- serious and concerned -- spelled competence. Thank goodness, he was here, Margaret thought. "I'll look him over," he said, "and then we can decide what to do." Looking out the window into a complete abyss, he shrugged. "Not much we <u>can</u> do in this weather." He started up the stairs.

295

"Is Grandpa sick?" said Katy.

"We don't know," said Margaret. "Uncle Andrew thought so last night, but maybe it was just the cold." She didn't say anything about Henry's plan to sleep in his car. Even thinking about it, as she, too, looked out the window, made her shudder. "Come, let's start working on the place cards and figure out where everyone will sit." She and Katy walked into the dining room and looked at the long table. "What do you think?"

Little by little, they arranged the seating, and then Katy sat down at the kitchen table and began writing out the names. "How do you spell Erik?" she asked.

"With a 'k' at the end," Margaret smiled.

And then Andrew came hurrying down the stairs. "Mom, I can't find Dad. He's not in my old room, and not in the bathroom, either. Where the hell could he have gone?"

A stab of fear ran through Margaret. Surely he wouldn't have gone out to the barn? And then she knew. "Come with me," she said, and ran upstairs, followed by Andrew. She opened the door to her own room, and there he was, sound asleep in her bed -- <u>his</u> old bed, of course. "He must have got up to go to the bathroom, and automatically, from long habit, made his way back here." Destiny was bringing him closer to the center of her life again. In <u>her</u> bed, for God's sake, as if he'd never left.

"It's okay, Mom," said Andrew, looking at the shock on her face. "I'll take care of Dad. Go back and get ready for Thanksgiving."

And in the middle of the chopping and slicing -- assisted by Molly and David, who were now up and had finished their breakfast -- Erik knocked on the back door. "Could you spare a cup of coffee for a snowman?" he asked. He was completely covered with white crystals, his eyes running with tears that seemed to have turned to icicles.

"Oh, my God," said Margaret. "You're absolutely frozen. Come in and get warm." She pulled off his jacket and, shaking it, hung it over the back of a chair near the hot oven. She found herself wishing she were alone with him and could warm him up with a big hug. She handed him some hot coffee and even before he took a sip, he wrapped his fingers around the mug. Shivering, he looked up at them all, half-smiling. "You haven't met my daughter Molly and her fiancé, David," she said.

Nodding, he waved his hand in their direction and sank into a chair, obviously too exhausted right then to speak. After a minute or two, Erik had recovered enough to look around. "It's really bad out," he said, still shivering a little. "With that wind, I'm sure we're going to lose power. The trees are groaning, and some of the weaker ones, those big old elms, infested by disease, are going to fall, and hit the power lines."

There was something ominous, Margaret thought, about that phrase. There <u>was</u> an old elm in the Larsons' yard next door, and it was close to all the power lines.

Erik wrinkled his brow. "I'd best drive home now, while I can still get through the streets, pick up Will, and then come right back." He looked around. "I see you've brought up wood for this fireplace -- a good idea -- and set up a lot of candles." Reluctantly, he rose to his feet, putting on his cold, icy jacket and moving slowly into the mud room.

"Here," said Margaret, "let me get that door for you." And when they were out of sight of the kitchen crew, she reached up and kissed him quickly on the cheek. "Thank you for everything."

Back in the kitchen, now crowded with Bluestones, since Charles, Anita and Everett were all up and munching muffins, Margaret tried to get her thoughts back on dinner. While she was thinking about what to do next, Andrew reappeared. "Mom," he said quietly, "I need to talk to you. Let's go into the living room."

Apprehensively, Margaret followed him. There was bad news written on his face.

"Dad is really sick. He's got pneumonia -- in both lungs. And a high temperature." He paused. "But it's more than that, Mom. Of course, it could be the pneumonia, but he's really out of it. It was the same last night. He hardly knew where he was or, worse yet, where he'd been. I couldn't get any coherent information out of him -- like how long he's been sick, or anything!" Now Andrew didn't seem so much like the grownup doctor as he did an exasperated son, with his furrowed brow and the fury in his voice. It was as if his father had deliberately withheld information about himself.

"Did he know who <u>you</u> were?"

He shook his head. "I don't think so. He called me 'Doctor' at one point, but I don't think he had any idea that I was his son or who the hell I was."

"So what do we do now?"

"Ideally, we should put him in the hospital, but it wouldn't be worth taking him out in this storm, even if we could. I gave him a double dose of antibiotics, and some Tylenol to try to bring down that fever. But I had trouble even getting him to swallow water." He paused. "He's sleeping now. I guess we'd better tell the rest of them, but let's not frighten them at this point. I'll keep checking. We can take turns going up to see how he is."

When they came back into the kitchen, the rest of the family had finally gathered. Anita looked upset, angry that she had not been the first to know something -- her lower lip slightly protruding. Once when she was a little girl, her feelings hurt because they'd forgotten to tell her that it was her Daddy's birthday, she had put her lip out in that same way. Henry had commented: "Oh, look, a little birdie could perch on that lip!" And, of course, that remark had just made Anita even angrier.

"Charles just told us that Dad spent the night here, that he might be sick. What's happening?" She looked to Andrew for information.

"Well, I was just telling Mom," he said. "It looks as if he has pneumonia, so I've given him a double dose of antibiotics. He's sleeping now, but we'll keep checking on him."

"Can we go up to see him?" asked Anita.

"That's a good idea, Anita," Margaret said. "Just a quick visit. "Anita would fuss less if she were allowed to carry out this task, and she'd feel even better if she saw him asleep. "And you could do us a favor: take up one of these candlesticks, and leave a lighted candle on the mantelpiece. He's sleeping in my room and I wouldn't want him to wake up and wonder where he was, particularly if the power fails." Margaret realized she'd fallen into an old pattern, setting things up so that Anita would not cause trouble.

Anita came downstairs after a few minutes, looking solemn, her long face pulled down in concern. "It's strange to see him sick," she said slowly. "And breathing in that noisy, raspy way. I always thought he was magically immune from all bodily ailments." She turned to Andrew. "Is he going to be okay?" Andrew shrugged. She took a deep breath and joined the group that was finishing up the dinner preparations.

Shortly after eleven, Margaret heard, in spite of the noise and confusion in the kitchen, the familiar sound of Erik's pickup. "I think I hear Erik's truck," she said, realizing that she sounded a little overly-enthusiastic. She glanced around and saw Charles looking at her intently. "Charles, could you help? Erik might need assistance with the wheelchair."

Ever the gentleman, Charles grabbed his jacket from the hook in the mudroom, and pulled on his gloves. His face was without expression. Oh, oh, thought Margaret. Charles <u>would</u> be the one to spot the evidence of a relationship between herself and Erik.

Charles opened the latch of the back door, and a gust of wind blew it against the wall. A burst of snow came whirling in, making them all gasp. Margaret, who'd followed Charles to the doorstep, felt as if she'd become part of a maelstrom: she could see nothing, and the force of the wind was frightening; the hanging lamp over the big table began to sway. Over the sound of the wind, she could hear Charles shouting his offer of help, and the answering assent of Erik. Finally, with the help of David and Everett, they were able to bring the wheelchair into the house and to close the door.

"Here," said Molly, "let me just sweep you all off with this broom." Briskly, she accomplished her task and gradually, the new arrivals were brought into the kitchen.

Will looked at Margaret. "It smells wonderful," he said, in his slow, deliberate manner. He grinned, and again Margaret saw how much he resembled his father, with that red hair and a warm smile. He was wearing a thick, white Irish sweater, and she realized that whatever happened between her and Erik, she'd always love Will. Erik, too, was dressed up. What a handsome man he was!

After introductions, Will joined the crowd in the living room in front of the TV set, while his father began roasting his giant pumpkin. Andrew went up several times to check on Henry, and Molly made the trip once as well. Julia even took advantage of the continuation of electric power to start a washload of baby clothes.

Margaret also went upstairs. She wanted to change her clothes for this festive occasion, especially since Erik had put on holiday garb. Entering her own bedroom, she looked over at Henry. Poor Henry, he would hate having people look at him as if he were on exhibit. He was breathing noisily, sounding almost like a branch rubbing on the window sill, but shallowly, as if he had lost the strength to take a deep breath. She looked at his face, and saw a much thinner version of Henry, his complexion almost yellow, and he seemed cold, almost frozen. But when she put her hand on his forehead, she found it hot. He certainly had a fever, but he didn't look like himself anymore. Perhaps it was because it wasn't really Henry: the real Henry had gone away, leaving this hollow shell behind.

She moved over to her closet and looked at the clothes hanging there. Finally, she selected her old periwinkle blue wool dress, the warmest thing she owned, but also the most flattering. Then, with new-found modesty, she moved into the bathroom to change her clothes. Even though Henry seemed to be unconscious, it didn't seem right any more to undress in front of him, since she had another man in her life. She spent some extra time on her makeup and in brushing her hair, wondering if all this would make Charles even more suspicious, and then telling herself: so what? I'm alive and I want to look nice. Slowly, she left the room and moved down the stairs to join the family.

Finally, at one o'clock, they all sat down to pumpkin soup, served, as promised, in its own pumpkin shell. There was a great deal of variety in what people were wearing: Everett and David, being new to the family, were wearing jackets and ties. Her own children had made some effort to "dress up," but poor Katy, with no mother to help her select the appropriate outfit, was wearing last year's best dress, her thin, bony wrists sticking out below the cuffs of the sleeves. Margaret made a mental note to herself: she would offer to take this child shopping when she went up to their place for Christmas. Matt, too, was outgrowing his clothes at a rapid rate.

The occasion had not turned out the way Margaret had pictured it -- a triumphant celebration of the new house, with all her favorite people around her, everyone looking gorgeous. No, it was more like the grouping of family members in a hospital waiting room, trapped together there, until the doctor arrived to give news of the patient.

The storm added to Margaret's sense of isolation. Gathered around the table, with the wind still howling, the snow swirling and obliterating the world outside, Margaret felt as if this family were all alone on the planet, that the house was another Noah's Ark, floating to an unknown destination. At least they were all together, but their ship was carrying a sick, doomed member as well. Even if they landed on some mountain top, they would be marooned with Henry.

Then Charles and Matt carried in the enormous turkey. It had the varnished look of all great turkeys. As Andrew began his careful dissection, Margaret announced that each of them should be prepared to tell the assembled multitude -- before the dessert was served -- what he or she was most thankful for that year.

This announcement seemed to quiet everyone down, as each one thought about his assignment. Glancing at the children, Margaret remembered how frightened she used to be, especially when she was very young and lived at Granny's house, when Grandfather would remind everyone they'd have to say something. She could never decide what to say, and whatever it was, everyone always laughed.

Looking at Katy, the youngest person there, she didn't think any such thoughts were bothering that child. She'd probably worked out her answer in a minute. Right at the moment, she was dreamily coloring her mashed potatoes with cranberry juice, while her brother was already finishing his first drumstick, seemingly without a care in the world. But if you looked closely, you could see that he was tapping out, with his left hand, the rhythm of what was no doubt the latest piece by his favorite rock band. As he tapped, Margaret saw Charles speaking seriously to Anita, and then watched as Anita broke out laughing. It always surprised her when she had evidence that these four children had a secret life among themselves, things that had happened that she was not privy to. She reminded herself that perhaps it was just as well.

Every now and then, she sneaked a look at Erik. He was dividing his time between Will's plate -- cutting his turkey, checking his napkin -- and talking to his neighbor, who happened to be Molly. It was such a treat to see him sitting there, obviously enjoying getting to know her child.

Just at that moment, the lights flickered. "Oh, oh," said someone. The lights came back on again, bravely, as they all held their collective breaths, and then, suddenly, the power went out for good. Everything stopped.

Margaret could hear her various appliances clicking off, including the dryer which had been merrily turning Duncan's little sleepers round and round, the microwave that had been warming the next course, and, most ominously, the furnace. There was a silence. The Larsons' elm must have crashed. Outside the window, what should have been a mid-afternoon late November light, was a dark gray nothing.

"Well," said a voice that Margaret recognized as Everett's, "there goes my Thanksgiving statement. I was going to say I was thankful that we hadn't lost power." During the gentle laughter that followed, Molly stood up and began lighting the candles on the dining room table, and then Charles went out to the kitchen and did the same. Already it looked much better, quite beautiful, Margaret thought, like an old-fashioned Thanksgiving, with the crystal picking up the flickering light of the candles, the polished silver reflecting the bright spots of cranberry, red wine, golden squash, and the green salad. Perhaps Thanksgiving could be salvaged.

And then, from the stairway, there was a loud crash. Matt got there first. "It's Grandpa," he said in a scared voice. And there lay Henry, stretched out, all six feet six of him, indeed like a giant tree. He'd evidently fallen -- in the dark --from the top to the bottom of the stairs. Andrew knelt at his side. Charles carried over one of the candles and stood nearby. Andrew had his hand on Henry's wrist. "His pulse is thready," he said, also now observing his breathing.

They all stood in a circle. While it was almost too dark to see their faces, in the flickering light of the candles, Margaret looked at each of them. Molly had a frozen look, while Katy's eyes were focussed on Charles, who was standing straight and tall like a soldier on watch. Anita looked drawn and almost more like a little girl than her niece. Margaret noticed again that Andrew had become the complete professional, even in this strange setting. "Could one of you call 911?" Anita hurried into the kitchen.

"Look at his foot, Uncle Andrew," said Matt. "It's in a funny position." It was sticking out in an unnatural way, Margaret could see. She could also see that Henry had no color, and seemed to be breathing with difficulty.

"There's certainly some kind of fracture," said Andrew, "but I'm more concerned about his heart and lungs."

Just then Anita came back. "The phones are out, too," she said. "That could have happened earlier, for all we know." She looked frightened, and helpless. Everett put his arm around her and pulled her close to him.

Andrew looked up and caught Erik's eye. 'We've got to get him to the hospital. Could we put him in the back of your truck?'

Erik bit his lip, thinking. "If you could get him splinted to a board -- there are some in the cellar -- we could maybe get him in under the Cap of my pickup -- slide him in -- and with the plow, drive to the hospital. It's only four miles and on a wide street, as long as no trees have fallen across the road." He turned to Matt. "You know where you picked up those logs for the fireplaces? Right next to them are a bunch of long, wide boards. See if you can bring up one of those. And two shorter, narrower ones for the splint. Better get my flashlight; it's in my green jacket pocket in the mudroom." Matt hurried into the kitchen, and soon they could hear him going down the cellar stairs. "What do you suppose happened?" said Anita. "He must have got out of bed, started for the old bathroom -- he probably didn't realize that you now have one off your own room, Mom -- and then when the lights went off, he didn't know where he was."

"I'm not sure he knew where he was, anyway," said Andrew, still sounding very worried. "Charles," he said, "upstairs, in that armoire where we found those old clothes of Dad's, I think there were some old shirts and things we could use to splint him onto the board. Would you see what you can find?" Andrew looked around anxiously. "Isn't there another flashlight somewhere?" No one answered. So Charles took another candle.

"I have some Ace Bandages in the upstairs medicine chest in the bathroom off my bedroom," said Margaret. "Bring them as well, Charles," she called up to him as he went up the stairs. "And someone should look for his wallet. The hospital will need to see his health insurance cards. It's probably in Andrew's old room." Katy ran up to help her father.

"I think I'd better go clean off the truck and put something in the flatbed," said Erik. "Maybe you've got some extra blankets, Margaret. Will," he said, turning to his son, "you don't mind staying here while I drive to the hospital?"

"No, Dad," he said, slowly, almost as if this were all part of a religious ceremony. "Of course not," Margaret heard him say as she hurried upstairs to get the blankets.

In a few minutes, Andrew and Charles had lifted Henry to the board, and tied him to the make-shift splint, covering him with blankets. It was decided that Charles should sit with Erik up front and Andrew would lie down next to his father in the flatbed. Quickly they got their boots, coats, hats and mittens. As they were strapping Henry into place, they could hear Erik revving his truck.

Then he came to the door. "Okay, we're ready to roll. One of you should turn on your car's headlights so we can see what we're doing as we lift him into the truck." Matt and David helped Andrew carry the home-made stretcher out the door, while Charles ran over to his car, and turned it so the headlights could shine on the back of the truck. Margaret looked out at the snow, still coming down furiously, making little whirlwinds. Even before they'd slid Henry into the back of the truck, the snow had wiped out the picture. Standing in the doorway, she could not see them, but she could hear them: "Watch it, there. A little more to the left. Wait, his foot is caught. Thank God, it was the other foot." And then a silence. "All right. I'm in. Let's go. No, wait a minute," said Andrew. "Get my bag, Matt," he called out, "it's right inside the door." Matt retrieved the bag, handed it to Andrew and then came back with David as the truck drove slowly off. The storm had swallowed them up, rescuers and victim alike, leaving the survivors to peer into the white void. Margaret closed the door tightly.

* * * *

Molly and Anita had already put a big pot of water on the stove so that they could have hot water for the dishes, and they'd begun rinsing and stacking the plates. When Margaret came back into the kitchen and started to help, Molly said: "Mom, you've done enough for the past few days. Go sit in the living room by the fire, and relax." She and Anita agreed that they would have dessert when everyone came back from the hospital. As Margaret walked out of the kitchen, she could hear them beginning to reassure each other: Dad would be okay. Maybe the fall was a blessing in disguise, Molly said. At least it got him to the hospital so he could recover from his pneumonia. But as Margaret moved toward the living room, she began to hear echoes of an old argument, as Molly began to explain to Anita that there was only one logical way to do dishes by hand: "You have to put the glasses in first when the water is the hottest; then the silverware, then the plates, and last of all the pots and pans."

And as Margaret could have predicted, Anita replied: "That's a lot of crap. It's quicker just to take each thing as it comes and wash it. We have plenty of water, for God's sake. The plumbing still works!" Why was it that these old disagreements were magnified by a family crisis? Well, she'd have to let the two of them work it out. Margaret couldn't do everything.

She wanted to take their advice and stretch out on the couch, but she was a little worried about Will, who'd been thrust into this family without too much preparation. He was sitting in the living room in his wheelchair, looking around, and glancing over at the two kids who were staring out the windows. What could she find for the three of them to do that would absorb and distract them and make things comfortable for Will? She frowned as she reminded herself that this was one time when you could not count on television to take care of the children. What had families done in the old days?

Then she remembered the attic. It was full of toys and games, even puzzles. She turned to Matt. "Matt, aren't there some games and things up in the attic that you two could bring down for the three of you? Take a couple of flashlights and go up and look around?"

The kids looked at her, as if wondering whether they had the right to refuse, but, finally, with some reluctance, they went upstairs together. I'm really sounding like Goody Bluestone right now, Margaret thought, telling everyone to "play nice."

A few minutes later, the kids came down again, each carrying several boxes. "Look, Gran, we found a Monopoly game, a chess set, and a bunch of jig-saw puzzles," said Matt, sounding a little more enthusiastic. He turned to Will. "Have you ever played Monopoly?" he asked, casually.

"Of course," Will said, in his slow, deliberate way, "my Dad and I play it all the time."

"Well, let's set it up," said Matt cheerfully, clearing off the old library table. Bless him, thought Margaret.

Then David spotted the Monopoly game. "Ah, hah," he said, cheerfully, "this is the game that made me decide to go into finance as a career." He and Everett moved over to join the kids, and Margaret closed her eyes.

* * * *

The rescue squad did not come back until eight o'clock. There'd been, of course, no way for them to call, since the phones were still out. But the snow seemed to be tapering off and they were able to drive home with only minor difficulty. They came into the house, breathing heavily, as they

312

stamped the snow off their feet and hung up their jackets. All three, each in his own way, looked exhausted and stressed out.

Andrew, in addition to being just plain tired from the usual fatigue of having a new baby in the house, was doubly stressed. He probably felt guilty, Margaret realized, that he hadn't acted sooner last night when he decided to let Henry sleep at the house, and then this morning, when he diagnosed the pneumonia.

Charles, too, she realized at she looked at him, was at the end of his rope. His silent face, now cold and forbidding, demonstrated that he'd been pushed from both sides, by an outsider to whom he'd had to give way -- Erik -- and by a much younger brother who had been giving him orders all day. But Charles was not the sort of man to let this exasperation out; he was just pulling into himself, more every hour.

Margaret didn't know Erik well enough to imagine what it must have been like for him, but it was bound to have been difficult. Spending five hours in a hospital waiting room with two men he'd never met before, could not have been easy, especially when those two men were her sons. And she was sure he was concerned about Will, and how he'd been getting along.

As soon as he'd shucked his jacket, he went into the living room to check on his son. Andrew and Charles followed slowly behind. The Monopoly game -- or was it the second or third in a series? -- was still in full swing. Will was holding his own, with one hotel and a few houses on his properties, but the pile of money in front of David was bigger. Erik looked at Margaret and smiled, a lot of his tension dropping from him. He sank into a chair. "Will, keep in mind that we're going to have to head for home pretty soon."

"Fifteen more minutes, please, Dad," said Will, obviously having a great time.

"Okay," Erik said. He closed his eyes briefly and then, after a minute, opened them and looked about the room. "I haven't been in this room, Margaret, since you put everything back together. It looks wonderful." And then he turned to Charles. "I remember the first time I saw them, last summer, and how struck I was by these paintings, especially by your use of light. They are really magnificent." These remarks seem to have brought Charles alive again. He smiled his thanks, and Margaret wondered if Erik had known intuitively how much her son had needed that reminder that he, too, was a talented professional.

Half an hour later, Erik and Will were on their way, taking with them a pecan pie -- Will's favorite -- and the sincere thanks of Andrew. "We never could have managed without you," he said, as he helped Erik out the door with the wheelchair. Margaret stood in the doorway, waving. She had wanted to say something special and personal, to hold him for a minute or two, but it just wasn't possible with everyone there. Then, as the family sat down in the kitchen over four kinds of pie and coffee, Andrew gave them the preliminary diagnosis. He'd been right: Henry had bi-lateral pneumonia, a serious case, but his temperature had gone down a little and he seemed to be responding to the antibiotic. His heart was okay. The fracture would take some time to heal. At this point, Andrew said slowly, the hospital staff was almost more concerned about his mental state. Unable to get a history, they wanted to keep him over the long weekend to be evaluated, after he'd recovered a little from the trauma of the fracture and the effects of the pneumonia.

There was a long silence after Andrew had delivered this news. No one wanted to ask -- or answer --what to Margaret was the most important question: what was going to happen to Henry after he left the hospital? Would he be able to go home? And, if so, where was home? How long, in these days of managed care, in fact, could he possibly remain hospitalized?

And no one would be asking or answering these questions until she, herself brought them up. Suddenly, she was more tired than she ever remembered. Her afternoon nap had not helped. "I'm afraid I have to go to bed," she announced. "I'll see you all tomorrow, that is, if it's light enough to see." She picked up one of the candles and walked slowly up to her room, feeling like a heroine in a nineteenth century novel.

She lit the fire and it blazed up immediately. Matt had done a good job. She began to wonder: if the storm continued, would they be able to keep warm, with just the fire places? Would they run out of candles? She frowned, thinking about the baby, and then reminded herself that the house was over a hundred years old. People had babies in those days, too, when there were no furnaces. Somehow they'd managed.

But when she went over to the bed, there was a strange smell, like ammonia. Then, when she started to lie down, the bed felt very cold. It was wet. Oh God. Henry had wet the bed, <u>her</u> bed. It was the last straw. She began to cry. It was more than she could bear, a bad omen of things to come. Andrew never told me, she sobbed to herself, that Henry was incontinent. Perhaps he hadn't known. Perhaps it was his high fever, the pneumonia, and not knowing where he was. It might just be temporary. But she would have to get up and remake the bed, normally not a big deal. But on this night, she was mortally tired. What did it mean when a sixty-five year old man wet the bed? Was that a common symptom of pneumonia? Perhaps the hospital was right in wondering about his mental status.

Poor Henry. If he knew, he'd be mortified. And as she moved slowly to the linen closet, she began to wonder about that word -- mortified -- it must have something to do with becoming dead. Suddenly she felt as if she were a hundred years old.

Chapter Seventeen

The noise of the plows woke Margaret on Friday morning, a wonderful, energetic noise, spelling freedom from confinement. It had stopped snowing! She could see the barn, and the humps of all their cars. While the sky was still gray and the snow more than two feet deep, she felt more optimistic. Quickly, she put on all the wool clothes she could find, and hurried down to the kitchen to light the gas stove.

But Julia had gotten ahead of her. She'd lit the stove, started the coffee, and even made a fire in the fireplace. Wrapped in a big blanket, she and the baby were nestled in the rocking chair. "Good morning," said Julia, rosy-cheeked and smiling, as she nursed the baby. "Yesterday was quite a day, wasn't it?" She paused. "Thank God, we had Erik's truck." She looked down at the baby, and he pulled away from the breast and grinned at his mother. "Look at that," she said, with delight in her voice. "He's never done that before. He'd rather smile at me than finish his breakfast. Don't you think that's very advanced?" she asked Margaret.

"Absolutely," said Margaret, delighted to see that this doctor daughter-in-law was like any other mother. She leaned back in her chair, enjoying the fact that she didn't have to do anything special at that moment. "Thank you so much for all you've done this morning," she said yawning. "Why don't you let me take the baby so you can get dressed, or go back to sleep,

317

whatever you want. I've hardly had any time with Duncan and I want to get to know him."

"Well, he's finished for now, I guess," said Julia, passing the baby to Margaret. "I'm going to wake up Andrew. I know he wanted to go to the hospital this morning to check on his father." After Julia had closed the door, Margaret sat quietly, smiling at the baby and making faces at him. For a long moment, he stared at her, with a sort of frown on his forehead as he focussed his eyes. Then he broke into a broad grin. "Hi, cutie," she whispered. "This is your Gran. Welcome to family life."

* * * *

Duncan had fallen asleep by the time other family members began to turn up. A very grumpy, silent Charles was the first intruder. Margaret had to smile when he opened the refrigerator, and, as he used to do every morning growing up, he said: "There's nothing to eat in here." Looking over his shoulder, Margaret could see a full larder, and on the pantry shelf, several pies that had hardly been cut into. But she knew better than to point them out. When Charles was cranky and hungry, he was impossible to reason with. He found his own coffee, and in a few minutes, he'd cut himself a piece of pumpkin pie.

"So what's with you and this Erik?" he said sharply. He was not looking at her, but was picking at the sleeve of his sweater. He must have planned to ask this question.

Oh, boy, thought Margaret. He's going to give it to me with both barrels. "I'm not sure what you mean," she said, as she moved the baby into his car-seat. "He's been a wonderful architect and a good friend." She was pleased with the way that sounded.

"Well, he seems pretty bossy," he said. "I hope you're not letting him push you around." Now he was facing her, almost defiantly, his chin firm, his blue eyes blazing.

"I've had quite a bit of experience along that line," she said quietly. "And I'm enjoying the management of my own life right now." She was reminding her son that she was an adult. Charles was silent, looking down at his plate. She wondered whether he felt as if he'd been rebuked. Margaret could feel that she was blushing, but hoped that in the half light, it wouldn't show.

And then Anita joined them. "Is there any news of Dad this morning?" she asked, as she, too, opened the refrigerator. "Ah, we seem to have plenty of eggs," she said, pulling out the carton and beginning to start an omelet.

"Andrew's planning to go to the hospital pretty soon," said Margaret. "Maybe, when he gets back, we should have a family conference."

"What about?" said Anita, as if there were no unanswered questions. Charles was looking at her. Usually, when Anita seemed on the verge of attacking Margaret, Charles would jump to his mother's defense. Automatically, Margaret looked at him.

And sure enough, he turned to Anita and said calmly: "Well, all of us need to decide what should be the plan for Dad. We can't expect Mom to take care of him at this point in their relationship: they're getting divorced, for Christ's sake."

And, as always happened, Margaret would step in and try to make peace between them. Quickly, she said: "Why don't we wait until we have some definite news about his prognosis, and until all four of you are in the room and we can discuss it rationally.

"There's not necessarily going to be a rational solution to this, you know," Anita said angrily. She took down two plates and set places, probably just for herself and Everett.

"Let's not raise our voices," said Margaret. "We don't want to wake this baby." Suddenly, Margaret realized she was hungry. She looked wistfully at the frying plan with its cooking omelet.

"So," said Charles, warming up to the fray, "are you prepared to take Dad into your apartment in Seattle if it's necessary?"

Anita looked startled. "I'm sure he'd be completely confused if we tried to settle him with us - - he's never even <u>seen</u> our new apartment."

"Kids," said Margaret, "let's not jump to any conclusions yet. Or start blaming each other for things that haven't happened yet."

"Mom, you never want to face the inevitable," said Anita. And then about-face, she said suddenly, "would either of you want some omelet? I seem to have made enough for an army."

"Actually, I haven't had any breakfast this morning," said Margaret. "Maybe Charles would like some as well?" She looked toward her son, but he shook his head, pointing to his pumpkin pie. And then Everett came downstairs, and the discussion ranged as to who would make the walk to the store, and who would start shoveling. Sighing, because it was just one more task, Margaret wrote out a short grocery list: eggs, candles, bread.

* * * *

It was after noon before Andrew returned from the hospital. When they'd all finished lunch, Margaret called all the family members into the living room for a meeting. She realized that she was terrified, not just that they'd find no solution to what she hoped they'd see as a common problem, but also that the fabric of the family, which she'd always thought of as strong and flexible, would turn out to be a thin shroud.

Margaret had seated herself in her mother's old high-backed damask chair, with her back to the edge of the fireplace, facing out into the room where they were all seated or sprawled. Anita lay stretched out on the floor, reminding Margaret of the way she'd studied when she was a teenager. Margaret had always suspected that her long frame just didn't fit into most chairs. It was difficult, in this light, with the gray, cloudy view from outside and the flickering firelight, to see her expression, but Anita looked wary, as if she were crouching, ready to spring if anyone said anything that roused her.

Charles sat upright, as always, in a straight ladder-back chair, his legs crossed neatly at the ankles, his hair carefully combed, his lips tight. Out of the corner of his eye, he could keep a watch on Anita. Molly sat cross-legged at Margaret's feet and she couldn't see her face except when she turned to look at Andrew, who'd chosen to stand. Margaret wished that he would sit down and not feel that he had to be the authority here. She reminded herself to suggest he take a chair as soon as he'd given his report on his father's condition. Charles was frowning at him already.

Margaret felt she had to begin the meeting. She said: "First I want to thank you all for being willing to participate in this discussion of your father's future." Shit, she told herself, I'm sounding like some CEO announcing a major downsizing. But she went on, bravely. "These meetings are never very comfortable, but I really need all your input since you'll be leaving in a day or two and I'll have to figure it all out by myself. So I need your guidance." She paused. Not one of them seemed to want to take her off the hook or run with the ball. Well, she told herself, I'll have to throw in the kicker, here, and I might as well do it now. She swallowed and cleared her throat.

"I think we all need to be reminded that your father and I are really no longer man and wife at this point. We are legally separated and a divorce hearing is on the docket for early January. It is really not up to me to make decisions about his care now. His lawyer, Paul Kosinski, has his power of attorney and health care proxy, and theoretically, should be with us today. I plan to have my attorney talk to him in this coming week. But right now, I'm sure we'd all like to hear what Andrew found out at the hospital this morning."

Andrew, too, seemed nervous, and he began to stroke his beard. He let out his breath. "Well," he said, "I'm not sure what you want to know." He stopped, uncertainly.

"For Christ's sake, Andy," said Charles. "Just tell us what's wrong with him and how he is. You don't need to make a speech and you're not in front of medical students at rounds. Was he conscious?"

"Well, not at first," said Andrew, oddly more comfortable now that he was once again being yelled at by his older brother. "I peeked into his room and he was sleeping. So I looked at his chart and saw that his temperature had gone down to about 100, and his breathing was much better. They had made a beautiful cast for his ankle." He smiled. "Then I went to talk to the nurses, and they called the orthopedist. The internist came in later, but the general consensus was that he was making a good recovery from the pneumonia. He'd had an uncomplicated fracture of the ankle, which would take six weeks before it heals. They were hoping to put on a walking cast in a few weeks."

"Was that all?" said Molly. "Are they going to send him home in a few days?"

"Oh, no, I don't think so," said Andrew. "They were concerned because they had a lot of trouble getting any kind of history from him. Of course, they're hoping that the effects of the fracture and the pneumonia will wear off and he'll gradually be more rational. But I had the impression that his mental status was their biggest concern. They're planning to have a neuro consult in a day or two and then go from there. The internist seemed to think that it wasn't just accidental that he had pneumonia: he thought that he'd been neglecting himself for months, sleeping in the cold, not getting good nutrition." Andrew paused for a minute, as if reluctant to go on. "The

324

orthopedist suggested that the broken ankle could have been the result of some dementia."

The word hung in the atmosphere like a poison cloud, and for a minute, no one breathed, as if they feared they would fill their minds and lungs with that poison. "What the hell does that mean -- dementia?" Anita asked, finally.

"That's what they use to describe a loss of mental capacity, particularly in older patients, or people with certain organic cerebral deficiencies." Margaret thought that Andrew was using these words to put a distance between himself and the rest of them. But she could see that Anita wasn't going to let him get away with that.

"Come on, little brother. Don't give us that jargon. We live in the real world. We know about senility and diseases like Alzheimer's. Is that what you're talking about?"

Andrew swallowed. Margaret could see that he was in an unenviable position. "I'm not talking about any diagnosis or condition. I'm trying to tell you that they don't know what's wrong. But they're a little suspicious that it's not just pneumonia and a broken ankle. But they don't know." He paused. "And neither do I." Now he sounded irritated.

There was a long silence. Margaret turned to Andrew. "Why don't you sit down, Andrew. No one's blaming you for anything. In fact, I don't know what we would have done without you yesterday. It's good news that he's

recovering from two of his diseases, and that's to your credit." She paused,

aware that she was trying to put out a potential fire. She went on: "It's hard

to make plans when we don't know what the outcome will be, but I need to

know what all of you think. Let's assume that, in a week or so, the

pneumonia is gone and they've put a walking cast on your father. He'll still

need a place to recover. Maybe the hospital will send him to some kind of

rehab place. His insurance will probably cover that, and if not, his lawyer

has some control of his money and could pay for that care." She looked at

them. Speak up, kids, for God's sake.

Anita was still looking wary, as if waiting for a particularly unpleasant

shoe to drop, while Charles was just frozen in his manner. Andrew looked

just plain tired, while Molly was looking at her watch: did she have some

kind of appointment? Perhaps she and David had made plans. But Margaret

found herself feeling angry.

"That would be the best case scenario," said Margaret. "But the worst

case would be -- what? That he would have some kind of dementia, and

need, perhaps, a nursing home?" These last two words hung in the air even

more frighteningly than "dementia" had done. No one spoke for a minute.

Then Anita scrambled to her feet. "I, for one, do not want my father to go to a nursing home!" Her voice was loud and she looked directly at her mother.

"Well," said Charles, almost as if he had been waiting for this statement, "are you prepared to take him in, to nurse him on a 24-hour basis for God knows how long? That's what I was asking you over breakfast."

"Anita, Charles, all of you. Listen to me," said Margaret. It seemed to her that she had spent many years using that same phrase. "Part of the problem is that none of us is really able to take your father into our homes. The day when there was always a dependent female relative in every house, available to nurse the invalids, is long gone. Anita and Everett live in Seattle, in an apartment your father has never seen. No one would suggest putting him there."

"And what about a nursing home?" said Anita. "He's never been in one of those, either." Standing by the mantelpiece, she banged her fist on it. "Being in a god-damned nursing home isn't exactly a day at the beach."

"Let's get down to realities," said Margaret. She could hear her voice rising. "Every one of you has a life that would be totally disrupted by having to take care of a sick man. Molly is getting married in a few months, Andrew and Julia have a new baby, Charles not only teaches and paints full-time but has full custody of two children. And it's out of the question for

Anita and Everett." She paused. "I, myself, have a full-time job, and I need the money to survive. I can't just quit it and take care of a man who chose to leave me five months ago, and from whom I'm getting a divorce." She looked at all of them, suddenly openly angry.

"There's something else, something people don't like to talk about." They all looked at her blankly. "I'm talking about money. Did you know that a nursing home can cost as much as a hundred dollars a day -- that's more than $36,000 a year." She paused, to let that sink in.

"Mom is right," said Molly, the financial advisor. "I'm always having to explain to my clients, when they make their long-range financial plans, that, except in rare short-term situations, insurance does not cover the cost of nursing homes."

"Then how do most people manage?" asked Anita. "Millions of people seem to end up in nursing homes. How do they pay for it?" She glared at Molly, almost as if she were the cause of the problem.

"Well," said Molly, warming to the question, "they have to do what's called 'spend down' their funds, until there's virtually nothing left, and then the government -- Medicaid -- takes over, and pays for minimum care."

"I have no idea how much money your father has," said Margaret, "but I'd hate to think that, whatever it is, it would all go to a nursing home. Or be spent down so that he could qualify for government subsidy. I'm sure he'd rather it went to you kids." She paused. "I'm not coming up with a solution, but I want you all to know that we have a problem."

"So why did you get us all together?" said Molly. "Surely it was not just to get us fighting?" She stood up, stretching. "Besides, I don't know what we're all worried about. There's nothing wrong with Dad's mind. He's one of the brightest men I've ever known." With her round face, curly hair and big blue eyes, she looked like a five-year telling her kindergarten friend that her Daddy was smarter than anyone's.

"Molly," said Anita, sadly, "you just want it all settled so that he can walk you down the aisle on Valentine's Day weekend; you can't bear to think that it won't work out."

"That's not it," Molly said. "I figured out a few weeks ago that I could walk down that aisle by myself when the time comes. I'm a grownup."

"Right on," said Charles, who always thought that anything Molly did was fine.

"I got us all together, Molly, just in case," said Margaret. "None of you will be here next week when the hospital begins to decide what's wrong with him. I guess what I'd like -- and it doesn't look as if I'll get it -- is some kind of vote of confidence from all of you, a vote that says: we'll leave it up to you, Mom. Do what you think is best. I don't want any of you blaming me for the rest of my life for doing the wrong thing."

"Well, of course, Mom," said Molly. But no one else said a word.

Anita finally spoke up. "I don't see how I, for one, can give you that kind of blank check, to do what you want." Raising her voice and trying to push her hair back up off her neck, she said: "You don't love him anymore. That's the bottom line. So why should you be the one to decide?"

"Well, Anita, then maybe you should have that power of attorney and the health care proxy that your Dad gave to his lawyer. But if he's now demented, and I hope to God he's not, he wouldn't even be able to make that change. It may have to stay with Paul, and I'll be happy to leave it up to him." She looked around the room. "Is that okay?"

Charles sighed. "What else can we do? It's a mess." He stood up. "I think I'll check on my kids."

Molly and Andrew also walked out of the room, not angrily, just sadly. "Thanks, Mom," said Molly. "Let's hope for the best." Andrew put his hand on her shoulder.

Margaret was left in the room with Anita. "You know -- what you just said?" She paused. "The funny thing is that I do love him; I probably always will, but maybe in a different way now. He's not the man I married, that's for sure, and he's been incredibly cruel to me for many years. I haven't told you kids because I figured it was my problem. And it still is. He was particularly cruel to me when I was sick. And now I wonder if I could even take care of him when <u>he</u> is the one who is sick."

Anita stood there, looking at her mother and rubbing her eyes. She was trying to make the tears go away, just as she did when she was a little girl. "Mom, how did it ever get to this point?"

Margaret shook her head, unable to answer at first. There seemed to be a big lump in her throat that kept her from swallowing. Finally, she gulped and turned to Anita. "I guess I should be proud that at least one of his children is still his advocate." She put her hand gently on Anita's arm and began to move toward the kitchen. "I need to be by myself this afternoon," she said, and went into the mudroom to pull on her boots, her warmest jacket and scarf, mittens and the hat with ear flaps.

* * * *

Much to Margaret's surprise, the late-afternoon sun was just coming out. All around the edges of her roof, icicles were forming and catching glints of the orange light. Ice had also coated even the smallest branches of the trees, making them look as if they were burning from the top down. This storm was tiring itself out. Looking up at the sky, she saw blue patches gradually outnumbering the scudding gray clouds. She began to walk, carefully at first, stepping over downed wires and uprooted trees. There were utility trucks in almost every block, men in trees with power saws, all very reassuring. The fresh air felt good in her lungs and she looked about, seeing her neighbors all out shoveling, making snowmen, and bringing out sleds for their kids. It was good to get away from her own children.

She trudged on, just enjoying the squeak of her boots in the deep drifts, and the crunch of the snow as she picked up a handful in her mitten. It was good packing snow, perfect for making snowballs. All she needed was someone to throw the snowball at. From time to time, a heap of snow would fall, all at once, from a big pine tree, dusting her with a fine mist. It felt good. She began to walk faster, almost to run. Then she realized where she was going. She was on her way to Chloe's house; she needed to see Chloe and tell her all -- well, maybe not quite all, not the part about Erik -- that had happened since the storm had begun.

She walked even faster, and almost ran up Chloe's newly shoveled front steps to ring the bell. Chloe, herself, answered the door. "Margaret! Have you run away from home?" she asked, looking beyond her and seeing that she was alone.

"I guess I have," said Margaret. "I need sanctuary." She was remembering the medieval tradition in which the hunted criminal would be safe from capture if he could reach and hang onto the big round door handle in the lion's mouth on the door of the cathedral. Chloe's house looked warm and inviting, and in fact, as she soon discovered, their power had been turned on that morning and they were luxuriating in heat and light.

"Come in and have some brandy, or whatever they give frozen travelers." said Chloe. And actually, brandy sounded like a good idea. Margaret took off her outer clothes and stood among Chloe's grown children and grandchildren and felt at home. She sighed a deep sigh and sank into the soft couch. In the meantime, Chloe had brought her a glass of brandy and had taken a good look at her. "Kids," she said, "I think Margaret needs to talk to me by herself. Scoot!" They all headed for the kitchen or into Saul's study, and there was peace and quiet. After a minute, Chloe said: "Tell all. You look as if you've been through some kind of hell. Maybe I should have given you one of the kids' teddy bears to stroke."

Margaret started to laugh and then it all turned to tears, and once she'd started crying, it was hard to stop. Gradually, when the hiccups slowed down and she'd wiped her eyes, she started to tell the saga of the return of Henry, beginning with Thanksgiving eve and running through the family meeting. At each surprise, beginning with Henry's arrival in the storm and his plan to sleep in the car, Chloe groaned. "Oh, no," she kept saying. And then the fall down the stairs, the trip to the hospital, and the possibility, now, of dementia. She also understood that the worst part was not having the kids backing her, especially not having Anita on her side.

After Margaret had finally finished her saga, she felt sleepy but somewhat better. "I think you could use a nap," said Chloe. "Come on, we'll find you a spot upstairs. No one will bother you, and when you wake up, Saul will drive you home." Obediently, she followed Chloe up the stairs, and stretched out on the bed to which she had been assigned. She fell asleep almost immediately and slept for nearly an hour. It was not until she had wakened and sat up that she realized where she was. Chloe had put her in Athena's old room. Thank you, Athena, she whispered.

* * * *

It was dark by the time Saul drove into her driveway. When she walked into the kitchen, the room was still a little cold, the fire going out. She wondered where everyone was and wandered out into the living room. The whole family seemed to have gathered there, near the fireplace, and when Molly looked up and saw her, she shouted: "Here she is! Oh, Mom, we were so worried. It was getting dark. Where were you?"

Margaret smiled. "I was at Chloe's. Where else?" Then she remembered that this was not the first time she'd played hookey by going to Chloe's. It usually happened when the kids had been particularly awful, like the time she found out there was hashish in the Brownies that she'd made for the P.T.A. meeting. And often, when she'd finally come home, the kids would be sitting together, evidently scared that she was never coming back.

"Sit down, Mom. We're all going to make supper -- steaks in here by the fire, and a big salad and baked potatoes."

Shortly after dinner, the power went back on, and life returned to normal. On Saturday, the kids all went to see their father in various combinations and at various times, but Margaret didn't go, feeling that she needed to make a statement that she was no longer responsible for Henry's care. They were, after all, soon to be divorced.

By Sunday noon, they'd all gone back home, and Margaret spent Sunday afternoon putting everything back together again. She was going through the motions, and from time to time, trying out the phone. But it was still not in operation, and she was beginning to wonder why Erik hadn't come by, at least to see how she was doing. It seemed a hundred years since they'd filled the bird feeder together. Perhaps Henry's arrival had put an end to the fragile beginning of a new relationship. Or had it all been just one of those things? A flare-up of the conjunction of two fading galaxies.

* * * *

Early on Monday morning, just before Margaret left for work, the telephone rang. Thank God, she thought, phone service must have been restored. It was the hospital calling, a woman's voice, with a slight accent. "Mrs. Bluestone? This is Doctor Reiner."

She rolled the 'r' in Reiner. "I'm calling about your husband." She explained that she was the neurologist who'd been assigned to evaluate him, and she wondered if Margaret could come to the hospital that morning to give her some history. "It hasn't been possible to get coherent information from Mr. Bluestone," she said pontifically. "Could you come at eleven o'clock?" Margaret agreed. She'd call the office right away to see what was on the docket, and just cancel whatever she had that morning.

Dr. Reiner was relatively young -- about forty, Margaret thought -- with her chestnut hair carefully braided into a French knot. From the accent, Margaret decided she probably came from Vienna. She seemed to have a permanent frown between her eyebrows, as if she had spent her professional life trying to make sense out of what people tried to tell her.

She listened as Margaret outlined Henry's life history as she knew it, his temper, his tirades, and, in the last three years, his paranoia. "Ah, so," she had said when Margaret talked about that aspect of his life, noting it down on a sheet in her folder. She was particularly interested in his plans to journey to the west and in his behavior as he prepared to leave. When Margaret mentioned how he'd got lost going to Albany, she carefully wrote that down as well. She didn't seem the least bit interested in the fact they were separated and planning to divorce. But when Margaret mentioned the postcard Anita had received and how small Henry's writing was on the card, she sat right up. "Ah," she said, "the micrographia." Now Dr. Reiner was nodding her head.

"Why is that so significant?" she asked the doctor.

"It helps us with the diagnosis," she said enigmatically. There was a long silence. Margaret had begun to feel that she was doing all the talking and learning nothing. She decided to keep quiet for a while.

After a bit, Dr. Reiner looked at her notes -- Margaret saw that she had quite a number of what looked like test results in her folder -- she asked whether Margaret had noticed any tremor in his hands. Margaret shook her head.

"Problems with his gait? Or a mask-like expression on his face? Incontinence?"

Margaret shrugged. "I've not seen him, you know, since July. I don't know about his face or his walking." Then she hesitated, feeling as if she were giving away family secrets. "On the night before we brought him to the hospital, he did wet the bed. He really didn't seem to know what was going on or where he was. I wondered if that might have been part of it as well."

The doctor looked at her. "Have you seen him since he came to the hospital?"

Margaret shook her head. "No, I told you. We're not really man and wife any more. My children brought him here, and they've been visiting him." There was something strange about the doctor's expression.

"Mrs. Bluestone, there are still times when your husband doesn't know what is going on or where he is. That is why I was asked to consult on this case, to evaluate what is wrong with him neurologically."

Margaret looked at her. "Well, I see you've taken a lot of tests, and you've written down some of what I've told you. So what is your diagnosis?" She'd had enough of this game.

Dr. Reiner looked down at her notes. She sighed. "At this point we just have to call it dementia."

Margaret found herself getting angry. "Could you at least give me some idea of prognosis, then? Is this, whatever it is, going to get better? Or worse?"

"There are a number of possible diagnoses, Mrs. Bluestone. The most well-known, at least these days, of course, is Alzheimer's Disease, which can last a long time. And I should tell you that one of the early symptoms of Alzheimer's is getting lost on a familiar road." As she paused to look at her notes, an invisible chill went through Margaret's body. Oh, God, please don't let it be that one.

Dr. Reiner went on. "From what you've just told me, it could be some form of Parkinson's. You're probably familiar with that."

"Yes," said Margaret, "my mother had Parkinson's. She wasn't -- well, crazy -- in the way that Henry is. And she did have a tremor. She took a medication that helped her for a long time."

"There are other forms than the one your mother probably had," said Dr. Reiner. "Your husband may have a more lethal one, which would explain both the dementia and the paranoia, and his urinary incontinence. Both kinds involve micrographia, and gait problems. By the way, it might have been the beginning of a gait problem that caused your husband to fall and break his ankle. This form of Parkinson's does not respond to the drug your mother probably took -- L-Dopa -- and its course is rapid."

Margaret could see now that Henry had been a puzzle to Dr. Reiner, an interesting one that would intrigue her until she'd figured it out. But she wasn't going to make Henry well. After a pause, she began to speak of other diseases -- small strokes, and others that she knew well enough to call by their initials. It was a long list, and the only one Margaret remembered was Diffuse Lewy Body Disease, which sounded like something that went wrong with your car, something akin to rusting out. And maybe that was what was happening to Henry.

After a bit, she stopped listening and promised herself that she would dump this whole mess, as quickly as possible, into Andrew's lap, and let him translate it for her. She, herself, had only one agenda. And that was to make sure that Dr. Reiner and the hospital understood that <u>none</u> of this was her problem. She told the doctor that if they needed any kind of authorization to perform any kind of medical procedure, they should call Henry's lawyer, who had not only power of attorney, but was also his health care proxy.

"Please," she said earnestly to Dr. Reiner, "take down this name and number." And she wrote it all out for her, and saw her put the piece of paper in the folder.

The doctor looked puzzled. "Well, of course," she said, "we would turn to the lawyer if it were ever necessary. But you have to understand that the patient is usually the person who makes these decisions. These are his 'patient's rights.' He decides what care he will accept or reject."

What the hell was she talking about? The doctor had just been telling her that Henry was probably demented. How could he make any decisions about his care?

As she left the doctor's office, she looked at her watch. It was only one o'clock. She would have a decent lunch somewhere, and then go back to the office.

* * * *

It had been just as well that she decided to return to the office. She'd had a call from Deborah Breen. Once again, Joe Breen had become furious with his wife, had slammed her head into the wall, and then rushed out of the house, but not without smashing her car with his own. Deb had called the police, and when they came to the house, they were able to persuade her, finally, to take out a restraining order.

Once she had done so, however, she began to have all kinds of doubts. She'd called Margaret and asked her, again and again, whether this was the right thing to do, whether she had any right to deprive her children of a father's love, and whether it was fair to Joe, who was, after all, a sick man, to put him out in the cold.

"Deborah," said Margaret, "he does have an illness, but this one -- the one he has -- can kill you." Deborah said nothing for a long while. "Are you still there?" said Margaret.

"I'm here," she said. "And thank you for reminding me that the important thing is for me not to deprive my children of me." Margaret knew that this was only the beginning of her figuring it out. Pretty soon, she reminded Deborah, Joe would start calling her, and sending her flowers. He would be crying. "This will be the hardest time for you. It's more difficult to stand up to flowers and tears than it is to brutality."

341

"That's true," said Deborah, after a long pause, during which she was probably remembering many bouquets of flowers. "I'll see you on Friday for our regular appointment. And thanks, Margaret. I'll probably be calling you before then."

Margaret thought about going home. The combination of Dr. Reiner and Joe Breen was just too much. It had been a long enough day as it was. She thought about the peace and quiet of her lovely house, its order, its shiny floors, and its green kitchen. She would straighten up her desk and then leave. And then the phone rang.

Oh, dear, not Deborah Breen again. But it was Paul Kosinski, Henry's lawyer.

"Oh, Paul, I was going to call you later this afternoon," she said quickly, "to bring you up to date on what happened to Henry."

"Please," he said, his voice sounding strained, "let me interrupt you. I've just had a call from Continuing Care at the hospital and they told me he'd come back to town, had become ill and is now a patient there. But, Margaret, what's important now is that they're planning to discharge him this afternoon."

"You're kidding! I was just talking to his neurologist a few hours ago, and she didn't say anything about a discharge. It sounded if as they'd be keeping him until they figured out what his diagnosis was." She paused. "Where are they sending him?"

Paul cleared his throat. "Well, that's the problem," he said slowly. "They're sending him home."

"Home? You mean to <u>my</u> house? But we're separated. How can they do that to me?"

"Well, it seems that placing him in a rehab center or a nursing home is a long-term process. I think they plan on your home as a temporary solution."

"But Paul, you have power of attorney and you are his Health Care Proxy. Don't <u>you</u> have some kind of authority? Couldn't you just say no?"

"I tried, Margaret, I really did. But they insisted on sending him home today."

"How? I'm at work. There's nobody home."

She could hear Paul sighing. "I told them I'd call you and then call them right back."

"But what if I'd been out of town?"

"Well," he said sheepishly, "you're not. I didn't know what else to do. You'll need to get some help in, that's for sure -- nurses, whatever -- until this is straightened out. Naturally, I'll pay for all that out of Henry's funds."

Margaret was speechless. What in God's name could she do?

343

Paul was speaking again. "I asked them about putting him in a nursing home and they said that it takes weeks, first of all, to get permission from the State agency to get him accepted -- anywhere."

Margaret was so angry she thought about hanging up on him. "Exactly <u>when</u> is all this supposed to happen?" Her voice was sharp, her tone bitter.

"They want to send him home in the ambulance around five o'clock. Can you be home by then? Continuing Care will be calling with instructions."

Margaret had the feeling that saying yes would be like locking herself into prison, for a term of God knows how long. But what else could she do? This man was still legally her husband, and what was more important, the father of her children. They'd probably never speak to her again if she refused to take him in now. There were still two feet of snow on the ground, and it was cold outside. And by five o'clock it would be dark. She could hardly put him out on a night like this.

Chapter Eighteen

Next to the bed where Henry lay sleeping was the rocking chair that Margaret had borrowed for the Thanksgiving weekend. Gratefully, she sank into it, and, kicking off her shoes, she began to rock, soothing herself as she tried to come to terms with what was ahead of her. Soon she realized that she was rocking to the rhythm of his labored breathing, and that the creak of the chair was adding to this strange symphony. One of his hands was twitching, and she now saw that it was the hand of an old man, with prominent veins, covered with liver spots, thin-skinned, almost fragile. His hands were what had first attracted her to him, his long tapering fingers looking so capable, so sensitive when he tapped a rock, as he carefully rescued its inner crystal. She'd wondered then what it would be like to have those hands make love to her.

And now he needed care, and nursing. Sighing heavily, he turned in bed. The blanket -- it must have belonged to the hospital -- slipped off his shoulders, revealing his wasted arms. He'd always had such beautifully sculpted muscles. Now all of that was gone. How could there have been this much change in only five months?

She looked at his hands again, at those long fingers, almost spider-like. She glanced down at her own hands. Never her best feature, short and almost plump, still tan from her sailing trip. She had a liver spot or two, but there was a look about her hands that spoke of capability, of strength. She would need all of that and more, she thought, if she were going to straighten out the mess she was in, and it wouldn't help just to sit there and rock. She needed to get on the phone and find some solutions. Or, as her grandson Matt would put it, she needed to "kick-ass."

Moving into the kitchen -- leaving the door open a crack in case Henry woke up -- she began to list people to call: Dr. Reiner at the hospital to find out why they'd decided to discharge him; Eleanor, her lawyer; Andrew, in Atlanta, who as a doctor would have more influence than she would in dealing with the hospital; Chloe, who always knew what to do; and Erik, because she missed him and couldn't understand why he hadn't called her.

Of course, when Margaret got the hospital, it turned out that Dr. Reiner had gone for the day, and it seemed that none of the doctors who were familiar with the case were available either. The nurse, obviously busy, suggested she call Social Service.

"But what am I supposed to do right now?" Margaret asked, her voice rising. "I just learned today that my former husband was being discharged to my care and to my house without my permission! You people could be sued for malpractice!"

"I'm sorry," said the nurse, a little more rattled now that the word "malpractice" had been tossed into the picture, "I'll try to reach one of the administrators and have him call you. Let me just find a piece of paper, and I'll take down your name and number." There was a silence, as she evidently went looking for a place to write all this down.

Wearily, Margaret gave her the data, but she had no sense that anything was going to happen. The little scrap of paper would undoubtedly be lost within the next hour, as the nurse became involved in other, more immediate crises.

She would have to turn this part of the process over to Andrew. But when she called their home in Atlanta, Julia explained that he hadn't yet come home from work, but she'd call him and ask him to get in touch with Margaret. Julia was horrified to hear that Henry had been "dumped" back at home, and it felt so comforting to have someone sounding sympathetic that Margaret began to cry. But she soon realized, as she heard the sound of the baby wailing in the background, that Julia wouldn't be able to do much right then, either.

Luckily she had her lawyer's home number and was able to reach her. Eleanor listened carefully as Margaret described the events of the last several days. "I can't believe it," she said finally. "They discharged him to you? And Paul let this happen?"

"Right," said Margaret. "Please, tell me what to do. He's here. In bed. Wearing a diaper." Margaret could hear her voice rising.

347

"Margaret, listen to me," said Eleanor. "I'm going to get on the phone right now and call Henry's lawyer. All this should be Paul's responsibility, not <u>your</u> problem. You have a separation agreement. I'll call you right back, whether I reach him or not."

Margaret sat by the phone, banging on the table with her fist, beginning to realize that no one was going to be able to do much at this hour. The problem was going to be hers, at least for this one night. She couldn't decide whether she was furious, or terrified -- probably a combination of both. She peeked into the room where Henry was still sleeping. Thank God, he wasn't moving. It crossed her mind that he might have died, and then she realized, at that same moment, that she was actually wishing that it could be so. Then she heard his breathing again. She heard her inner voice say: no such luck.

Perhaps she'd feel better if she could talk to Erik. She'd not heard from him since he'd left her house on Thanksgiving night. As she dialed his number, she felt a little shiver of fear: why hadn't he called her or at least dropped over to see how she was doing? It felt as if he'd abandoned her at a time when she needed all the help she could get. Finally, after many rings -- perhaps, she tried to rationalize, he'd been involved in the complicated process of helping Will get ready for bed -- he answered, sounding tentative. As she told her story, his voice was concerned, but somehow distant. She was reminded of the period when she'd been angry at him for cleaning out the barn. Now <u>he</u> was the one who was pulling back. Margaret wasn't sure just what she wanted from him; she was not asking for his help or even for advice. Maybe she just wanted him to stroke her hair and comfort her. But there was a difference in his attitude: he was not the same man who'd gone out in the snow to help Henry and the whole family.

"What's wrong, Erik?" she said, frantically. "You seem . . . well, almost angry at me."

"Margaret," he said slowly, "I don't know how to say this. But I realized the other day, when we took your husband to the hospital, that it just wouldn't be appropriate for me to be involved with you, at least not right now. Your kids, although they didn't say anything, gave off those vibes. And I think they were right." He paused, and cleared his throat. "I should have called and told you so, but I kept putting it off, maybe hoping that your situation would change."

Margaret couldn't understand anything he was saying. She noticed that he was referring to Henry as her husband. "Erik," she said. "Listen to me. I don't give a damn <u>what</u> my kids say or feel about you and me. I'm an adult, and they should behave like adults, too. I'm not going to let them dictate to me about whom I should see or what I should do. My marriage is over. I'm going to court in the middle of January for a divorce, an un-contested divorce that both Henry and I agreed to."

"Margaret," he said, with sadness in his voice. "I'm thinking of what it will be like down the road. I liked your kids and I want them to like me." He sighed. "I guess I want them to like me as much as Will likes you." There was another pause. "He talks about you all the time, and he keeps asking me why we can't all be one family. I don't want him to end up disappointed. He's had enough losses in his life."

As he was speaking, a part of her had already turned him off. She was too overwhelmed to care; it was almost as if he'd never existed. Part of her had heard what he was saying, and she'd filed it away as one little nugget of good news: he was saying he still loved her, but didn't want Will to be hurt. Wearily, she hung up the phone.

As she started to dial Chloe's number, the phone rang. It was Eleanor. "Listen, I was able to reach Paul. He said right away that he'd guarantee to pay medical expenses, whatever they would be, for Henry's care -- for a rehab center, whatever."

"That's all very well," said Margaret, realizing that she was sounding like a small child. "But what I need right now is a box of adult diapers." Tears were now filling her eyes. She wanted to tell them all, the hospital, Eric, and the whole legal profession, to go fuck themselves! What good were any of them when it came right down to a crisis?

But Chloe would understand, she decided. And quickly, she dialed again. As she'd hoped, it was as if Chloe had needed a project: she sounded ready and willing for action. "Listen, I'll come right over, and bring a box of diapers as well. Remember, I had my mother with me in the last years of her life. Before I come, however, I'm going to call Mrs. Mahoney -- you remember that wonderful nurse I had for Mother? -- and get a little advice. It's even possible she could give you some help for a few days while the experts straighten all this out." Chloe paused. "Have you had any dinner?"

Margaret looked at the clock. "I haven't even given it a thought." It was past seven.

"Well, I'll bring some. I made spinach pie tonight and there's some left over."

As she hung up the phone, for the first time Margaret felt that someone really had heard her. And suddenly she was hungry.

* * * *

Chloe arrived with a smile on her face. It was as if Margaret's crisis had given her a purpose and a task. She looked a little more like her old self. And she had good news. Mrs. Mahoney was free to come over in the morning and to help out for at least a few days if it were necessary. "So we just have to get you through the night somehow." She put down the big pink box. "And here are your diapers."

Margaret picked them up and looked at the label. She laughed out loud. "It says they're for women -- maybe that's why the box is pink."

"Oh, God," said Chloe. "I picked that box because that's what I used to buy for my mother, all those months. I wonder if there's really any difference? Let's look inside."

She ripped open the box and took out a pale pink diaper and unwrapped it. "Look," she said, "how sexist! There are ruffles on the legs." She laughed. "We'll put them on backwards. While you eat your spinach pie, I'll find some scissors and cut off the ruffles."

Margaret handed Chloe her kitchen scissors and then sat down at the table to eat her dinner. "I'm pleased to hear you using the word 'we' when you talk about changing the diaper. I would have no idea of how to do this on a grown man." There was something almost disrespectful about taking that role with a man who used to be your husband.

"Well," said Chloe, snipping away at the ruffles, "my expertise is with the other sex, but the good news is that Saul is coming over soon and he can show us how."

While Margaret continued to eat Chloe asked a few questions. "Did they give you any pills for him? Supplies?"

Margaret nodded. "Some antibiotics and one skimpy hospital blanket. He arrrived wearing a hospital johnny and a green diaper." She paused. "It seems to me I could sue them for malpractice. How could they send a patient home from the hospital practically naked? After all, he'd had pneumonia!"

"Well, first things first," said Chloe, always the practical one. "You can't sue anyone at this hour of night, and right now we'll have to make a shopping list. Saul can pick up a few things for us. Do you have a male urinal?" Margaret shook her head. "How about a baby monitor -- you know, those electronic gadgets people use to spy on their babies?"

Margaret laughed, shaking her head. She took out a pencil and paper, and wrote: urinal, monitor. "What else?" adding, on her own initiative: large plastic bags.

"We should have a few padded rubber sheets, some baby wipes, and maybe a tray for meals. No, wait a minute. I'll have Saul bring ours. Tomorrow, if it turns out he'll be here for a while, you'll need a hospital bed for this room, with sides that lock in place."

Margaret looked at Chloe with widening eyes. "It sounds as if you think he'll be here a long time." All this equipment coming in made it sound almost permanent, as if they were setting up a small hospital.

Chloe shrugged, as she dialed her own number to call Saul. "Even a few hours without basic supplies could be harrowing. I'm wondering if he needs to be tied to the bed." She spoke briefly to Saul and then turned to Margaret. "May I look at Henry?"

"Of course." Margaret stood up and led the way. Henry was still asleep but seemed to be stirring. "It all sounds like an enormous project," she whispered, becoming more horrified by the moment.

"Oh, it is," said Chloe, also lowering her voice, "like bringing home a new baby, except when that happens, you've usually had nine months to get ready."

Then the phone rang. It was Andrew. "The news is not good," he said. "In fact, I have no news. I couldn't get hold of anyone at the hospital who knew anything. If only he'd had his own doctor! I'm going to find one for him, since no one is claiming responsibility. I'll call Dr. Reiner in the morning. But Mom," he paused, "I think you're going to be stuck with him tonight at least, and maybe even a while longer. You may need to take some time off from work, or get someone in to take care of him." He paused. "Look, Mom, would it help if I came back? Maybe I could get some time off for a family emergency." His voice didn't sound too eager, and Margaret couldn't ask him to do that since he'd taken family leave when the baby was born. But she realized that if she'd insisted, he might have agreed to come.

"No, it's okay," she heard herself saying. "I ought to be able to manage a night or two. And Chloe has called her favorite nurse to come tomorrow morning. But thanks for offering. If I'm desperate, I'll call you." She heard

the doorbell ring. "I believe Saul has arrived with our medical supplies," she

said, "so I'll let you go. Good night, and thank Julia for being so

supportive."

Chloe had opened the door and taken Saul in to look at Henry. "My

God, didn't they at least put a tag on his foot?" she heard Saul say. "Even a

corpse gets that courtesy!"

The three of them went back into the kitchen and checked his purchases.

"Here, I'll set up the monitor. See, you can move the second part into any

other room you want, even upstairs." They put the rest of the supplies in

Henry's room. Then Margaret looked at Saul. He was still thin and drawn-

looking. Perhaps, like his wife, having to help with this emergency would

give him a little energy, a goal of some kind.

"Let's have some coffee," Margaret said. "I'll make it. We should relax

while we have a chance and before Henry wakes up and needs to be

changed." She smiled. "I'm already talking as if he were a baby." And then

she felt the tears start again. Dammit, why was it that whenever she got

really mad, she would start to cry?

She put the coffee pot on and got out some leftover mince pie. "I really

don't know what I'd have done without you guys," said Margaret. "It all

feels like a nightmare from which I can't wake up." She shook her head, as if to remove the images. "The last few days have had many surprises, none of them pleasant, but I think the nightmare part began with my interview this morning with the neurological consultant. Nothing has made any sense to me since then."

Saul was frowning. "What did the doctor say was really wrong with Henry -- in addition to pneumonia and a broken ankle?" he asked as he pushed his piece of pie around the plate. Margaret could see that he still wasn't eating.

She shrugged. "She said we should just call it 'dementia' but I had the feeling it might be some rare kind of Parkinson's Disease." She could feel her eyes filling again. "It doesn't really matter <u>what</u> they call it, but it's clear they've dumped the problem on <u>me</u>." Just then, she heard a strange knocking noise coming from Henry's room. She stood up, glancing at the two of them. "I think we need to check on him," she said, aware that there was pleading in her voice.

The three of them moved slowly into the room. While he still seemed to be asleep, he was thrashing around, and Margaret could see that the noise came from the banging of his cast against the wall. She looked helplessly at Saul.

"I think maybe he needs to be changed," he said with some authority.

"Wait, then," said Chloe, "I'll bring in one of the diapers I've already trimmed." She hurried back into the kitchen and emerged with a large pink diaper which she handed to Saul. With professional aplomb, he opened it up and spread it out, and then moved carefully toward Henry, turning back the blanket and lifting up his hospital johnny.

"Where are the baby wipes?" Saul asked. As he waited for Margaret to hand them to him, he reached out and touched Henry's forehead. "He does feel rather warm," he said.

"I thought so, too," said Margaret. "Thank God the hospital sent him home with some antibiotics."

Then, suddenly, Margaret felt like giggling. It was either that, she decided, or else she would burst into tears. She brought the box over to Saul and opened it up, her lips trembling on the verge of hysterical laughter. There was a moment of silence.

"First we remove the old diaper," said Saul, his tone making it seem like a lesson in a first aid class in which the patient was only a manikin. "As you see, diapers no longer require pins -- just tapes to strip back." He, too, looked as if he were stifling a giggle. Glancing at Chloe, he said, more soberly: "There but for the grace of God could be any of us one of these days. I hope that when it's my turn you two ladies will be the ones officiating."

Saul then lifted Henry's legs. "Boy, with that heavy cast, this is not easy." He frowned. "I'm not sure you could do this by yourself, Margaret." Chloe passed him the clean diaper and he slid it under Henry with his other hand. In seconds, he had everything back in place and had pulled up the blanket. Margaret took the wet diaper and dropped it into one of her new plastic bags, and then they all returned to the kitchen, this time turning off the light, closing the door and turning on the monitor.

"I think," said Margaret, "that we could all use a shot of cognac." She took three small glasses out of the cupboard and brought out the bottle. Looking at Chloe and Saul, she asked: "Does it get any easier?"

They both nodded. "It does," said Chloe. "<u>That</u> part, anyway. What's hard is when the patient is no longer the person he was."

Margaret took a last sip from her glass. "I think that's already starting to take place. A few days ago when I looked at him -- just before Thanksgiving dinner -- I felt that the real Henry had gone away, leaving just a hollow shell behind." Then she stood up. She was feeling stronger, a little more like her old self. "I think the two of you should get on home. I need to begin managing all this by myself -- at least until tomorrow morning when Mrs. Mahoney gets here. I don't know how to thank you. I don't know how you did it, but between you, you've made it possible for me to carry on." She went into the mud room and got their coats. "Don't worry about me," she said, as they seemed to hesitate. "Go, while the going is good." Then she hugged them both and shooed them out the back door.

* * * *

In spite of Saul's faith in the monitor, she didn't feel comfortable going all the way upstairs and leaving Henry asleep way in the back of the house. After changing into her warm nightgown and robe, she took her pillow and several blankets and went down to the living room to stretch out on the couch. But as soon as she lay down, she felt overwhelmed again. The blanket on her chin felt too scratchy. Her feet were cold. She began wondering if the monitor was really working: maybe she should go back into Henry's room and move it closer to him.

God damn him, anyway, she thought. Remembering so many times in the past when she, herself, was ill, had he ever worried about her in this way? And what was she so worried about? That he would fall out of bed, maybe break another bone? Or somehow wander outside into the street and get hit by a truck? Would that be so terrible? Why was she lying awake, afraid to fall asleep because "something could happen?" It all probably had to do with the kind of person she thought she was: a good person, whatever that was, who would not take advantage of this man and set things up so that he could die.

Wearily, she crept out of her little nest on the couch and tiptoed all the way to the back of the house. Using the flashlight from the kitchen, she pushed open his door and went as silently as possible toward his bed. Carefully, she picked up the monitor and moved it until it was just above his head. Then she backed out of the room and reversed her steps after closing the door.

Back on the couch, she picked up her end of the monitor, and sure enough, she could hear his raspy breathing. It was reassuring, and she was able to lie down again and to try to relax. Then, loud and clear, coming over the monitor, she could hear Henry's voice. "What the hell is going on?" he was saying, and then, more muffled: "Shit, what is this place?"

Margaret struggled to her feet. She would have to go to him. But she stood there, in the dark living room, waiting and hoping that he would go back to sleep. Perhaps he'd been dreaming. Then, loudly, and strongly, he spoke again: "Help. Please. . . Please."

Taking a deep breath and putting on her robe, she picked up her blanket and walked back to his room. He was quiet for the moment, but she decided it made more sense, for now, for her to wrap herself in the blanket and curl up in the rocking chair in the darkness. It was a wooden rocker and it had felt very comfortable a few hours ago when she was rocking in it, but now she could feel every slat on the seat, and the arms got in her way when she tried to stretch. And then Henry began to speak again.

In a frantic voice, he called out: "Where is everybody?"

Margaret decided she'd have to put on the light. He looked up at her, startled.

"Nurse," he said, obviously not recognizing her, "what the hell is going on?" He was struggling to sit up.

"Henry," she said, trying to sound calm and soothing, "don't try to sit up. You've broken your ankle."

He looked down at the cast. "Broken my ankle?" He shook his head. "Where the hell is this place?" he asked, looking around.

"You're in your own house. You're home from the hospital. You're in those old rooms that were off the kitchen -- you know, we used to call them the maids' rooms. I had it made into a guest suite." From the look on his face, she wasn't sure he understood. In fact, his face -- now that he was awake -- was strangely changed. It was as if he were wearing a mask. His eyes were wide open and staring; he seemed to have forgotten how to blink. And now he looked permanently startled, wide-eyed and suspicious, unable to move because he was so frightened.

As he continued to stare at her, she decided to simplify her explanations. Pointing to his cast again, she said: "See, you've broken your ankle. You fell down stairs. You can't walk on it yet." This time he put his hand on the cast. Perhaps he was getting it. She went on: "You've been sick, too. You had pneumonia. And now, you need lots of sleep. Can I get you some water before I turn off the light?"

He didn't answer, so she carefully switched off the lamp. For a minute or two there was silence, and then, once again, but even more urgently, he began to shout: "Please, someone, please!" He was obviously panic-stricken and frantic. She reached out to touch him, to try to soothe his anxiety, but he began to hit her and to scream: "Get me out of here, someone, please!"

She reached up and turned on the light again. This time, he was looking at her as if she were a complete stranger, and quickly, she said: "I'm Margaret, your wife. You're in your own house."

The mask that was his face changed a little and he smiled, almost craftily, and said: "Oh, sure." He looked at her carefully. "My wife is a much younger woman. This is not my house. You can't fool me." He started once again to try to get out of bed.

"What are you doing?" Margaret decided it was better to keep him talking.

"I'm going to pack," he said. "I'm getting out of here. Where's my suitcase?"

That was actually a good question. Margaret had planned that -- sometime this week, when things settled down -- she'd go out to his car, which was still parked outside in the melting snow next to the barn, and see what was in it. One glance had told her it was a complete mess, with things piled to the roof of the wagon. But she suspected some of his clothes were in there somewhere, and possibly there were also some valuable items that should be brought in the house for safekeeping, and maybe some clues as to where he'd been all that time. But all she said to Henry was: "I don't know, but maybe in the morning we could look. Right now, it's time for both of us to sleep. I'll be here in this rocking chair tonight. Let me tuck you in." Quickly, before he could object, she added her own blanket to his bedding and wished him good night. She turned out the light and went upstairs to find more blankets for herself.

By the time she'd come back down, she could hear him again, anxiously shouting: "Please, please, somebody help me." If only there were some medication she could give him to calm him down. If she didn't stay close to hand, he'd probably fall out of bed in his efforts to escape. What in God's name was she going to do? Suddenly, she understood why the relatives and caretakers of these elderly patients often felt like hitting them, screaming at them, and even killing them. It wouldn't take much for her to cross that line.

How could anyone stand this night after night? "Please, please, please," that voice kept saying.

Then she remembered Andrew. He'd said she could call. It was after midnight, but this was an emergency. Quickly, she picked up the kitchen phone, and luckily, he answered right away, probably thinking it was a call about one of his patients.

"Andrew," she said, her voice rising with hysteria, "there's something terribly wrong with your father. Every time I turn off the light, he starts raving. He seems frantic and in a panic. He doesn't know who I am or where he is and he keeps trying to get out of bed."

Andrew sighed. "You've got a sundowner," he said sadly.

"What the hell is that?" Would this nightmare never end?

"A fair number of demented patients become totally disoriented after the sun goes down, and often remain that way until sunrise. The good news is that, of course, then, they sleep for most of the day, but the nights are terrible for the family."

"What can I do? Is there any sleeping medication that would help?"

"Not that I know of. A really strong anti-anxiety drug would be the best thing, but I haven't heard of any real success with anything. My own suggestion -- it's too late for this night, but you could try it tomorrow night if he's still there -- would be to keep the lights on. Total darkness is what seems to terrify these patients." He was silent for a minute. "Mom, you may need to get a night nurse on a regular basis if this keeps up. Whatever happens, you need your sleep."

"Thank you, Andrew. At least the problem has a name -- sundowning, you say." She paused, trying to translate this whole nightmare into some kind of reality. "And there's another problem, Andrew. His face has changed, almost as if he's wearing a mask. Even his eyes are different: they're wide open and staring, as if he couldn't blink."

"You've just given a perfect description of the face of a patient with advanced Parkinson's Disease, Mom. I suspect that's part of your problem."

Then in the background, she could hear Henry, begging again for help. "I'll have to go now," she said, "it's happening again."

"Listen, Mom, I want you to let me know if it turns out he's going to be there for a while. I'll talk to Molly and Charles, maybe even Anita, and we'll try to work out some way we can all help. And try keeping on the light."

* * * *

Later Margaret decided that she must have finally gone to sleep, because she found herself awake with the sun coming in the east window, and Henry fast asleep. She had a stiff neck. Looking at her watch, she saw that it was eight o'clock; Mrs. Mahoney was due any minute.

365

She'd just finished putting on a pot of coffee when the back doorbell rang. It <u>was</u> Mrs. Mahoney. She'd been picturing and hoping for a large, comforting woman with a red, round face and bright blue eyes, and maybe a trace of a brogue, someone who would mother her as well as take care of Henry. But this woman -- the real Mrs. Mahoney -- was a small, thin, sharp-nosed person. Yet, in spite of her appearance, as soon as she opened her mouth, she was everything Margaret would want.

"Mrs. B.," she said, accepting a cup of coffee, "you don't mind if I call you that? It's just easier." Margaret shook her head. "You look as if you've had a rough night."

Margaret nodded. "My husband was frantic; I couldn't get him to settle down."

"Sundowner, I guess," said Mrs. Mahoney. "Look, why don't you go upstairs and take a good, long nap. I'll wake up Mr. B., give him a bath and get him ready for the day. When was the last time he had something to eat?"

"I really don't know. Probably yesterday noon at the hospital, if then. We changed his diaper last night around nine, so I'm sure that needs to be done again." Margaret frowned. "Saul bought a urinal for him, so you might want to try that. Maybe we don't need all these diapers."

Mrs. Mahoney shrugged, as if it were no big deal. "And we'll have to see," she said, "if he can feed himself. Then you and I can figure out what you want to do next, depending on how long he'll be here. We may want to order a hospital bed, of course."

There was that awful word again -- hospital bed -- with its implications. But Margaret understood that the nurse was just trying to be helpful, and to make things easier for all of them. "Thank you, Mrs. Mahoney. I'm already feeling as if he'll be in the hands of an expert, and I'm so grateful that you've agreed to help out right now."

Mrs. Mahoney looked uneasy. "Did Chloe tell you that I don't have a lot of time to give you? I'm leaving in three weeks to visit my sister in California for Christmas."

Margaret's heart sank. But maybe the problem would be solved by then.

* * * *

Later in the morning, there were several calls. The first was from Margaret's lawyer.

She'd been looking into the possibility of a nursing home for Henry, and had discovered that, before he could be accepted anywhere, a team of nurses would have to interview him and Margaret to discover if such a placement were medically necessary.

"But what if we were divorced by that time?" Margaret asked.

367

"This would not be the first case where the divorced spouse took responsibility for a demented partner," Eleanor said. Oh, Jesus, thought Margaret. Till death do you part?

The second call was from Molly who offered to come for the weekend to help. And then Charles said he'd be able to come for the whole Christmas vacation, since the kids would be spending the holiday with their mother in Florida. Andrew must have got in touch with both of them. And by late afternoon, Margaret had finally found a nursing agency who would send in a night nurse beginning the next day, but not for the weekend.

The only person she hadn't heard from was Anita, but perhaps no one had called her to tell her what was going on. Anita would probably say that it was Margaret's duty to take care of Henry, no matter what. How strange it would be if it turned out that she actually had no choice, that State regulations would require her to take on this burden.

She should probably call Anita right now, but as she looked out of the window, she saw that there was a magnificent winter sunset, the deep reds and oranges staining what was left of the snowstorm. Under normal conditions, such an event would lead her to open the front door and stand on her new little front porch to enjoy the spectacle. But now, the going down of the sun had other portents: Mrs. Mahoney had left for the day, and she was once again in full charge of Henry. Would this moment mark the beginning of another night of horror?

She needed to go in and talk to him. She told herself that they'd not really had a chance to exchange remarks that day. But, she thought, in all honesty, she didn't particularly want to talk to him. He wasn't the real Henry anymore. Hesitantly, she moved through the house, but as she turned on the lights in the various rooms, she realized that probably his room was getting dark. She hurried now, hoping that the magic of turning on a switch would make all the difference.

And then she heard the dreaded words: "Please, someone, please, please, please."

Chapter Nineteen

Months later, long after that December was over, Margaret would try to remember just when and how she'd made the important decisions that were to affect her life. Things just seemed to happen on their own, each occurrence like the odd-shaped stones in an old stone wall, each one supporting the next, and becoming thereby inevitable.

The first of these events was the house call, on Wednesday afternoon, just two days after Henry's arrival back in the house, by Andrew's friend and fellow medical student, Dr. William Pennypacker. A tall, serious young man, who looked barely old enough to carry a stethoscope, he told Margaret -- in his Brahmin prep-school voice -- that he'd just opened up his practice as an internist, and was planning to specialize in the care of elderly patients.

Margaret brought him into the sick room, explaining to Henry that this doctor had gone to school with Andrew. Henry had evidently been dozing but he opened his eyes wide and looked up at the man. After the doctor had seated himself in the chair next to Henry's bed, Margaret told them she'd leave them alone and went back to the kitchen to share a cup of tea with Mrs. Mahoney. Through the partially closed door she could hear Dr. Pennypacker's clipped tones and Henry's murmured answers. For a few minutes, she felt as if she was off the hook: someone else was at least temporarily in charge. Stretching out her legs, she sighed deeply.

"Not easy, is it?" said Mrs. Mahoney. She set her cup down and looked sharply at Margaret. "Mrs. B, I bet that husband of yours was a piece of work before he got sick."

Margaret smiled. "A real piece of work," she said. "And one of the things he hated most was sickness. If he were in his right mind now, he'd be so upset at having other people take care of him. He never went to a doctor in his life; I just hope he'll let this fellow examine him." She looked up at the nurse. "Does he let you do for him?"

Mrs. Mahoney nodded. "But I just keep jabbering at him all the time, talking about this and that. Sometimes I think he knows perfectly well that I'm changing his diaper, or whatever, and that he's playing a game, too." She paused. "But other times, -- I don't know -- I get the feeling he doesn't know where he is or why, or even who I am."

Then the doctor came out of the room and suggested to Margaret that they go into the living room to talk. Dr. Pennypacker leaned forward in the easy chair. "Mrs. Bluestone, you've got a complicated situation here." He took out a little notebook. "I'd like to begin -- before we talk about the future -- to make some suggestions as to what we can do to make things easier for all of you right now." He took a deep breath. "To begin with, you need a hospital bed; I'll call the medical supply store right now to order it for you, and maybe they can bring it out this afternoon. Otherwise, I'm

371

afraid Mr. Bluestone will try to get up: he could have a nasty fall. And he needs to stay on that antibiotic -- there are still noises in his chest and he's got a low grade fever." He paused, clearing his throat. "Andrew told me he has been sundowning; is that right?"

Margaret nodded. "Yes, is there anything you can do about that?"

"We can try him on some anti-anxiety medication, and maybe combine that with a pain-killer. That ankle may be hurting him, too. The pills come in suppository form as well." He looked at his watch. "I suspect all of this could be here this afternoon." He picked up the phone and quickly placed his orders. Sighing, he looked directly at Margaret again. "The broken ankle and the pneumonia will heal, I'm sure, but he appears to have a form of Parkinson's Disease -- alas, the kind for which L-Dopa is of no benefit -- plus some serious dementia, that includes some confabulation -- making up stories to explain things he's forgotten. For instance, when I asked him about his trip West, he was evasive, but came up with a tale about his journey that was almost believable, but some parts of it didn't ring true." He shook his head, admiringly.

Margaret smiled. Even though Henry was evidently losing his mind, he was doing it in his own unique way. "But doctor," she said, "What about a nursing home? I really can't manage to take care of him at home. I'm sure

Andrew must have told you that Henry and I are separated and planning to be divorced."

The doctor took a deep breath. "I'm afraid that the Commonwealth of Massachusetts, which now has the power to approve or reject all nursing home placements, will be the final authority about where Mr. Bluestone can be taken care of." He stood up. "But I plan to talk to the neurologist. Maybe she can help us." He smiled at her. "I'll be back in a few days to see him, unless I hear from you that you've made some other arrangement. Please feel free to call me." He gave her his card.

As Margaret closed the door on him, she walked back into her house, her feet dragging, her spirits drooping. She tried to tell herself that she was better off than she'd been this morning. At least, there'd be medications she could give Henry, and perhaps one of them would make this coming night a little better. Something Dr. Pennypacker had said about family had jogged her memory: in all the confusion, she'd never called Henry's sister Rosa to bring her up to date. At least she could give her a tentative diagnosis: Parkinson's Disease with Dementia.

There was no way to soften the blow. Margaret explained what had been happening. Rosa listened very carefully and sympathetically, sighing and making consoling noises. When Margaret had finally finished her story, Rosa's first words were supportive.

"What can I do to help?" she said. And then interrupted herself: "My God, this is my baby brother we're talking about, the kid I took care of for many years when my parents were walking the picket line. And now, here I am -- ten years older than he -- still offering to help take care of him." She paused. "And it doesn't make much sense for <u>you</u> to be taking care of him, either. You two are supposed to be getting divorced! Why can't you put him in a nursing home?"

"The doctor's not too encouraging about that possibility," said Margaret, "but I'm going to look into the regulations, myself. It seems the State makes the initial decision."

"You know," said Rosa, "I'm really not surprised at your news. When he was staying with us last summer, both George and I thought he was certainly not himself. He was fine when we talked about our childhood, but when we asked him about the trip from home, or his plans for going West, he was pretty vague. In fact, I had the feeling he was making up a lot of what he said." She sighed. "Oh, dear. Now tell me what I can do, if anything."

"I'll probably be calling on you for some weekend help. Molly will be here this Friday, and Charles may be able to come over the holidays, but I can't get night-nursing help on the weekends. If you can, I'd suggest both you and George should come. It's not a one-person job." As she said these words, Margaret realized she was about to cry. "Thanks, Rosa," she said, putting down the phone and starting to sob.

The arrival of the hospital bed did not cheer her up, either. Its very size and complexity did indeed make it seem like a permanent addition to the house. But Mrs. Mahoney was pleased and was able to convince the delivery men that they should help her move Henry from his old bed into this new one. But for Margaret, the bed felt like one more inexorable stone in the wall that someone was building around her.

* * * *

As long as she had Mrs. Mahoney on hand to deal with Henry, Margaret didn't have to spend much time with him during the daytime. The nights, even with the help of the nurse who was there from ll P.M. until 7 A.M., were something else again. The man she saw during those early evening hours was a complete stranger, a frightening intruder who'd forced his way into her life.

On Wednesday evening, he'd started again with his "please, please, please," but when she couldn't figure out what he wanted, he became more demanding, saying "do it now!" over and over. When she leaned over his bed to ask what he meant, he grabbed her by the throat. It was as if he were Dracula, and needed her blood to survive.

In spite of his various illnesses, he was still very strong, and in order to free herself she found herself pushing his chest and screaming back at him, "You're killing me." She threw herself into the chair to catch her breath. Even though he was in a hospital bed with the sides up, she was frightened. He was draining her, if not of her blood, then of her capacity for sympathy. She stood up and went to the door of his room. "Henry," she shouted, "I'm going into the kitchen to have my supper, and I'm not coming back in there until you calm down. And there's no point in your yelling, because I'm going to turn off this fucking monitor and have some peace."

It was more easily said than done. Even with the monitor turned off, she could hear him, first screaming, and then muttering, over and over: "please do it, please do it." Well, she told herself, he was a polite vampire, anyway: he never forgets to say please!

Sitting over her supper -- left-over, cold meat loaf that Chloe had sent over -- she tried to imagine what it was that Henry wanted. Probably he didn't know himself, so there was no point in asking him.

She knew that she was avoiding being alone with him, partly because he seemed to save all his angry words for her. Mrs. Mahoney and Dr. Pennypacker handled him better. Finally, on the Friday morning of that first week -- following another bad night on Thursday -- she made up her mind to go into his room and talk with him.

Assured by Mrs. Mahoney that he was awake and able to converse, she moved slowly into his room, feeling a combination of uncertainty, fear, and underneath it all, fury. The bed had been cranked up and he was reclining; he seemed to be aware that she was present. She was pretty sure that he had no memory of his nighttime behavior.

"Good morning, Henry," she said tentatively, trying to put some cheer into her voice, and realizing that it all sounded very artificial. "How are you feeling?"

In spite of the mask that now governed the expression on his face, a spark of the old Henry was still there -- inside -- because he answered, although in a muffled voice: "How the hell do I know? I'm stuck here in this goddamn bed, and can't even get out to take a leak!"

"Well, Henry," she said, trying to sound soothing and reasonable, "as soon as your ankle heals, maybe you can begin to walk again. You've still got pneumonia, of course." She stopped, wondering what to say next, something cheerful to promise him. If Dr. Pennypacker was right, there wasn't going to be too much to look forward to. Then she thought of one cheerful thing: "Molly will be here tonight, Henry. She's flying up from Philadelphia."

"Molly?" he said, almost as if the name of his younger daughter meant nothing to him, his expressionless face giving out no clues. But then he

377

smiled a vapid grin, like someone at a cocktail party who had forgotten where he had known the person he was talking to, and said, "That's nice." His voice was raspy. She wondered how she could help him understand that they were talking about his own child. She'd have to warn Molly not to expect much from him. Henry might not even recognize her. And then she had a thought. Henry was not wearing his glasses; in fact, she hadn't seen those glasses since he'd come home from the hospital. Where could they be?

She left the room: a short visit was about all she could stand. The walls were closing in. Henry was not going to get well, the old irascible, cantankerous bastard! While there was still a touch of that former self, the new Henry was a fragile, persistent burden, who had become entrenched in her life and house.

* * * *

Margaret had decided to wait until Molly's arrival before she called Anita. And because she didn't dare leave Henry to meet her at the airport, she'd told Molly to take a cab. The sun would be down by the time she got to the house, but Margaret had decided to keep the lights on in the early evening, hoping that, when Molly arrived, Henry would be able to recognize her and understand that she was his daughter. She was also able to convince him to take one of the anti-anxiety pills, telling him that it was a pain-reliever. While she waited for the cab to arrive, she found herself pacing --

first, into the living room, then all the way back to Henry's room, reminding him that Molly was coming soon, and then back again into the front part of the house, peering out the oval window of her new Victorian door.

A bright yellow taxi pulled up, and Molly came up the steps. Margaret burst out crying. "Molly, I'm sorry. I didn't mean to do this. I'm so glad to see you, so relieved that someone else in the family is here: I must have been storing up these tears." Molly reached out to hug her Mom. "You're probably thinking that help has arrived, but don't count on me for any skills. You'll have to show me what to do." Molly, looking a little scared, was still very much the young financial advisor in her light blue suit and pink scarf, and she brought a breath of the outside world into Margaret's life. She'd been dragging around in sweat pants and an old pullover for almost a week.

"Come on inside, and get settled," she said to Molly. "You'll want to change your clothes. Did you have dinner?"

"Well, a sort of snack on the plane. Can I see Dad, first? Before he goes to sleep?"

"Oh, Molly. He doesn't sleep -- he's what they call a sundowner. As soon as it gets dark, he gets frantic. I've left the lights on in his room, however, in the hope that he'll still think it's daytime -- Andrew's suggestion." As Molly began to move toward the back of the house,

Margaret stopped her. "But, Molly, I should warn you. At this time of night, especially, he may not know you. I'm not even sure he knows me."

Henry was propped up in bed, staring at the two of them as they came into the room. His eyes were wide open, his face, pale and thinner, was wearing the new mask. She could feel Molly's arm tighten on hers as she spoke. "Oh, Daddy, it's so good to see you." She bent over him and kissed his cheek.

In a stilted, mechanical voice, hoarse now and muffled, Henry said: "So, our paths cross again!" What a strange thing to say to his own daughter, Margaret thought, but trust Henry to come up with a phrase that could cover almost any social situation involving people he may have forgotten. Glancing at Molly, Margaret saw her swallow and clear her throat as she was evidently trying to think how to talk to her father. Oh, God, Margaret thought, it gets worse every day.

"I'll be spending the weekend, Dad," she said finally. "Tomorrow, we'll have a long talk and I'll tell you all about my wedding."

"You got married?" Henry said, with formality. "Congratulations." Obviously, thought Margaret, he had no idea to whom he was speaking.

Molly looked stricken. "No, Daddy, not quite yet. The wedding will be in February. I'm hoping you'll be well enough to come."

"Come, Molly, I'll help you unpack and you can change into something more comfortable. We'll see you later, Henry," she said, noticing that Molly was on the verge of tears. Margaret remembered Molly's words just last week, during the family meeting, that there was nothing wrong with her Dad's mind, that he was one of the brightest men she'd ever known. Seeing the Henry of today must have been a real shock.

* * * *

After Molly had been settled in her old room and changed to jeans and a sweater, she and her mother sat down in the kitchen for a cup of tea and some cookies. Molly sat with her head in her hands. "I had no idea, Mom, that it was this bad." Her eyes were full of tears. "You were right; he didn't know me." She laughed, with some bitterness in her voice. "But he did a pretty good job faking it!" Margaret also heard some pride in her tone.

"That, too, is part of his illness, so the doctor said. But cheer up. He'll appear much better in the morning. I'm pretty sure he'll know you then."

"So, Mom," said Molly, her voice sounding frantic, "what are you going to do? You stayed out of work this week, but then what?"

"Well, I'll have Mrs. Mahoney all next week, so I'm planning to go in to the office part time. Mrs. M will be here the first three days of the following week, and then Charles is coming, to spend the whole Christmas vacation. The kids will be with Elena in Florida. So I'll take it a day at a time."

"How about next weekend? Do you want me to come back?"

"Let's decide later. Your Aunt Rosa is available, too. I actually need you, my financial expert," -- she smiled to think that this child was a professional financial advisor -- "to help me now to make some more long-range decisions." She stood up and went over to the kitchen desk for some paper and a pencil. "I'd like to figure out some comparative costs." She handed the pencil to Molly and put the paper in front of them. She began to explain to Molly what it was costing her to have a trained nurse -- like Mrs. Mahoney -- here in the daytime for five days a week, so that she could go to work and feel confident that Henry was getting good care. The night nurse, also available only Monday through Friday, was a nurse's aide, and somewhat cheaper; she was here while Margaret was upstairs asleep, from eleven P.M. till seven A.M. The evenings -- the four-to-eleven shift -- she could handle herself. And she was planning to keep the night nurse, Monday through Friday, during the time that Charles was here -- the two weeks of Christmas vacation. But if, God forbid, Henry was still in the house after the holidays, she'd have to go back to something like what she was doing now.

Molly sat there, adding the figures. "And all this will be paid for out of Dad's money, is that correct?"

"Right. His lawyer has said there will be no problem in paying for these nurses. The real problem is what happens in the long run. You probably know better than I what a nursing home would cost. Maybe we should compare these two sets of figures."

"I can tell you, from my clients' experiences, that they come out pretty much the same," said Molly. "But, of course, a nursing home would make your life a lot easier. You wouldn't have the weekends to worry about, nor these long evenings. And also, there are times when the nurses don't show up, for one reason or another, and then you're stuck." She looked at her mother quizzically.

"The truth is, Molly, that in Massachusetts -- maybe now in other states, too -- you can't just park your relative in a nursing home, even if you're a millionaire. The State has to agree that he needs that kind of care and couldn't get it at home. Your father's new doctor, Dr. Pennypacker -- Andrew's friend from medical school -- doesn't seem to think we have much of a chance getting him into one of those places. The lawyer is supposed to be calling around, to rehabs and other institutions, but he hasn't called me back. Something tells me your dad will just end up here, unless a miracle happens."

Molly looked at her with wide eyes. "But Mom, you're supposed to be getting a divorce -- when is it? -- next month, I think you said, January 15th.

383

How can anyone expect you to take responsibility for someone you're no longer married to?"

Margaret's laugh was short and bitter. "You know what my lawyer said when I asked her that? She said: 'this would not be the first time a divorced woman had to take care of a demented spouse.'"

"Jesus," said Molly, her face falling.

"And either way, Molly, if our figures are right, this is going to be a very expensive proposition. It will very quickly use up his capital, the money the lawyer said would go to the four of you on his death." There was a long silence. Then Margaret spoke again. "Of course, there's another solution. I could take a leave from work -- under the family leave policy -- and take care of him myself, until . . .whatever happens. And from what the doctor has implied, that might not be such a long time, after all."

Molly looked at her. "Mom," she said, putting her hand on her mother's arm, "no! We can't let you do that."

"It's the last thing I want to do, Molly. I can't tell you," she said, and realized that she was now shouting, "how angry I am that this situation has developed: the world seems to be expecting me to take on the burden of a man who was cruel to me, especially when I was sick, a man who left me after over forty years, without a backward glance." She glanced at Molly who looked astonished. "I'm not mad at you; you know that."

In the silence that followed, Margaret got up and rustled around in the cupboard. She was looking for cookies, and she wanted to hide her tears. "Here," she said, "Chloe made these. You probably remember them from your childhood. Kourambiedes -- Greek butter cookies." She stuffed one into her own mouth.

Molly bit into one of the round, powdery cookies. "Oh, God, I do remember these!"

She smiled, and her face relaxed into its usual warm, pink roundness.

Then there was a clicking noise coming from the monitor. Margaret put up one hand. "Listen," she said, "I hope we're not in for one of those awful nights. I gave him some of that anti-anxiety medication." The noise continued, like a crackling.

And then Henry spoke: "I need my goddamn suitcase. Where the hell is it?"

Molly looked puzzled. "What is he talking about?"

"He doesn't know where he is, and he's decided it's time to go. He wants to pack and get out of here. He was asking for that suitcase the other night as well." She sighed. "I'd better go in to him." She got up, feeling stiff, her whole body resisting the idea.

"I'll come, too," said Molly. "I've got to learn how to handle him. Maybe tonight, we should take shifts, like nurses, or watches, like sailors on a ship. Four hours on, and four hours off." She stood up, ready for the challenge, but from the tremble in her voice, she was clearly frightened underneath.

They moved into Henry's room. There was a bad odor. "Oh, shit," said Margaret. "He needs to be changed. There's no reason for <u>you</u> to have to be involved in this part of it," she told Molly. "You're his <u>daughter</u>."

"But this is a job for two people. Have you ever done it by yourself before?"

Margaret shook her head, reaching for the baby wipes and a clean diaper. "No, but I'd better start learning. Go in the kitchen, Molly." She tried to speak firmly.

Molly said quietly: "I suspect this is what they had in mind when they put those words -- for better or worse -- in the wedding ceremony. This part is probably the 'worse.' Move over, Mom, and I'll hold up the leg with the cast."

With Henry cursing and using every four-letter word he knew, they did the job together, working as a team. As soon as they'd finished, he calmed down and went right back to sleep. They went into the bathroom and washed their hands together, like a couple of surgeons who had just performed some delicate operation.

"You're right, Molly, we should take shifts. Why don't you go up to bed now and I'll sit here and read. I promise you I'll call you at -- she looked at her watch -- 2 A.M., four hours from now. And then you can take, you should pardon the expression, the graveyard shift."

"Okay, Mom, I'll do that, but only if you promise me two things: that you'll really wake me at 2, and that if you need me before that, you'll let me know. And I'll do the same for you."

Margaret nodded. She reached over and kissed Molly goodnight. "I'll never forget this night," she said. She paused. "And now we have just one more hard thing to do tomorrow. We'll have to call Anita. I've been waiting until you got here."

* * * *

When they finally reached Anita at noon the next day, she was, of course, twice as angry, when she learned that Molly was there on the spot, and she was 3000 miles away.

And it didn't take Anita long to catch on that, once again, she was the last to know. As Margaret tried to explain that they were all so busy, so involved with trying to find solutions, she saw that Molly was becoming impatient. "Let me have the phone," she said, taking it from Margaret. "Anita, none of us really had any idea how bad the situation was. I think Mom was trying to spare us, hoping that things would improve and we'd never have to know the worst. But now that I see what's happening here, I wanted you to know." Molly stopped to catch her breath. Watching her face, Margaret saw that Anita had begun her tirade again. She wondered if she should go into the study and pick up the other phone, but perhaps she was better off <u>not</u> hearing what Anita was saying. Molly was now holding the telephone several inches away from her ear.

"Anita," Molly said finally, "would you shut the fuck up and listen. You have no idea what's going on here, and what it's like for Mom. What happened twenty years ago is neither here nor there. Dad has <u>dementia</u>, for God's sake. He's out of his mind! And he's wearing diapers!"

Margaret took the phone again. "Anita," she said calmly, as if she were talking down a two-year old with a temper tantrum, "let's talk about where we all are <u>now</u>." As she spoke, she was aware that her stomach was tied in knots; what was there about this child that she still had the power to do this to her mother?

Anita continued her torrent of words. "And now <u>nurse Molly</u> is on the scene, taking care of her Daddy, while I'm out here in Seattle!"

"Anita, I wish you were here, too. You can't be a back-seat driver from 3000 miles away. And this is a job that takes more than two of us. In fact," she said, suddenly inspired, "I could use your help <u>next</u> weekend, when I'll be all alone here. The night nurse isn't with us on weekends. Could you come next Friday by any chance?"

Being asked to help seemed to calm Anita down, but she was still sulking. "I wish you'd asked me about this several days ago," she said. "Now I'll have to try to find someone to trade days with me, because I'm on duty next weekend. Working for the weather bureau, as you know, is a seven-day-a week job."

"Well, at this point, taking care of your father is also a full-time job, but it's twenty-four hours a day," said Margaret. "I wish you could come. It would mean a lot to him." There was a long silence.

"I'll see what I can do," said Anita, in a softer voice. "I'll call you back as soon as I get it organized. Maybe I could take the day flight on Friday, so I won't be so exhausted." As Margaret hung up, she made a thumbs up sign to Molly.

"I'm sorry," her mother said, "that you had to hear all that. Half the time, I don't think Anita knows what she's saying."

"Don't worry about me," said Molly laughing. "I grew up with her -- remember? I learned to ignore her when it got too bad, and just go about my business." She sighed. "But I feel bad for her sometimes: she gets in her own way." She was quiet for a minute, then looked up. "But she does have a nice boyfriend, doesn't she? I really liked that Everett. I wonder why they don't get married?"

Margaret shrugged. "Maybe it works well because they're <u>not</u> married. Who knows?"

* * * *

On Monday morning, Margaret went back to work. The very act of driving there, being able to wear "grownup" clothes, a suit, pearls, and a soft white blouse, made her feel like herself again. At the same time, she realized she must have told Mrs. Mahoney, over and over, that she should call her if anything came up. Mrs. Mahoney smiled, and gently pushed her out the door. "Go," she said, "Trust me. Mr. B. knows me now, and I can handle him."

Before she saw any clients, she went in to talk to Brian, her boss. "I wish I could tell you about my schedule," she said, "but I'm not sure what my situation will be on a day-to-day basis."

Quickly, Brian said: "Listen, Margaret, you've been here a long time. Whatever you need -- sick leave, vacation, leave without pay -- you're certainly entitled to it."

The rest of the day was a combination of paper-work catch-up and arranging to see the clients who were most in crisis. The secretary had, in fact, greeted her with the statement: "Whatever you do today, you've got to call Deborah Breen. She's been calling every day." As it turned out, in spite of the restraining order she'd taken out, Deb had allowed Joe to come for Thanksgiving dinner, a big mistake, as it turned out.

* * * *

It was just a little before four on Friday when Mrs. Mahoney called up the stairs to say that Anita had arrived. When Margaret came down she found Anita already talking to her father, and Mrs. Mahoney in his room, too, but putting on her coat.

"You two have introduced yourselves, I assume," said Margaret, watching Henry out of the corner of her eye. It was difficult to tell whether he knew what was going on.

"Sure did," said Mrs. M. "I'd a known this was Mr. B.'s daughter, all right. Spittin' image of him, that's the truth -- the two of them, both long drinks of water."

Anita looked pleased, as she always did when people pointed out the resemblance, and Margaret quickly took advantage of the mood by adding: "She's her Daddy's girl, too, always was." She reached up to hug her. Then she remembered that earlier in the week, she'd started to clean out Henry's car and had found his glasses on the dashboard. "Here, let's put on your glasses so you can really see her." Awkwardly, she fitted them over his ears, but he continued to stare at Anita as if he couldn't figure out what she was doing there.

"Anita," he said, proudly.

Margaret sighed. "He recognizes you now," she said to Anita. But Anita was also staring at Henry. Clearly, she was not prepared for the change in him. Then she saw that Anita was twisting a lock of hair. "Henry, "she said to her husband, "I think Anita's having some jet lag and probably needs a nap. We'll be in to see you at supper-time," she added, taking Anita by the arm and leading her into the kitchen. Anita did not protest, but allowed herself to be steered out of the room.

Much later, after Anita had napped for two hours, she and her mother were in the kitchen, putting together a light supper for themselves. As they worked together, Margaret began to talk about Henry, what the doctor had said, what the days were like, and particularly, the problem of sundowning. On the weekend, without the night nurse, she said: "I'll really need your help."

Anita was silent, obviously thinking it over. After a bit, she said: "Mom, what are the long-range implications of all this? You can't keep it up, week after week," she said at last, evidently beginning to get the idea of what had been happening.

Margaret put her head in her hands. "I don't know. The doctor says that we probably won't be able to put him in a nursing home, even if we wanted to, at least not now." She paused, realizing that Anita was mulling this all over. "I hate to think of spending all your father's money on nursing care. I know he'd rather the money went to you four kids. That's how he's set up his will. It turns out that the cost is just about the same: full-time (or two shifts, as I have it now) nurses in the home, or nursing home care."

"I don't suppose we could all take turns," said Anita, after a long silence, "coming up here to help, taking time off from work. . ." her voice trailing off. "As you pointed out at Thanksgiving, all of us have complicated lives."

"No," said Margaret, "none of you can do very much, although everyone has offered. Charles will be up for two weeks around Christmas, and your Aunt Rosa could put in some time. But, the bottom line . . . is me." And then her eyes filled with tears. "I could consider taking care of him until the divorce; I see no other solution."

The two women sat, eating a simple soup and salad supper, no longer enemies, but colleagues in misery and sadness. Someone out there was building a stone wall around her. The various stones were falling into place: the doctor's diagnosis, the lawyer's inability to find another place for Henry, the State's regulations that he couldn't get into a nursing home, and finally,

393

her children's conviction, especially Anita's, that their father shouldn't be put out into the cold.

Chapter Twenty

On the Monday morning of Mrs. Mahoney's last week Margaret had several cancellations, so there was time to make a few phone calls, to find out what the possibilities were for getting Henry into a nursing home. Why am I so anxious? she asked herself, phone in hand. If she were calling on behalf of a client, she'd have no trouble at all. Always a good advocate for others, she'd actually enjoyed that part of her job. But when the request had to do with her own needs, she found herself tongue-tied.

After several tries, she finally got the right person. Explaining that her husband was sick and might need a nursing home, Margaret said she wanted to find out about the regulations governing possible admission. She was told that she needed to call her local Elder Affairs office and request a visit from the Long Term Care Screening Team. Two nurse-practitioners would come to her house to interview her and the patient, and then talk to the attending physicians. An Occupational Therapist would survey the layout of the house, and then the whole team would make an assessment of the need. They could decide that, with extra help, the patient could do better at home, or in another setting.

Margaret felt a chill. What if that happened in Henry's case, that the "team" would decide that he was well-cared for at home and didn't need a nursing home? She would be stuck with him until he died. The very idea was like a prison sentence, possibly a life sentence, she thought, shuddering. "Could they make that decision even if the family was willing to pay the full cost?" she asked.

"They could indeed," the official told her. "The problem is: what happens when the money runs out? Sooner or later, if the patient lives long enough, the money could be gone. Nursing homes don't want to start the Medicaid application at that point, and this system provides what is called Prior Approval. It assures that Medicaid can legitimately take over when that time comes, without having to move the patient."

Margaret sighed. "How long does all this take?" There was weariness in her voice.

"Well, it could be a month or more. First you have to get an appointment with the Team, and depending on how busy they are, that could take some time. Then they have to talk to the doctors. If the team approves the need, of course, the family has to find a nursing home that can take him." The official paused, hesitating, and then added: "Of course, you could apply for a few days of Respite Care in the meantime. Sometimes there's a last-minute cancellation, and you might be able to get a respite bed for your husband at the local center. Just call our number and ask for Respite."

Margaret hung up the phone and sat there, trying to put it all together. Respite, she thought, God knows she needed it. Then she got a call from Dr.

Pennypacker, reminding her that Henry had a follow-up appointment with Dr. Everson, the orthopedist, for the day after Christmas. When she talked to the receptionist, she found out that she'd need to get a wheelchair to take him to the hospital. That meant a call to her lawyer; Eleanor promised to arrange it right away.

* * * *

Thursday was Mrs. Mahoney's last day. When Margaret arrived at her office that morning, the secretary reminded her that the clinic would close at noon, a custom that allowed its employees to take a half day for Christmas shopping. Thanks to catalogs, most of her shopping for her far-off relatives was done, but she did want to go to a fancy toy store to pick out something for her newest grandchild. Later, browsing about the shop, she found a crib mobile for Duncan, and arranged to have it sent. Feeling for the first time in weeks that she had all the time in the world, she moved slowly among the toys and games. Then she spotted a lovely ivory-colored Domino set, with bright red, blue, yellow and purple dots, all the colors of the rainbow. It would make a wonderful present for Erik's son Will who, she remembered, had enjoyed the Monopoly game on Thanksgiving Day at her house and who, although hampered in his ability to speak, had a good sense of numbers. Before she could change her mind, she'd bought it and had it gift-wrapped for Christmas.

Drifting out of the busy Mall, she wondered what she should do next. What a luxury a few hours of free time had become! It felt so good to be standing in the parking lot, and to know that no one knew where she was. Maybe she should drop off Will's present at Erik's house. Looking at her watch, she calculated that the boy would still be in school -- until 3:30, she recalled. She and Erik hadn't talked since shortly after Thanksgiving, and that had been a rather unproductive conversation, to say the least.

But even as she mulled over these thoughts, she saw that she was driving in the direction of his house. His red pickup truck was there. He was home. Carefully, she got out of the car, and carrying Will's gift before her like an offering, she climbed up the brick steps and rang the bell, licking her lips. Her heart was beating fast.

Then Erik opened the door. "Maggie," he said, and then he stood there, just looking at her, with a question in his face. But there was a hint of a smile, too.

"I've brought a little present for Will," she said, thrusting it at him as she moved into the house. Carefully, he put it down on the hall table and gathered her in his arms. She began to cry. "Don't make me go," she said. "Don't abandon me. I couldn't stand it." He took out his handkerchief and began to wipe her face. Through her tears, she could see his warm brown eyes, concerned and wet as well, his sandy-gray hair flopping down over his forehead, and she could feel the soft scratchiness of his beard against her cheek. For the first time in weeks -- since the day before Thanksgiving -- she felt safe, and as if someone would be there for <u>her</u> if she needed help.

"Let me get us some brandy," he said. "You look as if you could use it." Taking her coat, he settled her on the couch. While she waited, she looked up at his Christmas tree. It was decorated with crude ornaments, obviously made by Will with a little help from his father. Reaching out, she touched, first, a lop-sided red paper star, sprinkled with gold spangles, and then she pulled on a silver paper chain. Overwhelmed by both her own responsibilities and now by Erik's, she started to cry again.

Erik came back into the room with two glasses and a squat brown bottle. "More tears?" he asked, putting his arm around her.

She pointed to the tree. "It was those ornaments," she said. "Will made them."

He began stroking her hair. "I think we're a lot alike: we spend our days taking care of people who depend on us, and worrying about them." He sighed deeply. "We need to take care of ourselves sometimes, Maggie, and make each other a priority."

Margaret nodded. "Isn't there some way," she asked, "when we could have a few moments -- like now -- in which our kids, or Henry, don't have to be involved? When we can just be together? Can't we just put off planning for the future and take some time for ourselves?" She sniffled. "Please don't abandon me," she said, almost angrily.

"I won't," he said. "I promise. And don't let me get away with making unilateral decisions that involve the two of us," he said, putting his arms around her. "I'm so impressed that you had the guts to fight for us, to come here today. You're right. We need to take some time for ourselves -- right now." He looked at the kitchen clock.

"When do you have to leave to pick up Will?" she whispered.

Later, driving home in a warm daze, she wondered how much stored-up anger had fueled the afternoon's passion.

* * * *

The next morning, Mrs. Mahoney was gone, but not before a tearful Margaret had extracted a promise from her that she'd try to be available to escort Henry to Molly's wedding on February fifteenth, even if he were in a nursing home by then.

On Friday morning, on her own with Henry once again, she was able to tell him that their son Charles would be arriving that afternoon to spend the Christmas holiday with them. Henry actually smiled and then asked, clearly but slowly: "Kids coming, too?" Margaret was relieved that he remembered them and associated them with Charles.

She shook her head. "No, they're going to visit their mother -- Elena -- in Florida."

She paused, wondering how much he could take in, but decided to go ahead. "Charles and Elena are getting a divorce." She hesitated. "Like us. Like you and me. We're going to Court to get a divorce in a few weeks. We decided, you and I, before you took your long trip, that it would be a good idea." It was difficult to tell whether he understood what she was saying. He seemed to be thinking it over.

"Paul. . . will. . . help. . . me," he said, with a small gap between each word.

"That's right. We all have to go see a judge. After that we'll be divorced."

There was a long silence. He looked pale and exhausted. He'd been sitting up all morning. "Would you like to lie down now?" she asked. Henry nodded, and she cranked down the bed. Suddenly, it crossed her mind that she should kiss him goodnight, a little peck on the cheek. Good Lord, where had that come from? What was happening to her? Something was going on inside her that was changing her attitude toward Henry. In his illness and helplessness, he'd become a different kind of burden, a pull on the part of her that made her want to take care of people.

* * * *

Margaret was just finishing her lunch when a delivery man rang her back doorbell. He was bringing the new wheelchair. He opened it up for her and showed her how the brakes worked, but she decided to wait until Charles arrived before trying to deal with it. Pushing it into the front hall to get it out of the way, she saw that Henry's living space was going to be expanded. He might be pushing himself all over the first floor, getting into everything. Once again, she was seeing him as a troublesome toddler. Oh God, would it never end? Would she ever get a chance to live her own life, to join the living? Or was she going to be dragged down into a nether world of decay, delirium, and depression, never free of this demanding infantile being? She began to sob.

It was a little after three when Charles pulled into the driveway. As always, the sight of this child lifted her spirits. She and Molly were close and very much alike, but Charles was the one who understood her without asking, who always made sure that her needs were taken into account. She would never forget how he'd defended her at the yard sale last summer, against Anita's charges that she was putting her father down by wanting to sell the phone booth, and at the family meeting a few weeks ago.

"Come in, come in," she said, grinning, and giving him a big hug. "It's so good of you to be doing this. I really have no idea what I'd do now if you weren't here."

Charles lifted his duffle bags out of the wagon and looked around. "But Mom, where are all your Christmas decorations? You don't have a tree, or any of your wreaths!"

"You're right," she said. "I've barely thought about Christmas; I've hardly had the time." She looked around. "It does seem kind of gloomy, now that you mention it."

"Well, listen, I'll go out and buy you a tree. This is ridiculous." He smiled. "I even brought you a present, and I've pictured it under a tree." He headed out the door again.

Goodness, thought Margaret. She hadn't yet decided what to give Charles. And what a dear boy he is, she mused. This would be a sad year for him, his first Christmas without Elena. She walked upstairs to the attic to dig out the boxes of Christmas ornaments and strings of lights, then laid everything out on the big table in the living room. Some of the ornaments had been Granny's and she still remembered each of them. Her favorite was an elaborate Victorian ivory-colored bulb, almost like a budding tulip.. There was also a bright green globe with a tiny ruby interior world, like a geode with its hidden jewel.

* * * *

While Charles decorated the tree Margaret made supper for the three of them. Just as she took the chicken out of the oven, she heard Henry stirring, and went quickly to get Charles. "Your father is waking up," she said. "Come, and I'll take you to him -- he may have forgotten you were coming. And let's bring the wheelchair and try it out."

She couldn't help but look at Charles's face as he first spotted his father. She should have warned him. For one thing, they'd let his beard just grow since it had become too difficult to shave him. Charles was now looking at a scraggly, frail elderly man. She saw her son swallow and then speak in the hearty fashion that everyone seemed to use when they talked to Henry: "Well, Dad, I'm here, and I guess one of my jobs will be to fatten you up." Charles was right: Henry had lost weight, even in the last few weeks. "Let's get you into your new wheelchair, so you can have supper with us in the kitchen!"

Margaret set the brakes while Charles leaned over to scoop him up and set him in the chair. Even though Henry was six foot six, he was so thin that it was almost easy. After Margaret buckled the strap, they pushed him into the kitchen. Suddenly she realized that Henry had never seen that room, or any other part of the house since it had been done over. Quickly she explained. "This is the new kitchen, Henry."

Henry looked around, and then said proudly in his new husky voice: "Painted green." Well, that was one way to put it, thought Margaret, reminding herself that interior decoration had never been his strong suit. He looked comfortable, as if being out of bed was actually pleasant. As she cut

up his food and guided his fork to his mouth, she glanced at Charles, hoping

that these changes in his father weren't going to be too upsetting. But

Charles quickly fell into his new role: he was now the parent, and Henry

was the child.

"Here, let me," he said, putting the chicken on the fork. "Now you can

manage it," he said to his Dad, and Margaret was reminded of how patient

Charles had always been with his own kids.

As the meal progressed slowly, Charles talked about his kids to his

father: "Katy helps me on the boat." He waited while Henry absorbed this

information, and then added: "She's the navigator." Henry seemed to smile.

"And Matt is a big help, too. He can be skipper." He spoke slowly, seeming

to catch Henry's rhythms. And between bites -- each taking what seemed an

interminable time -- Henry tried to be part of the conversation as well.

"Your boat -- how big?" he asked very slowly, reminding Margaret of

Will.

"I got a new one last year," said Charles, proudly, "thirty-seven feet."

He smiled. "Mom was on the boat this last summer. We taught her to steer."

Henry looked at Margaret, and she felt, just for a minute, that he was

seeing her new self. "Good girl," he said, and Margaret was so touched that

she had to turn her head to hide the tears. That look and those words brought back the early years of their relationship, when he was her teacher and showed her the difference between sedimentary and igneous rocks, eons ago.

"Katy showed me how," she said, quietly, after swallowing a few tears.

After dinner, Charles pushed the wheelchair into the living room. He'd placed the Christmas tree near the front window, and dimmed the room lights. All the tree lights were turned on and the ornaments were shining in reflected glory. Henry looked startled. Then he glanced around at the two of them, and smiled his artificial smile. "Christmas," he said, as if he had been put in charge of naming the holiday.

Charles stood up. "Let's try something. Maybe some music would jog his memory."

He put a CD on the machine and turned it on. It was a medley of Christmas carols, normally not the kind of music Henry would have liked. But clearly, the familiar tunes tapped into another part of his brain that was still unaffected. Henry began to sing, softly but in tune, along with the songs. It was ironic, thought Margaret, that a man who was at least nominally Jewish, would be responding to these particular cultural icons. But of course, it was probably impossible to grow up in America and avoid learning them.

Margaret looked at Charles. "How did you know that would work?"

"I've been doing some reading -- about dementia -- and it was one of the things they suggested. Even long-time Alzheimer's patients can sing along with songs they've known all their lives." He sighed. "It's not much, but it's something. Maybe tomorrow we can try some Beethoven or something that he liked more recently."

"Thank you, Charles," said Margaret. And then the three of them sat in the half-light, Margaret remembering her own early Christmases at Granny's house, Charles, whose face rarely reflected his sadness, now looking drained and miserable, and Henry -- who knew how far back his damaged mind was traveling?

* * * *

Christmas day itself was bittersweet. Ghosts of Christmas past were always there. After opening their presents -- Charles had given Henry a new bathrobe and her gift from her son was a painting. Remembering how moved she'd been by the panoply of stars as she'd seen them from the sailboat last summer, he'd created one of his silhouetted scenes with the mast and rigging of the boat in stark contrast to a sky-full of whirling galaxies and brilliant constellations. And Margaret had bought Charles a new sports jacket, having noticed that the one he had was even beyond elbow patches.

The rest of the day turned out to be a pleasant outing. Chloe and Saul had invited them all for dinner, and between Charles and Margaret, they'd figured out how to get Henry transferred into the car, with the wheelchair folded in the trunk. She couldn't help but remember the many times the two families had shared the holiday, and she was haunted by memories of Anita and Athena, their two heads together over a new book or game. Today she could see the shadows that crossed Chloe's and Saul's faces as they looked around the big table. Mentally, there would always be an empty chair.

She and Charles left early in order to get Henry to bed -- he looked pale and tired, not used to all this excitement. The next day was his appointment with the orthopedist at the Hospital. Once he'd been tucked in for the night, Margaret realized that she, too, was exhausted, and went up to bed, even though it was barely nine o'clock. She'd just stretched out under the covers when the phone rang. It was Erik.

"Merry Christmas, Maggie," he said, his voice warm and immediately reassuring. "I've been calling you all day."

"We were at Chloe's," she said. "Were you at your sister's?"

"We were," he said. "Maggie, I want very much to give you a Christmas present." He seemed to pause for a minute, then went on bravely. "You are, after all, my girl."

"Oh, that sounds so lovely," she said, feeling that she was about to cry. "That's better than any present you could think of. My present to Will was really for you, too, as you know. In fact, it was really just an excuse to get me into your house."

He laughed. "I think I figured that out a little later, after you'd gone home that day. And by the way, we played Dominos over at my sister's house. We all had a great time, and Will just loved it. It was the perfect game for him." He paused again. "But I do have a present for you, and I hope you'll be able to make use of it."

"What is it?" What was there about his tone that alerted her?

"It's a weekend in New York with me. You know that the Mackintosh Exhibit is at the Metropolitan Museum right now? He's a special favorite of mine and I've decided to go. My sister will keep Will that weekend, but I don't want to go without you."

"What weekend did you have in mind?" said Margaret, wondering how in the world she was going to manage this.

"Friday, January third, through that Sunday." There was a long silence. Oh God, thought Margaret. I've never wanted anything more in my life. She remembered that Charles and the kids would be leaving that day, going back up to Maine. Was it possible she'd be free that weekend? Perhaps Henry could go to the Respite Center.

"Erik, listen. I'm going to try. I really am. Oh, God, I can't believe we'd really have a whole weekend to ourselves, in New York. In a real hotel?" She realized she was sounding like a child. "You're talking about the Scottish architect? From 1900?"

"That's right. And we'll stay in a real hotel. We'll spend the whole day in bed if we want to." He laughed softly. "And we'll want to, I'm sure." He paused again. "Listen, I know your life is complicated, and if you can't do it, I won't be angry -- just disappointed as hell. But see what you can do. I love you."

Suddenly Margaret wasn't sleepy any more. She lay there, racking her brain, trying to think how she could manage a whole weekend away. She knew she could not count on Respite, although she'd certainly call them. Somehow, she wasn't comfortable asking any of the kids to stay with Henry. Rosa had offered to come whenever she was needed, but something told her that even Rosa would not be happy about taking care of her brother when Margaret was spending the weekend with another man. But I need it, she thought, I need -- not just time with Erik -- but time away.

* * * *

They were on time for their eleven o'clock appointment the next morning, but of course, it was past noon when the nurse finally came for them. They were ushered into Dr. Everson's office, and right away,

Margaret decided she didn't like him because of the way he spoke to Henry. "So, young feller," he said loudly, probably assuming that everyone over sixty-five was either deaf or stupid, "let's have a look at that leg."

"Mr. Bluestone is still recovering from pneumonia," Margaret said, "and possibly has Parkinson's. He hasn't been out of bed except to sit in the wheelchair for the last couple of days. Actually, Doctor," said Margaret, hurrying to get her message across, "we were wondering if there was any possibility, down the road, of your referring him to a rehab center, where he could get some help and training in using his legs again."

"Slow down, young lady. Before we start talking rehab, I want you to take him down to the basement to the X-ray department, so we can see the status of the fracture."

Swallowing her anger and disgust, Margaret joined Charles and they pushed Henry into the elevator. They had to wait in the X-Ray Department, as well, and by that time Henry had fallen asleep. After the films were taken, they were sent to the elevator again and on to Dr. Everson's waiting room, which seemed to have filled up with young victims of skiing accidents. For the first time, Henry looked completely disoriented and frightened.

"It's okay," said the receptionist in a soothing voice.

Henry looked up at her. "Take me home?"

"Not yet," said Charles. "Dr. Everson wants to see you again." He turned to Margaret. "Part of the problem, you know, is that Dad hasn't had any lunch yet." He laughed. "And neither have we, come to think of it."

The receptionist suggested they all go to the hospital cafeteria but they decided to wait. It was two o'clock before they met with the doctor once more. Frowning, he looked carefully at Henry. Then he spoke to Charles. "Tell me, do you think your father could learn to use crutches?"

"Not as he is now," said Charles. "I could picture, down the road, maybe his using a cane. But I think crutches are just too complicated for him." He also looked at Henry.

"What do you think, Dad, would you like to start walking?"

Henry stared at him, and finally answered slowly: "Wheelchair."

The doctor shrugged. "I don't know. Maybe later, after several more weeks, and after we get him onto a walking cast, we should give rehab a chance. They could try him out for a few days, and make a determination of his capability. If it works out, he could stay a few weeks and maybe start actually walking." He looked down at Henry's record. "He's still young," he said. "Sixty-five." Then he looked up. "And so tall. So far to fall." He shook his head. Then he sighed and for the first time, looked almost human. "Good luck," he said. "The fracture, at least, is healing."

The next morning Margaret took a chance and called the Respite Center, hoping that there might be a cancellation for the weekend of January third, when she and Eric had hoped to go to New York. No such luck, the woman said, but then she asked if Margaret could use some time this coming week. Could he be ready by Monday?

By Saturday afternoon, Margaret found herself -- once again, after many years -- sitting in the rocking chair in her kitchen, sewing on name tapes. The respite center had made a point of saying that all the patient's clothing should be labeled. It was as if Henry was going off to camp: the cycle of life seemed to be circling backward. It occurred to Margaret that he might not be a happy camper.

While the center had offered to pick Henry up in their ambulance, both Margaret and Charles agreed that it might be less frightening for Henry if they drove him there on their own. In fact, Henry began to look apprehensive when he saw them carrying his suitcase out to the car, and as they drove in what was an unfamiliar direction, he became more agitated.

"Home!" he shouted, "my house!" Each time he spoke of "home" Margaret felt a twinge. Poor man, what must it be like to feel you have no control over where you are going, and to feel that you were being forced to leave home against your will? It was all so strange, especially when she recalled how Henry had never thought of their house as home, and had seemed -- only five months ago -- anxious to leave it for good.

Margaret, who was riding in the back seat, reached over and tried to soothe him. "It's a nice place, Henry. They'll take good care of you." Nothing they said had any effect on Henry, who kept looking anxiously out the window and talking of home. And when they pulled up at the center, there were two attendants waiting to help them get Henry out of the car. They lifted him out and quickly strapped him onto a gurney and took him into the building. Margaret and Charles followed with his suitcase and wheelchair.

After they'd signed Henry in and watched the staff tuck him into bed, Margaret felt like a mother leaving her child at nursery school, being hustled out by the staff before the kid started to cry. But as they headed for the stairs, they heard a voice: "Please!"

"Come on, Mom, I'm going to take you to dinner," said Charles. "It's time you had a night out!"

In the restaurant, after several glasses of wine, and some fresh Italian bread, waiting contentedly for their meal, they sat in a companionable silence. Margaret yawned several times and finally said: "Charles, I never could have done this without you -- this whole week. How can I thank you?"

Charles shook his head. "I'm just glad it worked out," he said, looking uneasy, "and I'm glad we have at least this one night to talk. The kids will be here tomorrow and we'll be busy again." He swallowed. "I guess I wanted to apologize again for having been so nasty -- during that Thanksgiving weekend -- about your friend Erik. I want you to know that if there's a romance or anything like that going on, I think you deserve a real life -- whatever."

Margaret sat silently, trying to decide what to say next. "Well, actually, Charles, your instinct, or whatever it was, is right. I'm glad you brought the whole subject up, because I don't like secrets. However, I'm not sure the rest of your siblings would feel the same, so let's keep this between us for a while." She hesitated, not sure how much to say. At the same time, she had wanted to tell somebody, and maybe Charles was the right person. Little by little, she told her story, and then added: "Erik doesn't want to do anything that would upset either my children or his son. Erik doesn't want Will to have any further disappointments: the boy's mother walked out on him four years ago." She paused. "The other thing, Charles, he feels that as long as Henry is living in my house, he should do nothing to make him uncomfortable, either."

Charles reached his hand across the table. "I'm really happy for you, Mom. I hope something like this will happen to me someday. But I'm not rushing it."

As they continued with their meal, Margaret wondered if she should tell Charles about her invitation to go to New York with Erik on this coming weekend. Why not? Sighing heavily, she plunged in. "Actually, Erik has invited me to go with him to New York on Friday. He's going down to see the Mackintosh Exhibit."

"Oh, my God! I'd give my eye teeth to see that show. I hope you're going."

"How can I? Your father's only going to be in the Respite Center for a few days. And even if they took him next weekend, what if they needed to call me?"

"Well, then," said Charles reasonably, "the kids and I still stay at your house. We can manage. The kids don't start school until that Monday." Margaret's eyes filled with tears. She'd been afraid he'd say that.

She shook her head. "No, I wouldn't have told you if I thought you'd offer to do that. I'm a grownup: I can wait. And there'll be other chances. I've been thinking about this and I decided I couldn't ask any of the others, either. Molly, Andrew and Julia are too busy, and Anita would have a fit at the idea of my going to New York with a man! And I decided that Rosa might be shocked if I told her everything."

"Did you definitely say 'no' to Erik?"

"Actually, I said I'd try to find a way," she said sheepishly.

"Then let me work on it. Please. I'll figure out something. At least let's wait until I have a chance to work on an idea or two. I think you need that weekend away, Mom. This is the first night off you've had in over a month!"

"I did go to a movie with Chloe one night," she said, laughing. "Saul baby-sat."

"Now there's a true friend," said Charles thoughtfully. "Well, anyway, leave this problem to me for a while. I'll see what I can do."

Early the next day, the respite center called to say that Henry was not able to handle being away from home at this point. What now? Margaret asked herself. When Charles woke up, she'd ask him to go to pick up Henry. In the meantime, she looked up the number of the local Elder Affairs office and asked for the Long Term Care Screening Team, and after a few false starts, actually got one of the nurses on the team, and was able to make a request for a home visit. The nurse said she'd look at their schedule and call her back to give her the date of the appointment, probably in two or three weeks. Well, that at least was done.

When Charles came down for breakfast a half an hour later, she was sitting gloomily over her coffee. "What's wrong?" he said. She told him about the call from the center.

He shook his head. "Do you want me to go get him? I can drive out this morning." She nodded. Looking up at him, she saw a strange look on his face. "Mom, listen, I hope you're not going to be mad at me, but I did something the other day."

"What did you do?" she said, completely mystified.

"I went to see Chloe." Margaret waited. "I told her about your invitation to go to New York -- no, I didn't tell her who invited you. She called me yesterday, and she and Saul are offering to come over here for the weekend."

"Oh, my God. You didn't. Oh, Charles, could I let them do something like that?"

"I had the feeling they really wanted to, Mom. Chloe said you were so wonderful to them when Athena died; I think they really want to do something for you. So what are you waiting for?" said Charles. "Get on the phone and tell Erik that you can come. Here," he said, handing her the instrument, "take it. I'll give you some privacy; I've got to wake up the kids, anyway." He left the kitchen, and she could hear him walking up the stairs, whistling.

She picked up the phone and dialed. "Erik, it's me, Maggie. Guess what?"

Chapter Twenty-one

Margaret and Erik had decided to take the train to New York on Friday morning. Sitting next to him on the window side, with the sun pouring in, deliciously warm in her favorite blue cashmere sweater and matching skirt, Margaret felt as if she'd been transported to a desert island, a place where no one could find them, where neither of them had any responsibilities. Of course, she'd given Chloe and Saul the name and number of their hotel, but for the next four hours, they were incommunicado. Here on this train, the seats were wide and comfortable. There were no seat belts, and she could stretch out, without worrying about whether the pilot was keeping track of his instruments. An engineer, like the man with the red bandana who'd always waved at her when she was a child living at Granny's, was driving the train; he was someone they could trust. Curling up like a cat, Margaret soaked up the sunshine.

Erik looked down at her. "You're having happy thoughts," he said, taking her hand. His bulky down jacket felt like an additional safety feature, like a crib bumper.

"We're two kids who've run away from home. And no one knows where we are."

He nodded. "It's true. This is the first time I've left Will for a whole weekend." Margaret yawned, leaning against his jacket. She felt her breathing slowing down, and a lovely lassitude sweeping over her. In bed the night before, she'd worried about what they'd say to each other this weekend. In the past when they'd been together, they'd dealt with problems: renovating the house, Thanksgiving dinner, her kids, Will, and Henry. Their time together had been limited. Now there would be a vast canvas on which they could begin to sketch out a life with each other. But last night, tossing and turning as she'd tried to get some sleep, Margaret wondered: what if they discovered they had nothing to say to each other? Of course, she told herself, she could always ask him to tell her his life history. She really knew very little about his childhood or any of his past. But it would be awkward, to say the least, if she were to clear her throat and say: excuse me, where were you born? where did you go to school? what made you decide to become an architect?

"You know," said Erik, hesitantly, a little frown appearing between his round glasses, like a little bridge between those two bushy red eyebrows, "thinking about this trip yesterday, I was nervous. I began wondering what we would talk about."

She laughed, but quickly added: "We're two of a kind. I had the same fears. I finally decided, if all else failed, that I would ask you to tell me the story of your life. I really don't know that much about you!"

421

"And here you are, going off for a weekend with a complete stranger!" He grinned. "Didn't your mother ever warn you?"

It was going to be all right, Margaret realized. Suddenly she remembered the first day they met, how they'd sat side-by-side, in the loft of the barn, already aware that they shared the same sense of magic.

"Why don't I go to the club car," he said, "and get us some coffee? And then, by God, I <u>will</u> tell you my life history, beginning with the fact that I was born in Denmark and came to America when I was two years old!" As he stood up and moved down the aisle, she watched him go with a sense of well-being. That big red-headed, red-bearded man was hers, at least for the next three days.

Each time she was with him, the experience was like being on a desert island, a secret garden with tropical flowers set down in a wintry world. It reminded her of the Boston Flower Show, artificially full of spring when outside the snow was whirling. What would happen to them if they were living an ordinary life? What if they had to deal with all the minutiae that often ate away at marriages? Or even nibbled at relationships?

* * * *

As Erik had predicted, they spent most of Friday afternoon in bed, emerging into the sights and sounds of the early evening world of New York City. Blinking like dark-adapted forest animals, they were confronted by millions of lights, almost frightened by the noise of horns, shouts and sirens. Instinctively, Erik put his arm around her and said: "Let's walk a bit, uptown maybe, toward the Plaza Hotel. Perhaps we could take a carriage ride through the Park. Have you ever done that?"

She shook her head. "It's exciting here, but overwhelming. I feel like a country girl."

The carriage ride, the intimacy of being wrapped in a big blanket, and the trees and grass of Central Park, restored some of their sense of themselves. Afterwards, they both agreed that a simple supper in the hotel coffee shop was all they needed. Later they strolled around the lobby with its Art Deco designs. "You'll have to compare the way this place is decorated," said Eric, "with what you'll see tomorrow in the Mackintosh exhibit. There's a connection." Margaret felt as if she were on a special guided tour.

She loved everything about the hotel -- the big, fluffy towels, the little bottles of shampoo, the shoe-shine cloth, and the sewing kit. And she enjoyed the illusion of domesticity as they brushed their teeth together. She was even pleased with his striped red and white pajamas: there was so much about him that she wanted to know. But best of all was sleeping all night in the same bed, like a pair of spoons in the silver drawer.

Saturday was their day to attend the Mackintosh exhibit at the Museum. Margaret found Erik a good teacher: he let his pupil make the discoveries herself. "His designs don't look the way I expected," she said. "I was thinking I'd see just geometrical, repetitive forms, one after the other. But I'm finding tulips, fruit, and little flowers everywhere I look." She smiled. "I really love this stuff. And I see what you meant about its connection to Art Deco."

Erik's warm brown eyes lit up as he looked down at her. "You have a good sense of line. It's a shame that no one else picked up on his style, or never with the same delicacy. Maybe this exhibit will produce some changes in the architectural world."

At lunch, in the Museum cafeteria, their talk naturally led to the years when he lived in New York. "I ended up at Columbia for my undergraduate work. After living in a small town in Michigan, I wanted to see the big city."

"How did your family feel, with your being so far away from home?"

He shook his head. "It wasn't easy, especially for my mom. My parents were pushing for the University of Michigan; my sister had gone there." He looked down at her, evidently pleased that she was interested in his early life. "My father was an engineer, a designer, really, of luxury car interiors -- which were still made of wood in those days. He'd been brought to this country by one of the big auto makers; that's why we ended up in Michigan.

My mother grew up on a farm in Denmark, and she insisted that we live in a rural area. In the end, I won the battle and was allowed to come to New York."

As he was speaking, Margaret tried to picture life in that small community, and she wondered if it could have been similar to the Iowa town where her grandparents had lived. Strange that for her, most of her life she'd been striving to get back to that time and place, where you knew the rules, who you were, and how you fitted in. Erik had evidently pushed to get away, and maybe that was healthier.

"The minute I got to New York, I fell in love with the buildings: the brownstones, the town houses, the mixtures of architectural styles, from the Triangle Building to the Cloisters." He sighed. "I wish we had time to go up there. Perhaps we can arrange another New York weekend sometime." Gradually his smile faded, and Margaret realized that this casual remark had reminded both of them of their real lives back home: it was as if he'd brought up a forbidden topic. She put her hand on top of his. What were the chances of their having another weekend together? For a few minutes they looked at each other bleakly.

"My favorite part of the city was Greenwich Village," he went on, perhaps trying to restore some of his earlier enthusiasm. "In fact, I took a summer job before my senior year, with a construction firm that did restoration in the Village. I was an apprentice carpenter. I loved that job, working with real carpenters, getting to know those wonderful houses down there. That was when I decided to go to Architecture School, and how I ended up at the Harvard School of Design." He paused, and then said: "Have you been to the Village?"

Margaret shook her head. "Just once, a long time ago, with my mother, shopping."

"Maybe we could take the Fifth Avenue bus down to Washington Square, so I can show you some of the houses down there." Then he stopped, blushing. "Here I go again, organizing your life for you. I think you should be the one to decide how we spend the rest of today. Maybe you'd rather look for tickets to a play, whatever."

Margaret could see that he was trying to show her that he wasn't making decisions for her, but she was already intrigued by the idea of seeing the Village. She smiled. "I vote for the Village. It's a nice day, and we could walk. I want to spend my time talking to you, without being stuck inside a theater."

The Village was crowded on this warm January afternoon, with a wonderful mixture of couples like themselves, just strolling and window-shopping, and people wearing outfits that could only be called costumes, with enormous earrings, long gowns or very short skirts. Erik and Margaret had taken off their jackets. Erik was carrying his over his shoulder, and Margaret had tied hers around her waist.

They walked through a section that seemed to feature Italian pastries and piles of red and green vegetables, and then, in the next block, craft shops and antique places. Margaret was reminded that she wanted to buy a thank you present for Chloe and Saul. Drawn to the window of one store, a pottery shop with swirling designs on its bowls and hand-made lamps, she said to Erik: "Oh, look!" She pointed into the shop and pulled his hand. "Here's a green and orange bowl that would be perfect for Chloe's early spring flowers." When he didn't answer, she glanced up at him. He didn't seem to be sharing her interest in the pottery, but was looking down at her, beginning to stroke her hair.

"I was looking at you," he said, "with your curly hair, your bright blue eyes and your enthusiasm. I was thinking about how much I loved you: you're so easy to be with; you enjoy life so whole-heartedly." And right there, on the street, he took her in his arms and kissed her. "Oh, God, if only I could do that whenever I wanted to." He paused. She looked up at him. The light coming through the awning of the shop had made stripes on his body. With his furry bright red hair and dark flannel shirt, he looked like one of those wooly-bear caterpillars, the kind country folk insist are useful in predicting the onset of cold weather. "Sometimes," he said, "when I'm at home, just a few blocks from you, I want to come right over and hold you --

like this."

Margaret's eyes filled with tears. "These are happy tears," she said

grinning. "Come, let's go in the store and you can help me buy the

Solomons a present, and then we'll go find something for Will, maybe in

that little leather store we passed back there."

After dinner, they agreed that an early bedtime made a lot of sense since

they had to catch the 9 A.M. train on Sunday morning. Taking a taxi back to

the hotel, they leaned comfortably into each other. Margaret yawned, and

Erik's eyes were closing by the time the cab pulled up at the entrance to the

hotel.

As they climbed into bed, Erik turned to Margaret. "I've a confession to

make," he said sheepishly. He leaned up on one elbow. Oddly enough,

Margaret thought he looked even more like an owl when he had his glasses

off. "I find I'm not so sleepy after all," he said. "With you so close to me,

I'm full of ideas." He laughed. "Can we keep the light on so I can really see

you? I want to memorize all of you."

Margaret was blushing but she was pleased. She smiled. "Now I'll have

a chance to find out how furry you really are!" They didn't get much sleep,

after all.

* * * *

The return train trip was the dark side of their journey. The train was crowded and they had difficulty finding two seats together. The car they finally settled in had erratic heating, a continually crying baby, and nothing to see out the windows except pouring rain. But the real problem was that the train was going in the wrong direction: it was taking them back to their real lives.

"Maggie," said Erik, after a long silence in which both had tried to sleep, "What's going to happen to Henry after you get your divorce. It's only ten days, right?"

Margaret nodded, and then sighed. "I wish I knew."

"Could he end up still living in your house, under your care?"

"Not if I can help it!" she said. "I've applied for a screening interview by the Department of Elder Affairs. He can't get into a nursing home without their approval. But you seem to be implying I haven't thought about it." She could hear the anger in her voice. "Believe me, I <u>have</u> been thinking about it. I'm trying to understand where I am in all this." She paused. How could she explain it? "We're really not talking about the Henry that I knew and was married to for forty years. That man was a real bastard." She shook her head. "I don't owe <u>him</u> anything. The man who's living at my house now, wearing a diaper and barely able to feed himself, is someone else.

While he looks a little like the old Henry, though thinner and with a scraggly beard, he's <u>not</u> Henry."

Erik was looking puzzled.

"Well, for one thing, this person, the one I'm taking care of now, is a <u>nicer</u> person than the old Henry. I can't believe I'm saying this, but this man is a pussy cat, compared to the old bastard I used to be married to. He's frightened. He doesn't know what's going on, or what's happening to him. He's become attached to where he's living now, and he calls it 'home.'" She stopped, and frowned. "Like a cat. But I'm not sure he's talking about the house where he and I lived all those years -- it looks so different now. I think he knows who I am, and he trusts me." Her eyes were becoming wet. "Last week, we took him to a respite care center, and I felt as if I were abandoning him." Now she began to cry. "Erik," she said, "I feel <u>responsible</u> for him. If I could find <u>someplace</u>, or <u>someone</u> that would take good care of him, I think I could let go. But I can't just walk away." She wiped her eyes. "You wouldn't like me if I were the kind of person who could just dump him on the street, would you?" Erik shook his head. "Do you understand what I'm saying?"

He put his arms around her and she laid her head on his soft down jacket. "I understand it all too well, Maggie. It's the story of my life." There was a long silence.

Finally, Margaret spoke up again. "Of course, you're right. You may have to take care of Will for the rest of your life. It's different for me. I know that this problem with Henry won't go on forever. But I can tell you, Erik, that there were times when I wanted to hasten his journey to the grave, especially when I remember that he wouldn't even permit me to be sick when the kids were little." And then she began to cry again. "He was cruel to me, Erik, when I was ill. Of course, after a while I learned never to let him know about it when I was coming down with something." She looked up at him; his brown eyes were full of concern. "I'm not trying to get your sympathy, Erik. I guess I'm trying to tell you that it's complicated. But I just can't play the game of tit for tat."

"Come, put your head on my shoulder, Maggie. Try to get some sleep."

* * * *

Margaret had arranged to take the next two weeks off from work. Except for the night nurse, she'd have no one to cover for her at home until Henry's sister Rosa and her husband George arrived. They'd agreed to help out until after the divorce hearing.

And in the meantime, Anita -- thank God -- would come for the weekend, and also be around when they went to Court. She seemed to think that Henry needed someone who would be his ally, and the more Margaret thought about it, the more she wondered whether that meant she and Anita would be adversaries. It was hard enough, she thought, wrinkling her brow as she went about changing all the beds to get ready for these guests, to get the skein of a marriage disentangled without snarling the children.

Her lawyer had told her that they had to be at the Probate Court, at ten A.M. on Wednesday, January 15, and that there'd be other divorces scheduled for that same day, plus other related hearings. There was no way to tell which time slot they'd be given. Eleanor had told her the name of the judge, a woman named Sheri Donabedian. Margaret pictured a dark, brooding Armenian, wrapped in her black robes, aloof but even-handed as she weighed the scales of justice.

On Friday of that first week, Rosa and George took an early flight from Cleveland and arrived at Margaret's house in time for lunch. It had been several years since she'd seen Rosa, and Margaret was amazed at how little she'd changed. A thin, wiry woman with a lot of energy, a tiny version of Henry with a long face like his and snapping brown eyes, there was a no-nonsense air about her. Tight-lipped, she always made Margaret feel as if she were in the presence of an authority, a person who knew -- not only the answers -- but the questions as well. As soon as she'd taken off her coat, she marched into Henry's room and said: "Well, what have we here?"

And much to Margaret's surprise, Henry grinned and said: "Rosa." Margaret suddenly felt like a proud mother of a toddler. Dear God, how had it ever come to this? But she was happy for Rosa that he recognized her. Of course, it was early in the day. Later on, he probably couldn't have performed as well.

"Henry," she said, "George is here, too, and we're all going to have lunch together in the kitchen." She released the brake on the wheelchair and pushed it out of the room.

George hadn't changed much, either. White-haired now, and rounder, he was a little more twinkly as he gazed over his half glasses. And he was still, as Henry had pointed out many years ago, a true "little Sir Echo" of whatever his wife said or thought. But it was sad to think that while both George and Rosa were more than ten years older than Henry, the person who looked really old was her husband, even thinner than Rosa.

After lunch, while Henry was napping, she tried to explain to both of them how to care for Henry. "I'll be here most of the time, but I wanted you to know the bare essentials, about his medication, the monitor, where everything is kept."

She'd started to tell Rosa about the diapers, but Rosa interrupted. "Margaret, dear, I've been changing that boy's diapers since he was born. I was really a second mother to him most of the time when he was little." Like most of Rosa's pronouncements, these words had come out like a speech. It was a speech Margaret had heard before, and each time she had wondered what it must have been like, years ago, when Henry was little, to have had <u>two</u> mothers, one of them a bossy junior high school student.

But then, to Margaret's surprise, Rosa began to cry. She was human, after all. "I should have known," Rosa said, wiping her cheeks with a well-ironed handkerchief, "last summer when he came to see us, he wasn't himself. Isn't that right, George?"

George nodded. "The worst thing was he didn't know where he was going. Honest to God, he didn't know north from south." He shook his head. "I got out the atlas, to show him how to get out of Cleveland and head west, and I could tell -- he didn't know what the hell I was talking about!"

"It goes with his disease, the doctor told me, inability to read maps and getting lost," said Margaret. How lucky she was that this aging couple was willing to come all this way to help out! "I can't tell you how glad I am that you're here. And here I am, about to divorce your brother."

"Margaret," said Rosa. "It made sense to me that the two of you should get a divorce. He wanted to be free, he told us, so that he could go exploring or whatever he was trying to do." Margaret had a feeling she'd memorized this speech in advance as well. Rosa paused, for the first time looking ill-at-ease. "After the divorce, Margaret, where will he go?"

"I wish I knew," said Margaret. "I'd hoped he'd be placed somewhere by now, but I'm still waiting for the State to make up their minds if he's eligible for a nursing home. The people who decide about that will be coming over soon, I hope, to investigate the whole situation. None of the kids could take him, not as he is now." She sighed. "Listen, if you feel comfortable being alone with him, I'd like to go to the grocery store. We're out of everything. Anita will be coming in later this afternoon and we'll have more help. If she calls, tell her to take a cab."

* * * *

On Wednesday morning, as they were all getting ready to go to the courthouse, there was a knock at the back door. Margaret hurried to answer it, thinking it might be Eleanor arriving early. But it was Charles! And he was all dressed up. "Oh my God, what are you doing here today? Didn't you have to work?"

"I took the day off," he said. "Arranged for a substitute, got up at six, and here I am." It felt so good to see him, with his carefully combed blond hair, his straight nose and serious expression. Just then Anita came into the kitchen. He looked at her and smiled. "Hi, big sister," he said, evidently trying to forestall any arguments. Always the peacemaker, Charles's antennae were up.

Anita looked startled, but pleased. She, too, was dressed like a professional, in a wine-colored suit, and her hair neatly braided in a French knot. "We need all the help we can get today, I guess. It's a sad day." She looked as if she might start to cry.

"Well, we're still a family," said Charles. "They're both our parents, no matter whether they're married or not." And he gave Anita a big hug. Then Rosa and George came into the room, with their coats on, pushing the wheelchair, with Henry tucked in, looking almost handsome in a real suit. It was loose on him now, but it was the first time he'd worn anything other than pajamas and a bathrobe in over six weeks.

"I think you're ready to go," said Margaret. "You have the directions; it's only a few miles, Anita. I did a dry run the other day and saw that the handicapped entrance is right off the parking lot. All you have to do when you get there is ring the buzzer and the court officer will let you in. He'll take you to the elevator." She was sounding like a fussy old hen. She'd taken on a new role -- caretaker for a man with a superficial resemblance to the man she married forty years ago. But she couldn't stop herself. "Now that Charles is here, he can help with getting your father into the wagon. I'll wait for Eleanor." She stood in the open doorway, watching them maneuver Henry into the front seat and the wheelchair into the back. Anita climbed into the driver's seat and Rosa and George sat behind her.

Then Charles came back into the house. "I'm going to ride with you and Eleanor," he said. They stood together as Anita backed the wagon out of the driveway. Margaret looked up at the sky. There was a heavy, leaden look to it, and the wind was raw.

"I hope it doesn't start to snow," she said, shivering.

"Come on in, Mom," Charles said, putting his arm around her shoulder. "I think freezing rain is predicted, but not until afternoon. Do you have some extra coffee?"

Margaret looked at her watch. "Yes, and there's time for some toast or something if you want it. Eleanor won't be here for another fifteen minutes."

As they sat down together at the kitchen table, Charles frowned. "Just getting divorced isn't going to solve anything. We're still going to have to decide what to do with Dad. But at least you won't be legally responsible any more." They sat silently, drinking their coffee. She could hear the toast crunch as he bit down.

And then the doorbell rang. It was Eleanor. She was dressed in a well-cut cherry-colored suit, with a crisp white blouse. It was time to go to court. She said she'd follow them in her own car, so that Charles and Margaret could ride together.

By the time the three of them reached the parking lot of the courthouse, sleet had begun to fall. It was only a little after nine in the morning, but already it was dark and dreary. The building itself was impressive -- at least

437

on the outside -- with big pillars holding up the portico, and a long flight of wide steps up to the double doors. Inside there was a metal detector just like the ones at the airport, and then a marble staircase that led to the courtrooms upstairs. At the top, a large square waiting room was already crowded with worried men and women whispering to their lawyers in corners, while unsupervised children were climbing on the big wide bench. Sooner or later, Margaret thought, one of them was going to lean right over that railing and fall onto the marble steps. She looked the other way. She couldn't save everybody. Not today.

On a bulletin board was a printed list of all the cases for that day, with the names written out for all the world to see, including theirs. There was no privacy. They'd joined a multitude.

As Margaret was reading the list and wondering if they'd printed it in the newspaper, she was interrupted by Eleanor. "Paul wants to speak to us in one of the small conference rooms."

Margaret followed her down the long corridor and went with her into a room that was furnished with a large table and several chairs. Henry was sitting there in his wheelchair, looking dazed and confused. Paul was standing near the window, frowning. Rosa and George stood up as she came in, and Rosa said: "We'll be outside when you need us," and they quickly left the room.

"Margaret," said Paul, "I've just been talking to Henry, and frankly, I'm not at all sure, at this point, that he's able to understand and go along with the concept of divorce." He looked unsure of himself, biting his lip as he looked at her.

Margaret was stunned. "But you talked to him last week. Why didn't you say something then?"

"Well, I had a few doubts even then, but today Henry seems quite confused, as if he doesn't know why we're all here. I reminded him of our conversation last summer, when we talked about divorce, but he doesn't seem to remember it -- or anything else. Have you noticed that he's less able to keep things in mind?"

Even as he spoke, Margaret was glancing at Henry and wondering what he was thinking as this conversation unrolled. From time to time, she'd been puzzled about his capabilities: his ability to speak seemed to be shrinking as time went on; his sentences were shorter, often only one or two words, but he usually understood the subject. Or seemed to. Right now, she couldn't tell <u>what</u> he was thinking.

"So what do we do today?" Margaret asked.

"Let me tell you what Paul and I came up with," said Eleanor. "Neither of us knows this judge -- she's new -- but we'd like to go ahead with the request for the divorce, and see what happens. Perhaps we can squeeze by.

439

She may grant it on the basis of the agreed-upon separation agreement, but it's a risk. We may have to spend all day here and go home with nothing."

Margaret shrugged. "I guess we have nothing to lose except the time."

"Well, we'd better get back into court," said Eleanor, moving out into the corridor.

She led them into a large courtroom. Rosa and George pushed Henry's wheelchair up to the front row where Anita was already sitting. Paul joined them there. Eleanor took Margaret and Charles to the back row. The room was almost full.

Seated at a desk near the door was a young woman in a police uniform, and at a larger desk, just under the judge's empty bench, another court officer was leafing through a pile of pink and white case files. People kept walking in and out, some with briefcases, others with sheets of paper. In spite of the court officers, it looked as if no one was in charge, as if this were a place with no rules, no guidelines.

Finally, one of the officers stood up and spoke loudly: "All rise. The court of the honorable Judge Donabedian is now in session." Everyone quickly stood up and looked toward the bench. Judge Donabedian was nothing like Margaret's fantasy of an even-handed weigher of the scales of justice. She seemed very young, very blond, and was wearing high heels, in patent leather. Holding her gavel in one hand, she glanced at her clerk and began to leaf through some of the cases. Gradually, conversation in the court room picked up again, as latecomers hurried in.

Suddenly, the officer shouted: "Order in the Court," and conversation died back down to whispers. "<u>Johnson</u>," said the clerk, and a large pale woman took her place in front of the bench. Margaret could hear the judge when she spoke, but not what the plaintiff was saying. And there were no court reporters to take it all down. The interchange was brief, and ended with the judge's saying: "All I can give you is twelve dollars. Do you understand?" The woman nodded and left the courtroom. They weren't even following the order of the list. This could be a long day.

As the morning wore on, with one case after another, Margaret began to worry about Henry. Although he was sitting way up front and making no sign of being upset, she kept wondering if he was all right. She reminded herself that Rosa was very capable of handling whatever came up. There is something wrong with me, she told herself. Why am I not worrying about myself at this point? Then she saw Eleanor leaving the room.

Margaret put her hands over her face. "What's wrong, Mom?" whispered Charles.

"This whole thing is a nightmare, like something out of Kafka or worse," she said. "How can justice come out of this mess?" She shook her head. "Could you find out where Eleanor has gone and ask her whether she thinks they'll get to us today?"

Charles eased himself out of the row of seats and left the room. Now Margaret glanced over at the other half of her family group, and she saw that Paul had also left the courtroom. She looked at the clock. It was getting near noon. She supposed there'd be a break for lunch. And sure enough, after a few minutes, the court officer spoke again: "All rise." And after they'd all stood up, the judge tripped delicately out of the courtroom, to have lunch in the peace and quiet of her chambers.

The regulars in the crowd began to leave, too, and Margaret asked one of the worn-out women if this was, indeed, lunchtime. "Yeah, right," said the woman. "We gotta be back here by one-thirty." She paused. "Court begins at two."

"Is it always like this?" Margaret asked. "So confused? No one seems to know what is going on." She shook her head. "And there's no privacy. Everyone can hear."

"Yeah. It's always like this. You gotta spend the day. And for what?" she asked, under her breath. "For goddam justice, if you're lucky." Gradually, the room emptied, and Margaret went over to join the rest of the family. By now, Henry was looking totally blank, wide-eyed and uncomfortable. Someone -- probably Charles when he got back -- needed to take him to the men's room for a diaper change, while someone else went out for sandwiches.

* * * *

The afternoon session seemed more organized. It was as if they were getting down to the serious business now. The first case involved the guardianship of a child. It seemed to go quite quickly, with the grandmother evidently getting temporary custody.

Then, without any warning, the judge's clerk announced: <u>Bluestone.</u> Eleanor led her before the bench, and there they met Paul and Henry. They all waited quietly while the judge looked at their case record. When she looked up, Paul said: "Your honor, this is an uncontested divorce. I represent Mr. Bluestone." He pointed to Henry who was looking up at the judge with his eyes wide open.

"Mr. Bluestone," the judge said loudly, as if she assumed Henry was deaf, "you are here to get a divorce, is that correct?"

Henry didn't answer. Margaret wished she could explain that it was time for his nap.

The judge turned to Paul. "Counselor, does your client understand my question? Is he here under his own free will?"

Paul looked uncomfortable. "I think this large courtroom is confusing to him, but he understands the issues. He came to me six months ago requesting I help him get a divorce. We have formal separation agreement."

The judge frowned. She looked up at the clock on the wall. "I'll see you in my chambers at four o'clock," she said, dismissing them with a wave of her hand.

"Paul," said Margaret. "I think Henry is used to having a nap at this time, and he would do much better if someone took him into one of those private conference rooms and let him doze off. Then, when he wakes up, you can explain to him what's going to be happening, and what he needs to say."

"We'll take him," said Rosa, and she and George pushed the wheelchair down the corridor. Paul looked at Eleanor and the two of walked together in another direction, an odd couple, with Paul, not only fat but tall, leaning down to speak to the much shorter Eleanor. Margaret was left with her two children. The three of them sat down on the wide bench, and for a few minutes, no one spoke. Anita stretched out her long legs.

"What do you think is going to happen?" she asked, sighing.

Margaret shrugged. "I wish we could have gone before the judge earlier in the day. I think your father would have done much better then. I suppose it could end up that they'd ask us to come back tomorrow, or something." Then she laughed bitterly. "How did you like the judge?"

Anita shrugged. She looked tired and confused, and her hair was beginning to hang down on both sides of her face. "It was nothing like the kind of courtroom you see on TV. She didn't even attempt to control the crowd."

* * * *

It was after four-thirty before the judge's clerk summoned them to her chambers. Henry had awakened and talked briefly to Paul; he looked more alert. He and Paul sat on one side of the judge and she and Eleanor on the other. Once again, the judge turned to Henry and began to question him. She was a little more gentle this time, and seemed determined to get a response out of him.

"Mr. Bluestone, you are here to obtain a divorce, isn't that right?" Slowly, Henry nodded his head. "How long have you been in a wheelchair?" she asked.

"Broke my leg," said Henry, evidently expecting a slightly different question.

"And when was that?" the judge asked.

Henry looked at Paul, obviously hoping to get a little help.

After a minute, Paul said to him: "Wasn't it around Thanksgiving?" And Henry nodded. The judge looked sternly over at Paul, as if to say: don't interfere.

"Where have you been living since then?"

This time, Henry answered more quickly. "My house."

"Do you mean the house where you and Mrs. Bluestone have been living for some years?" The judge asked, looking puzzled. Henry nodded uncertainly.

"And who has been taking care of you?"

Henry turned and looked directly at Margaret. "Margaret," he said, smiling as if pleased that this time he had given the right answer.

The judge looked at Eleanor and asked: "Is that correct?"

"Yes, your honor," said Eleanor. "Mrs. Bluestone has been the primary caretaker ever since his accident at the end of November."

The judge frowned and was silent for several minutes. She looked down at the papers on her desk. "If you get divorced, Mr. Bluestone, who will take care of you then? And where will you live?"

Now Henry looked almost frightened, his eyes wide and staring out of his Parkinsonian mask. He took a deep breath, and finally said, slowly: "My house? Please, please, please."

Now it was the judge's turn to take a deep breath. "Mr. Bluestone, do you know what year this is?" Henry didn't reply.

"Do you know who the President is?"

Henry frowned. From the look on his face, it was clear that he was not sure. Oh, dear, thought Margaret, that does it. Henry shook his head, as if he were trying to clear away his confusion. And then, pleading, he turned to the judge, and said once again: "Please, please, please."

The judge stood up. "Counselor," she said to Paul, "your client is certainly not competent to understand what a divorce entails. Let me remind you that this court looks with disfavor on attorneys who clog up its busy schedule with inappropriate cases." She paused, and Margaret glanced over at Paul; he looked like a child who was being reprimanded by his kindergarten teacher. "What your client does need," the judge went on, "is a guardian -- someone to look after his interests -- and I would urge you to petition the court to that end." Gathering her black robe about her, she said to the four of them: "Divorce denied," before she swept out of the room, like the wicked witch of the west. All she needed was a broomstick, Margaret thought.

There was a long silence. Margaret felt as if she had been condemned to a life sentence of hard labor, that there was no reprieve. The bottom had dropped out of her life. Suddenly, she was mad at everyone except Henry.

None of this was his fault, she realized. This whole experience must have been a torture to him. She rose to her feet. "I think we need to get Henry home and into bed." She got behind the wheelchair and began pushing it out into the corridor. Now she felt like Sisyphus, doomed to roll a large stone up a hill, and, having almost reached the top, condemned to have it fall on her, and then to start pushing it up again.

"Let me do that, Margaret," said Paul.

"You've done enough," she replied. "Or maybe the answer is that you've done nothing. I just want to go home." As they moved along the corridor, they met the rest of the family.

"What happened?" asked Charles. "What did the judge say?"

She sighed. "She said your father isn't competent enough to understand a divorce, and that what he really needs is a guardian, and of course, she was right. Your father told her that he wanted to be home." She sighed. "Here, Charles, would you mind pushing the chair?" All of a sudden, she was exhausted. "You'll have to take him in the elevator."

When they all got to the bottom of the marble stairs, Eleanor turned to Margaret and said: "I'm so sorry it turned out like this. We had a good divorce agreement, but the judge was right. Henry's incompetence obviously precludes a divorce at this time." Margaret looked at her in astonishment. Didn't she understand that this was a disaster? The two lawyers walked together toward the parking lot. Margaret wondered if they were discussing what they were going to bill her and Henry.

* * * *

When supper was over and Henry had been put to bed, Margaret sensed that the rest of the family seemed to be needing to go their separate ways. It was as if they were suffering from a kind of culture shock, perhaps from too much togetherness all day long in a hostile environment. Charles had already told them that he had to get back to Portland that night, and then Anita had said she was still having some left-over jet lag and wanted to go to bed early. Rosa and George, who'd hardly said a word during the meal, looked completely exhausted. Quickly, before they all disappeared, Margaret felt she had to make some kind of statement. "I don't know how to thank you all for being here today. Maybe tomorrow, after we've had some sleep, we should get together and make some decisions about where to go from here." Again, she was sounding like a CEO whose company had gone into receivership. And maybe that was true; she was certainly feeling emotionally bankrupt. She sighed, and reached up to give Charles a hug as he put on his jacket and prepared to leave. She kissed Anita goodnight and ushered Rosa and George up the stairs.

Now she needed to call Erik, to tell him what had happened. Forcing herself to do so, she dialed his number. "Erik," she said when she heard his voice at the other end, and then she began to cry. She could hardly say the words: "The judge said no divorce."

"Oh, Maggie," he said. "Oh, shit." He was quiet for a minute, and then sighed. "What happened?"

As she sobbed, she tried to explain. "The judge said Henry wasn't competent to understand even the idea of a divorce. And she was right." She paused, wiping her tears with the edge of her sleeve. "Poor Henry, he had no idea what it was all about -- it was really horrible."

There was a long silence. "Listen, Maggie, whatever happens, from here on, I want to be there for you, to help in any way that I can. I don't care what the fuck the courts decided. For my money, you're not married to that man any more. I understand you want him to have good care, and I'll help with that if I can. But I'm not going to play games anymore. I'm going to be part of your life. Do you hear me?"

"Oh, Erik. God, I needed you to say that to me." For a minute, she wondered if Erik was thinking of moving into her house and helping her take care of Henry. Now there was a fantasy. She went on quickly. "And somehow -- I don't know exactly how, we need to see each other. In person. This talking on the phone is no good." She felt a little better, and was able to whisper: "Goodnight. I love you."

Chapter Twenty-two

After breakfast, Margaret knew that she should start the discussion, but she hesitated. She was tired of being chairperson of the world. And she saw that Anita had become her cool self again. Wearing her dark brown slacks and a light velvet pullover, she'd braided her hair and tucked in all the stray pieces. Margaret remembered how, even as a child, Anita had presented these two different faces to the world: one, a soft, helpless rumpled look -- like an unmade bed -- and the other, on display today, -- aloof, efficient, and remote.

Margaret usually avoided confronting that second Anita, but not today. Addressing her directly, she said: "I've been thinking -- most of the night -- about what to do about your father. The Screening Team will be here next week to tell us if he's acceptable for nursing home placement, but I also need to decide what's right for me." She looked around. No one said anything, and it was impossible to tell what Anita was thinking. "I've made a few decisions. First, I'm going to ask Paul to go ahead, as the judge recommended, and have a guardian appointed. I'd like Henry to attend Molly's wedding; and by then, I'm sure, the State will have approved his placement in a nursing home." Her voice was not questioning, nor was it begging. It was a straight-out decision, and it was hers to make. The judge, after all, had decided that they were still married.

451

"Mom," said Anita, quietly and slowly, "I think we should go to look at some nursing homes while I'm here." Margaret sighed with relief. There was a sound of acceptance in Anita's voice, as if she were willing to move forward. Perhaps her daughter was also responding to the fact that her mother had made a definite decision.

Then, thank God, Rosa spoke up. She had a determined look on her long, thin face, but her tri-focal glasses gave her eyes a cubist character, as if there were, indeed, several ways of looking at things. "George and I talked last night about this whole situation." This sounded like one of Rosa's pronouncements, giving the impression of having been rehearsed in advance. "We want you to know, Margaret, that we think you deserve a lot of credit. We'll back you whatever you decide." With a "that's that" look on her face, Rosa tightened her lips and sat back. George, his usually jolly round face looking serious, just nodded. Did they ever disagree?

"We decided," said George, now belatedly seconding the motion Rosa had made, "that we could stay here and help you for a while, anyway. But we'll need to go home toward the end of next week to take care of our bills and check on the house. We'll be back, of course, for Molly's wedding on Valentine's Day weekend."

Margaret sighed with relief. "And Molly's coming a week before the wedding, so I won't be on my own too long."

452

Anita looked directly at her mother. "Mom, I'd planned to be here anyway through Monday." She paused, her brow furrowed, her warm brown eyes looking concerned. "Maybe you and I could look at some nursing homes in the next few days, if Aunt Rosa and Uncle George can keep an eye on Dad. This job is getting to be too much for all of us. I'd certainly feel better if I could see some of these places."

Margaret sighed with relief. Her oldest child was finally looking at the world through her mother's eyes. "Oh, Anita, thank you."

The monitor began to indicate, by its rustling noises, that Henry was waking up from his post-breakfast nap. "I'll go," said George, evidently happy to be useful.

Suddenly Margaret felt, in spite of the disaster of yesterday, as if she had a support team: Erik, last night, Rosa and George, and now, Anita!

Friday seemed to be a good day to start looking at nursing homes. Margaret had thought about calling the hospital for suggestions, but when she saw Anita looking at the Yellow Pages to see what was nearby, she decided to let her go ahead.

"Oh my God," she said to her mother. "Look how many there are, just in our own phone book, and two right here, Mom, close to home. Why don't we call them and make appointments for today or tomorrow?"

Margaret and Anita's first appointment was at two o'clock that afternoon. Margaret recalled the way she'd felt when she was applying to nursery schools for her children. Does the mother admit that the child occasionally has "accidents," or temper tantrums? Does he or she need to have "time outs" for biting other kids?

The Raleigh Hills Nursing Home turned out to be located on the grounds of what Margaret remembered as an old country club, and the place was clearly named after that club. The admissions social worker, Mrs. Tarantino, met them in the waiting room. Efficient and brisk as she walked in, she was even shorter than Margaret, but she radiated confidence.

"Let me take you first to the community area," she said proudly, leading them down a corridor into what looked like the main floor of a hotel. She pointed out a gift shop, a library, and a crafts room, all at the moment unoccupied. At the end of the hall was what looked like a cocktail lounge. Margaret glanced up at the sign hanging over the door: *The Nineteenth Hole*, it said.

"Do you actually serve cocktails to the patients?" she asked.

"With the permission of their doctors, of course," said the social worker. "A nursing home is not a prison, you know."

They passed a large conference room where a group of elderly women in wheelchairs -- and one lone man -- were being led in song by a young woman who seemed never to have left the sixties, with her long hair, her guitar, and her torn blue jeans. They were singing, trying to make a round out of it: *Row, Row, Row your Boat.*

Anita shook her head. "Not quite Dad's cup of tea," she whispered to Margaret, starting to giggle. They passed another group room, and here a number of patients were sitting at long tables, playing Bingo. Oh, dear, thought Margaret, this is not the place for Henry, that's for sure.

Perhaps reading their minds, or at least picking up on their lack of enthusiasm, Mrs. Tarantino said: "Why don't we go upstairs and see the patients' rooms?" She took them into the elevator and pressed the button for "2." "I'll show you the men's corridor," she said smiling. "There aren't too many male patients -- only 20% of our population, actually. We have two men, occasionally three, in each room, and of course, we try to match the gentlemen, if we can. What are your husband's interests?"

Anita and Margaret were quiet. Finally, Margaret said: "My husband was a geologist, but he's not very verbal anymore," suddenly feeling once again that she was about to flunk the entrance interview. They peeked into several double rooms where patients were evidently napping. In one of these rooms, there was an empty bed, with its bedspread neatly in place. "I see you have a vacancy," said Margaret.

"Oh, that one is spoken for," said the social worker quickly. "That patient will be checking in tomorrow. We took his name off the top of our waiting list," she said, deftly indicating that admission wasn't quite so easy.

Margaret's heart sank, not because she was anxious for Henry to end up in this particular nursing home, but because the woman's remarks indicated that admission could be a problem everywhere. "How long is that list?" she asked.

"The men's list is shorter by far than the women's," she said. "There are five or six names, if I recall rightly, but there would be a minimum of a month or more before we can expect any vacancies."

As they continued down the corridor they passed a room entitled: Patients' Lounge. Sitting inside, were ten or more blank-faced women in wheelchairs. The chairs were positioned so that they were facing a large television set that was blaring at top volume -- presumably to accommodate the more hard-of-hearing patients. The program seemed to be a soap opera. None of the patients was speaking; several had fallen asleep and were canted over to one side. One kept muttering that someone had stolen her purse. "No one believes me," she was saying, reaching out to grab Margaret's wrist.

"What's up on the third floor?" said Anita, the crispness of her voice indicating that she'd had enough of this area.

456

"Oh, that's for demented patients, who've regressed to a childlike state. We don't want to bother them with visitors like yourselves." Mrs. Tarantino looked uneasy.

Anita and Margaret looked at each other. Anita spoke up: "My father is rather regressed, too. I think we need to see that floor. We won't disturb them."

The social worker shook her head. "It's more like a hospital or an infirmary up there, and most of the patients are not continent."

"Neither is my father," said Anita. "If you're talking about diapers and things like that, we're quite familiar with the problem. And we really need to see that floor, since that's probably where my Dad would go. He's not going to be singing *Row, Row, Row your Boat*, or bending his elbow in the Nineteenth Hole."

"All right," said the social worker, leading them back to the elevator. Her voice sounded angry, and Margaret could hear the unspoken words of: you'll be sorry.

As soon as the elevator doors opened, Margaret was aware of the smell. That's funny, she thought, Henry's room doesn't have an odor. You'd think they could solve that problem somehow. She glanced over at Anita and saw that she, too, was wrinkling her nose. And she was mouthing, for her mother's view only: NO WAY, shaking her head.

They walked along the corridor, following the social worker, whose erect posture seemed to say: you asked for it; don't blame me. Margaret took a quick peek into one of the rooms. Curled up in a fetal position, entwined in her sheets, was an emaciated, wispy-haired woman. And she was moaning, over and over, Mama, Mama.

And from further down the hall, you could now hear, again and again, hoarse screams coming out of one of the rooms. In the waiting room for that floor, a concerned looking elderly man in old-fashioned high shoes was patting the hand of his demented wife as she sat in her wheelchair. With his other hand, he kept trying to pull down his wife's skimpy bathrobe, to cover her knees. He was saying over and over: it's gonna be okay; Edith, it's gonna be okay. Well, Margaret thought with one part of her mind, at least they let the relatives come up to this floor. But the other part was saying: Oh God, is this how it's going to end for Henry? And, who knows, maybe for me?

The social worker looked at them, as if to say: have you had enough? And they nodded, indicating that they were ready to leave. As they passed the rooms again, this time Margaret saw another female patient, lying on her back on her bed, stark naked. Quickly, Mrs. Tarantino closed the door to that room, muttering that they were short-staffed that day since one of the nurses was out sick.

They spoke very little, going down in the elevator, except to say that they would get in touch with her if the Screening Team gave their okay for Henry to enter a nursing home.

In the car on the way home, they were both silent. Then Anita said, looking at her watch:

"It's a little early for the Nineteenth Hole, but by God, I could use a drink!" And Margaret laughed, since Anita was well known in the family for never taking more than a little sip of any alcoholic beverage.

"Well, maybe the place we're going to see tomorrow will be better. I hope so," said Margaret, "because I can't go through too much of this. Oh, those poor patients! How would you feel if you went to visit a relative and found her either stark naked, or wound up in her sheets in a fetal position, calling for her Mama?"

"Well, we both vote no on that one, anyway," said Anita. "If they're all like that, I'm quitting my job and moving in to take care of Dad!" She shook her head. "Bingo, and *Row, Row, Row your Boat*!"

* * * *

Eastman House, on the outskirts of town, had been donated by the family of that name only seven years ago. The brochure, which Margaret and Anita found in the waiting room, mentioned that they could accept a few chronic cases, but that their main purpose was to serve the families and friends of those patients who had only a limited time to live. The House was very quiet. After a few minutes, a tall, very lean man, came into the room and greeted them.

"Thank you for coming," he said, "they call me Father Geoffrey. I'm the Director here. And you must be the Bluestones." Margaret noticed that he was wearing the round, backward-turned collar of man of the cloth, but she decided not to ask which cloth. "You're looking us over because your husband is ill?" he asked Margaret.

She nodded. "I'm not sure whether he falls into the category of 'terminal' but I'm beginning to think that may be the case. I'll know better in a few weeks when he sees the neurologist again."

"This is a small place compared to most nursing home. I'll take you around. Let's go first into the kitchen." He led them into a moderately-sized kitchen. Several women were sitting at the table, drinking tea and eating crackers. There seemed to be soup cooking on the stove. "We encourage family members -- some of whom may spend most of the day here -- to use the kitchen in any way that they want."

Father Geoffrey commented, as they walked toward the front of the house, "The kitchen seems to serve as a sort of 'group therapy' place. Toward the end, when the patient is dying, these people probably feel that no one can understand what they're going through except other people who

460

are going through the same thing." Then he smiled. "People always wonder why there isn't a cook in the kitchen, making meals for the patients. But most of the patients have lost interest in food: the kitchen is for the living."

Margaret noticed that there were no Bingo rooms, no Happy Hour place, no TV room, and no library. Most of the house consisted of large single rooms with high ceilings. The patients she saw were in bed, some struggling to breathe, but there was usually a family member or a nurse with them. It was very quiet; people spoke in murmurs. And there were no odors. She looked over at Anita. Her daughter was looking thoughtful, but taking in everything she saw. Margaret thought she saw a tear on one cheek.

As they finished the small tour, Father Geoffrey took them back into the waiting room. "Do you have any questions?" he said.

"Just a comment," said Margaret. "This is a very peaceful place, isn't it? It makes me feel that maybe dying doesn't have to be so awful." Anita was nodding her head.

"Good," said the man, "that's what we hope people will feel. But we don't kid ourselves: the families and friends -- the survivors -- will be feeling a lot of pain and sadness for a long time." He looked at them quizzically, as if wondering what they weren't asking.

Margaret felt she should say something. Looking up at him, she said: "I'm really impressed. We're still thinking about whether we can manage by ourselves at home, but if we need a place to take him, this is the kind of setting that would make us comfortable. Am I right, Anita?" Again her daughter nodded. She squeezed Margaret's hand.

"So we may hear from you?"

"You will," said Margaret. "We're having the Screening Team next week. Even if they approve placement, I gather that it can take a month or so. Do you have a long waiting list?"

He shook his head. "No. That's because we're basically a hospice. Turnover is, sad to say, rapid here." He took them to the door. "Call me whenever you need us. And thank you for coming."

* * * *

On Tuesday, after Anita had gone back to Seattle, the Screening Team came to make their assessment. Margaret noticed that even Rosa and George were nervous; for all of them it was like having the teacher make a home visit. The two nurses were wearing civilian clothes, but looked very professional, with their clip boards and printed forms. Rosa and George excused themselves and went to sit with Henry, while Margaret took the women into the living room to answer their questions. They introduced themselves: the smaller, darker one was Rosaria Escobar, and the other, a tall, pale, lanky blond, was Helen Parker.

462

They began by taking a history of his illness, focussing on the period since Thanksgiving. Then they said they wanted to ask about six items in particular. They got out their clip boards. "Please tell us, Mrs. Bluestone, about his bathing," said Ms. Parker. "Is he able to do this himself?"

Margaret shook her head. "Since his leg is broken, he can't get out of bed to go into the bathtub. So he's had to be bathed by one of us, every day. Sometimes we hand him the washcloth and tell him to do part of the job himself, but mostly he just looks as us as if he didn't know what we were talking about."

Ms. Escobar looked down at her list. "What about dressing? Can he do any of that, or help with it?"

"Well, he mostly wears pajamas, or even hospital johnnies -- one of my nurses suggested I buy them since they're more convenient for the caretakers. And it's easier, of course, when the patient is wearing diapers."

"Oh," said the tall one, "he's wearing diapers. I didn't know that. So he is not continent?"

"That's correct. In fact, even before he broke his fracture, he wet the bed."

"Can he feed himself?"

"Yes," said Margaret, proudly. "Sometimes he might need a little help, but the nurse I had last month urged me to let him do it by himself as much as possible. We do cut his meat. It takes him a very long time to chew each bite, but the doctor said that's typical in this kind of Parkinson's."

"So his illness has been described as Parkinson's Disease?"

"The neurologist he saw in late November -- Dr. Reiner -- made that tentative diagnosis, but she's going to see him again soon and could perhaps be more definite by that time. I could have her send you a copy of her report."

"That would be good, and we need one from his primary care physician as well." Ms. Escobar was quiet for a minute. "His disease seems to have gone downhill rather quickly," she said, frowning.

"Dr. Reiner told me he probably had a more devastating form of Parkinson's, the one that includes dementia and has a more rapid course."

There was another long silence, and then Ms. Parker said: "We have one more question for you. Can he get out of his wheelchair or bed and into a car or other place? Either with or without help?"

"No, he can't," said Margaret. "In fact, that's one of the hardest things for us to accomplish, and it takes at least two of us to do it."

"Mrs. Bluestone," and this time it was Ms. Parker who spoke for both of them, "out of the six areas that we've asked you about, there was only one -- feeding -- which your husband was able to manage. I would guess, although we have to wait to get all the medical reports in, as well as the reports from the Occupational Therapist, that with this history we are probably going to agree that he needs placement in a nursing facility." She paused. "Of course, after we see him, we might change our minds and decide that your family is providing such good care for him that it makes more sense for him to remain at home."

Oh, God, thought Margaret. She could end up being punished for having done a good job. "I have to tell you," she said, "that I don't think I can do this much longer. It's too much, and I have to get back to work. I didn't tell you -- because you didn't ask -- but he's a sundowner who gets agitated and really out of his mind as soon as darkness falls." And now she was crying in earnest. "I just don't think I can do it anymore, really."

The two women stood up. "Let's go in and see Mr. Bluestone. We'll want to give him a complete physical exam, and then ask him if he has some thoughts as to where he should be." Margaret suspected they were going to check on Henry's cognitive ability.

"Yes, he does have some thoughts on that subject." Margaret could hear the sarcasm in her own voice. "Just ask him where he wants to be. The judge in the Probate Court asked him that the other day and he said 'Home, my home.'" She wiped her eyes.

Margaret told Henry that these two women were nurses and that they wanted to examine him and ask him some questions. Rosa and George waited in the kitchen until the physical exam was completed, but Rosa came into his room when the nurses began to query him. Henry only looked at the nurses blankly, with his wide-open stare. After a few unproductive attempts, the nurses seemed about to leave. Rosa, Margaret could see, was unhappy that Henry wasn't giving a better performance.

"Henry," said Rosa, "tell these two nurses who I am."

Henry smiled and said slowly: "Rosa."

"That's right," she said, "and tell them where you are, right now."

"My house," he said proudly. And then pointing to his cast, he added triumphantly, "broke my leg." Perhaps remembering the time he was in the hospital when other nurses had done so, he pointed to his leg, and said to them slowly: "sign my cast."

Rosa was beaming. As the nurses leaned down to sign the cast, she said: "no one knows him the way I do." Margaret wondered again about Rosa's role in Henry's life. Grandma Bluestone had probably figured out long ago that she was only the half-mother. Smiling, Margaret couldn't help wondering where that left her. Maybe she was just a half-wife. It sounded like something from atomic physics.

She was recalled to the present as one of the nurses turned to Rosa and asked her to assist them with a series of questions. "Would you ask Mr.

Bluestone what these various objects are and what they're for?" She opened up her handbag and pulled out a small screwdriver, handing it to Rosa.

"Henry," said his sister, "What's this?"

Henry looked at it and frowned. Margaret thought, from the look on his face, that it was vaguely familiar, and suspected that he might have forgotten the name, but probably knew what it was for. "Henry," Rosa said, "what is it for?" He reached out for it and took it in his right hand. Automatically, he turned it back and forth, as if his body recalled its purpose.

The nurse took it back from him and handed him a key. "And what's this?" asked Rosa, and the look on her face showed how much she wanted to give him some kind of hint. She leaned forward and began to mouth the correct answer.

This time, Henry seemed less confused. He held it as one would hold a key and said:

"Door?" Even he knew that wasn't it, but his smile indicated that he felt he was on the right track. He handed it back to the nurse.

"One more," she said, as the pulled a small hammer out of the bag. It reminded Margaret of one of Henry's geological tools -- his old rock hammer.

Henry's whole face lit up, and for a few seconds, he looked like his old self. "Rock hammer!" he said, hefting it gently, as if tapping a crystal. Then he looked around at all of them, puzzled, it seemed, as to what they were all doing there, and most of all, who and what was he. Oh God, thought Margaret, none of this was going to be easy.

As the nurses moved toward the front door, Margaret leaned down and kissed Rosa on the cheek. "Thanks," she whispered, wondering at the same time whether Rosa's pride might have queered the whole deal. It was all so confusing.

* * * *

On Saturday, January 25, Margaret was alone with Henry all night for the first time since that week -- right after Thanksgiving -- when he'd been sent back to her house from the hospital. By evening, she'd lost whatever patience she had. Trying to calm herself, she walked out of his room and went into the living room. Perhaps some music would help. She was reminded of Charles's success with the Christmas music. They'd never got around to trying Beethoven as he'd suggested. Maybe that would help <u>her</u>, and Henry as well. What would be soothing? Finally, she selected one of Beethoven's last quartets, the one that started out very slowly -- Opus 132. Putting it on the machine, she flicked the switch that would carry the sound to the back of the house. Just hearing those beginning notes did indeed calm her down. Taking a deep breath, she went back into Henry's room. He was tapping slowly in rhythm on his dinner tray, quietly and with a gentle smile on his face. Settling herself in the rocking chair, she hummed the melody softly to herself. After a bit, she looked over at Henry. As she'd hoped, his eyes had closed. When the quartet was over, she tip-toed out of the room and went up to bed. She dropped into a deep and dreamless sleep.

She had no idea what time it was or how long the monitor had been making these strange noises, but she woke in total darkness to the sounds of what sounded like the old "please, please, please." She'd have to get up and see what was wrong. When she walked into Henry's room, she saw immediately that he was not in his bed. Terrified, she looked around. Not in the chair, nor the bathroom. Then her glance fell upon the floor. He'd got out of bed and was lying, face-down, his head on the carpet, spread-eagled at the foot of the bed, naked except for the green diaper. He wasn't moving. She leaned down, hiking up her nightgown, to see if he was still breathing. Just then, he muttered: please, please. So he was alive. She felt a tiny wave of regret.

He'd evidently wanted to get out of bed, couldn't climb over the sides which had been pulled up to keep him in, so he'd crawled, cast and all, to the end of the bed and fallen off. As far as she could see, he wasn't hurt, and the fracture, itself, was, of course, protected by the cast. But now the problem, insurmountable as far as she could see, was to get him back into bed. But he might be less frightened if she could turn him over and cover him. But how was she going to do that?

Kicking off her slippers to give herself better traction, she unzipped her robe and dropped it to the floor. She needed leverage to flip him over. It was going to be something like turning a large tortoise onto its back.

Kneeling now, with one knee on each side, she reached for Henry's right arm. It was too far away. She'd have to stand. Putting her weight on one hand, she stood up, awkwardly, grunting as she did so. Jesus, she thought, she was getting too old for this kind of stuff! She looked at the problem again. She would need to bring both his arms down next to his sides so that she could roll him over.

"Henry," she said firmly, "Let me move your arms down this way, so I can turn you over." Slowly, she slid the right arm out and down, tucking it next to his body. Switching then, bending over, to the left arm, she saw the right one begin to move on its own. "No, Henry, keep your arms <u>down</u> so I can turn you." She could hear the exasperation in her voice and felt tempted to give him a little swat, as if she were training a dog.

Well, here goes, she told herself, leaning forward again. She tucked Henry's right arm in close to his narrow chest, then quickly, before he could move it, pulled the left one down as well. Then she stepped over to the right side of his body, her toes pointing to his waist, took both her hands, slipped her fingers under his back, and pushed him over. Much to her surprise, it worked. The legs followed the rest of him obediently. And there he was, her upended turtle, looking at her in Parkinsonian astonishment. And, as far as she could see, he wasn't hurt, just cold and shivering.

Trying to calm him down -- he still seemed frightened and began again to say his "pleases" -- she said to him: "Henry, it's okay. You just fell out of bed. See, I'm putting this pillow under your head and I'm covering you with your blankets." She paused, because he still looked terrified. "It's me, I'm here, I'm Margaret, and I'll find someone to help us." That sounded good, and seemed to settle Henry for a few minutes, but who the hell could she get at this hour -- she looked at her watch and saw that it was after two -- to come to lift this man into bed.

There was always the police, she thought, or the fire department. That was whom you called if your kid locked himself in the bathroom, or if your kitty was up in a tree. And now they had the EMT's, but she suspected none of these organizations would consider this an emergency. She could call Saul, Chloe's husband, and he'd probably come, the dear man, but she already owed him a debt she could never repay for his willingness to take care of Henry that weekend when she went to New York with Erik.

Erik. . . He'd told her to call if she needed help. But could he leave Will in the middle of the night? Then she remembered that on the night he'd had her for dinner, way back last summer, he'd driven her home, explaining that he sometimes left Will for short periods like that, and it was okay. Quickly, before she could change her mind, she dialed his number.

"Erik. It's Maggie. I hate calling you like this, but you said I could. Henry has fallen out of bed. He seems to be okay, not hurt or anything, but I can't lift him back into bed again, at least not by myself. I thought about calling the police or someone, but then I thought about you."

"I'll be right over," he said. "Let me just wake up Will and tell him where I'm going and leave him your number."

In ten minutes he was ringing her back door bell. "Come in," she said, reaching up to hug him, and already feeling some of the tension go out of her body, and a sense of security taking over. He stood just inside the doorway, his feet hastily shoved into his untied sneakers, the bottoms of his red and white pajama tops beneath his brown sweater. Under his wool cap, his bushy red hair curled out around the edges. She'd never seen anyone look better! "Thank you," she said. "Come," and she led him into Henry's room.

"This is Erik, Henry," she said simply. "He's the man who fixed up the house. He's going to help you get back into bed." She took Erik's jacket and put it on the rocker.

Erik moved toward Henry. "Margaret," he said, "could you unhook the side of the bed here? Thank you." He took the blankets off and laid them aside. "Okay, now, I'm just going to pick you up and put you back into bed. Margaret, can you keep your hand on the leg with the cast? I don't want to knock it into the frame here." Then, in one quick motion, with Margaret's help, he gently lifted him to safety. Tucking the blankets around him, while Margaret repositioned the pillow, he pulled up the side and locked it into place. Safe and secure, Henry closed his eyes and seemed to drift off immediately.

Looking around the room, Erik said: "Maybe we should move that chest of drawers down to the end of the bed, so this won't happen again. He's probably getting more mobile, now that the leg is healing, and he'll keep trying to get out." Without even bothering to empty the drawers, he picked up the chest and moved it into place at the foot of Henry's bed. "Okay?" he asked Margaret.

She nodded. "Thank you so much. You've thought of everything." How easy it would be to dump this whole problem of Henry into this man's capable hands. What a temptation it would be to ask him to move in -- lock,

473

stock and barrel, including Will and his wheelchair -- to be on hand for emergencies like this one! But it wouldn't do.

Moving out of the sick room, they walked together into the living room. Quickly, he reached out for her and they held each other closely in the half-light. "Oh, God, right now, here in this place, I want you so much." His hands moved under her thin nightgown. "Come, let's go upstairs," he said, taking her hand. "I have to admit, it feels strange, even to be thinking about all this, when we're only a few rooms away from him."

"I have the monitor hooked up," she whispered. It was also true that it wouldn't take long, not the way they were both feeling.

As they walked up the stairs, she noticed they were both tiptoeing. This time she led him into her own bedroom. "Here," she said, "let me undress you." As he pulled the sweater over his head, she began to unbutton his pajama tops. Then she pulled down his pajama pants, and seeing what awaited her there, she quickly took her own nightgown off and pulled him into bed. "Don't wait," she said, breathing rapidly, "now, please, now."

Chapter Twenty-three

Early Sunday morning, still in bed, Margaret lay awake, smiling as she thought about the night before. And a few minutes later, standing before the bathroom mirror, toothbrush in hand, she looked at her face. Her cheeks were pink, still a little creased from sleeping, and she was grinning. She should call Erik right now, to thank him for his help last night. And for everything else. She smiled. She dialed his number.

"Erik? It's Maggie." Suddenly, she was embarrassed and didn't know what to say.

"How's my girl this morning?" She could hear the smile in his voice.

"I'm feeling wonderful," she said, "thanks to you -- for everything."

"Listen," he said, "I had an idea. Have you looked out the window?"

"Not really," said Margaret, still warm from his words, "I've just got out of bed. What's happening? Don't tell me it's snowing?"

"No," he laughed. "It's a beautiful day. I was wondering if we could bundle Henry up and take him, along with his wheelchair, and with Will and his wheelchair, for a ride somewhere? Maybe down to look at the ocean -- Will and I do that sometimes on sunny winter days -- and it would make a nice change for Henry. What do you think?"

"Oh, Erik. What a wonderful thought! Just tell me what time and I'll have us ready." Even as she spoke, she was aware that they were entering new and uncharted country.

* * * *

Henry slept for most of the ride to the beach, while Margaret leaned back and listened to the interchange between Erik and his son. She noticed that when Will was talking to his father and feeling no stress, his conversation went more smoothly. It was difficult to tell whether he was actually retarded, or if he had a muscular problem that involved speaking. "Look, Dad," Will said, pointing across the Charles River to a lofty crane that stood poised over a half-finished building, "there's a man up there, in that little cabin, in the crane." Erik slowed down and pulled over. "See?"

"You're right, and today's Sunday. I wonder what he's doing?"

"What I'd like to know," said Will, now speaking slowly once more, his rosy-cheeked face flushed with pleasure, "is how does he get up there?"

"Good question," said his father, frowning as he looked up at the crane. "I don't know, myself. Maybe we could figure it out." The morning sun had picked up the fiery red of his hair and beard. He was enjoying this conversation. And so was Margaret.

"There ought to be an elevator," said Will, sounding puzzled, "but there isn't. Maybe they bring the crane down every night and then he takes it up after he gets in."

"Could be," said his father, slowly starting up the car again. Margaret thought it was good he didn't come up with another and better answer. He was letting Will figure it out. Later on, at the beach, Erik pulled the car up close to the sand and took a big blanket out of the back. Opening the passenger side of the car, lifted Will out and sat him down. By this time, Henry had waked up and was looking around. "Beach," he said cheerfully.

"Would you like to come out and sit on the blanket?" Erik asked. Henry nodded, and Erik lifted him out as well. Soon the four of them were sitting in the bright sunlight, not that far from where the waves were coming in. The wind was down and it felt comfortably warm. They were alone on the beach with the gulls. Margaret stretched out and looked up at the sky. Pale blue and far away, it was still a winter sky. Suddenly, she felt the need to test the water temperature; she walked down to the ocean's edge, bravely waiting on the sloping sand for the waves to reach her outstretched hand. Oh, God, it was cold! Well, it could have been worse. She laughed and then moved down the beach, waving back at the three of them. Looking for shells, she walked along, thinking of Chloe's daughter, Athena, and how she'd spent the last days of her life collecting sea shells. Soon Margaret had found a few remnants from the wrack of the winter's storms. Carrying them carefully, she brought them back and laid them on the blanket.

"Oh, look," said Will, holding up a long narrow shell. He showed it to Henry.

"Razor clam," said Henry. And he was right. Will looked puzzled. "Here," said Henry, taking the shell and holding it up to his face, pretending to shave. "Razor."

"That's what razors looked like in the old days," said Erik to Will. He looked over at Margaret, smiling a very tender smile. The smile said: they're talking to each other.

* * * *

Later, after Erik had dropped them off at her house, Margaret thought about the day. Were they in the process of setting up a little family here? Mom and Pop: that would be herself and Erik, then Will, the handicapped son, and what role was being set aside for Henry? Grandpa? Something about this vision made her shiver.

But by mid-week, in spite of her reservations, she'd asked Erik to help out again. They took Henry to both doctors on the same day -- a long day for Henry, but the good news was that the cast could come off, and would be replaced by a walking brace, for a two-week period. The orthopedist was concerned that Henry seemed to have no interest in walking: when he suggested he try, Henry only said: "Wheelchair," in a frantic voice.

"I think he needs some physical therapy as well as some occupational therapy," the orthopedist said to Margaret. "Your husband may know better than we do what he's able to do." Everyone kept telling her that Henry knew what was best for him. She'd heard this from the judge, the lawyers, the nurses on the Screening Team, and now the orthopedist. "You're off now to see the neurologist," he said, "so ask her about it."

When they got to Dr. Reiner's office, Margaret asked Erik to sit with Henry while she talked with the doctor. As she explained why she needed an updated report for the screening team, Dr. Reiner was leaning towards her, listening as she listed Henry's symptoms, and nodding sympathetically as Margaret described the difficult nights. When she told the doctor what had happened in Court, she shook her head sadly.

"It sounds as if he has deteriorated quite rapidly, Mrs. Bluestone. It's been very hard for you, I can see that." She paused. "Well, let me talk to him and I'll see what's going on now." As Margaret went out into the waiting room to get Henry, she wondered what had happened that had changed Dr. Reiner so much. On her previous visit, she'd seemed arrogant, unsympathetic, uncaring, and condescending. Of course, maybe the person who'd changed was herself.

479

Dr. Reiner's seemingly random questions to Henry -- where he lived, who was taking care of him, how he'd got to the hospital that day -- elicited little or no response. If anything, Henry just seemed frightened. He didn't resist when she tested his reflexes, and cooperated a little when she asked him to move his hands and nod his head. Margaret had told the doctor about the tests carried out by the screening team, and how he'd been able to identify the hammer. Dr. Reiner tried one test like that of her own, asking Henry what a pencil was -- he didn't reply -- but when she asked him what you did with it, he pretended to write in the air, and she nodded her head.

"I think that's all we'll do today," she said to Margaret. "Why don't you take him out to the waiting room and then we'll talk again briefly."

Margaret pushed him back to Erik's care and returned to Dr. Reiner's office. "Sit down, Mrs. Bluestone," the doctor said quietly. "I am going to put in my report that your husband is suffering from the end stages of atypical Parkinson's Disease and that he could use the full-time care of a nursing facility."

"What does that mean? End stage? Does that mean he's dying?" How strange it was to hear herself use those words about Henry. Why hadn't she been expecting Dr. Reiner to say something like that? He'd indeed been deteriorating at a rapid rate, but she realized that she'd continued to assume that he'd remain at the stage he'd now reached, a place where he was rather pleasant -- in fact, easier to get along with than he'd ever been since she'd known him. She'd begun to think that he might go on for a long time in this way, a person who needed loving physical care, and a place to live. Of all people, she told herself, she should be familiar with the concept of denial. But in a funny way, she was a perfect example of someone who could not accept a plain fact. Somewhere, hidden in these thoughts was a glimmer of relief: Henry would be dying soon, and she wouldn't have to carry this burden forever. She was feeling guilty, and it was the guilt that led to the denial.

As she was thinking these thoughts, Dr. Reiner was nodding her head. "I can't say just when, but I think we're talking about only a few months or less. He'll begin to lose interest in eating; eventually he'll stop taking liquids; and finally, he'll go into a coma. In fact, even in the last month or so, he'll be quieter. That sundowning behavior will stop, and he'll sleep more and more. You could have hospice care at home, or he could go to one of those hospice nursing facilities."

"My daughter and I visited one, right here in town, that seemed very good," said Margaret, still trying to come to terms with this new information.

"Father Geoffrey's place, I imagine. Excellent. Like home care." The doctor was quiet. Amazingly, she didn't seem to be in any hurry. "In answer to your earlier question, about walking, he needs physical and occupational therapy to give him the best chance to walk."

Margaret was quiet, too. Knowing that Henry would soon die made her feel as if she were in the presence of something overwhelming but inexorable.

"There is one thing I'd like to suggest to you, Mrs. Bluestone," the doctor said. "I'm going to give you a list of dementia support groups. I think you would find it helpful to attend their meetings regularly. There's one that meets on Thursday mornings in a room off the kitchen of Saint Boniface's Church, in town here."

Margaret took the list, but she was surprised. In her role as a social worker, she'd run a number of support groups over the years, none for families of dementia patients, as it happened, but for many other problems. And now she was being referred to a support group. But maybe the doctor had a point.

After thanking her and going out to collect Henry and Erik, she found herself wondering why was she no longer angry at Henry. What had changed? It was Henry who'd become different. This dying man in his final months was no longer the cruel, verbally abusive man she'd been married to for so long. It was as if his disease had burned away his outer prickly hide, leaving a soft inner person who needed tenderness and assistance in the last phase of his life - - its ending.

As they drove home she was quiet, mulling all this over, and Erik left her to her thoughts. As they drew up to her house, she looked back at Henry. He'd fallen asleep. "Don't go yet," she said to Erik. "He's asleep. I need to tell you something."

Erik looked down at her and took her hand. "Bad news? What did the doctor say?"

"She told me Henry was going to die, maybe in a few months, but pretty soon."

"Oh, Maggie." He was quiet for a moment. Margaret wondered if he, too, were struggling with some guilt at the idea of relief. "It must be so complicated for you with all that's gone before, and all that's happening now." He didn't outline what he meant, and Margaret thought maybe that was just as well. And he was right. She wasn't sure how she felt, except that she was stunned, numb, and suddenly very sad. Tears came to her eyes, surprising her. How short life was. It was only yesterday, it seemed, when Henry had been climbing mountains, taking his children camping, testing out his earthquake theories. Perhaps she needed to talk to other people who were going through this process. Maybe she <u>would</u> try the support group.

Chloe might be able to come over for an hour or two this Thursday and she could try out the local group.

* * * *

Saint Boniface's Church was just a mile away. She was the first arrival. She looked around the room, at the chairs set out in a circle, at the old piano in the corner, and at the blackboard with its tired piece of chalk on the end of a string, It was like every Sunday School she'd ever attended, or every A.A. meeting she'd visited, and similar to the sites of many committees she'd belonged to as a social worker representing her agency.

As the members gathered, she looked them over, waiting to see where each of them sat and where there would be an empty chair. She ended up sitting in a kind of back row, behind the primary group, sitting tentatively on the edge of her chair. She looked down at her hands, and pulled off a protruding hangnail, wondering why she was so anxious. The men and women in this group seemed pleased to see each other. Several people introduced themselves to Margaret, and she was glad to see there were other newcomers as well.

In fact, the meeting began by the lay leader's suggestion that each of them, including the new members, should introduce themselves and tell the group briefly what was happening at home. The leader, a tall thin middle-aged woman with short gray hair and thick glasses, began with herself, giving her first name only -- it <u>was</u> going to be like A.A., -- and the fact that she had been taking care of her mother for the last three years. Her mother, she said, had Alzheimer's Disease, and was getting to be a real problem in that she had recently begun to "escape." She kept running out to the street.

As the other members spoke of their own situations, Margaret began to feel that she didn't belong, after all. Some of them spoke so lovingly of their sick and demented relatives, and while sometimes what they said was amusing -- one elderly man with advanced Alzheimer's had told his wife that he couldn't believe he could ever have married <u>her</u>, such an ugly old lady? -- most of them were compassionate. A few evidently preferred to say nothing. When it was her turn, Margaret decided she would just tell them the truth.

"I guess I'm in a different place than the rest of you," she began. "My husband and I, after forty years of a not very happy marriage, had decided to get a divorce. We'd finally separated and he'd gone across the country. Then, suddenly, after five months, he came back, and moved in again with me, demented and disabled." She paused, watching their faces. "I'm taking care of him, but I'm so angry at him for doing this to me!" She sat back, wondering if they would reject her, maybe even throw her out of the group.

The leader laughed. "I must have forgotten to mention that my mother has always been a cruel witch. My sisters are married and live on the West

485

Coast, so I'm stuck with a woman I've hated all my life." Others in the group were nodding. As it turned out, quite a few had similar stories to tell.

Perhaps what they all had in common was that none of them had really accepted this burden willingly, but fate, or being an only child, or the economics of the situation, had thrust them into the position of being caretakers. Several of the members mentioned that many years ago, they'd promised their parents or spouses or sisters that they would <u>never</u> put them in a nursing home. And now they were <u>stuck</u>!

"All my friends tell me I must be some kind of saint," said one man, a tall thin African-American with grizzled hair. "But I'm not. There are days when I feel that taking care of my wife has turned me into some kind of devil. I didn't know, until all this happened, what a horrible person I could be."

One of the other newcomers, a thin little white-haired librarian, sighed. "You're making me feel better, actually. I thought I was the only person who'd thought about strangling the person she's taking care of. My sister's been keeping me up all night, screaming and yelling, and all I can think of is how much I want her to die."

Margaret decided that maybe she needed this group, after all.

* * * *

But by the next day -- in the middle of the morning, when she'd finished her basic daily chores -- she was aware of a new feeling: except for Henry, who was sound asleep, she was alone in her big house. The house felt strangely empty, and she, herself, felt empty, too, as if her whole life had no meaning whatsoever. It was a dull, gray day outside, the ground looking hard and lifeless. And the house was cold; even putting on an extra sweater and pushing up the thermostat didn't help to take away the deep chill she felt. Aware that she was sloppily dressed in old, baggy sweat pants and a cotton turtle neck that was beginning to shrink -- it barely reached her waist -- and realizing that she hadn't even washed her face that morning, she leaned against the hall radiator, pressing its ridges against her body, trying both to warm herself, and to feel <u>something</u> beyond this emptiness.

She looked out toward the street. The only thing moving was an old vine, still clinging to her last elderly elm, being blown by the slight breeze that barely tickled its dried-up tendrils. No one walked by; there was no traffic on the road. For all she knew, she was alone in the world. Maybe Henry had died in the last few minutes. She thought about the other members of the support group, the dullness of their lives, and the sense she'd from them that by the time their husbands, mothers, whoever, had finally died, they'd be so used up that there'd be nothing left of them to find the joy of life again.

Barbara Selling

Ever since she'd been an adult, she'd filled her life up with people: a husband and four children, and then, as they began to leave the nest, a cadre of clients who needed her, and whose growth she nurtured as if they were a new batch of children. Wistfully, she thought about the agency, her own lovely office, and the way in which working there was like being part of a second family, a group of people who really wanted to know what you'd done over the weekend, whether your dinner party had worked out, and where had you bought those lovely shoes?

She tried to imagine her whole life continuing on as it was today, with a demented husband sleeping in a back room, a huge house in which to wander about and no real goals, nothing to look forward to. How did people stand it? For her -- and how lucky she was -- it was temporary. She'd be free when Mrs. Mahoney arrived early the next week, and then Molly, and all the excitement of the wedding. But after the wedding, unless she were able to put Henry in a nursing home, life <u>could</u> go on like this.

How had she managed when she was stuck at home with sick children? And then she remembered: that's what friends were for; that's how women had always done it, even in primitive societies, down by the brook, washing their clothes together on the rocks, sharing their miseries -- and joys, if any -- with each other.

What really helped was to talk to a friend, someone like Chloe. The two of them would exchange horror stories, laughing at their own or each other's stupidities. Or one could put it all on paper, and write to a good friend, whose return letter would lift your spirits, and you'd find out that you were not alone in your feelings. She still remembered from twenty years ago a letter from a wonderful friend, written just after Christmas, about her disappointment in the whole holiday: what ungrateful little monsters her children had been, how the tinsel-choked vacuum cleaner had given up the ghost, and how ashamed she was for being such a Scrooge. That letter had pulled her out of the kind of funk she was in today.

And then she smiled. She could call Chloe up right now, and make a date for lunch sometime next week when Mrs. Mahoney was here. They could dress up, go to that lovely restaurant near Chloe's office and be what they used to call Real Ladies. Somehow, she should be able to manage until then. Quickly, before Henry could wake up, demanding God knows what, she would hurry upstairs to take her shower and put on something clean and decent.

* * * *

And sure enough, on the day after Mrs. Mahoney's return, she and Chloe were sitting at a table for two in that restaurant, dressed like ladies, and ordering rosé wine and nibbling on fresh-cut bread. There was a starched pink tablecloth, some pink hyacinths in a pale pink vase, a giant

pink-flowered menu whose specialty of the day was poached salmon with

zucchini blossoms. And the sun was shining.

Chloe was wearing a deep red suit, that set off her black hair, her thick

dark eyebrows, and her Greek nose. The effect emphasized the look she'd

always had, of a tragic but queenly Greek matron, a Clytemnestra, in fact,

whose daughter had been sacrificed. Today Margaret saw dark circles under

Chloe's eyes. She was probably having troubles with sleeping. She knew

that she should ask Chloe about her grief, but she wasn't sure how to bring it

up. An unassailable dignity in Chloe almost said: don't ask. But Margaret

would find a way, she promised herself.

"So how is Henry?" said Chloe, after they'd ordered. "I tried to prepare

Mrs. Mahoney for the changes in him when I saw her the other day. He

seems to be fading."

"That's what the doctor told me last week. In fact," she paused, still

finding it difficult to say these words aloud, "she said that he might only last

a few more months." She was watching Chloe's face as she spoke.

"Oh, wow," said Chloe, taking a minute or two to digest this piece of

information. She took a deep breath, and that mask of tragic dignity was

replaced with real concern. She reached across the table and took Margaret's

hand. "Oh, Margaret. What a sad end for Henry. He was the sort of man who should have died on the barricades, raising a flag to something." How like Chloe, thought Margaret, to concentrate on one of Henry's best qualilties. "Are you thinking about putting him in a nursing home at this point?"

"Actually, I am. I'm waiting for the Screening Team to send me a certificate indicating that he needs nursing home care." Margaret sighed. "I think I needed to be able to tell myself that I'd done my best, that I'd suffered, so that I wouldn't feel guilty. I was also worried about what the kids would say, particularly Anita, but now I've decided that it's my decision. After all, I'm still legally his wife. The judge said so."

They sat there quietly while the waiter brought their salads and went through the fresh ground pepper routine. "You know, Chloe, it's funny, but Henry has changed with his illness. He's pretty nice now, and it's hard for me to remember how cruel he could be."

"I know what you mean. When Saul and I took care of him that weekend, he was quite docile." Chloe paused to take a sip of wine, and then said casually -- almost too casually -- "and speaking of that weekend, how are things with you and Erik?"

Margaret smiled. "I called him the other night when I was desperate. Henry had fallen out of bed and I needed help to get him back in. Since that day, he's made me part of his life." She frowned, trying to think how to explain. "Well, for instance, he took us all to the beach on Sunday, a week ago, Henry and me, and his son Will. We traveled with two wheelchairs. We had a lovely time, with Henry and Will communicating."

"That doesn't sound so bad," said Chloe, as she took another piece of bread, and then, after hesitating, evidently decided to go ahead and put butter on it as well.

"But what does it all mean? That we're taking care of each other's disabled relatives? And I asked him to take Henry and me to the hospital for his check-up appointments as well. He's been wonderful. But I guess I'm thinking I've signed a blank check that says: after Henry is gone, I'll have to start taking care of Will. And then I hear my inner voice saying that, and I start accusing myself of being selfish, and I decide that I'm using Erik without being willing to reciprocate."

Chloe sat there, thinking. "Margaret," she said quietly, "are you in love with him?"

"I'm afraid so." She had to smile, thinking of their time in New York. She shook her head. "Maybe it's just all too soon. Right now, I've got to say goodbye to Henry and to forty years of our life together."

The waiter brought them their checks, but Margaret felt the pressure to ask Chloe about herself. "Chloe," she said, firmly, "we haven't talked about you at all. You've been so good to me during this time. But it's been only six months now since Athena died. Have you been getting enough sleep? You have circles under your eyes. You had said a while ago that you were worried about Saul, but aren't you worried about yourself?"

Chloe put her hands over her eyes. It had never been easy for her to deal with her own sadness, Margaret remembered. Wiping her eyes with the linen napkin, Chloe said, her voice muffled: "It's like a hole inside me. Every now and then, I forget about it for a minute or two, and then it's worse; it's as if it's all happening again, brand new, and so painful." She wiped her eyes again. "One night I had a lovely dream in which Athena was her old self, whistling happily. When I woke up, I felt wonderful. And then, as I got in the shower, I realized it was all just a dream, that she was dead. It hurt more at that minute than it did when we first found her." She looked up at Margaret. "You're going to tell me to get help, or join a group like the one you go to now. But I don't know if I could do that, come right out and say that my daughter . . . <u>killed</u> herself."

Margaret reached out and put her hand on Chloe's. "Actually, I <u>was</u> thinking about that. There's a group just for parents whose children have committed suicide. It could help, both you and Saul. The other people have gone through the same experience, and some may even have learned ways to cope. I can find out where it meets and who runs it if you like, and then you can think about it." Chloe nodded. Margaret couldn't tell whether she was agreeing just to be polite, or whether she might actually join such a group. Now Chloe was looking at her watch.

* * * *

Molly arrived promptly on Thursday evening. It was raining, but Margaret ran out to the car to welcome her and to help with the luggage. Cautiously, Molly carried her wedding dress in its garment bag, draping it over her arm. She was smiling a special tender smile, almost as if this were her newborn baby that she was presenting for the first time. In spite of her long drive, she looked fresh and young, her curly blond hair a little frizzy from the rain, but her eyes sparkling.

"Your father's asleep," said Margaret, "so we can unpack or whatever." She hoped they could open the garment bag and take a peek at the dress. "Did you have dinner?"

"Briefly, some fast food on the turnpike, but I was a little nervous that someone would break into my car and steal my dress, so I wolfed it down. Would you like to look at it?"

"Yes, please," said Margaret, grinning. "Shall we take it up to your room and hang it up?" Together they brought suitcases and dress to Molly's old room and were able to hang the garment bag on the curtain rod. "You'll be wanting to put it back in that bag when it's all over," Margaret said, "so let's open it carefully."

Molly reached up and began to pull on the zipper, and Margaret was able to free the tissue-bound dress. Then they stood back and looked. "Oh, God," said Molly, "I had forgotten how fancy it was. Look at all those sequins! Somehow, it doesn't look at all like me, does it?"

"It looks like you as a bride," said her mother, beaming. The two women sighed. "Well, change your clothes," Margaret said, "and then come to the kitchen and we can have some kind of snack, with a cup of tea. Then you can tell me what your schedule is for this week, what we have to do."

Ten minutes later, Molly joined her in the kitchen. "Tomorrow night, Mom, I'd like some help with the seating for the big dinner." Margaret nodded. "Tonight I just want to say hello to Daddy before I go to bed. We haven't talked about him -- is he okay?"

There was a long silence, as Margaret wondered whether to tell Molly what Dr. Reiner had said. "I think we're going through a process of letting him go, piece by piece. He hardly eats anything . And he seems quite content, very different from his healthy self which always fought against everything. It bothers me that he's not -- well, raging against the dying of the light. He's just given up, and almost cheerfully." With Molly there, it suddenly became all right to cry, to begin to mourn. Margaret put her hands over her face and sobbed. She took off her glasses and rubbed her eyes.

"Oh, Mom, it's so complicated, isn't it? Here you were, the two of you, getting ready to be divorced, and now you're becoming a widow. Oh, dear, I didn't pick a very good time to get married, did I?"

"Oh, my dear, you did pick a good time," she said, still sniffling. "We all needed this wedding, just as we needed Andrew's and Julia's baby, to remind us of life's going on. Even in the middle of death, we shouldn't forget life." Margaret picked up a tissue and wiped her eyes. And just then, the monitor signaled that Henry was waking up.

"That's your father," said Margaret. "Let's go in and say hello." With Molly trailing, they walked into Henry's room. For a minute or two, he looked closely at Molly.

He smiled, and said cheerfully: "Molly." Thank God, he'd recognized her.

After dinner the next evening, Margaret and Molly sat down at the dining room table to plan the seating for the wedding dinner. Molly took out a big diagram and laid it in front of them. "We have our work cut out for us, don't we?" said Margaret. "How do people do this?" She was tired. It had been a long day. Why had she offered to help?

Molly looked over at her mother. "You know, you're looking tired. Why don't you go up to bed. I can manage by myself.

* * * *

The next morning, Margaret got a letter from the Department of Elder Affairs, telling her that Henry'd been certified as needing specialized nursing care. She realized that she'd been waiting for it for a long time, but that she no longer felt a desperate need to get Henry out of the house. Today she would call Father Geoffrey and ask him if they could accept Henry on February 18, the Tuesday after the wedding.

As she was thinking these thoughts, the phone rang. It was Chloe. "Margaret, I have bad news. Helena and her husband can't come to the wedding. Their youngest is sick and they didn't feel they could leave her with anyone at this point. She needs surgery and they want to be with her in the hospital."

"Oh, Chloe! Is the child going to be all right?"

"She has a mastoid infection and the doctor is confident that everything will turn out okay, but they have to operate today, and then there will be a long period of recovery."

"When you talk to her, tell her we're thinking of her. I know Molly will miss her."

As Margaret was hanging up the phone, she saw Molly coming down the stairs. She was still in pajamas and bathrobe, with the sleepy-eyed look of a young child. She was even wearing her old bunny slippers. "Someone's not coming, is that it?" she said.

"That's right. Helena Solomon and her husband have a sick child who needs surgery. So there's room for two more at Chloe's table." Even as she was speaking, Margaret had a thought, but she wasn't sure how to put it to Molly.

"So what are you thinking?" said Molly. "Who will be the replacements?"

"I was thinking of Erik Jensen and his son, Will. Erik has been so helpful with your father, driving him to the doctor. He even came over the other night and put him back into bed: your father had fallen out and I couldn't move him. And the day after that, he took Henry and me to the beach with him and Will." She felt as if she were babbling, and so stopped abruptly. But then she thought of something else. "We could seat them at Chloe's table. She knows him."

Molly looked closely at her mother. "Let's go into the kitchen," she said. "I need some coffee." She sat down at the table and poured herself a cup. Stirring her coffee, she looked her mother in the eyes. "You don't have to tell me, but there's more to this than your just being grateful for his help, isn't that the truth?"

Margaret let out her breath forcefully. And then she smiled. "Well, now that you mention it . . . yes." Then she realized she was blushing. "Oh, Molly, I didn't want to complicate your wedding day, and I hadn't planned to say anything until after you got back from your honeymoon." She paused. "I did tell Charles. He was like you: he guessed. And Chloe knows. But no one else, and I'd like to keep it that way for now."

"So let's invite him and Will to the wedding. Call him up. We'll send him two invitations." Again, she looked searchingly at her mother. "You really like this guy, I guess." And then she grinned. "At your age! I'm impressed." She got out of her chair and came around to Margaret. "You're a good role model, I'll have to say." She gave her a big hug. "I thought he was nice, myself! As long as the two of you don't smooch on the dance floor, I think it will be fine."

Chapter Twenty-four

As the mother of the bride, Margaret had told herself that she was entitled to take a quick tour around the hotel for a last-minute check an hour before the ceremony. If she weren't there, master-minding this upcoming production, she thought, something would go wrong. So, rather than wait for one of her kids to drive her, she'd ordered a cab. And, as she walked into the lobby, she was drawn, as if by an invisible magnet, toward the huge, gilt-encrusted mirror. She barely recognized the woman who looked back at her. Like a baby who is just learning what mirrors can do, she waved her hand at the willowy long-waisted fairy godmother she saw portrayed there. Yes, it was she.

She saw a taller, more dignified person. Her high-heeled shoes, dyed to match the periwinkle blue velvet gown, actually made her taller, and the hairdo that piled her hair on top of her head, with the blue velvet ribbon, added a few more inches. She made herself smile for the mirror. Her eyes sparkled and she was pleased that she'd found that same blue for the dress. But mirrors do lie, she thought. This one didn't show how scared she was, nor that she was still little Maggie MacPherson, just a little over five feet tall.

Looking around, she had to admit that the venerable Boston hotel had done itself proud. The brass had been polished; red-jacketed bartenders were setting out bottles and every kind of stemware. Stacks of plates and rows of silverware had been laid out for the hors d'oeuvres. Everything seemed to be ready -- like a stage set when the curtain first rises. In the dining room, spring flowers bloomed on every table, and big fires were laid in the giant fireplaces at both ends of the room.

Finding nothing wrong on the first floor, she walked up the broad stairway to the second floor, picturing Molly and David coming down after the rabbi had pronounced them man and wife. Here, too, the photographer was supposed to take several shots of them as they descended, and then more pictures of the wedding party and various family groupings. Peeking into the room where the ceremony itself would be held, she was pleased to see that the flowers on the white wicker chupa also included the brightness of spring. Chairs were lined up in rows, and little white ribbons designated where family would sit. Everything seemed in order here, too.

She knocked, then, on the door of the hotel room that had been assigned to Molly and her attendants for their last-minute dressing and makeup and found all the women, including Katy, giggling as they stood in their underwear. Katy was obviously enjoying being part of the grown-ups' world. Then Molly looked at her mother. "Mom, you look absolutely gorgeous. That dress is perfect, and you'll see, when we come down the aisle, that it matches our gowns perfectly."

"Well, unless you need me to pin up something, I'll continue with my tour. I'll have to admit everything looks wonderful!"

Molly grinned. "You almost sound as if you'd like to find something wrong."

Maybe Molly was right, but it made her nervous to see other people being so casual. After all, there was less than an hour to go before the wedding march, and there they were, still not dressed at all. "Would you like me to help Katy get dressed?"

Anita shook her head. "No, I'll do it." She turned away and started brushing her hair.

Clearly, they wanted her out of their way. "Well," she said finally, "I'm going to talk to the wedding consultant and see how things are going."

She had to make sure that Henry and his wheelchair were going to be taken care of, and she wanted to see how Charles and Matt looked in their tuxedos. Back in the lobby, she saw Maureen waiting for her. She'd promised, when she and Molly met with her early in the week, that she would be there to tell them all exactly what they had to do.

A lovely Irish blond and surely only twenty-five or so, Maureen seemed pleased to see her. "Mrs. Bluestone, I have your corsage here, along with all the others, so let's start with that." Pinning it on, she said: "Perfect! Now let's sit down and go over the schedule, and then we can look at the menus one last time." She settled Margaret on a long couch and took out her clipboard. Soon Margaret realized that this young woman knew exactly what she was doing, where everyone was, and what would happen minute to minute. The hotel had even set aside a special room where Mrs. Mahoney could attend to Henry if necessary. Perhaps Margaret could let go and start to enjoy herself.

* * * *

In no time at all, it seemed, Margaret had been led into the ceremony room on Charles's arm and up to the front row. Henry's wheelchair was parked at the end of that row, on the main aisle, facing back so that he could watch the wedding party coming toward him. As she passed, Margaret bent over and kissed him on the cheek. Mrs. Mahoney was in the seat next to him, and Margaret sat beside her. Seeing Henry in real clothes made Margaret realize how emaciated he was, but he looked wonderfully distinguished in his tuxedo, and the addition of the black eye patch -- recommended by Dr. Reiner to prevent double vision -- gave him the appearance of an elegant pirate.

Margaret had never discussed with Mrs. Mahoney what the nurse would be wearing, but her choice was perfect. She had on a sparkling white uniform, and on her head a cap that designated the nursing school from which she'd graduated. The cap looked like a ether cone, since her school

503

had been the Mass General Hospital where ether was first used. Over the dress, Mrs. Mahoney wore a black wool cape, buttoned at the neck, the whole effect reminiscent of World War I.

"You look terrific," Margaret whispered to her, and then, as Mrs. Mahoney was about to reply, the rabbi, along with David and his best man, came out of a side door. The rabbi stood calmly, facing the congregation. David was licking his lips and flexing his fingers, his eyes firmly fixed on the back of the room, his face downcast, as if someone had told him not to count on Molly's showing up. Then the music began.

Everyone turned to look as Katy, the first bridesmaid, moved slowly down the aisle, matching her steps to the downbeat of the march. The green velvet floor-length gown complimented her coloring perfectly. Her brilliant emerald-green eyes and her reddish blond curly hair looked better than any jewels she might have worn. Even more appealing was the look on her face. Still only ten years old, she was the picture of dignity, and at the same time, of joy. No person in the audience could miss her dedication to this ceremony. Several people caught their breaths, and then Margaret heard Henry say, loud enough for everyone to hear: "Katy." A little smile trembled at the corners of the child's mouth, but she maintained both her pace and her poise. Margaret began reaching for her Kleenex.

Next came David's sister Terri, striking in her ruby red velvet dress, with her black hair and eyes. And then, at the back of the room, she saw Anita appear. <u>She</u> was a true princess. Her dress was gold, and she carried herself with true regal grace. Her hair, a lovely French knot pulling it all together, was caught up by a gold ribbon. As she passed her father, she whispered softly: "Hi, Dad," and Margaret saw Henry smile.

Lastly, of course, was Molly. What was it about getting married that gave women that radiant look? Like a newly-whipped meringue, she looked both soft and shiny. She was smiling and nodding to people she knew. Margaret looked back up at the bimah and saw that David had relaxed. Molly was smiling at him and he obviously felt a hundred percent better.

The service was conducted in both Hebrew and English, and occasionally included the participation of the audience. The chupa with its arch of spring flowers was a bridal bower, and Molly and David looked like young children, maybe on the first day of kindergarten, as they listened to the rabbi explain the meaning of marriage.

Then the rabbi said, smiling, "I now pronounce you husband and wife; you may kiss the bride." David stepped firmly on the napkin-wrapped glass, a fine performance that brought a hearty *l'chaim* from the audience; the couple turned and faced them all. But before they walked back down the aisle, Molly leaned over and kissed her father.

505

"Thanks, Daddy," she said, loudly and clearly. Many people were wiping their eyes.

A few minutes later, marching back on Charles's arm again, Margaret saw Erik and Will in the rear area where there was room for the wheelchair. Erik was beaming as he looked at her. But Will spoke out: "Hi, Margaret. You look so pretty!" Erik added a ditto with his thumbs up gesture.

* * * *

Later, after the photographs had been taken and the receiving line had run its weary course, Mrs. Mahoney took Henry to the rest room and the guests moved into the dining hall. As Margaret walked toward her table, she remembered that Molly had seated her with Charles and his family, along with Rosa and George, and Henry and Mrs. Mahoney. Matt grinned at her as he picked up his fork. "Do you know what we're eating?" he asked.

She frowned. "I should know; I helped to plan this meal, and I just looked at the menu. Ah, this must be the mushroom vol au vent!" Watching Matt as he dug into his meal, she realized that, whatever it was, the boy's teenage appetite would make it taste good to him. But she noticed that Katy was less enthusiastic.

Mrs. Mahoney had brought Henry back to the table. And now the band had begun to play again. Margaret recognized the tune as the one Molly and David had chosen as "their song." What was it called? *Let it be Me*, by the

Everly Brothers. Slowly and self-consciously, David stood up and led his new wife out on the dance floor for their solo.

Charles leaned over to his mother and whispered: "May I have this next dance?"

Suddenly, Margaret knew that everything was going to be all right at this wedding.

* * * *

After the obligatory dances and several toasts, the main course was served, and the band took a recess. It was time, Margaret decided, to make the traditional "mother-of-the bride" walk from table to table, greeting everyone. She came -- finally -- to Chloe's table. Chloe looked magnificent, dressed in black and white, giving her a sort of Mata Hari look. She was leaning over, talking to Erik, when Margaret approached them.

"Margaret," said Chloe, "everything is so lovely, and you look magnificent in that dress."

Smiling her thanks, Margaret looked over at Will. He was clearly enjoying himself, and now that the band was playing again, he began beating the arm of his wheel chair in time to the music. "Thank you," he said, slowly and clearly, "for inviting me. I'm learning a lot." He'd been well trained.

Chloe laughed. "Saul has been telling him about Jewish weddings, the meaning of the chupa, the purpose of the ketuba." She looked over at Will. "I'll test you on this one: what is a ketuba?"

He grinned. "That's easy," he said slowly but confidently, "it's the contract the groom gives to the bride." His ease in talking showed her that Will evidently felt comfortable with Chloe. But, of course, Chloe had always had a way with teenagers, even those with special problems.

Erik smiled as he got to his feet. "He's really had fun here. Listen, I'm glad you came over. I wanted to tell you that I'd be happy to take Henry and the nurse home whenever they're ready to go. Chloe has agreed to keep an eye on Will. Would that be okay?"

Margaret nodded. "Thank you so much." Then she looked directly at him for the first time. She tried to say with her eyes what she was really thinking, that she would love to dance with him, but thought it would be inappropriate. Erik nodded. He seemed to have understood.

"One of these days," he said, grasping her hand.

* * * *

When the band came back, they switched to a heavy rock and roll beat. Margaret was surprised to see the number of people who knew how to dance to that kind of music. A frenzy seemed to have taken over. Even Chloe and

Saul were among the dancers. She spotted Everett dancing with a flushed and bright-eyed Katy.

Mrs. Mahoney said she thought it would be a good idea to take Henry home now, that he was getting drowsy. Margaret glanced over at Erik who seemed to have been waiting for her signal. He stood up and threaded his way through the dancers. "I can take him now," he said. "It shouldn't take too long, but Will is definitely not ready to leave." He pointed out to the dance floor. Andrew had pushed Will in his wheelchair into the middle of the throng, and was dancing with him. The boy was laughing and wriggling in time to the beat.

Margaret waved to Molly and pointed to her Dad. Molly came over and even though Henry was fast asleep, she whispered: "Good night, Daddy, and thanks for coming to my wedding."

* * * *

The next day, Sunday, gradually turned life back to normal. Mrs. Mahoney came at her usual time, giving Margaret a chance to sleep in. The house was quiet except for baby Duncan's little chirps, and Margaret came down to an empty kitchen, playing the part of Cinderella the day after the ball when she was back in her rags again. Somewhere in the process of moving into Andrew's old room, she'd also lost a slipper. She was glad to have some time to herself, to sort out yesterday's events and to store away some special memories: the look of Molly coming down the aisle, her sweet gesture of kissing her dad, Everett's dance with Katy, Andrew's with Will. All these thoughts were interrupted by the arrival of Anita, who was also looking pleasantly disheveled. What a change from the regal, golden-gowned princess of last night to today's rumpled sleepyhead, her hair halfway unraveled from its French knot.

"Good morning," said Margaret. "Did I tell you how gorgeous you looked yesterday? Absolutely stunning."

"Yes, but you can tell me again. It was fun to dress up -- and that's what it felt like, the kind of dress-up games Athena and I used to play over at Chloe's. She would let us wear her old gowns and high heels, and we'd put up our hair to look like grownups." She sighed. "I wish Athena had been with us last night. Chloe looked so sad." She sat down and began to nibble on a bagel. Her eyes, the droop of her face, hair hanging widdershins, as Margaret's old Scot-descended Granny used to say, proclaimed her own sadness.

"I guess events like this wedding will often make us all think about Athena," Margaret said, trying to tune in to the look on Anita's face.

"It's funny, but I was actually feeling sad about something else," she said hesitantly, as if wondering whether to continue. Margaret held her breath, conscious that she was about to hear something that was coming from the inside of Anita, some sadness, rather than the usual anger.

"Seeing Molly get married, of course, made me wonder if I should be getting married, too," she said, after a long pause, and then she added: "Everett wants to; he's been begging me for years."

"Well," said Margaret, slowly and carefully, not wanting to dam up this stream now that it had found a small hole in the log jam, "you'd never find a nicer man." She paused. "But I guess you have your doubts about him."

"Not about Everett. No, not at all. I love him dearly." And now her eyes were shiny, with unshed tears. "It's me, and the whole institution of marriage that I worry about." She paused. "I'm not the easiest person to live with, as you must have noticed." Her laugh was bitter.

"Well," said Margaret, slowly and sadly, "you grew up in a house where the marriage wasn't too good an example." She frowned. "Your father and I . . ." how to say it? "We were certainly in love, especially in the beginning. And even today, taking care of him, I realize he's . . .dear to me in a special way. I guess I love him a different way now, as someone who needs my care." Thinking, as she spoke, she went on: "But I feel bad if we gave you a sour view of marriage."

Now Anita's eyes really filled with tears. "Mom, it's nobody's fault. It's mainly me. I keep feeling that Everett and I get along so well because we're

<u>not</u> married. These ten years have been lovely, and I wonder if that would all change if we made it legal." She sighed. "I'm just afraid that -- once we were married -- he'd begin to advise and suggest in that same way he does now about my investments, only about our lives in general."

"It sounds as if you're saying you fear for your independence?"

"Exactly." Anita looked pleased at being understood. Then she laughed. "You know, Mom, I never really knew before how good you were at your job!"

Margaret was taken aback. "Gee, I'd hoped I was being a mother just now, and not a social worker."

"I know, I was just kidding. But you're good at both. Our problem has always been that I wasn't good at being a child."

Margaret smiled, remembering. "There's something to that. Even when you were very little -- before Charles was born -- and I'd be crossing the street with you, and you'd always say: 'I can hold my own hand!'"

"That's me, all right," said Anita. "I'm still holding my own hand, I guess." She paused. "But, of course," she said, standing up, obviously about to end the discussion, "that also means giving up the occasional joys and comforts of being dependent and having someone to lean on." But, for once, Anita evidently hadn't minded this "invasion" into her privacy. She leaned down and gave Margaret a big hug. "It felt good talking to you like this. I keep things inside too much -- except for my anger. That always seems to find its way to leap out." She started toward the stairs.

"Oh, wait," said Margaret, the word 'anger' triggering her next thought, "sometime today, I'd like to get all you kids together -- while I've still got you in the same house -- for a brief family meeting."

"Oh, God," said Anita, "I hope it won't go the way the last one did!"

Margaret smiled. "No, I just need to tell you all about what the doctors have told me lately about your Father's prognosis and the decisions I've made." How good that sounded, she thought. I'm the mother and the wife, and I make the decisions around here.

* * * *

By four o'clock on Sunday afternoon, the kids were all back from their various excursions. They'd settled themselves in the kitchen and were looking at her expectantly. She picked up a sense of urgency, as if her children were all saying, by their actions rather than by words, that they were all anxious to leave. Molly and David's luggage was parked next to the refrigerator. Although they'd told no one where they were going on their trip, one couldn't miss the skis on the roof of their car. Charles's station wagon was also already packed, and the kids -- who must have been told that this was a grownups' meeting -- were out in the yard, kicking the dirt and poking each other, clearly anxious to be on their way. Margaret knew that Andrew and Julia had seven o'clock reservations on the Atlanta plane; she, herself, had offered to drive them. Andrew kept looking at his watch. Anita and Everett were spending the night, but they were having dinner with friends and planned to get home early so that they could catch their morning flight. And Margaret, too, was glad that this was evidently going to be a short meeting. It meant that no one had a stake in prolonging the discussion.

"Why don't we just stay right here in the kitchen and have a quick cup of tea while we talk. Chloe brought over more Greek cookies and this seems as good a time as any to serve them." She paused, glancing at these grown children of hers. Of all of them, only Andrew looked apprehensive, perhaps afraid that, once again, he'd be put on the spot medically. "Let me begin," said Margaret in a forthright tone, "with what the neurologist told me the last time your father had an appointment with her -- about two weeks ago. I didn't want to talk about it until the wedding was over." She swallowed. "Dr. Reiner said that he was 'at the end stage'" -- she said it in quotes -- "of a particularly virulent kind of Parkinson's Disease." In the silence that followed, she gulped and then went on. "She said he had not too long to live." As she said these words, she thought: oh, my God, these are his children, hearing this for the first time. While most of them may have suspected this outcome, they were probably like herself, assuming that he'd be in this current plateau for a long while. "Dr. Reiner said he'd be sleeping

514

more and more, eating less and less, becoming a little more demented and finally he'd go into a coma." She stopped talking and looked at all their faces. While she'd actually hinted at this news in talking to Molly the other day, and Charles and Anita had both seen him during the aborted divorce hearing, it was Andrew for whom this would be a shock.

He was sitting with his shoulders hunched over, looking down at his tea cup, stirring it round and round, almost as if this stirring would keep his father alive. Julia put her arm around him, and this gesture seemed to turn on the tears. "Here I am," he said between tears, "crying. I'm a doctor and I tell people this kind of news every day. But it sure is different when you're the one being told." Julia passed him a tissue and he wiped his eyes. The rest of them just looked at him.

Carefully and gently, Charles asked him: "Are you surprised?"

"No," he said swallowing. "I was just hoping for a miracle." He looked up. "And between Mom and Mrs. Mahoney, and all of you who came and helped, if anyone could have got better, it would have been Dad. He's had wonderful care."

"Thank you for saying that," Margaret said. "I sure couldn't have done it without all you weekend helpers, and that great doctor you sent us, Andrew, not to mention Rosa and George. But Mrs. Mahoney was the backbone of it all." She paused, realizing that Andrew's words had given her a bridge to the other half of this discussion. "But Mrs. Mahoney, unfortunately, has to leave this week."

There was a silence. It was as if they were all still little kids. Mom would fix it, whether it was a hornet in the bathroom, or a frightened bird in the basement. They looked at her, waiting for her to tell them what she was going to do.

"So I've been thinking it over -- what to do when the time came. When Anita was here a month ago," -- thank Heaven, she thought, that the two of them had worked so well together at that time -- "we did some research and looked at two places where Dad could go next." Since no one said anything, she quickly continued. "Of course, ideally he should stay here, but without Mrs. Mahoney, I just couldn't do it. And it will get harder. It's reached the point where we need experts on duty twenty-four hours a day." She looked over at Anita, who nodded. "One of the places was just awful." Margaret shuddered, remembering the Happy Hour and the wheelchairs parked facing the TV set. "We both agreed we could never put your father there. The other one was a hospice, a peaceful place where people can live out their last days." She looked again at Anita, hoping for more support.

"Yes," said Anita, "the atmosphere made you feel as if" -- she paused, evidently trying to put it just right -- "as if dying might not be so bad, that it was part of life." She glanced carefully over at Margaret, as if wondering if she had caught the spirit of the place.

"Exactly," said her mother. "And Dr. Reiner also recommended it. 'Like home care,' she said."

"So is that what you decided, Mom?" Anita asked. "To put him there?"

"Yes," said Margaret, simply. "I think on Tuesday. Mrs. Mahoney will help me get him ready."

Now Charles looked anxious. "What do you plan to tell him, Mom? You remember how he hated going to that respite center, how he kept saying: 'My home, my home.'"

"Well," said Margaret, "I think your father is in a different place now. And I'm sure Mrs. Mahoney has had a lot of experience with these kinds of situations. I'm also going to ask Father Geoffrey, the Episcopal priest who runs that place, about how to prepare a patient for this move. This hospice is called Eastman House, by the way, and it's right here in town. And the people in my group should be quite helpful as well."

"What group?" asked Molly, looking puzzled.

"Oh, I keep thinking that everyone knows. It's a group for people -- like me -- who have relatives or spouses with dementia."

"Oh, God," said Anita. "That must be a laugh and a half. How depressing."

"Well, we need each other, which is why it works," said Margaret, realizing that while Anita might have softened a little, she was still her old caustic self.

Molly was looking at her watch. Margaret realized she'd better wind this up. "Just one more thing. You may all want to say goodbye to your father today, but I suspect he'll be confused with so many people. It might be better if you come back individually in the next month or so, to spend a day with him at the hospice. Anita and I saw several families who seemed to be hanging out there, making themselves little soups in the kitchen."

"You'll have to let us know when would be a good time," said Andrew. "And call us, especially if it's an emergency."

Gradually, they trooped into Henry's room. He was awake. Molly spoke first. "David and I are about to go on our honeymoon, Dad, but I want to thank you for being at the wedding."

To Margaret's surprise, Henry seemed to understand, and was able to respond: "Have a good trip." Molly looked enormously pleased. But then his eyes closed; he was asleep. He'd shot his wad when he spoke to Molly. Oh, Henry, Margaret thought, this may be the last time you'll ever see all your kids together. Or even worse, perhaps he won't see any of them again. But it was not really Henry she was sad for, but these nice kids.

"It was a very tiring weekend for him," said Margaret. "He'll do better the next time you see him, with a one-to-one." She hoped that was true.

Mrs. Mahoney then appeared at the kitchen door. Her thin, sharp-nosed face looked tired, too. There were long lines on both sides of her mouth. This had not been an easy job for her, Margaret thought, although it usually didn't show. "He's still exhausted from yesterday," said the nurse. "But I wanted to say goodbye to all of you." And then she added, with a trace of Ireland in her voice: "He was a lovely man, your father."

Margaret had never thought to hear anyone say that about Henry.

* * * *

Henry slept for most of the evening, and once again, Margaret had the house to herself. She would have to stay awake until the night nurse came at eleven. If only she could go right up to bed! Maybe a bath would help. Rubbing her eyes with sleepiness, she picked the monitor off the kitchen table, and took it with her as she slowly started to climb the stairs.

Lolling in the tub, she was aware that she was in danger of falling sleep. To distract herself, she looked down the length of her short body. Mostly submerged, she could see all the way to her feet. In the past, her plumper tummy had blocked her view. She must, indeed, have lost some weight, as Chloe had said. Now there was only her little mound, blond but now sprinkled with gray, still proclaiming her femininity.

519

Wearily, she climbed out of the bathtub, and after drying herself and putting on a flannel nightgown, she went back downstairs to wait for the night nurse. No heavy thinking, she told herself. But she found herself thinking wistfully that all the kids were leaving. Once again, they were all taking a trip somewhere.

She'd like to take a trip, herself. She began to picture herself, heading west. Right there on the coffee table, where Molly and David must have left it when they were planning their route, was the atlas. Idly turning the pages until she found the map of the whole United States, she began to trace her way slowly westward from Boston. It would be wonderful to take a trip all by herself, stopping whenever she wanted to, staying any old place, taking the back roads instead of the interstates. Maybe, after all this was over, this sad goodbye that was surely coming up, she could start to think about her life and where it was going. On a trip like that, there'd be no one to take care of, only herself.

She could go by car, stopping at Rosa and George's place in Cleveland, and stay there for several days, go back to visit Granny's old town. She hadn't been there since Granny's death ten years ago. She could take old Route 34 -- if it still existed -- and find her way back to where she'd lived with her parents in the mountains of Colorado. Closing her eyes and imagining the whole scene, she saw herself heading for the west coast, to California and maybe up to Seattle to visit Anita and Everett.

Smiling, and realizing that all this was pure fantasy -- she had, after all, a dying husband to take care of, and a full-time job that was waiting for her -- she reminded herself that there was another factor in this whole equation, the one that involved Erik and his son, Will. These two people also had a place in her life, or so she'd begun to assume. How would they react if she told them that she was planning to take off for parts unknown, for an unlimited amount of time? And how would she feel, if she were cut off from the warmth and support that Erik had given her?

And then she laughed out loud. A trip like this would cost a lot of money! Even if she drove -- and it occurred to her that maybe she could take Henry's old Volvo -- there would be all kinds of expenses. And right now, money was tight. She'd taken a lot of time off from work -- unpaid time, a lot of it -- and there'd been all the expenses in connection with Henry's illness: nursing fees, both in the daytime for Mrs. Mahoney, and for the night nurse, the doctor, and all the medicines. And now she was planning to place him in the Hospice. Theoretically, Paul could pay some of these bills out of Henry's funds, but who knew how long that money would last?

Of course, it had been her decision to put money into the house, but that decision had been made before Henry got sick. Molly's wedding had been another big expense, and she would never regret a penny of that, she told herself.

She closed the atlas and stretched out on the couch, wondering why she was suddenly thinking about escaping. Perhaps long-term prisoners who had been cooped up for months and months had fantasies of this kind. Long vistas and roads that went on forever were probably their favorite daydreams.

Chapter Twenty-five

While Henry napped the next afternoon, Margaret and Mrs. Mahoney sat together, sewing on name tapes and discussing what they'd tell him about going to the hospice. "Maybe just the truth?" said Margaret.

"That's right," said Mrs. Mahoney, firmly, "tell him the truth. Just say the place is called Eastman House." She paused, frowning. "But you know, Mrs. B., I'll bet he knows he's dying." She pursed her lips. "It's as if he's accepted it. He's very different from when I first came, when he fought us all the way."

"So let's tell him in the morning," Margaret said. Mrs. Mahoney nodded. There was a comfortable silence. "I don't know how I could have managed this whole time without you," Margaret said, smiling warmly at Mrs. Mahoney. "You've been so nice to have around. Andrew made a point of saying that Henry had received wonderful care."

"You have a nice family, Mrs. B. They really rallied 'round. And good friends, too. Chloe thinks the world of you, as I'm sure you know, and that Mr. Jensen -- Erik -- has been so helpful."

Her tone of voice had been casual. Margaret hoped she hadn't guessed about anything else. But maybe she was giving her blessing. She didn't miss much. And as soon as she'd left for the day, Margaret put in a call to Erik, telling herself that she needed to thank him for his help at the wedding, and to let him know that they were placing Henry in the hospice. But, of course, as soon as he answered, she realized that she'd called him because she needed to hear his voice.

The next day, as they were giving him breakfast, Margaret simply told Henry that Mrs. Mahoney was leaving and that he needed full-time nursing now. They were taking him to a place, just a mile from here, where he could get good care. Henry continued to open his mouth like a baby bird as Mrs. Mahoney spooned in his oatmeal. "I'll come to see you every day," Margaret heard herself promise.

There was a silence. "Mrs. Mahoney, too?" he asked, his voice hoarse.

"Of course, Mr. B. I'll come visit. I'll miss you," she said, her eyes tearing. "After breakfast, we'll get you dressed so you can ride in the big van. We'll follow you."

By the time Margaret and Mrs. Mahoney had reached the hospice, Henry was already settled in his room. "This is such a wonderful place," Mrs. Mahoney said to Margaret. "Mr. B. seems perfectly at ease. It was a good choice. Look, he's already falling asleep, as if he were in his own bed at home."

Margaret's life took on a whole new pattern. She began to have a regular routine: a long visit to Henry in the morning, sitting in the rocker in his high-ceilinged room, often listening to music on the radio since it seemed to soothe him, going out to the kitchen for a cup of tea when he napped, talking to the other regular visitors.

Nurses came quietly into Henry's room from time to time, giving him routine but gentle care, changing him, offering but not insisting that he try a bite of some food or other. Henry seemed oddly content. He spoke less and less, and he seemed to understand her when she kept it simple. She told him that Matt had written a paper for school about rock-climbing with his grandfather. The teacher had loved it and had given him an A-plus. At first she wasn't sure that Henry knew what she was talking about, but eventually, he replied, slowly but clearly: "Good boy!"

She spent her afternoons at the office, doing paperwork, seeing a few clients. It was amazing how well they'd done without her, even Deborah Breen, who'd been going regularly to Al-Anon. In the evenings, Margaret often went back to the hospice, sitting with Henry while he slept. Her house was back to its pristine shape: the medical supply store had removed the hospital bed and all the other accouterments of patient care. The place had an empty feeling now, and she preferred staying with Henry till bedtime.

One night, when she came back to the hospice, the nurse told her that Henry'd had a visitor that afternoon, and that he'd brought a card. She handed it to Margaret. It was from Erik. He'd chosen one of the Charles Mackintosh cards they'd bought at the museum in New York. Inside, he'd written only: From Erik and Will. It was his way of reminding her of that special time, and it brought tears to Margaret's eyes. That weekend together seemed so long ago, now almost just a dream. She shuddered, feeling as if it had been an uncharted island in the ocean of life, and now there was no way she could find her way back there. When she called Erik that evening -- she'd been doing that every night before bed -- she told him about her fantasy.

"We'll find it again, my dear," he'd said in a confident voice. "It's there, waiting."

The next day, as she sat rocking herself quietly, she found time to think about what kind of funeral Henry should have. It was clear, as he ate less and slept more, that the end was coming soon. When he was admitted to Eastman House, she'd been asked to give them the name of a funeral home, and she'd listed Aronson's. All she knew about the place was that it was Jewish, and that it was less than a mile from her house. When she raised the subject with each of the children as they came up to see their father, they looked startled, either because they felt this decision was hers to make, or because it was somehow unseemly to be thinking of these matters as long as their father was still alive.

In the last week of March, Henry began to refuse food altogether, and it was even becoming difficult to get him to sip water. He was, indeed, sleeping most of the time. Dr. Pennypacker made regular visits, and Margaret made a point of being there when he examined Henry. Each time he came, he would pull back the sheets and look at Henry's feet and lower legs. One day he said to Margaret: "Perhaps you've wondered what I'm looking for."

Margaret nodded.

"I'm looking for a kind of red or purple mottling that begins on the feet and slowly moves up the legs. It usually doesn't start until after the patient has gone into a coma, but I suspect that will be soon." Dr. Pennypacker was calm, and gentle as he told her about this. The Brahmin authority that rang in his voice was oddly soothing. It was almost as if God were speaking.

"But what does it mean?"

"It's a sign that the body is instituting a last-ditch defense against death. Recognizing that it needs all the strength it can find - - since the upper body and head need blood to function - - it borrows from the lower extremities, whatever it can get. Of course, it's just borrowing time. But when you see the mottling, you know what is happening. And if you do see it, that would be the time to call your children."

But Henry's strong body kept fighting. Margaret continued to sit in the rocker, wondering, as he slept, if this was the coma everyone had talked about. But occasionally he was more conscious and would ask a few disjointed questions: "Who?" was one he often asked, and she would always tell him that <u>she</u> was there, his wife, Margaret. Another was "Where?" and she would explain that this was Eastman House where people who were very sick were taken care of. The last one was more difficult: "When?" he would ask, and at first she would pretend not to understand, but she suspected that he was asking when he would die. Finally, she began to reply: "Pretty soon." That seemed to satisfy him, and he would turn over and sleep some more.

As he slept, her thoughts would return to the subject of his funeral. In the last few years, she'd gone to a number of funerals and memorial services. People her age were beginning to die. How short life was! But she was still only sixty-two, she comforted herself. Some of these ceremonies or services had been held outdoors, on the edge of a beautiful meadow, in a grove of trees in the woods, or on a beach.

She wondered if Henry would have wanted that kind of ceremony. And to her surprise, she decided the answer was no. In fact, she seemed to recall his saying, years ago, something like: when my time comes, just dig a hole and throw me in the ground as fertilizer, so I can be recycled!

But did the deceased have a right to determine what was done and said about him after death? Margaret didn't think so. Death and its aftermath belonged to the living, and she was pretty sure her children wouldn't like the sort of ending Henry had envisioned. <u>She</u> would have to decide.

* * * *

On the first of April, a bright spring morning, Margaret went to the hospice for her usual visit, bringing along a small bouquet of early perennials from her garden -- snow drops, crocuses, and bluebells. She pulled up the blinds to bring the sunshine in, and went to the kitchen for a small vase. And back in the room, even though he usually didn't respond, she talked to Henry. "It's such a lovely spring day," she said. "I've brought you flowers from our garden." His lips looked dry. "Here, let's try some ice."

The ice water trickled down his chin. Henry was quiet, hardly moving. She wondered if this was the coma that the doctor had talked about, and sure enough, when the nurse came into the room, she looked closely at Henry and then nodded. "I'll call Dr. Pennypacker," she said. As soon as the nurse was out of sight, carefully, almost furtively, Margaret turned down the covers and looked at Henry's feet. Yes, there were strange red and purple mottlings there, but nothing on the legs. At least, nothing yet. It was time to call the kids. A feeling of inevitability came over her: she knew just what to do. She began with Anita, waking her at dawn Pacific time. Andrew was next since he had almost as far to come. And then Molly and Charles. It looked as if all of them would make it by nightfall.

As she waited for the children to arrive, once again she thought about the funeral. She wondered how people would feel about a service at a geological site of some kind, one of his favorite places. But most of the people who'd be invited were getting a little old for rock-climbing. Maybe that part of the mourning could take place at a later date, with just the kids, their spouses and the grandchildren attending a family memorial. The funeral itself should be shortly after his death. Someone would have to officiate. Margaret wondered if having a rabbi would make it a travesty. A Jewish funeral for Henry would be a gift of respect to his sister Rosa, to thank her for her help during this terrible time.

Henry had <u>never</u> defined himself as Jewish. He'd even gone to work on Yom Kippur, puzzling his fellow employees who would ask: "Isn't this one of your high holy days?"

"It's none of their goddamn business," he would say to Margaret. "I don't <u>look</u> Jewish." He was right, but somehow, people always knew. Henry was the sort of man who'd bring non-Kosher French wines to a Passover dinner, and he'd always put butter on his Matzos. He'd even refused to sit Shiva for his father. And he'd absolutely <u>never</u> go to movies about concentration camps.

Margaret, on the other hand, had never forgotten some of scenes from these films, where the long rows of Jewish men were laid out like kindling just outside the gate, in striped suits or stark naked, eyes staring, bodies emaciated from starvation, dehydration, and torture.

* * * *

By evening, when the kids had all assembled at the hospice, Henry was still alive. The mottling on his legs had moved up to his knees, and his breathing had slowed down. Dr. Pennypacker predicted that this would be his last day. The hospice had brought in extra chairs so that all of them could sit together in Henry's room. One of the other hospice visitors had made a big pot of soup for them, and served it to them in mugs.

Each of the children reacted in his or her own way. Anita, who'd left Seattle at dawn, kept falling asleep, and then jerking awake, embarrassed at not being vigilant. Her eyes were red, her hair loose. Charles, on the other hand, was sitting straight up, looking ahead, almost as if he were a statue, his classic features expressing both expectation and resignation. His eyes were on his father, but his lips trembled from time to time, as if he were about to speak. Andrew was pacing around the room, and Molly kept jumping up to wait on all of them. Margaret was watching Henry's breathing. The spaces between breaths were getting longer, and each time, she would think to herself: this will be the last one. But he struggled on. The

531

breaths were also shallower, so that it was hard to be sure he really <u>was</u> breathing. Finally, just before eleven o'clock, he took a very faint breath. Margaret waited for another. "It's okay, Henry," she whispered, "you don't have to try so hard. You can let go. We're all here." Now the silence stretched out further, and then there were no more. "Good night, sweetie," Margaret said, surprising herself, and then, softly: "Good bye." It was 10:56 P.M. on the first of April.

Andrew reached over and closed Henry's eyes, while Molly went out to the desk to call the nurse. Anita put her face in her hands and began to sob. Margaret reached up and pulled down the sheet. She wasn't sure what she was looking for now, but when she saw his incredibly thin, still very long body, his shoulders now quite narrow, stretched out on the bed, she knew she'd seen this somewhere before, on TV or in a movie. With his taut skin over an emaciated frame, he'd joined a multitude. He'd been gathered to his kin. There would have to be a Jewish funeral. It was where he belonged. He would, as they said in the Torah, sleep in the dust with his fathers. There was no other choice for this man. After a lifetime of pushing away and often denying his Judaism -- perhaps as part of the wall he'd built around himself -- Henry was now going to be counted, along with all the other Jews, on Judgment Day. Charles pulled the sheet over his father's face.

* * * *

The next morning, while her children were still asleep, Margaret had called Erik to tell him of Henry's death. His response was subdued and respectful. And of course, he offered to help in any way that he could. Then a strange sort of energy seemed to take over and she felt suddenly very efficient, organized and ready to make decisions. She began to make lists in her head, of people she needed to call.

She began with Aronson's Funeral Home. Explaining that she was not Jewish, she told the man who answered the phone that she wanted them to help her plan a Jewish funeral for her atheist husband who'd died the previous night at Eastman House. "Come over to my office now, and we can talk," said the man. "My name is Nathan Aronson." Mr. Aronson was a tall, very thin man in his mid-forties, with a long face, a shock of white hair, and thick, black bushy eyebrows. "What made you decide to have a Jewish funeral? You said your husband was an atheist." After some hesitation, she said: "Well, I guess I saw a Jewish funeral as a mark of respect for my husband's sister. And we have four children, two of whom have chosen to be Jewish." She decided not to say anything about how Henry's appearance, right after he died, had reminded her of those concentration camp films.

533

"Tell me about yourself? What do <u>you</u> want? It's up to the widow to decide," he said, gazing at her under those bushy eyebrows. The widow, thought Margaret. That's what I am now. Strange, she mused.

"Well, I was the one who always pushed for Seders, Hanukkah candles, and I supported my son when he wanted a Bar Mitzvah. My husband would always object, but eventually he'd go along. If I chose a Jewish cemetery, he'd maybe not be turning over in his grave, but he'd be kicking and screaming." She laughed and Mr. Aronson joined her.

"It sounds as if you've made up your mind on that point," said Mr. Aronson. "Let me ask you a few questions first: have you decided where you want him buried?"

Margaret shook her head. "Let me suggest the local city cemetery. It's close by; you've probably passed it many times." She nodded. "It has advantages for you; fortunately, it's inter-denominational, and since 1945, has accepted Jews along with everyone else. Unlike a strictly Jewish cemetery -- which wouldn't accept <u>you</u> if you wanted to be buried next to him -- you could be there as well. Most rabbis are willing to conduct graveside services there."

"Oh, I like that idea. When the children come home to visit, they could go there."

"Well, you'd better call the cemetery right away as well. Here's their card. When you get home, call me and let me know if they can arrange it." He paused. "Now let me tell you how we work. Everything is dependent on the casket you purchase; all the rest comes with it." Margaret looked puzzled. "If you buy an expensive casket, the cost of everything else goes up, too." He paused. "So now we go look at caskets."

He stood up, and she had no choice but to follow. They went upstairs into an enormous room. She felt as if she were buying a bed in a giant furniture store. She saw caskets in every direction. For the first time, she felt a little queasy. Picking out a casket really told you, if nothing had before, that someone -- Henry -- had died. She felt a hollow in her stomach and a sort of chill. Mr. Aronson was looking closely at her. "Are you okay?" he asked.

She nodded. He took her first to a plain pine box that Orthodox Jews would select. Margaret found it beautiful, with the lovely smell of fresh wood, and the fact that it was made without nails -- just wooden pegs -- appealed to her sense of simplicity. The price was incredibly low as well. But she had a feeling that it wouldn't do for Henry. That would be a travesty. You'd have to be really Jewish to deserve that lovely box.

The director was looking at her. "I can see that you like this one," he said, in some surprise, raising his bushy eyebrows.

"But it's not right for my husband to have it," she said regretfully. "He hasn't," she paused, trying to think how to say it, "he hasn't paid his dues for that privilege."

Looking a little puzzled, Mr. Aronson said: "Well, let me show you another. Actually, it's the same basic box but it's been stained and varnished so that it looks just like all the fancy ones." He pointed across the room. "Of course, it's twice the price of the plain pine box."

"That would be just right," said Margaret, "but does it have to come with that awful fluffy pink lining?"

He looked a little offended, but quickly replied: "No, of course not." On the way back to his office, he asked: "Before we decide on what kind of services you want, you're going to need a rabbi. Did you have anyone in mind?"

"The only one I know is the nice young man -- he's probably not so young any more -- who conducted Andrew's Bar Mitzvah." But she couldn't recall his name. Perhaps the funeral director would know.

"Who's the rabbi now at Temple Beth Shalom?"

"Rabbi Shulman. Does that ring a bell?"

"That was his name. I'd love to have him do the service. He actually knew my husband: it was he who persuaded Henry to participate in the Bar Mitzvah ceremony."

"I suspect he'd be happy to do it, if he's not all booked up. When do you want the services to be?"

"Would Friday be okay? Our children are all here now."

"That would be fine. I'll check our schedule and set you up with a cost estimate. Then if everything works out, I'll send a notice to the papers. Maybe one of your children could help with the obituary. And you'll need to call Rabbi Shulman."

* * * *

Back at the house, Margaret continued to feel this surge of energy. Perhaps it was inevitable after all those weeks of just sitting, waiting for his death. No, it was more than that: taking care of Henry had been an enormous responsibility. For the last six months, she'd been in charge, helping to smooth his path from illness into death. And that job was finished now. And she knew, deep inside, that she'd done a good job. She thought about being a widow, and had to admit that she didn't <u>feel</u> like a widow. It was more as if she had just been divorced. An image flashed before her eyes, a picture that she'd once seen in the newspaper of some famous Hollywood star, tossing her wedding ring into a river after her divorce.

Margaret looked down at her ring finger. The ring, which she herself had purchased at Sears for $29.95 more than forty years ago, was a little loose now and it came off easily. She decided, after the children had left, that she wasn't going to wear it any more. She didn't deserve to be called a widow, and if it hadn't been for that judge, she told herself angrily, she'd have been divorced by now.

Her children, who were gradually appearing in the kitchen, looked almost stunned. They moved slowly, cautiously, and didn't seem to know what to do next. Margaret was making lists when Charles, the first one up, appeared on the scene. She'd already called Rabbi Shulman and they'd chosen eleven o'clock on Friday, and then she'd made a call to the cemetery. She had an appointment there that morning.

Charles, first, and then the rest of them, were looking at her in astonishment. "Mom," said Anita, "you're a whirling dervish today."

"There's a lot to do," she said. "The funeral will be Friday morning."

Anita looked as if she had no idea what her mother was talking about. She stared at her. Margaret reached over and gave her a hug. "It's hard to get used to, isn't it, even when we all knew it was coming? But I think it helps to <u>do</u> things; it makes it all real." Anita continued to stare at her. "I went out this morning and looked at caskets: it's just one of the things one has to do." The rest of them looked equally confused. Molly was biting her lip, as if it had never occurred to her that anyone needed to do that. "There is one thing you kids could do for me, when you feel up to it. A lot of people need to be called, out-of-town relatives, your own friends, and some of our close friends here. I'll leave a list here by the phone and if you reach any of them, check them off. Just tell them the funeral will be at Aronson's, here in town, at eleven o'clock on Friday." She stopped, still not sure that she was reaching them. "I'll call Chloe, myself, a little later." As she looked at her children, she decided maybe she should make that call right now, so they could hear how it was done.

She picked up the phone. "Chloe," she said, and suddenly she felt as if she might cry, realizing at the same time that this was something important she <u>hadn't</u> done. She hadn't cried for Henry. And now the tears were running down her face.

"Margaret?" Chloe's voice was already full of concern. "Are you okay? Is it over?"

Swallowing and catching her breath, Margaret replied, slowly: "Henry died last night, a little before eleven. We were all there. It was slow and gentle, I guess you'd say, and he was never in pain." There, she thought, looking up at the children, that's how you do it, and it's okay to cry.

As she moved out of the kitchen, on her way to the cemetery, she saw Andrew reach over and pick up the list.

That evening, over the Chinese take-out the kids had ordered, Margaret began to talk about the program for the ceremony. The rabbi, of course, would speak. He'd be coming over tonight to talk to them all about their father.

Charles quickly spoke up. "Mom, I'll have to leave tonight right after dinner to go back to Portland and pick up the kids. I'll need to organize their clothes -- I'm just hoping that Matt's one suit will still fit him. But we'll be back late tomorrow. I'm sorry to miss meeting the rabbi tonight." He paused, looking slightly harassed. "I don't know, Mom, what you had in mind for speakers, but I'd like to suggest that -- if he'd be willing -- it might be nice if Matt could read his essay about his adventures in rock-climbing with his grandfather."

"Oh, Charles. That would be perfect." She paused. "I was hoping that one of you kids would also say something,-- or even all of you, whatever you like. Talk it over among yourselves. I don't think I'll say anything at the ceremony; it just wouldn't be proper, since a lot of people knew that we were trying to get a divorce." No one said anything, but they all looked at each other, probably hoping that someone would come forward. "One of your Dad's colleagues at the University has offered to speak, and I think, from what he said, that one of the students will also say a few words."

The kids still looked uneasy and uncomfortable. "Are all of you angry with me?" she asked. "Am I doing all the wrong things?" She looked at each of them. Charles was looking down at his plate, pushing his noodles around.

Molly was wearing her "old stone face," and Anita had turned away so that it was hard to tell what she was thinking. Only Andrew made eye contact with her and he, at least, showed his distress. He'd picked up one of the unused chopsticks and was rolling it back and forth.

For a long time no one answered her question. "It's not that, Mom," said Anita slowly, trying at the same time to get her fortune cookie opened, "I can't speak for anyone else, but I'm grateful that you can be so organized. I feel paralyzed, myself, as if my feet were stuck to the floor. I guess I feel that I should start mourning him and I don't know how to start."

Margaret felt she should speak again. "I suspect I've been mourning your father all during these last four months, when I've had long times alone with him, and especially in these last few weeks when I've sat in that rocking chair at the hospice and watched him die. You kids have had some of that, but probably not enough for it to be real." At least they were all now looking at her and Andrew had put the chopstick back in the box. "I had another idea that I'd like you to think about. I thought maybe the day after the funeral -- on Saturday, when you'll all still be here -- we could have a family memorial, maybe go to Mount Monadnock, right over the border in New Hampshire, and spend the day there, climb it and have a picnic, unless it turns out to be too cold up there." Now the silence was profound. No one said anything, and they'd lowered their eyes. She couldn't tell if they were furious with her, or just confused. Turning to Andrew, she said, finally, "I don't know . . . could you bring Duncan in a back pack? I'd want him to be part of the occasion." She held her breath, waiting for a response.

"No problem," said Andrew in a muffled voice. "We've taken him everywhere on our backs and he seems to enjoy it."

Margaret noticed he was not exactly endorsing the idea of the climb.

Normally, at this point, she would have started backpedaling, apologizing for her idea, taking them off the hook so they wouldn't have to be forthright in their rejection of her plan. But this time, she decided to make it a definitive decision. This was one time, by God, when being in charge should give a mother some perks!

"I think we should leave early in the morning so that we'll be able to have lunch at the top," she said, and then she noticed that Charles had stood up and was putting on his coat to take off for Maine. It would probably be up to him to put the seal of half-hearted approval on her idea, she thought, and sure enough he turned and looked at her.

"I'll bring stuff for the kids to wear for climbing," he said, and turning to the others, he waved. "I'll see you guys on Friday morning." He stopped, obviously feeling that this was not a casual goodbye, but the end of a day like no other. "I'm sorry I can't be here to help," he said, and then moved out the back door.

In the silence that followed, Margaret could hear Anita muttering, more or less *sotto voce*, but definitely expressed for public consumption, something about the possibility of deep snow up there so early in the season, but it appeared to be a token protest. Then Anita said: "Do we have enough room for all of us to drive up there?"

"Well, actually," said Margaret, "I was thinking we'd have to use your father's Volvo, along with Charles's car and mine."

"When has anyone last driven that old wagon?" said Andrew.

"Well, not since Thanksgiving," said Margaret. "I cleaned it out before Christmas, but I don't think I started the engine." She frowned. "I suppose the battery might be dead after all this time." It was strange how much easier it was to talk about cars.

"I'll try it tomorrow," said Anita, thus endorsing, in her backhanded way, the trip.

After a few minutes, Molly got up and started putting the trash in the basket, and gradually, the rest of them dispersed. Margaret continued to sit at the big table, wondering what had made her come up with this idea.

All during the years of their growing up, she'd tried to present Henry as someone nicer than he really was, a brilliant and eccentric scientist with his head in the clouds. This trip up the mountain would be another attempt to

543

show him at his best. Perhaps all mothers did something like that when they talked with their children about their dad.

The funeral that she was planning would be more of the same, including a non-existent Jewish version of this man. Maybe she could find a way to make this expedition to Monadnock an opportunity for all of them to talk about the <u>real</u> Henry, a last chance to look at this man before they all went their separate ways. Sighing heavily, she gathered herself together and moved toward the staircase. She needed to figure out what she would wear for the funeral.

* * * *

One of the big surprises at the funeral was the number of people who showed up. Somehow, Margaret had pictured a small circle of friends and relatives, sitting together in the smallest chapel at Aronson's. But they'd been given the biggest one, and by the time the family moved out of the back room to take their places in the front left section there were well over a hundred of people already seated, and more kept arriving. She wondered who all these people were. She could see Chloe and her family, along with Mrs. Mahoney right behind them, a group of her near neighbors in the middle, fellow social workers toward the back, several clients, including Deborah Breen, and a large group of older men, probably fellow faculty, scattered here and there. In the rear, reminding her of Molly's wedding, were Erik and Will in his wheelchair. But there were also lots of young people in the chapel, people she didn't know. It was puzzling.

Charles also kept turning and looking around, both at the audience and toward the back of the chapel, almost as if he were expecting someone. And at the last moment, just before eleven o'clock, Margaret saw a strange young woman hurrying up the aisle. She was dressed neatly, all in black, and was even wearing a small black hat. It wasn't until she took her place on the seat next to Charles, where he'd piled their coats, that Margaret recognized her. It was his soon-to-be ex-wife Elena. In all the years that she'd known her, Margaret had never seen her dressed so conservatively. Her usual "presentation" was on the wild side, bright, flowing, unevenly matched draperies from thrift shops, picking up the variegated colors of her hair. Charles had obviously been either expecting her or hoping she would come, but the children's faces showed surprise, and perhaps an admixture of hope or delight. Katy immediately reached out her hand to touch her mother, and Margaret could hear her intake of breath and the word "Mom!" Matt's face had frozen in a look she'd often seen on Charles's face.

Just then the rabbi walked to the podium. He began by telling about his first meeting with Henry, when he'd come reluctantly to the Temple to discuss his son Andrew's Bar Mitzvah. On that occasion, the rabbi said, Henry had expressed his many doubts about religion in general and spoke

545

quite vigorously of the fact that he didn't believe in God. Smiling at the memory, the rabbi told him that he guessed that God must have believed in Henry, or else he wouldn't be there that day, talking about Andrew's coming of age. Margaret glanced over at Andrew and saw that he was wiping his eyes. The rest of the rabbi's talk was more conventional and ended with his point that in this kind of service people often said: May his memory be a blessing for you. Jews, he pointed out, do not actually believe in immortality, but do understand that as long as the deceased is remembered, he lives on in us.

Matt then got to his feet and read his essay. Now Margaret began to cry. Matt stood tall and self- assured as he told about his early lessons in rock-climbing, how Grandpa had always told him: remember, keep three points on the rock, two legs and one arm, or two arms and one leg. That wasn't so hard to remember, Matt said, because I always figured I had another secret point that would keep me from falling: and that was Grandpa, himself. And now, I guess it's the memory of Grandpa that will keep me safe.

Oh, dear, thought Margaret, wiping her eyes, this isn't going to be easy, this whole service. The next person to speak was Anita. The kids had got together and picked her, perhaps, or maybe she'd volunteered. She looked magnificent today in a deep brown velvet dress, a perfect match for her eyes and hair, and she walked proudly to the podium. She talked about Henry as a father and how she'd always seen him as a teacher. "He took us," she said, "to wonderful places and taught us how to look at things -- stars in the sky, seashells at the shore, rocks in the mountains, and the secret world that you could find under a microscope. We always felt as if our dad was the best, and we were sorry for other kids who had ordinary fathers." Anita stood there for a minute, looking out at the audience. Although she looked appropriately sad, Margaret felt that there was a special quality about her at that point, a maturity and an openness, almost as if the death of her father had finally made it possible for Anita to open up, like a late-blooming flower. She had blossomed and become her true feminine self.

The last two speakers were from the University, one the chairman of Henry's department, and the other a current student. What the chairman said was the other big surprise for Margaret. He spoke of Henry as the department's iconoclast, the person who dared to think the unthinkable, to predict the unpredictable. "It will be a long time," he said, "before we'll be able to find a replacement for Henry Bluestone. Such a person would have to have enormous reaches of imagination, and at the same time be able to defend his or her theories with solid data and research. And that person would also have to be a great teacher." Then he turned to a young woman who was sitting in the front row. "Before I introduce Sumi Asaka, I'd like everyone in the audience who had been Henry Bluestone's student to put up

547

his or her hand." A forest of hands went up. So now Margaret knew who all the unknown young people were!

As Ms. Asaka got up and moved toward the podium, Margaret became aware that she was annoyed. She wanted to stand up and say: "But this man was a bastard, a cruel and insensitive bastard. He looked down on all of his colleagues; he thought all of you were wrong-headed, stupid conservatives who were out to thwart him at every turn." But of course, she couldn't do that. Funerals were for praising and glorifying, not for condemning. And then she wondered why Henry had given her such a false picture of the way he was viewed at the University. He'd always spoken of himself there as a misunderstood genius, a man whose ideas were looked down on, and whose theories were considered suspect. Perhaps he really had been paranoid, or had a need to be the outsider, the rebel of the academic world, just as his parents had been radicals in their world. Maybe it was only to her that he'd turned this tortured face. She shook her head, confused, and bitter. She'd always assumed, from what Henry had said or implied, that he was not really regarded as competent at the University, that they'd only kept him on because he had tenure and had showed promise at the beginning of his career. Now it appeared that whole picture was a false one. Listening to his department chairman, one would have thought they were thinking of nominating him for the Nobel Prize!

But now Sumi Asaka was beginning to speak. "It would be hard for me," she said, in her precise accent, "to improve on what Dr. Bluestone's daughter has told us. He was a man who made us discover by ourselves what the truth was. When I came to the university, I had planned to study political science, but after I took his Freshman Geology, I was a changed person. I would come home from the classes with my brain humming, unable to sleep because my mind was churning out all kinds of new ideas. Now I am in the graduate school, taking Dr. Bluestone's old course: Plate Tectonics 304. Next summer I will be a fellow in a seminar that is going to Utah to look at his earthquake theories. I wish he could go with us, but we will be thinking of him."

As Margaret was puzzling over what to her was still brand new information, the rabbi stood up to deliver the final prayers, asking that the family and all those who wished to do so, should join him in saying Kaddish. The familiar words rang out -- Yit-gadal ve-yit-kadash shmei raba -- and her mind went back to what the rabbi had told the family the other night, that the final prayers were in praise of God, to tell the mourners that only God knew why this person had died at this point, and that we had to trust Him.

Chapter Twenty-six

Walking down from the grave site to where the cars were parked, Margaret finally had a chance to connect with Elena. She was overcome with sadness as she was reminded that these children needed a mother. All the grandmothers and loving fathers in the world were not going to make up for that loss. As they fell in step together, she put her hand on Elena's shoulder. Margaret wanted to thank her for coming, and then she told her, truthfully, that Henry had always enjoyed talking with her.

"Oh, Mom," she said, stopping then as if she realized that she might have forfeited the right to call her that. "I wanted to write you when Charles told me how serious Dad's illness was, but I didn't know how you'd feel -- hearing from me, I mean," she said, dissolving in confusion, her eyes beginning to tear up.

Elena's parents had separated when she was small, and she'd never really known her own father. Perhaps she'd even wished that Henry could have played this role for her. And he, in turn, had always enjoyed this outlandish and outspoken young woman.

In the silence that followed, Elena pursed her lips, looking rueful, and said: "I want to thank you, Mom, for all you've done this year for Katy and Matt." Now she was really crying, and Margaret took her in her arms and gave her a big long hug. It was a hug that said everything that words could not say, that there were no happy endings when a marriage fell apart, that no matter who had custody of the children, it was painful for everyone, especially these children, and that all the extended family was left with complicated feelings -- anger, regret, and lingering love.

They stood by the limousine, waiting for the rest of the family to sort itself out as to who would ride with whom. Margaret wanted to ask her how long she was staying, and where, but she decided to let events take their course . It was Charles's problem, after all. Several hours later, Charles and the kids went off with Elena, evidently for dinner.

But by early evening, Charles and the children came back without her, and after Matt and Katie had gone into the sun porch to listen to some CDs, Charles joined his mother as she tried to reorganize the kitchen for the next day's picnic. They worked, companionably, side by side, filling the ice chest with sodas, and laying out the bread and mustard for cold cuts. After they'd finished their work, Charles looked directly at his mother and said: "Why don't we have a cup of tea, and I'll tell you about where things are between Elena and me." He filled the kettle and set up the cups.

"You don't have to tell me unless you want to," Margaret said quickly.

"I want to," he said. "What happened was this: I called Elena the morning after Dad died, to tell her, because I knew she'd want to know. She was always crazy about him, you know, and I think she felt he liked her."

"He did," said Margaret. "I think he saw her as a fellow rebel or something, an outsider in society."

"Well, as soon as I told her, she said she wanted to come up and asked me if I minded, or if I thought you'd mind."

"Of course, I didn't mind. I was impressed that she came."

"That's what I told her," he said, "so we left it that she'd try to get a reservation, but she asked me not to tell the kids, so they wouldn't be disappointed if she couldn't make it." Margaret nodded, and then stood up to pour the water into their cups. "So I was only halfway sure she was coming, until the moment she showed up."

"I was very impressed with how she was dressed,"said Margaret. "She looked quite dignified." She smiled. "And the kids, particularly Katy, were so pleased to see her!"

"It's a little more complicated with Matt. I suspect he thinks he's defending me when he stays aloof from her." There was a long pause, and then Charles said: "She was giving me double messages, Mom. Even coming was a kind of double message. It was as if she were saying: ask me to stay and maybe I will. But I was sure I didn't want her back. I suspect all is not wine and roses with the fellow in Florida, and I'm not surprised. I finally told her that she couldn't treat me and the kids like an accordion, in and out every few months. I said that it had been hard on us all in the beginning but that the three of us were now recovering and doing a little better, and I didn't want, either for myself, or for the kids, to have to do it all over again." He sighed. "So we dropped her at the airport after dinner." Margaret looked at Charles and realized that he was feeling almost proud of himself. And she was proud of him. Elena had been leading him in a kind of in and out dance ever since he'd met her and it was time, finally, for him to be free She was reminded of the times when he was being the skipper of his own boat. He was in charge of his life.

* * * *

On their arrival at the parking lot of Monadnock State Park, Margaret was pleased, first of all, to find that it was unseasonably warm that day, although they'd spotted a few traces of snow at the higher elevations. And it was good to see that a new and neat-looking set of restrooms had replaced the old outhouses, and that posted in plain sight was a map in full color, outlining the various trails. Well, Margaret told herself, this might not be as difficult as she'd thought, but she decided to make the little speech she'd rehearsed last night while she was tossing and turning in bed. And the kids were all grouped together, almost as if they were aware that she wanted to address them.

Clearing her throat, she said: "Listen, why don't we each go at our own pace? I'll probably take my time, but I'm sure I'll get there and we can have lunch at noon." She looked at her watch; it was still only nine. They continued to stand here. "Come on, get going," she said, realizing that she wanted them on their way and out of sight before she started. She didn't want anyone giving her advice about trail walking. And she also wanted to use the rest room once more. "I'll see you at the top, I promise."

Katy and Matt turned, finally, and ran toward the beginning of the trail they'd selected. "Bye, Gran, see you later," Katy said as she disappeared from sight. One by one, the rest of them followed suit. Everett seemed to have inherited the lunch pack, and before he turned, he waved.

Ten minutes later, Margaret started up the trail, trying to remember her three previous trips. The first had been when she was a freshman in college. In spite of a favorable forecast, it had begun to rain lightly when the Wellesley Mountaineer Club started their bus trip to New Hampshire. Margaret was wearing a brand-new pair of blue jeans. As she recalled, she'd had no problem reaching the top, scampering up like a goat as the rain fell. But by the time they started down, the rain had become heavy; she remembered sliding in the mud most of the way back to the bus. Later, at the dorm, when she took off those soggy pants, she discovered that the blue dye had come off on everything -- her socks, underpants and her skin. It was a week before she turned back to her normal pink.

If it hadn't been for Henry, she'd probably never have tried this mountain again. But in the spring of her senior year, he'd taken her up on a lovely late spring day. Among other delights, the trip turned out to include a lecture on the geology of that mountain. Henry could make this kind of story fascinating and their relationship was at the stage where almost anything he said was compelling. She still remembered that "monadnock" had become the common name all over the world for mountains like this one -- a rocky promontory surrounded by a flat plain. It had made her feel special to be climbing such a famous mountain, with so knowledgeable a tutor.

They'd climbed the mountain again when she'd been pregnant with Andrew. Henry had carried Molly on his back, while Anita and Charles had run on ahead. Her memories of this trip involved the effort of climbing: it had been hard work. It had seemed as if the middle part of the mountain was made up of large, six-foot whitish slabs, all sloping down at the same angle, and just as she'd climbed up one of them, there'd be another of the same size to clamber over. Henry had smiled and explained that in French these kinds of slabs were called "roches moutonees" -- sheep rocks -- since from a distance they all looked like sleeping sheep. With some apprehension, Margaret began to wonder if those sheep were still there, still sleeping after all these years. She'd soon find out.

The lower part of the mountain sloped up gradually, but little by little, she became aware of a series of logs that had been laid across the trail to help the climbers over the spring mud and make walking a little easier. But for Margaret, barely five feet tall, these logs were just a little too far apart, so that when she put her foot down on one of them, the other foot would end up in the squishy, soggy soil in between. And the mud was cold and sticky, and after a few minutes, had worked its way into her socks.

By now, she was beginning to perspire, and her hair was sticking to her head. Breathing was not as easy as it had been down below, and she was starting to feel that the muscles in her thighs, while not exactly hurting, were making themselves known in a new way. Several climbers who passed her seemed to leap from one log to another, but her legs were just not long enough. Some of the children who went by, of course, simply jumped into the mud, happily sloshing it over the tops of their boots. She saw that, at this rate, she was going to fall far behind the rest of the family. She wondered why she'd ever thought up this hike. For the first time, she wondered if perhaps she'd bitten off more than she could handle.

After a half an hour of rigorous walking, Margaret saw that the trail changed. It had begun to seem like a real climb. The logs had become steps in a long staircase. As she rounded one of the corners, she saw that the trees were getting shorter, and she could see open space. Then suddenly, ahead of her, her old enemies, the sleeping sheep, came into view. Now she remembered that Henry had said they were slabs of schist, a flaky sort of rock that tended to come off in your hands. Whatever she had done in previous climbs wasn't working now. How had she managed? Each of these slabs had to be scrabbled up, using her finger nails, and her knees. She should have thought about bringing gloves, and maybe even knee pads. In fact, now she recalled that this kind of climbing was called "slabbing," a word obviously invented, she thought, by some poor soul like herself. Soon she was sweating heavily. Stopping to take off her sweatshirt and to tie it around her waist, she saw ahead of her, more rows of sheep. No point in counting how many rows there were, either. Now she was becoming short of breath, and breathing faster. Luckily, it was sometimes possible to work her way around one of the slabs, and she could rest a bit. It was at one of these places that she looked up and saw Matt and Katy, leaping joyfully down from one sheep to another, obviously searching for her. At ages fifteen and eleven, they'd evidently been considered capable of a rescue mission. She'd never been so glad to see anyone in her life. Matt gave the impression of being loose-jointed, with various pieces of clothing hanging out at inappropriate places, his uneven hair falling below Henry's old fishing hat, while Katy, in spite of her sweaty face, still looked pulled together in neat Navy shorts and a bright red T-shirt.

"Gran," said Matt, "can we help?" Already taller than his father, he took her hand, while Katy, still plump from mid-childhood, but beginning to show the legginess of days to come, began to push from behind. All of a sudden, the whole enterprise became possible again. Margaret began to laugh at the ridiculousness of their situation. And in what seemed like no time, they'd passed through the sheep section and were able to climb up more easily on plain rock to the top!

The whole family was assembled, obviously waiting for her, with the lunch laid out artistically on a wide, flat stone, the paper napkins fluttering in the strong breeze. When they saw her, they broke into spontaneous applause. Suddenly, she felt enormously lucky. What a beautiful family they were! Her glance fell first on Charles who was perched on top of a large boulder, his long legs folded into two isosceles triangles, one side of his Tilley hat pulled up to the brim, with strands of his blond hair hanging at both sides. His chiseled face was in profile as he took in the horizon, but from the neck down he was a hodge-podge, in his worn, old paint-spattered clothes, a wardrobe built around a pair of blue and white striped overalls, and a thick, worn green and brown flannel shirt.

Everett and David, the sun shining brightly on their balding heads, were kneeling on one of the flat rocks, peering at the geologic topographical map, trying to figure out exactly where each of the other nearby mountains were.

Since they'd both come from out of town and hadn't brought clothes suitable for mountain-climbing, they'd worn what they had -- chino pants and shirts open at the neck with light jackets. In spite of sun block, Everett's nose was already quite red, and David was looking quite pink.. But they were grinning and enjoying, not only the day, but each other's company.

Molly and Julia had settled into a shady spot under an overhang and were talking seriously. Molly's curly blond head was nodding as Julia's smooth auburn hair bounced when she made a point. Both women were in jeans, and wore long-sleeved jerseys with their sweaters tied around them, but they'd kept their hiking boots on. There were indeed patches of snow here and there on the northern side of the mountain. Margaret could see Andrew curled up, sound asleep. Where was the baby?

And then she spotted Anita walking up and down, carrying a chuckling Duncan. Now seven months old, he was a very handsome young man. Someone had put a Red Sox cap on his blond head. Anita looked wonderful, better than Margaret had ever seen her. She was laughing at the baby, her cheeks pink and her eyes all crinkled up with pleasure. She had on old stretch pants that she must have found in her closet, and a sweater with a hole in the elbow. But she was glowing.

"Thank you," said Margaret, huffing and puffing, as she sank down on a small boulder, "for the mountain goats you sent to rescue me." She looked at her watch. It was almost noon. "Well," she said, still breathing heavily, "I seem to have arrived just in time for lunch!" Wiping her sweaty face on the tail of her sweatshirt, she smiled as she accepted her ham and cheese sandwich. Then she looked out into the distance.

The view, of course, was magnificent. To the west was Mount Greylock, a little taller than their own peak, and to the northeast, a group of much bigger mountains, but cloudy enough so that no one had been able to spot the giant, Mount Washington. A big surprise was the two towers of the Prudential and Hancock buildings, clearly visible over Boston.

. "Mom," said Anita, "do you feel as good as you look?" She sounded surprised..

"Actually, I feel great," said Margaret, between bites. "But it's true that most of the way up here, besides cursing those sleeping sheep, I kept asking myself why I ever thought up this idea to memorialize your father, killing myself in the process!"

"Well, we've been wondering that, too," said Anita, her cheeks pink and her eyes shining. She seemed to be the spokesperson at this point. "And wondering about yesterday, too, -- why you decided to put on a Jewish funeral for Dad." Anita never avoided an issue. "Would he have approved?"

Margaret shook her head, putting the sandwich down beside her. "No, I don't think he would. But I'd started thinking, during the last few weeks, whether a person could call his own tune when it came to his own funeral. And I decided that it was really up to the survivors. They were the ones who were entitled to decide." There was a pause, and then she went on. "I decided that, in fact, it was up to me." She looked up at them, almost as if to challenge them all. "Years ago, your father told me that he wanted no funeral or memorial of any kind. I was pretty sure you kids wouldn't like that solution." Feeling herself becoming angry, she added: "If you recall, I started bringing the subject up with each of you during the last month or so. None of you wanted to talk about it."

Anita looked down at her sneakers, while Molly seemed to be fixated on the faraway White Mountains. Andrew was concentrating on feeding some applesauce to the baby, and Charles was opening a can of soda. "So I thought," said Margaret into this vacuum, "that I'd start by doing something for Aunt Rosa. The Jewish service was partly for her." She stopped. "And two of you, after all, have made Judaism part of your lives."

"But when I think of Dad," said Anita, "I think he'd have been upset, especially by all that Hebrew." She sounded as if she were trying to be reasonable.

"Well, that's one reason I thought this climb today would kind of be more for him, in his language, the language of rocks and mountains," said Margaret. Quickly, she continued: "I think our whole married life was kind

561

of like this week, where what I wanted was at one end of the spectrum and what he wanted was at the other."

"How do you mean?" said Charles.

"Well, just take the house as an example. He agreed to go ahead and buy the place, but he never wanted to make it look even halfway decent." There were nods of agreement at this point. "So that's how we compromised, you might say. I got what I wanted -- a house -- and he was able to live the same Bohemian life he would have if we'd continued to live over a cafe in Somerville." She looked up at the skies. It was true, the clouds really did seem closer up here. For the first time, she realized that she was glad they'd come. She smiled. "Can I have another sandwich? I'm starving."

Matt, who had been sitting there with his radio to his ear, trying to ignore the grownups, got up and handed her a nicely wrapped one. "Here, this is a roast beef, I think. Do you want a soda, Gran?"

Margaret nodded.

Charles looked up at his kids and Margaret heard him whisper to Matt: "Listen, if you kids want to go off exploring, please feel free. But try to be back in an hour, so that we can all start down together." Margaret thought Charles was wise: she had a feeling the discussion was about to become heated.

"But you know," she said, as the kids disappeared from sight, "it wasn't all like that. We weren't as different as you might think. We liked the same kinds of music." She looked over at Charles and saw him nodding. "And vacations," she said, with a glance at Anita. Since no one was responding to this assertion, she went on and spoke forcefully: "And we especially liked the same kinds of children, your kind." She stopped, still hoping for some response. But they only seemed embarrassed. "Children like you guys. He was really crazy about every one of you, you know, and Matt and Katy, too. I'm sorry he never had a chance to get to know Duncan, not to mention whatever grandchildren are still to come." She smiled warmly and pointedly at Molly and David.

But it was Everett who looked up, grinning. "Don't assume anything," he said.

"Everett!" said Anita, loudly. "We weren't going to tell people yet." But she was smiling, almost coyly, and suddenly Margaret knew why she'd been looking so much like a rose in bloom: she was pregnant!

Molly grinned, her blue eyes sparkling. "Anita, you sly fox. How long has this been going on?"

"Only for about a month," she said. "I really didn't want to talk about it so soon, but since we're all going back tomorrow, I'm sort of glad Everett spilled the beans."

563

Everett looked particularly pleased. "And in case you're all too embarrassed to ask, we <u>are</u> going to get married -- just a simple ceremony when we get back home, toward the end of next month when we both have time off. I hope no one's upset that we're doing things in backward order."

Charles laughed. "It's an old family tradition, although perhaps Everett doesn't know. Elena and I didn't get married until she was several months pregnant."

Margaret had never before heard him speak of all this so openly, and before she knew it, she heard herself say: "This family tradition goes back even further. Anita, your father and I also did this all in backward order."

"Mom, why didn't you ever tell me?" Margaret wasn't sure Anita was upset, or pleased or just puzzled. But she seemed to be smiling.

"Well, it was your father's secret as well as mine, and he never wanted people to know. But now he's gone, and I'm in charge of family secrets and family traditions. Actually, a few years ago I discovered that this tradition is even older. My grandmother MacPherson was also pregnant when she got married." She laughed. "Sometimes I think our family must have slept through all the courses in birth control."

"I can say amen to that," said Julia. "But look how wonderfully it has all turned out," she said, pointing to Duncan, who was sleeping peacefully on his blanket.

Margaret could feel her own eyes closing. Maybe it would be a good idea to take a nap before the return trip. Making a pillow of her sweat shirt, she leaned back.

* * * *

By Sunday evening, the children had gone and once again Margaret had the house to herself. Since it was still only early April, and the house was cold, she'd lit a fire. Sitting in front of it, toasting her feet and warming up her aching muscles, she took a deep breath. Perhaps this was the beginning of the rest of her life, the last third, if she lived as long as her granny. Some of her friends would say that this was the start of old age. But every fiber of her being resisted that idea! She was still the same energetic person she'd always been, and she could do just about everything she'd always done. In fact, thanks to Henry, several new possibilities had opened up.

Earlier in the day, his lawyer, Paul Kosinski, had met with the family to tell them about the contents of the will. After explaining that the deceased and his wife had made a settlement last summer in which she was given the house and half of his severance pay, Paul said that there were two outright bequests -- one to his sister Rosa, and the other a gift to the geology department at the University to support special projects in the field of plate tectonics. The bulk of his estate, as expected, would be divided equally among the four children. While Paul was unable at that point to give the exact amount at this point, Margaret could see that each share was substantial enough so that Charles was able to sigh with relief. Clearly, this inheritance would lighten the burden of planning for his children's education.

After the children had scattered to their packing, Margaret walked Paul to the door. As he stood in the hallway, he turned to her and said: "I assume you know that you are the sole beneficiary of Henry's life insurance policy."

"I am?" she said, completely astonished. "I knew he had some small paid-up policies for each of the kids, but I didn't know there was one for me."

"This was a special policy that was automatically given to tenured faculty. It's not large, but it will come to you as a matter of course. You should do something nice with it -- take a trip, or buy something you've always wanted. It's only $25,000."

"Wow," said Margaret. "That would be quite a trip." She smiled. "Thank you for telling me, and for coming over today. The children were certainly pleased."

She'd been planning to go back to work the next day, but by the middle of May, she would start an extended unpaid six weeks' leave. Her fantasy of a trip could now really happen! With this extra money from Henry's life insurance, she wouldn't have to worry about the expense. She could even go to Seattle, to Anita's wedding.

But there was a spot of anxiety in the pit of her stomach, and she knew it had to do with Erik. If only she'd met him after the care of Henry had stopped being a factor in her life! Right now, she knew, twisting her wedding ring round and round, she needed time and space away from Erik, from everyone. Then she remembered she'd promised herself she'd take off that ring as soon as the children left. She slid it off. Her hand felt free.

She went out into the kitchen to make herself a snack. The refrigerator was full of things people had brought: that little chicken salad looked appetizing. She put it on the kitchen table and then set the kettle on for tea. As she sat down, the back doorbell rang.

Looking out the window, she saw, by the shape of the shadow, that it was Erik. Now was the time to tell him that she was going away. But what could she say? Opening the door, she was not prepared for the rush of warmth that spread through her body. She'd forgotten, in these last weeks, the powerful physical appeal that this man had for her.

"Are you okay?" Erik said, looking down at her, and moving slowly into the kitchen.

She took a deep breath, and sitting down abruptly at the kitchen table, forced herself to plunge right ahead. She would just say it, quickly, before she changed her mind. But instead, to her surprise, she began to cry. She tried wiping her eyes, to stop the tears, but her glasses got in the way and became blurred.

Erik lowered himself into the chair next to her. "What's wrong?"

She put her hands over her face, and began to speak in a muffled voice. "This has been such an awful year. The one lovely thing in all of it was you." She stopped, trying to catch her breath, rubbing her eyes with the sleeve of her sweatshirt. "But I need some time when I don't have to take care of anybody." She hiccupped. "I've been doing a lot of that all my life, and it's time I stopped, at least for a little while. And I need space, too. So I'm going to drive across the country, on my own."

Now she glanced up at him. But he was not looking at her. He was looking at the ceiling, as if someone or something up there had an answer for him. His fingers began making tapping noises on the marble table. "Let me ask you something," he said slowly, and deliberately, his face taking on a severity she'd never seen before, almost as if his mouth was barely moving. "How much does Will have to do with all of this, your need to get away, to have time and space, not to have to take care of anybody?" He paused, and she realized there'd been an undercurrent of anger in his voice. "You would not be the first woman to bail out when that problem loomed larger. And I am <u>not</u> going to let that happen to Will again." The chilliness of his tone implied that he'd been thinking about this for some time.

Oh, God, she thought. I must be sounding like his former wife. Frowning, she spoke slowly, realizing that she was angry, too. "Listen, I love Will, Erik, and part of what I've loved about you from the beginning is that you are such a caring, responsible parent, and you've done such a wonderful job of bringing him up. But it's more than that. It's something about Will, himself -- his spunky enjoyment of learning new things, his ability to enjoy life and other people --" she stopped, remembering him at Molly's wedding, at the picnic last summer, at the beach with Henry, "Will is one piece of why I'm finding it necessary to go off by myself and concentrate on me. You're right. He doesn't deserve to be abandoned again."

How could she explain herself to him, without coming across as someone who wanted to escape from responsibility? Maybe that was the problem: she <u>was</u> trying to do just that! And would that be so terrible, once in her life?

"I think I've always made sure I had people to take care of -- my kids, even my mother when I was a teenager, a husband who, as Mrs. Mahoney said, was a 'piece of work,' and all my clients. One way to avoid being alone is to surround yourself with people who need you. It would be so tempting to jump in and join you in the care of Will." It was true. It would be easier, somehow, just to stay.

She tried to remember when she'd first learned that Erik had a handicapped son. "Chloe told me last summer, when I said I was looking for someone to restore my house, that she knew a terrific architect, a nice man, who had a disabled son to care for. I had several other people to choose from. But, without hesitation, and probably because I was attracted to you anyway, I picked you. And then, when I got to know Will, I began to feel an even stronger pull toward the two of you."

Now he really looked angry. He sighed in exasperation. "You tell me you love Will. Well, I have to tell you that he adores you. You remember, last winter when I told you that I didn't want this child to get too attached to you? This was after Henry came back into your life. Something told me that he might get hurt again." He paused, as if wondering whether he should tell her something. "I've had a time with him in this last week, I can tell you. He keeps asking me: 'Margaret's husband is dead now, so why can't you marry her?' I've tried everything from saying that this is a decision for the grownups, to explaining that people usually wait a year before they remarry, and everything in between. But he knows what he wants." Now he looked at her directly. "He wants you and so do I." Now he was shouting.

"Erik," she said quietly and firmly, "<u>Don't</u> <u>push</u> <u>me</u>. I'm going. And that's it." A warm feeling of satisfaction came over her as she said these words. She'd said it, she told herself. She'd got mad and she didn't even care <u>what</u> he thought or what he'd say.

He sat there, looking defeated, and then he shrugged. "Would you be willing to come to have dinner with Will and me before you leave?"

"Of course. But you must explain to Will somehow that my coming doesn't imply any kind of promise. Can you do that?"

"I'll have to," he said slowly. He stood up and put his arms around her.

"Erik, Erik," she said, leaning into him, "I'd like to have your blessing when I go, but you need to understand that I'm going, anyway, no matter what you say."

Now he was stroking her hair, but in an absent-minded way, as if she'd already gone. "I'm giving it to you," he said slowly, "because holding you too tightly is not the way to keep you, I can see that." She'd let him down, and maybe lost him in the process.

* * * *

Six weeks later she got into Henry's old car and drove it to the Volvo place. All she knew about the chief mechanic was that Henry had thought the world of him, and that his name was Leo. She'd driven to the dealer's that morning, hoping he still worked there.

571

In a few minutes, a short, wiry, sunburned man came out to the car. His teeth were stained -- probably from tobacco, she decided, noticing that he was carrying a cigarette -- but she found him quirkily attractive, her age or older, with a crooked smile, eyes with many wrinkles around them. And he looked familiar, although she was certain she'd not been to this dealer's before. He was smiling. "Mrs. Bluestone," he said, reaching out to stroke the apple-green finish on the car, "I couldn't stay to speak to you last week, but I was at Dr. Bluestone's funeral service, sitting near the back. It was a fine service."

Climbing out of the front seat, she said: "Thank you. Now I know why you looked familiar. I saw you there. You were one of my husband's favorite people."

"I'm glad to see you driving the car," he said. "Are you keeping it?" He looked at the car with love and reverence in his face. "This is the greatest car in the world. Dr. Bluestone used to say that he and I had kept this vehicle in mint condition, working together." He leaned into the open window and glanced at the speedometer reading. "Three hundred and eleven thousand miles." He grinned. "A tribute to regular maintenance and wise replacement of parts." He opened the hood. "Look at that engine. We put that in nearly two years ago -- that was our second replacement -- and it looks <u>clean</u>." He looked at the interior of the car. "And, speaking of clean," he said, grinning, "I see you've got the inside bright and shining. Dr. Bluestone was certainly a keeper, a real pack rat!" He dropped his cigarette on the floor and stepped on it. "Are you here because you want to sell it to me? I always told Dr. Bluestone that I wanted to be the first customer if that day ever came. It would be a treasure."

"I'm not sure," said Margaret. "Right now, I'm here for some advice, since you know the car. I'm thinking of taking a trip across the country in a couple of weeks, and while I have my own car, I was wondering if it made sense for me to take this one."

He looked at her closely. "Are you going by yourself?"

She nodded.

"Not taking that young grandson along? Nobody?" He looked worried, the lines around his eyes enhanced by his concern.

"Are you saying this car might not make it?"

He shook his head. "No, I was thinking of you, a lady by yourself, going across the country alone. The car," he said - - was there a slight hesitation in his voice -- "she'd do fine. I could go over her, bring everything up to snuff, but you couldn't do better for long distance than this baby." Once again, he stroked the finish, and then he looked at her seriously. "If anything did go wrong, you could take it to a Volvo place and have them call me." He scratched the back of his head. "It's the safest car you could ever drive.

Maybe you should have one of your kids buy you a cellular phone, so you could always call for help." He shrugged. "What can I say? So why don't you leave it with me and I'll check it over and make it perfect. I'll call you when it's ready."

She handed him the keys. "It's been a pleasure to meet you finally. And I really appreciate your coming to the service. My husband would have been pleased to know you were there."

"He was one in a million, Mrs. Bluestone, a lot like this car, you know." He paused. "I'll get one of the boys to drive you home and I'll call you when it's all ship-shape. And when you get back, if you don't know what else to do with it and you want to sell it, come to me first. I'd be honored." She could see that he really coveted it. But then he cast his appraising glance at Margaret. "You know, I bet you'll do just fine on this trip. You have a lotta spunk."

Now here was a man who was really giving her his blessing.

Chapter Twenty-seven

Margaret spent the rest of the week packing, but at last it was time to leave. Erik came over to say good-bye and to give her a little package to take with her. She felt a sense of distance on his part, as if he'd begun to write her off, and wasn't counting on her in the same way as before. Yet he held her for a long time, and she leaned her head against his chest, feeling as if she were saying good-bye to safety.

She'd deliberately made no plans about what roads to take on the first leg of this journey. Nor had she set any particular time to leave. Looking up at the sky, and seeing that it was about to rain, she'd put off going until nearly noon. Finally, she got into the car and headed north. She would start on Route 2 and take that west to New York state. Maybe she shouldn't go that far on this first day, she told herself, as the rain began to fall. Soon the windshield wipers, even at top speed, were having trouble keeping up with the storm. Well, it <u>was</u> an old car. The wind was rising, blowing branches across the road. Slowing down, she found herself behind a line of trucks.

Far ahead, she could hear the gears of the big eighteen-wheelers switching into low when they had to grind their way up the hills, and then, the pitch rising as they came down again. And when they passed her, she was almost blinded by the spray, barely able to see the blinking red lights of their trailers. Whatever had made her imagine that she could drive along and think about her life? Clearly, in this kind of driving, one had to concentrate on the road. Her picnic lunch -- which she'd pictured herself enjoying on a meadow somewhere in the Berkshires -- would have to wait until things cleared up, and she'd probably just wolf it down in the car. On this road, unlike the Mass Pike, there were no tourist eateries, or nice rest rooms.

At two o'clock she turned off the road at one of the exits, and after driving along for a mile or so, found a parking lot -- empty except for the cardboard fast food containers -- next to an abandoned restaurant, its sign partly unhinged by the storm. She opened the lunch box, and unwrapped the turkey sandwich. Turning on the radio was no help, either. It was mostly static and warnings of flooding in low-lying places. What in hell was she doing in this God-forsaken place?

* * * *

By five- thirty she was tired of the slow, stop-and-go driving, and even though she was back on Route 2, she decided to pick some town where she could spend the night. The next exit sign had been partially blown away, probably by this current wind, but the place was called something Falls. It probably had an inn or a bed-and-breakfast.

The main street was several blocks long. Most of the stores had closed for the day, and the only place to eat seemed to be The Falls Bar and Grill. Across the street was a small brick three-story hotel. She pulled over and parked the car. Grabbing her raincoat from the back seat, she ran into the lobby. Behind the desk was a thin elderly man with glasses, chatting with two old men who were sitting on the worn leather couch. One of the residents was grossly overweight, with a very red face, but the other, except for being covered with age freckles, looked a little more sprightly.

"Do you have a room with bath?" She was almost hoping the desk clerk would say no. "No rooms with bath here," he said. "But there's a bathroom down the hall, not far. Thirty dollars a night, cash."

She looked up at the clerk. "Well, I'll take it," she said. He stood there, waiting for something. Oh, my God, she thought, he wants to be paid in advance. She dug down into her purse. "Here," she said handing him three tens, "and could I have an extra pillow?" She'd brought several books along, figuring she could read in bed.

"You can have mine," said the fat man on the couch. "I haven't used it since my surgery."

"Oh, that's all right," she said quickly, hoping he wouldn't tell her about his operation. The desk clerk handed her the key. It came attached to a wooden marker that said 23.

"Well, I'll get my overnight bag. Is it all right to park right out there?" He nodded.

Quickly, she ran out to the car, and grabbed the bag. Upstairs, in Room 23, she looked around. There was a plain iron bedstead with a white cotton spread that didn't quite cover it. Underneath, a gray cotton blanket and sheets that appeared to be clean.

One pillow. A painted wooden dresser stood nearby, and in the bottom drawer she found an extra blanket, probably at least partly wool. The window shades didn't quite fit and one had a long rust stripe on it. A single unshaded light bulb hung down in the middle of the room: evidently reading in bed was not an option in this hotel, so she wouldn't need that extra pillow, anyway! She put her bag down and went into the corridor to explore the bathroom. Well, it was clean, but the line of green powder along the wall made her wonder if there had been cockroaches. She decided not to take a bath, although a hot shower would have been wonderful. Suddenly she pictured a modern motel with little bottles of shampoo and fluffy white towels. This bathroom had a towel but she wondered if it was hers alone. Maybe in this hotel, one shared towels as well as pillows!

After dinner at the <u>Falls</u> -- the special was meat loaf and gravy, with instant mashed potatoes and canned string beans -- she went back into the hotel, nodded at the three elderly men, and went up to bed. She tried to double-lock the door, but it had only an old-fashioned slide bolt. It was cold.

Thank God, she had her flannel nightgown, and that the hotel had provided an extra blanket. She put the cotton bedspread on top.

But once in bed, with the light turned out, she realized two things: one that the blinking neon light from the <u>Falls Bar and Grill</u> could be seen in the crack in the window shade, making an on-off pattern on the wall of her room, and two, that she should have tested the springs. <u>This</u> mattress must have been as old as the hotel, and it was shaped like a bow with a big sag in the middle. She got up and looked underneath. There was only a rusty iron spring, and it had sprung. Then she remembered one of Henry's sayings: when the bed spring is bad, put the mattress on the floor.

It wasn't easy, but gradually, she tugged on it until it slid, like a dying seal, right onto the bare floor. And Henry was right. Her back felt much better when she lay down. Perhaps she could get some sleep. Lying there now, for the first time, she thought about Henry, not the Henry that she'd taken care of in this last year, nor the paranoid man she'd seen for the two years before that, but the person she'd married, a man who could rise to this kind of occasion, and make it liveable. Henry had been adaptable, flexible, and he could come up with practical solutions to these kinds of crises. He would have made this experience into an adventure. But the charm of this kind of adventure seemed to be wearing off, as far as she was concerned.

* * * *

On the road the next day, Margaret felt more in command of her journey. Gradually, she made her way into New York state, and eventually, almost by chance, ended up on Route 20, one of Henry's old favorites. What if he were here with her now, sharing this joint memory, driving his old car? Maybe this was what the rabbi had meant when he'd said that as long as the deceased is remembered, he lives on in us. And perhaps all widows went through this kind of process, remembering only the good times, eventually putting the deceased husband on a pedestal. Was this trip going to be a rerun of all the best qualities of Henry Bluestone? After all these years of nourishing and reworking the negative aspects of living with him, here was a whole new version of him!

She had lunch that day at a diner in a tiny town called Richfield Springs. Sitting at the counter, on a little round stool, she watched the cook as he flipped omelets, turning the hamburgers at exactly the right minute, never forgetting the slowly cooking bacon, or the fried potatoes. After the lunch rush was over, she told him how much she'd enjoyed his expertise. He shrugged. "Goes with the job," he said. Looking up at her, he asked:

"So are you here to visit the Baseball Hall of Fame?"

Puzzled, she said: "Is that near here?"

"Turn left at the next crossroads. It's eleven miles to Cooperstown."

Henry had taken the kids there, years ago, combining baseball with geology.

Now she remembered they were going to look for some rocks with a strange name -- Herkimer diamonds -- that was it. The kids had taken picks and rock hammers and dug up a few of these clear quartz crystals. A cardboard box up in Margaret's attic, full of rocks the kids had found over the years, probably included some of them. Maybe she should drive to Herkimer, if it was also nearby. She'd ask the counterman.

"Well, when you get to the crossroads, instead of turning left to Cooperstown, turn right and go about that same distance, north -- to Herkimer. Just past the I-90."

Margaret sat thinking. Maybe she should skip Herkimer and drive up to the interstate and put in some good mileage today. The I-90 went all the way to Cleveland, near where Rosa and George lived, and she'd promised to stop by for a few days.

Of course, she could make a side trip to Cooperstown. She was as much a baseball fan as anyone. On the other hand, it might make more sense to wait until she and Erik could bring Will. He would really love it.

Standing up and taking out the money to pay her bill, she realized what she had just thought. Where had that idea come from? She wondered if this whole journey was just a screen to cover what she had planned to do from the beginning. It was almost as if she'd been making up excuses, trying to convince herself that she was a free agent, that she still had a choice as to which way her life could go. Perhaps she was, both in fact, and in her heart, committed to this man and his child. Yet the whole point of this journey was to concentrate on herself. It was beginning to look as if some of her life's decisions were already made.

* * * *

By mid- afternoon Margaret was driving west on the Thruway. It had been a long time since she'd had the pleasure of the wide open road before her. This part of upper New York state, where the highway followed the Mohawk River valley, was pocketed on the north side with little caves in the high palisades, and from time to time, right next to the road, the old Erie Canal ran parallel to her route. If Henry were with her now, he'd be telling her about the history and geology of this area, explaining what natural events had produced those caves, and good teacher that he was, he'd make it fascinating. How strange it was that, on this journey in which she'd hoped to begin to conduct her own life on its own terms, she seemed to be carrying an invisible passenger: Henry.

To distract herself, she turned on the radio. Today, she was in luck: one of the local stations was focusing on The Beatles. There was no one to hear her off-key singing, thank God, so she was free to join in. The station was working its way from "She Loves You" to the last songs the group had done together. As the afternoon wore on, Margaret began to feel that she was back in the late sixties and early seventies. Gradually, she became aware that tears were rolling down her cheeks.

Those were such innocent days, when it had seemed that anything was possible if you stood up for your beliefs, when young people -- even a young married couple like herself and Henry with small children -- could be part of the peace movement. They'd had the power to end a war! It was a time when all her friends were singing the same songs, shouting the same slogans, cheering the same heroes. But it was more than that. In her own personal life, it had been the last time she and Henry had been <u>together,</u> agreeing on fundamentals. What had happened to them?

Pushing these thoughts aside, Margaret realized she was finding it more difficult to drive. The sun -- now in the west -- was shining right into her eyes, and in spite of air-conditioning, the car seemed to be warming up. It was time to leave the highway, and maybe find somewhere to swim, although it was still only June. To the south of her, she could see the beginnings of the Finger Lakes. She turned off at the next exit, and began to look for a place to stay, something with facilities for cooking a light supper. She'd only just begun her trip, but already she was finding these happy memories painful.

* * * *

As it turned out, she stayed for two nights in a little cabin colony. The tiny cottage, advertised as providing light housekeeping with lake access, was just what she needed. There was even a small store, and each little house had a deck facing the lake. The kitchen was just one wall of a combination living and dining room, with a two-burner stove sitting on top of a tiny refrigerator. A single shelf displayed a frying pan, a saucepan, two plates, cups and saucers, some utensils, and an old percolator. A small oilcloth-covered table with two chairs completed that end of the room; the other was furnished with two easy chairs and a bookcase. It was enough. She could play house.

She began by bringing in all her luggage, so that she could repack. First she took out some of the books she'd brought along -- mostly things by Virginia Woolf that she'd never read -- and placed them carefully in the bookcase. She smiled. A *Room of One's Own* would be just right for this setting. She made a little "one-nighter," putting whatever she might need for such a night into one medium-sized suitcase, and then she took the little canvas airline carry-on and made it into a swimming bag, with a beach towel, flip-flops and bathing suit, and shampoo in case she found a pool with a shower somewhere. And here, too, was the little package Erik had given her. Carefully, she opened it, and then smiled. She'd always wanted one of these: a Swiss army knife, with all the gadgets one could ever wish for, from a can opener to a Phillips screw driver, and a little pair of scissors. She dropped it into her purse.

Changing into her bathing suit, and taking the beach towel, she walked out onto her deck and down to the water. At that moment, probably suppertime for the other residents, there was no one at the lake but herself. The water was still a little cool, but she forced herself to get wet and after a few minutes, she swam a few strokes, turning over on her back and looking up at the long lines of pink clouds, already reflecting the setting sun. Right at that moment, she felt as if she were complete, sufficient within herself, as if she could live forever in this little cabin.

After a long, hot shower, and supper on the deck -- pasta sauce on vermicelli and a can of white asparagus -- she walked into the woodsy section of the colony and found a bunch of wild daisies, some white bloodroot, and down near a little brook, some yellow cowslip. She picked a few of each and brought them back decorate her new little house, putting them in a water glass and arranging them casually. Climbing into bed, shortly after darkness had fallen, she stretched out and heard herself taking a deep breath that spelled a new kind of contentment. Right here, where she was at this very minute, she felt as if she were in the exact center of the world -- a world that was her own. Other parts of her life -- her children, Erik, her house, her job and all her clients -- were out there somewhere, spinning around like the edges of the galaxy, but <u>she</u> was here. Now. And no one knew where she was: that was the best part. She went to sleep early and slept long and deeply.

The next day she took a side trip into Seneca Falls, a center of the Women's Movement, birthplace of a number of pioneers in Women's Suffrage and Women's Rights. But as she poked around the town and visited the Museum, she was aware that this was a duty call, a pilgrimage she could mention to certain ardent feminist friends back home. She wanted to get back to her own little deck, to her books, and to the pay phone in the store so she could call Rosa to say that she'd be arriving the next day.

* * * *

It had been at least ten years since she'd last visited Rosa and George at their home. But Margaret had never felt as close to them as she did now. The weeks of nursing Henry had created a special bond, as if they'd all been in a war together, and she found she was looking forward to seeing them again. They must have felt the same way: when she drove into their driveway and honked the horn, the two of them came quickly out of the house and reached out to give her a couple of big hugs.

"Oh, Rosa," said Margaret, "my comrade in arms!" Rosa was wearing what Margaret remembered was called a "house dress," in flowered cotton or gingham, probably something that needed ironing. But it suited Rosa: it was plain, unpretentious and completely unstylish. Rosa's appearance seemed to say: what you see is what you get -- a plain, small Jewish housewife, who still spoke with the remains of a Bronx accent. At first glance, her mouth seemed prim and her face stern, but her features slid easily into warmth and softness.

George, Rosa's Little Sir Echo -- who'd always been ready to take on any task, never losing his temper no matter how cranky Henry had been -- he, too, looked his part. He was a short, slightly plump, baldish retired engineer, devoted to his wife and happy to go through life as her doppelganger, the person who always replied: Right! when she ended her sentences with: Right, George? At eighty-three, his jowls had become dewlaps, and little bunches of gray hair were beginning to sprout from his ears and his nose, while his eyebrows had taken to shooting off in several directions at once.

"Come on in," George said now, taking one of her bags and bringing it up the steps. "We've given you a nice room with a view of our garden. Hope you haven't had dinner yet?" he asked anxiously, "because Rosa has made you a real summer supper." They straggled into the house and dumped the luggage in the hall. Margaret looked around. The house had a nice, old-fashioned look to it, of post-depression plainness, comfortable and full of pictures of all their children and grandchildren. It looked exactly like what it was: the home of a Midwestern couple who had been married for nearly fifty years.

"It feels so good to be here," she said. "Is it okay if I take a nap before dinner?"

"Of course," said Rosa. "Come upstairs. I'll show you your room."

* * * *

It wasn't until the next afternoon that Margaret had a chance to talk seriously with Rosa. George had gone to his weekly Rotary lunch at the local hotel, while the two women had dined on leftovers at home. After a long, comfortable silence as they sipped on their ice tea, Margaret said: "You know, on this trip so far, I've spent a lot of time thinking about Henry, and I found myself wondering what his childhood was like. He never talked about it too much -- hardly at all -- and I've often wondered about it. I know you used to take care of him a great deal."

Rosa sighed. Biting her lip, she began to stir the remains of melting ice in her glass. And then she looked up at Margaret. "Actually," she said slowly, her face suddenly looking drawn, with deep channels on either side of her mouth, "if you want to know the truth, Henry had a miserable childhood. Our mom was a real career woman, and I don't think she'd ever planned to have more than one child." She laughed, shortly. "I, at least, was never any trouble to my parents. When I was little, my Granny took care of me while Ma went off to work. But Granny died when I was nine, and after that, I was kind of on my own after school. I went to a neighbor's for an hour or two." Margaret sat there listening, trying to absorb this view of her former mother-in-law, whom she'd only known as a quiet, elderly lady. She often wondered what had happened to that early feminist, who'd made a real life out of running a leftist bookstore.

"And then Ma became pregnant with Henry. It was in the worst time of the depression -- 1932 -- and Pa's union was on strike a lot; Ma needed to work, but she also liked to work. I don't think she ever wanted Henry, and I'm sure she resented his very existence. Even though I was still pretty young -- ten, when he was born -- I knew that she was neglecting him." She shook her head, sadly. "I remember one Sunday when we all went to Orchard Beach, up in the Bronx, not far from where we lived. You could get there on the subway -- one of those places that was lined with bodies on hot summer days. Henry was a toddler, and he kept heading for the water. Ma never seemed to notice, and I always felt that, if I didn't keep an eye on him, he'd drown." She looked at Margaret. "The social worker in you is probably wondering what was wrong with me! There I was, a healthy twelve-year old at the beach and I was spending all my time watching my baby brother." Her eyes were filling with unshed tears, but she shook her head, as if telling them to go away. "That was the story of my life, if you want to know the

589

truth. Until he went to high school -- you know, he got into the Bronx High School of Science; even then he was brilliant -- I ended up taking care of him every minute that I was not in school. Ma had a series of baby sitters, but he wasn't easy to handle. I think he knew Ma didn't want him, and he wasn't going to go out of his way to make it easy for anyone."

Rosa was quiet for a long minute, wiping her eyes with the clean handkerchief that she kept in her apron pocket. Margaret was trying to think of something comforting to say when Rosa sighed. "The worst time was when Henry was about eleven, too young, really, to stay by himself. He came down with scarlet fever that year and had a bad case of it. The doctors were worried it would affect his heart and told Ma that he had to stay in bed. I was in college and couldn't always get home, even to fix his lunch. Pa was back at work, finally, working full-time because the War was on, so sometimes Ma had to stay home with him. Once when I walked in, I could hear her yelling at Henry, blaming him for getting sick and making her lose time from work."

"It's no wonder," said Margaret softly, "that he hated illness so much."

"I guess I should have taken the semester off that year," said Rosa.

"It sounds as if you're <u>still</u> blaming yourself, as well as your mother," said Margaret, realizing that she was beginning to sound like a social worker.

"Not so much anymore. The best thing that ever happened to Henry was meeting you. As soon as I met you -- remember, George and I came to Boston to visit you when you two had that little apartment in Somerville - - I could see right away that you were just what Henry needed, so domestic, such a good cook, and a wonderful mother. I always thought that Henry knew right away that you were what he'd missed all those years, someone who could really love him and take care of him. In my heart, I turned him over to you at that moment."

"But Rosa," and now Margaret was starting to cry, "you must have felt terrible when you heard that Henry and I were thinking of divorce, that he was leaving me." She'd had no idea that she'd taken on a sort of sacred trust when she married Henry.

"Well, I felt bad for <u>you</u>, because I knew, having watched him all those years, that he really didn't like women very much. Oh, he called himself a feminist, but it was only skin deep. Once you went back to school and got a job, I knew he'd make life difficult for you. He probably saw all that as being neglected all over again." She looked up at Margaret. "And what's strange, you know, is that I think he really loved you, at least as much as he could love any woman." Wiping her eyes, she went on. "And I think he was crazy about the kids. That was a big surprise to him, I think, that he could really love children." She laughed. "When I had Louise, Henry was just

591

sixteen. He came to see me in the hospital, and when he looked at her in the nursery, he turned to me and he said, with real bitterness in his voice: 'I'm never going to have kids. There are already too many people in this world.'"

Margaret smiled. "By the time I met Henry, you had three children. I remember he told me once that you'd 'sold out.' As if getting married and having children was some kind of crime." There was another long silence, as Margaret poured herself another glass of iced tea. "Lately I've been wondering if I made him miserable by pushing for pretty much the same kind of life you had -- a house in the suburbs, children, the whole nine yards. A lot of our arguments turned out to be about things like that: you remember how upset he was about Andrew wanting to have a bar mitzvah. And he even refused to let the kids take music lessons; he thought that was just suburban foolishness. And I learned pretty quickly that there was no way we were going to buy any furniture. In fact, the only way I could get a couch, for instance, was to find one that had been dumped at the curb, waiting to be picked up by the trash men." She put her head in her hands. "And that couch was purple! The kids used to say: 'I never saw a purple couch; I never hope to see one.'" She smiled, remembering. "But now I'm thinking that he was right, that those material things weren't worth fighting about. Maybe he had better values than I did. I can understand why he thought of me as a conventional suburban housewife, and why he left when he finally had the opportunity."

Rosa stood up and came over to Margaret. "You're as bad as I am, blaming yourself for everything. He was a difficult man, no question about it. From the day he was born, he wasn't wanted, and none of that is your fault. I've finally decided that it wasn't my fault, either," said Rosa. "But in spite of all that, you know, Margaret, he was quite a person. He was someone we can be proud of, a great scientist, a good teacher, and a pretty good father. Can't we leave it at that, and get on with our lives?"

Margaret nodded. "That's probably the best we can do."

* * * *

As the sun was beginning to set the next day, Margaret was still in Indiana, driving slowly and contentedly along Route 24, the one George had picked out for her. She'd asked him to select roads that weren't well-traveled. It had been a relaxing day, with the road running parallel to several rivers. The first had been the Maumee, a brisk little stream that eventually came to a big dam where she pulled over and stopped to eat the picnic lunch Rosa had prepared for her. After lunch, locking the car, she'd taken a nap.

A little further on, she'd begun to travel along the Wabash, a much bigger river that nestled in a fertile valley. Small farms dotted the landscape, and at this time of the year, the corn was just beginning to come up; many of the vegetables were ready to be picked. At the side of the road one brightly painted vegetable stand tempted Margaret to stop. She wasn't sure whether she'd be cooking her own supper that night, but she couldn't resist the fresh young lettuces, the tiny new beets with their tender greens, the spring peas. It had been, she realized as it began to get dark, a day for dawdling. There was no traffic on this road. Perhaps everyone had switched to the interstates.

She'd seen a few motels when she passed through one town -- Logansport -- but at that point she hadn't felt ready to stop. On the map, she'd spotted what looked like a big lake and she began hoping she'd find another cottage colony. By the time she finally reached it, however, night had begun to fall. There <u>was</u> a motel, right on the lake, but out front, a sign read NO VACANCY. And the lights were out. She'd have to go on until she reached the place where Route 24 intersected with I-65, twenty miles further on. And now she realized that she was beginning to get hungry. There didn't seem to be any restaurants in this part of the country, either.

Now there were absolutely no cars. And it looked as if the farmers had gone to sleep early, since all the houses were dark. A couple of gas stations had turned out their lights as well. The moon, nearly full, was shining down on what could have been an empty world. She felt as if no one lived in this part of the country, as if they'd all gone away somewhere, leaving just herself, driving along in Henry's old car, the two of them ghosts from the past. Perhaps civilization had moved on to another planet. She was beginning to sound like one of the science fiction novels that Andrew used to read.

Now her imagination took over. What if this old car broke down, right here on this deserted road, or if she had a flat tire? What would she do? Of course, she had her cellular phone, but the other day she'd tried punching in some numbers and got nothing. There was probably no one there, wherever "there" was. The lights were out all over in this part of Indiana. And all she could hear were spring peepers.

She could picture herself, pulled over to the side of the road, in the middle of nowhere, about to be raped by someone coming out of those woods, or robbed and killed. All she would have to defend herself would be the Swiss Army knife that Erik had given her. And then she laughed. She was scaring herself to the point of being ridiculous.

An hour later, following a long hot bath, she was stretched out on a chaise longue, with a glass of brandy close at hand, in a big modern motel. The room was magnificent, with two queen-size beds to choose from, a bright, shiny bathroom, and a wonderful room-service menu. She'd just had a steak, with french fries, a big salad, and a dish of chocolate mousse. By God, she deserved it! This night was trying to tell her something. And not just <u>this</u> night; maybe the whole trip. She began to wonder if there was a pattern in the way she'd set it all up. Any normal person -- she paused: now there was an ominous phrase -- any normal person would not, first of all, have chosen to take a twenty-five year old car on a trip across the country, no matter how beautifully maintained it had been. And nobody in her right mind would have set off on Route 2 in a driving rainstorm, surrounded by enormous trucks. She could have waited for a day or two until the weather cleared. There was no hurry. She could have got a booklet from the AAA with a list of decent motels and hotels. That fleabag hotel was waiting for someone just like herself.

And she'd stayed there, and felt a sense of triumph that she'd turned it into an adventure. Who would have applauded her courage and inventiveness? Who, indeed, but Henry. Here she was, now that he was finally dead and gone, evidently trying to live out <u>his</u> life, instead of her own. In <u>his</u> car, with <u>his</u> set of values.

Henry would have been charmed by the little cottage colony where she spent two nights in the Finger Lakes. That was exactly the kind of place he would have chosen to stay. And what's more, she'd felt incredibly secure and at home in that place. She'd <u>liked</u> "making do" with her two-burner stove, and her little bouquet of wild flowers. She'd liked "playing house" in that setting. It had felt like the center of the world, <u>her</u> world. So maybe some of this didn't come from Henry; maybe it was part of who she'd always been. She'd always been willing to settle for so little, willing to marry a man who would make her go to Sears to buy her own wedding ring.

She seemed to have a need to <u>prove</u> to herself that she could manage, no matter what. And let's face it, she told herself, as she crawled into bed, she'd been asking for trouble this very day when she let George pick out a deserted road for her, and then to have stuck with it after dark. She was just lucky that nothing bad <u>had</u> happened.

* * * *

Sticking to daytime driving the next day, she made good time. By mid-afternoon she'd reached the Mississippi River. The river was wide at this point, looking across to Burlington, and it was still muddy and fast-flowing. She found herself thinking, as she'd always done when she reached the river, about Huck Finn and what it would have been like to ride down that rushing water on a raft. And then she remembered that she'd seen that book in Will's room, the other night when she'd gone to their house for a farewell dinner. She'd asked him if he'd read it, and he nodded his head.

"We read it in school," he said slowly. "And then I read it again, with my dad."

"So you liked it?" she'd asked him.

He nodded, and then added: "But it's so sad. It makes me cry."

"Me, too," she'd replied.

She wondered if he'd ever seen this magnificent river. It was another place she and Erik could take him someday.

There, she was doing it again, taking for granted the picture of a life for all of them together. If it was true that somewhere inside, her mind was already made up, why was she heading west instead of east?

* * * *

Approaching the outskirts of Granny's home town should have prepared her for the fact that there might have been changes since her last visit more than ten years ago. Indistinguishable now from every place of its size in America, the five-mile stretch that led into town -- an area that she remembered as dotted with small farms and an occasional gas station -- featured the same fast food restaurants, the same motel chains, and, to her surprise, even the same supermarkets, toy stores and giant hardware emporia. She was even more shocked and dismayed to see what had happened to the town square. The old bandstand was still standing in its center, needing a coat of paint, but the stores she remembered were mostly all gone, some of them empty and boarded up. What had happened to the old department store, where Granny had bought yard goods for house dresses and aprons? The little drug store had been replaced by one of the national chains, but the barbershop -- where she'd had her first professional haircut -- was gone altogether. Where in the world would those old men sitting on that bench in front of the court house go for their haircuts? Surely not to that neon-lighted beauty shop that proclaimed itself as UNISEX!

Driving slowly around that town square, she realized that her memories of life in Granny's home town were stronger and more persistent that what she was now seeing with her own eyes. She'd probably always remember the town as it had been, and not this strange, hybrid place it had become. She had a sense of dislocation, as if the past were stronger than the present, almost as if she could blink her eyes and wake up back in that past. The big old hotel, where she had planned to spend the night, was boarded up, and she was forced to drive back outside of town to stay at one of the chains.

The next morning Margaret took a long walk through town, heading for the location of Granny's former house. Somehow she was not surprised to discover that there were now three ranch houses on that property, and that the developers had managed to level off the hill as well. The whole neighborhood had changed. There were no longer any bird houses where purple martins could nest; even the trees that had sheltered them were gone. And where her best friend, Rebecca Peterson, had lived, there was now an elementary school. It was true. Margaret's memories of this place were part of her, they were built into her own house back in Massachusetts, into her values, her sense of what a home was supposed to look like. The world that Granny had lived in was no more. If Margaret wanted to look for her roots, it made more sense to look inside herself than to travel over a thousand miles to find them in this little town in Southeastern Iowa.

But then she began to wonder again why she'd really come to this town. If, as it turned out, her roots were inside herself, rather than here, what was the point of the trip?

Chapter Twenty-eight

As it turned out, it was the old Volvo that finally told her what to do about her trip. Looking back on the last ten days, she could see that perhaps the car had been trying to tell her something all along. That first day of her journey, when it had been raining so hard on Route 2, she'd noticed the windshield wipers were a little weak. And now, heading northwest from Granny's hometown, she noticed a slight hesitation when she changed gears. There were probably people who would say that it was really <u>Henry</u>, speaking through the car. But whoever or whatever it was, she began to feel uneasy, a little prickling in the pit of her stomach. It was a warning.

She'd gone only about thirty miles when she heard a strange noise in the engine. It was a deep, grinding noise that made her think of only one word: transmission. Wondering if it would be safe to drive any further, she pulled over to the side of the road. Getting out the list of Volvo dealers that Leo had given her, she also looked at the map. It seemed that the nearest one would be up in Des Moines, fifty miles further. Maybe she should limp along until the got to the next gas station. But it was a terrible noise; it made her feel as if she were tearing the engine apart. Forgive me, Henry, she said, your nice car doesn't deserve this. Now, why had she put it that way? <u>She</u> didn't deserve this.

Slowly, she moved out on to the road, proceeding at a very low speed. **Thank God there was a town coming up, and sure enough, on the outskirts, a** gas station. She drove in. A short, middle-aged man was standing next to the pump, his name embroidered on his shirt. *Fred.*

"Can I help you? I could hear you coming, that's for sure."

"Does it sound like the transmission?" she asked, hoping desperately that he would say it was some small benign lesion.

He nodded. "Yep." Then he looked at the car. "What a great car! How old is it?"

"Twenty-five years," she said. "It was my husband's, and between him and his mechanic, they kept it very well. It's gone over 300,000 miles, and this is its third engine. But I don't know when it had its last transmission. That mechanic gave me a list of Volvo dealers. Do you think I should call the nearest one? Or could you fix it?"

"Not me, I'm afraid. We don't do transmissions. And the nearest Volvo place is in Des Moines. Why don't you pull over and let me take a look, and then you could call them. It probably would need to be towed." He frowned. "I don't know if they'd come this far. We'll see what they have to say, and if they won't tow you, I can probably find someone around here who could do it."

"How long does it usually take to put in a new transmission?" said Margaret, trying to plan for the worst. She felt a slight queasiness, as if her stomach had already figured it all out.

"A while," he said. "Depending on if they have the parts. With a car of this age, they might have to send for some. Could be a whole week, or more."

A whole week? she thought. Climbing out of the car to make the call to Des Moines, she felt for the first time a sense of distance from the Volvo, as if it were no longer going to be part of her life. She was reminded of how she'd felt shortly after Henry had died. Once again, she was energized in a strange way, ready to line up the various possibilities and talk to the experts about what had to be done next. And sure enough, the dealer in Des Moines suggested she have the car towed to their place so they could take a look at it. When he heard that the car had been driven for over 300,000 miles, there was a silence at the other end of the line. Then he suggested she come along in the tow truck, because they'd need to discuss what to do. She'd already made up her mind not to make any decisions until she'd talked to Leo.

* * * *

Later, riding in the open tow truck next to a young, red-haired driver with a passion for hard rock, she made up her mind just to enjoy the trip, in spite of the noise of his radio. It felt good <u>not</u> to have to drive, and to be able to look around the flat countryside on a sunny morning. She took off the sweater she'd worn in the air-conditioned Volvo, and sat happily in her short-sleeved cotton shirt. The wind ruffled the hairs on her arms and her face felt the breeze when she looked out her side of the truck. The problem with driving, she thought, is that you had to keep looking at the road. There ought to be a way to get across the country and still be able to look out the window. She grinned. Of course, there <u>were</u> several ways: airplanes, buses, and trains -- something to think about!

Margaret spent the afternoon in the waiting room at the Volvo place. After she'd leafed through several issues of *Car and Driver*, drunk several cups of stale coffee, and watched a soap opera that seemed to involve doctors' wives, she began pacing around the showroom, looking at new Volvos, imagining herself driving one of their sedans. Finally, the service manager appeared and took her into his office.

"We've located the problem in your automobile, Mrs. Bluestone," he said. "You were right. It was the transmission, and you'll need a new one. But the car, as you know, is over twenty-five years old, and we'd have to send for the parts. We're talking ten days before we'd have it fixed." He paused, looking closely at her face, and then smiled. "Maybe it's time to get a new car," he said, slowly. "Of course, I understand that you have a valuable antique there, and you might not want to trade it in."

Margaret frowned. "It's more complicated than just the car. I'm on my way to the west coast. It wouldn't make sense for me to spend ten days in Des Moines. What would help me a great deal would be to talk to my mechanic back in Boston. He knows this car very well and, in fact, would like to buy it if I ever decide to give it up. Could I call him on your phone and talk to him? Maybe you could talk to him as well and tell him what you found, and then perhaps I can make a decision about what to do next."

"No problem. Let me get the number for you; we're all part of the same family, you know." He picked up the phone and dialed. "What's his name?" he asked.

"It's Leo. He's the service manager there, just as you are here." While she waited, she realized that while she'd been riding in the tow truck, she'd already made up her mind. It was time to sell the car to Leo, and then be on her way.

"Leo," she said, "I'm here in Des Moines, Iowa, and I'm thinking that it's time for us to start talking about a deal. Unfortunately, the car I'd like to sell you has a slight problem: it needs a new transmission! I should have listened to you in Boston, when it was doing fine."

"Hey," he said, and suddenly she could see his face, with a cigarette hanging out of the corner of his mouth, "you gave it a good run for the money; you got as far as Des Moines." He seemed to be chuckling. "Ms.

Bluestone, you remember I told you that you had a lotta spunk. You just

proved me right. Listen, can I talk to the fellow there? We gotta figure out

how to ship this car, if I'm gonna buy it." Margaret passed the phone to the

service manager, and listened to enough of the conversation to learn that the

Des Moines place could add the car to a shipment it would be making in a

week or so, and that it would end up in Boston where Leo could do the

transmission at his leisure. Then the man gave her back the phone.

"So, Leo," she said, feeling very comfortable talking to him, "what do

you think is a fair figure and how should we arrange the payment, since I'm

here and you're there?"

"You know what I'd suggest," he said. "Let's decide all that when you

get home next month. I'm sure we can work it out between us. Okay?"

That was fine with Margaret, and as she hung up, it occurred to her that

she was now really free of Henry. Her mourning period was over.

* * * *

The next day, having spent the night in a hotel, she went to a travel

agent they'd recommended. Right away, Margaret liked the woman who ran

the agency. When she realized that Margaret was in no hurry to get to the

west coast, the first thing she did was to send out for coffee for both of

them. Soon Margaret found herself telling her all about the old Volvo,

Henry's death, and all the places she'd stayed in along the way, beginning with the fleabag hotel, then on to the little cabin colony in the Finger Lakes. As she talked, Margaret realized that it had been a long time since she'd sat down with someone and talked about herself and where she was.

The woman was nodding her head. "Well, here's what I've been thinking as you talked. I think you should take the train. You could fly, of course, but you've probably done enough of that in your life, and the bus is a little grungy. I think I'm hearing that you've given up grunge at this point. The train is slow, but you said you were in no hurry."

"How slow?" said Margaret, the very words making her feel like yawning.

"Well, first of all, you have to understand that the train doesn't even come to Des Moines. You'd have to go to a place called Osceola, which is about thirty-five miles south of here. You'd have to take a limousine. And that train only comes through every other day." She smiled. "It's a gorgeous trip. It goes through the plains, where you'll see deer and antelope racing the train."

Margaret sat there, thinking. "Could you get me a nice bedroom, a private place all to myself, where I could just sit and look out, during the day, and sleep comfortably all night?" It sounded too good to be true.

* * * *

Sleeping on the train turned out to be almost the best part. Margaret could lie in her berth, with her big window shade up, and look right out at the stars, being rocked by the lullaby of the wheels. And in the daytime, there was the whole length of the train to walk in, once she'd learned to bob and weave with the motion of the cars. Best of all were those special places between the cars -- where you weren't supposed to stand because the doors were sometimes left open -- where Margaret and a few other hardy souls would spend their time, breathing in the prairie dust, and watching herds of wild horses, and storm clouds gathering, way off in the distance.

It was in the dining car that she got to know some of her fellow travelers. A few of them were train buffs, people who spent all their vacations riding the rails. Other passengers had the bemused look that she thought was probably mirrored on her own face, people who were taking advantage of a hiatus in their lives, being somewhere almost incognito, with no time demands, no decisions to make. Margaret had thought, as perhaps all of them had, that she could think on this train, but she found, instead, that her mind just drifted with the landscape. Of course, there were some passengers who kept working at their laptops, and there at least one young man who was always talking on his cellphone. When the train stopped at a place called Green River, Utah, Margaret remembered that this was the state where Henry had been heading. But even as she ran that idea through her mind, she felt it slipping away. Henry was gone.

She'd pictured herself, sitting in the privacy of her own little stateroom, reading one of the many books she'd bought in Des Moines, or else thinking serious thoughts about her future. She'd told herself she'd make up her mind about where Will and Erik fitted into her life. Will was easy, and required no thought at all. She loved Will, as she had told Erik, in the same way that she loved her own less than perfect children. But she couldn't focus her mind on very much else, not on the books, nor on the future after she got home to Massachusetts.

All she knew was that she was going to have a vacation in San Francisco and the Monterey Bay area. And then she'd take another lovely train up to Seattle to be a witness, as well as mother of the bride, at Anita's wedding.

After that, who knew? There was plenty of time to decide, all the time in the world.

Epilogue

A year and a half had passed since Henry's death. Once again, it was the day before Thanksgiving, and Margaret was preparing for the arrival of all her children, a stepchild, her grandchildren, and one guest. Much had changed in that short time, and most surprising, even for New England, was the difference in the weather. Two years ago, there'd been that terrible blizzard. Now it was unseasonably warm. Lazy, summer-like clouds dotted a pale blue sky, and Margaret found herself sitting out on the deck, reading the paper. She knew she should be making lists, deciding how to seat everyone at the table, planning the menu. She yawned, promising herself she'd get to work in a few minutes. In any case, the house looked nice, not perfect, like Chloe's, but nice!

Probably the biggest change in that year and a half was in herself. She was once again a married woman, with the complicated name of Margaret Bluestone-Jensen. Since her marriage, last June, she felt as if she were looking different as well, less wary, more satisfied, and with fewer lines around her mouth and eyes. She felt less driven.

Life seemed less complicated. Even though she'd had to make many more changes than she'd ever considered, adjusting to living in a house with Will and his needs, and living with a man who wanted to be part of her whole life, she found that her daily burdens were now shared. To her surprise, she discovered that the downside of this gift was that she was no longer always in charge. Someone else, usually Erik, was consciously or unconsciously deciding things, sometimes without checking with her. One morning she came downstairs to find that the wire whisks were now in a different place. Most of their disagreements were, in fact, around such minor issues.

Pulling herself to her feet and moving into the kitchen, she thought about some of those arguments. She and Henry, in spite of their differences, his diatribes and tirades, had never actually fought. She'd always kept her mouth shut and put up with whatever he said. It was no wonder she'd always looked drawn and tense. Now, she was learning how to disagree, to shout occasionally. One time she'd even ended up weeping when she realized how unhappy she'd made Erik. Then they would make up and find some compromise that would make things better.

This very day, before he'd gone to drive Will to school, they'd been discussing whether tomorrow's dinner should be a buffet or a sit-down dinner. (She couldn't imagine Henry caring one way or another.) What really made her angry was that it turned out that Erik had set up the table before she'd even gotten out of bed.

"Why didn't you <u>ask</u> me about it before you assumed this was the right way?" she'd shrieked, when she discovered what he'd done.

611

"Why should I have to ask you about every little thing?" he'd growled. "This is my house, too." And he'd stamped off to his car before they could get around to making up.

Walking into the dining room, she looked again at the table. Erik had put all the leaves in, so now it was big enough for twelve. She knew full well that they'd be more than a dozen. In addition to herself and Erik, all four of her children would be there with a spouse or significant other. Charles had told her last night that he'd be bringing a date -- that was the word he'd used to describe a fellow teacher that he'd been seeing for several months.

But in addition to these eleven adults -- Will was now nineteen and should, she felt, be counted as a grownup -- there was a growing army of children, beginning with Matt and Katy. Maybe it would be a good idea to have a teenagers' table this year in the kitchen: Will, with Katy and Matt. The two babies could sit at the big table in the dining room with their mothers, Duncan, on a regular chair with the big telephone book, and Hattie, Anita's daughter, in the high chair. Well, maybe Erik had been thinking of that solution when he'd set up the table that way. That was the trouble with arguments, she thought. No one had a chance to think of reasonable alternatives, or compromises, until much later. But, she thought wistfully, it would have been fun working it out together.

In these few short months since their marriage, they'd managed so far to avoid what was still probably the biggest issue between them: the barn. Ever since the time, two years ago, when Erik had completely cleaned the place out and set it up to look almost like a museum, Margaret had been wondering if he would approach her again and ask if he could turn it into an office for himself. She, of course, had occasionally thought about making it an office for herself, a setting for a private practice. Up until now, neither of them had even mentioned the barn, nor had either of them even unlocked it to peek inside. And Margaret had the only key.

Well, this was no time to be thinking about the barn. More exciting things were about to happen. Anita and Everett were, in fact, due that morning, flying in from Seattle with the baby whom Margaret hadn't seen since she was born. Just a year ago, she'd spent Thanksgiving week with them, waiting for the birth of this child. Her daughter had known since the amniocentesis that the baby would be a girl, and she'd told her mother that she was going to follow the Jewish custom and name the child after Henry, using at least the initial letter of his name. Margaret had spent several months wondering if they would choose Hortense, Hester, Henrietta, Helen, Hadley, or Hilary. But she'd never even thought of Harriet, a lovely name, and she'd liked the baby's nickname even more: Hattie.

And then she heard the noise of a car door opening. It was the cab from the airport. Everett, climbing out first, grinned broadly, his bald head shining, a seasoned dad by now, carrying the car seat that all babies seemed to need these days, plus a giant carryall, no doubt full of baby clothes and favorite blankets, and finally, Anita, rosy, hair askew, carrying a round-faced, wide-eyed baby girl with short, curly brown hair. Hattie looked directly at Margaret, and after a short hesitation, returned her grandmother's smile.

"I've been trying to teach her to say 'Nana,'" said Anita, "but I suspect she thinks I'm talking about her favorite food -- banana." Turning to her child, she said clearly and carefully: "This is your Nana." But the baby did not respond.

"Let me take her," said Margaret, "while you unpack. I've put you all upstairs in your old room, with the crib in there."

Anita handed her the child, and as soon as they got in the house, Hattie began to wriggle. Margaret put her down on the rug. Quickly, she pulled herself to her feet and began to toddle toward the stairs. "Oh, my God," she called up to Anita, "I never thought about gates!" She'd have to send Erik out to get them, one for downstairs, and one for the top as well. She picked up the baby and carried her into the living room. Spotting the wastebasket, Hattie reached for it and managed to dump it over. The baby beamed. "Oh, sweetie," Margaret said to her, smiling with delight, "You've reached that wonderful stage where you're into <u>everything</u>, and falling in love with the world!"

Later, as they sat in the kitchen together, Margaret looked at her daughter. Anita was holding the sleepy baby, slowly rocking in the chair, and while she was still the old Anita, there was an added softness to her, a gentle quality to the way she moved. Then Margaret saw that Hattie had put her thumb in her mouth, doing it just the way Anita used to do -- backward, almost upside down, with her hand turned around.

They sat quietly, as Margaret worked on her list, adding "gates." "So how's it all going, Mom?" Anita asked. "Being married again, and with Will, for instance. Is that complicated?"

"Adjusting to Will is the easier part." She paused, grinning. "It's really lovely being married to Erik. We get along well, except for stupid disagreements about household matters."

"Everett and I didn't start fighting until Hattie was born," said Anita. "I found myself resenting everything he did for her. I was looking at her as <u>my</u> baby, maybe because I was nursing her, but once I let him do things, we did much better. He's really a wonderful parent, I suspect a more natural one than I, and of course, she's crazy about him." They both looked down at Hattie, whose long lashes were now resting on her cheek, as she fell asleep.

"Why don't you take her upstairs and put her in the crib, and get a little nap, yourself. We'll have a late lunch, maybe on the deck, since it's so warm."

* * * *

Later, she could hear Erik and Will coming in the back way. Will smiled and waved at her and then wheeled himself into his room; he was beginning to value his privacy. He was also feeling especially good about himself these days since his school had recommended him for a part-time program at a local bank, where he'd have a chance to use his skill in numbers to learn their computers.

Erik walked slowly into the kitchen. Then, noticing the car seat on the floor, he said: "So they've arrived!" It was his way of opening up communication after an argument.

"They're all three asleep upstairs," said Margaret, in polite words, aware that they hadn't settled their early morning tiff. Then she met his eyes. He put his arms around her. He was still her giant red teddy bear.

"I'm sorry I yelled at you, Maggie," he said. "I think I got used to deciding things by myself when I was on my own, all those years."

She began running her hands through his sandy-gray hair. "I realized you were right. It made more sense for the adults and the two babies to sit at the big dining room table, and let the teenagers take over the kitchen." She sighed, as he started kissing her. "When are we going to learn to wait a bit and ask a few questions?" And then they got down to more pleasant domestic issues and she gave him the list. "I'm going to set the table out on the deck for lunch." She paused. "If that's okay with you." But now she was teasing him.

Erik grinned and tapped her lightly on the bottom.

* * * *

By evening, everyone except Charles and his family had arrived. Charles had already told Margaret that he would come down from Maine early in the morning with the kids and his "date," whose name, it turned out, was Pamela. Somehow the absence of Charles had changed the complexion of the Wednesday night preparations. No one wanted to take over his old job of peeling the apples for the pies.

"Well, I can manage that," said Molly, her yellow curls bouncing, "but I'm not going to do those chestnuts for the stuffing, not any more. I value my nails too much."

"Don't worry about it," said Margaret, cheerfully, her face and hands covered with flour. "We'll just use some of the stuffing that comes in a box."

There was a silence in the room. Andrew looked at his mother as if she'd turned into a different person, while Anita stared at her with her mouth open. "Gee," said Molly, "next thing we know, you'll be saying we're having instant mashed potatoes!"

Margaret laughed. "Not a bad idea! Do you think anyone would notice?"

After everyone had drifted off to bed, she and Erik were alone in their room. "Are you okay?" she said. "Not too overwhelmed by this mob scene?"

He shook his head and began stroking her hair. "You're wearing your pink summer nightgown," he said, "giving me all kinds of ideas." But then he paused, indicating that he understood she wanted to talk a little first. "I was more afraid," he said, "that Will would find it difficult, but he seems comfortable with everyone."

"I was very proud of him tonight," said Margaret, as she began running her fingers through the hair on his chest.

"You'll be in trouble if you keep that up, Maggie," he said, moving closer.

"I know," she said, as her body took over.

* * * *

The dinner, itself, the next day, was much less formal than in previous years. She'd ended up having to piece out her china with substitutes, and the glasses didn't match. Charles's date, Pamela, turned out to be much different than Margaret had expected. A large, big-boned brunette with frizzy dark hair, she took to the crowd easily, and soon had them all laughing as she described -- in her British accent -- her apprehensions at meeting them all. "Well, I thought that Charles's mother, being a social worker, would probably know exactly what I was thinking. And one of his sisters can forecast the weather." Anita grinned. "I wouldn't know an isobar from a candy bar." Pamela shrugged. "And the other sister is a bloody financial advisor, married to a broker. Somehow I figured they'd know that my credit cards are almost maxed out!"

After the laughter had died down, Andrew said: "And what about me? Surely you weren't afraid of Charles's little brother?"

"Are you kidding? Between you and your wife, you can probably tell exactly what operations I've had, what sickness I'm about to come down with, and how old I am! Well, I'll tell you the answers: I'm thirty-six, and healthy as a horse. And Molly, you'd be right about my credit cards. As for Charles's mother, it's still early days, but I'll have to confess to her that I think he's lovely." Her smile, as she said these last words, was genuine, and touched Margaret's heart. She glanced quickly at Charles, himself, and saw that he was biting his lip, and blushing. But he was smiling.

In the meantime, Margaret had been keeping one ear cocked to hear how things were going with Will and Charles's two kids, and had been reassured

619

to hear laughter and bits of conversation. She knew she worried too much about Will's ability to socialize with so-called "normal" kids his age, and often Erik had to remind her that Will needed to work all this out for himself. How easy it was to become an overprotective mother hen when one of your chicks was disabled!

After the main course, Charles went into the kitchen and brought out Pamela's gift to them all, four bottles of champagne. "I'd like to make the first toast," he said, clearing his throat, "to the woman who made all this possible -- our Mom!"

"Hear! Hear!" said Everett and David. Then several others joined in and Margaret smiled. "Thank you." She picked up her glass, and said: "And I, too, would like to make a toast to my wonderful husband, Erik, who began by making over my house, and then by making me over." She raised her glass and then drained it.

The toasts went on, and Margaret listened with her hand in Erik's, looking around at this wonderful group. Margaret knew there was much to be thankful for.

Following the main course, by common consent they all moved out to the deck, bringing their chairs and glasses for more champagne. The sun, of course, didn't understand that they were having an Indian summer, and it had begun to set at its usual late November time. The grownups leaned back and enjoyed the orangy pink reflection of the sunset in their fluted glasses, while the children turned the place into a playground. The long ramp that Erik had built for Will's wheelchair had become Duncan's roadway, a hill for his little cars and trucks. Later, when Hattie woke up, she was brought downstairs and introduced to the ramp. Little by little, first by creeping, then with faltering steps, she began to master the difficult skill involved in walking up and down a slope. Over and over, she repeated her efforts.

In the meantime, Matt and Katy had rediscovered the barn, and were peeking into the windows. Will wheeled himself over to take a look. "Margaret," he said, "you've never showed me the inside of your barn. Could we unlock it and see what it's like?"

Margaret hesitated, a little ribbon of fear running through her. She took a quick glance at Erik, but he was, deliberately, she thought, looking in another direction. Perhaps he was saying in his body language that this ball was now in her court. Well, this whole subject couldn't be avoided forever. "Sure," she said, as cheerfully as she could, "I'll get the key." She walked quickly across the deck and opened the back door, removing the bunch of keys. "Here," she said, handing the whole ring to Will, "it's this little one; it should fit the padlock."

Clumsily -- he was still having trouble coordinating his left hand with the more stable right one -- he managed to fit the key into the lock, and eventually pulled down the hasp. Matt reached up and opened the big door. At this point, Erik quietly moved over, put his hand inside, and turned on the light switch.

The barn was ablaze with light, the brass of the antique phone booth shining brightly, the windows clear and letting in the last rays of the setting sun, the floors polished, and the old tools, neatly hanging on the wall. It was, among other things, a tribute to Henry.

"Oh, Mom," said Anita, "what a nice thing to have done for Dad! It's so beautiful. When did all this happen?"

Margaret looked at Erik, and then waved her hand as if to say: now you're on stage.

"Well," he said slowly, feeling his way as he spoke, "I actually cleaned the place up last year when I'd finished with the house. I thought it deserved a special treatment. Some of those tools were historical, and that phone booth! -- it was a real gem." He paused. "The barn, itself, of course, is a classic, built in the basilica style."

"Can we go inside?" Katy asked. "I'd like to climb up the ladder to the loft. Is it okay, Dad?" she asked Charles.

He reached up and tested the rungs, and then nodded. "Sure, go ahead." Katy and Matt mounted the ladder, and the rest of the family crowded in. Meanwhile, Duncan had discovered the folding doors of the phone booth, and made a game of going in and out, while Julia kept reminding him to watch his fingers.

Suddenly Margaret turned to Erik and said: "Why don't we take a short walk before it gets too dark, and then come back and join everyone for dessert?" She felt that the two of them needed to talk privately about the barn. Erik took her hand and the two of them walked around the other side of the house and out towards the street. For a while they walked along in the warm night air. "Isn't it wonderful, having a second summer like this?" she said.

For several minutes they were both quiet, but they were still holding hands. Erik cleared his throat and then said: "Thank you for suggesting this walk. We certainly need to talk about the barn. That discussion is long overdue." Margaret waited to see if he would continue. But he was silent. Finally, he said: "I'd like you to tell me what you had in mind for the it, both then, and now. One of my mistakes was not asking."

"I'm not sure," she spoke hesitantly, clearing her throat, "but I thought, after Henry left, that I might want to open a private practice, gradually decreasing my time at the clinic." She swallowed. "The barn seemed like a good place for an office." She hesitated, since he'd said nothing. "It would need all kinds of improvements, of course, including a bathroom, heating

623

and plumbing, and so on." She laughed. "And it would be expensive." She paused. "I guess you'd like it for an office, too."

Erik laughed. "I think we've locked the barn door, and it turns out that there was no horse to steal!"

Thinking about the barn and what was inside, Margaret said: "Well, there's always been a sort of Trojan Horse -- that old phone booth!" She laughed, too. "Erik, surely the place is big enough for both of us. You're an architect; couldn't you draw up a plan?" She smiled. "It would be a good advertisement for your skills at restoration."

He seemed to be thinking. "That's a good idea. We'd have to cost it out. In the long run it could save us money, you know, because if we moved my office over here, we could sell the condo!" Then he laughed. "Can we go back now?" said Erik. "I'd like some of that pumpkin pie!"

As they turned back toward the house, the wind seemed to pick up. The leaves began to rustle and Margaret felt chilly. "I think winter is starting to come back," she said, but it was not a sad thought. Winter could bring fires in the fireplace, long nights curled up on the couch, and this winter, she'd have someone to curl up with. Erik put his jacket over her shoulders and they began to hurry home.

In their absence, the kids had cleaned up the dishes and re-set the table for dessert. The candles were lit and the place looked festive. As they came into the house, they were met by Anita, who was carrying the baby, now in her pajamas and ready for bed.

"Look, Hattie. Who's that?" she asked, pointing to Margaret.

"Nana!" said the child, reaching out her arms.

Barbara Selling

About the Author

Barbara Selling has been a long-term member of a class of experienced creative writers at the Radcliffe Seminars in Cambridge. She reached the Finalist Round of the Heekin Group Foundation's Writers and Education Fund, and was selected to join Sue Miller's Master Class at the Radcliffe Institute. Her poem, "In Memoriam," was published in the Smith Alumnae Quarterly.

Selling was named Social Worker of the Year in Massachusetts where she has practiced clinical social work for many years. She has four grown children, four stepchildren, and nine grandchildren. Selling and her husband, a retired physician, live in the suburbs of Boston, where, like her protagonist, they inhabited decaying Victorian houses.

Printed in the United States
928200002B